David Eddings was born in Spokane, Washington, in 1931, and was raised in the Puget Sound area north of Seattle. He received a Bachelor of Arts degree from the University of Washington in 1961. He has served in the United States Army, worked as a buyer for the Boeing Company, has been a grocery clerk and has taught college English. He has lived in many parts of the United States. His first novel, *High Hunt*, was a contemporary adventure story. The field of fantasy has always been of interest to him, however, and he turned to *The Belgariad* (also published by Corgi) in an effort to develop certain technical and philosophical ideas concerning that genre. Eddings currently resides with his wife, Leigh, in northwest America.

D0233761

and published by Corgi Books

David Eddings

Book One of the Malloreon

GUARDIANS OF THE WEST

CORGI BOOKS

BOOK ONE OF THE MALLOREON:
GUARDIANS OF THE WEST
A CORGI BOOK : 0 552 14802 4

Originally published in Great Britain by Bantam Press,
a division of Transworld Publishers

This edition published by arrangement with Ballantine Books,
a division of Random House, Inc.

PRINTING HISTORY
Bantam Press edition published 1987
Corgi edition published 1987

17 19 20 18 16

Set in 10/11pt Sabon.

Corgi Books are published by Transworld Publishers,
61-63 Uxbridge Road, London W5 5SA,
a division of The Random House Group Ltd,
in Australia by Random House Australia (Pty) Ltd,
20 Alfred Street, Milsons Point, Sydney, NSW 2061, Australia,
in New Zealand by Random House New Zealand Ltd,
18 Poland Road, Glenfield, Auckland 10, New Zealand
and in South Africa by Random House (Pty) Ltd,
Endulini, 5a Jubilee Road, Parktown 2193, South Africa.

Printed and bound in Great Britain by
Cox & Wyman Ltd, Reading, Berkshire.

Papers used by Transworld Publishers are natural, recyclable
products made from wood grown in sustainable forests.
The manufacturing processes conform to the environmental
regulations of the country of origin.

For Judy-Lynn:

A rose blooms and then fades,
but the beauty and the fragrance
are remembered always.

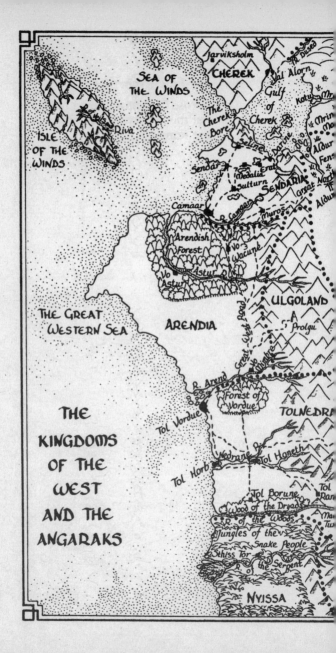

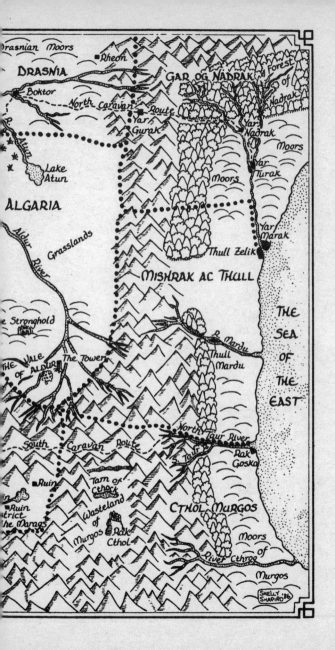

Prologue

Being an Account of those Events whereby Belgarion came to the Throne of Riva and how he slew the Accursed God Torak.
      — from the Introduction, *Legends of Alora*

After the seven Gods created the world, it is said that they and those races of men they had chosen dwelt together in peace and harmony. But UL, father of the Gods, remained aloof, until Gorim, leader of those who had no God, went up on a high mountain and importuned him mightily. Then the heart of UL melted, and he lifted up Gorim and swore to be his God and God of his people, the Ulgos.

The God Aldur remained apart, teaching the power of the Will and the Word to Belgarath and other disciples. And a time came when Aldur took up a globe-shaped stone no larger than the heart of a child. Men named the stone the Orb of Aldur, and it was filled with enormous power, for it was the embodiment of a Necessity which had existed since the beginning of time.

Torak, God of the Angarak peoples, coveted lordship and dominion over all things, for to him had come an opposing Necessity. When he learned of the Orb, he was sorely troubled, fearing that it would counter his destiny. He went therefore to Aldur to plead that the stone be set aside. When Aldur would not give up the stone, Torak smote him and fled with the Orb.

Then Aldur summoned his other brothers, and they went with a mighty army of their followers to confront Torak. But Torak, seeing that his Angaraks must be defeated, raised the Orb and used its power to crack the world and bring in the Sea of the East to divide him from his enemies.

But the Orb was angered that Torak should use it thus and it lashed him with a fire whose agony could not be quenched. Torak's left hand was burned away, his left cheek was seared and charred, and his left eye took flame and was ever after filled with the fire of the Orb's wrath.

In agony, Torak led his people into the wastelands of Mallorea, and his people built him a city in Cthol Mishrak, which was called the City of Night, for Torak hid it under an endless cloud. There, in a tower of iron, Torak contended with the Orb, trying in vain to quell its hatred for him.

Thus it endured for two thousand years. Then Cherek Bear-shoulders, King of the Alorns, went down to the Vale of Aldur to tell Belgarath the Sorcerer that the northern way was clear. Together they left the Vale with Cherek's three mighty sons, Dras Bull-neck, Algar Fleet-foot, and Riva Iron-grip. They stole through the marches, with Belgarath taking the form of a wolf to guide them, and they crossed over into Mallorea. By night, they stole into Torak's iron tower. And while the maimed God tossed in pain-haunted slumber, they crept to the room where he kept the Orb locked in an iron casket. Riva Iron-grip, whose heart was without ill intent, took up the Orb, and they left for the West.

Torak waked to find the Orb gone and he pursued them. But Riva lifted up the Orb, and its angry flame filled Torak with fear. Then the company passed from Mallorea and returned to their own lands.

Belgarath divided Aloria into four kingdoms. Over three he set Cherek Bear-shoulders, Dras Bull-neck, and Algar Fleet-foot. To Riva Iron-grip and to his line he gave the Orb of Aldur and sent him to the Isle of the Winds.

Belar, God of the Alorns, sent down two stars, and from them Riva forged a mighty sword and placed the Orb on its pommel. And he hung the sword on the wall of the throne room of the Citadel, where it might ever guard the West from Torak.

When Belgarath returned to his home, he discovered that his wife, Poledra, had borne him twin daughters, but then had passed away. In heartsick sorrow, he named his daughters Polgara and Beldaran. And when they were of age, he sent Beldaran to Riva Iron-grip to be his wife and mother of the Rivan line. But Polgara he kept with him and instructed in the arts of sorcery.

In rage at the loss of the Orb, Torak destroyed the City of Night and divided the Angaraks. The Murgos, the Nadraks, and the Thulls he sent to dwell in the wastelands along the western shores of the Sea of the East. The Malloreans he kept to subdue all of the continent on which they dwelt. Over all, he set his Grolim priests to watch, to scourge any who faltered, and to offer human sacrifices to him.

Many centuries passed. Then Zedar the Apostate, who served Torak, conspired with Salmissra, Queen of the snake-people, to send emissaries to the Isle of the Winds to slay Gorek, Riva's descendant, and all his family. This was done, though some claimed that a lone child escaped; but none could say for certain.

Emboldened by the death of the guardian of the Orb, Torak gathered his hosts and invaded the West, planning to enslave the peoples and regain the Orb. At Vo Mimbre on the plains of Arendia, the hordes of Angaraks met the armies of the West in dreadful slaughter. And there Brand the Rivan Warder, bearing the Orb upon his shield, met Torak in single combat and struck down the maimed God. The Angaraks, seeing that, were disheartened and they were overthrown and destroyed. But at night, as the Kings of the West celebrated, Zedar the Apostate took the body of Torak and spirited it away. Then the High Priest of the Ulgos, named Gorim as all such High Priests had been, revealed that Torak had not been killed, but bound in slumber until a king of the line of Riva sat once more on the throne in the Hall of the Rivan King.

The Kings of the West believed that meant forever, for

it was held that the line of Riva had perished utterly. But Belgarath and his daughter Polgara knew better. For a child *had* escaped the slaughter of Gorek's family, and they had concealed him and his descendants in obscurity for generations. But ancient prophecies revealed to them that the time for the return of the Rivan King was not yet come.

Many more centuries passed. Then, in a nameless city on the far side of the world, Zedar the Apostate came upon an innocent child and resolved to take the child and go secretly with him to the Isle of the Winds. There he hoped that the innocence of the child might enable that child to take the Orb of Aldur from the pommel of the sword of the Rivan King. It occurred as he wished, and Zedar fled with the child and the Orb toward the East.

Polgara the Sorceress had been living with a young boy, who called her Aunt Pol, in obscurity on a farm in Sendaria. This boy was Garion, the orphaned last descendant of the Rivan line, but he was unaware of his parentage.

When Belgarath learned of the theft of the Orb, he hastened to Sendar to urge his daughter to join him in the search for Zedar and the Orb. Polgara insisted that the boy must accompany them on the quest, so Garion accompanied his Aunt Pol and Belgarath, whom he knew as a storyteller who sometimes visited the farm and whom he called Grandfather.

Durnik, the farm smith, insisted on going with them. Soon they were joined by Barak of Cherek and by Kheldar of Drasnia, whom men called Silk. In time, their quest for the Orb was joined by others: Hettar, horse-lord of Algaria; Mandorallen, the Mimbrate knight; and Relg, an Ulgo zealot. And seemingly by chance, the Princess Ce'Nedra, having quarreled with her father, Emperor Ran Borune XXIII of Tolnedra, fled his palace and became one of the companions, though she knew nothing of their quest. Thus was completed the company foretold by the prophecy of the Mrin Codex.

Their search led them to the Wood of the Dryads, where

they were confronted by the Murgo Grolim Asharak, who had long spied secretly upon Garion. Then the voice of prophecy within Garion's mind spoke to Garion, and he struck Asharak with his hand and his Will. And Asharak was utterly consumed in fire. Thus Garion learned that he was possessed of the power of sorcery. Polgara rejoiced, telling him that henceforth he should be named Belgarion, as was proper for a sorcerer, for she knew then that the centuries of waiting were over and that Garion should be the one to reclaim the Rivan Throne, as foretold.

Zedar the Apostate fled from Belgarath in haste. Unwisely, he entered the realms of Ctuchik, High Priest of the western Grolims. Like Zedar, Ctuchik was a disciple of Torak, but the two had lived in enmity throughout the centuries. As Zedar crossed the barren mountains of Cthol Murgos, Ctuchik awaited him in ambush and wrested from him the Orb of Aldur and the child whose innocence enabled him to touch the Orb and not die.

Belgarath went ahead to seek out the trail of Zedar, but Beltira, another disciple of Aldur, gave him the news that Ctuchik now held the child and the Orb. The other companions went on to Nyissa, where Salmissra, Queen of the snake-loving people, had Garion seized and brought to her palace. But Polgara freed him and turned Salmissra into a serpent, to rule over the snake-people in that form forever.

When Belgarath rejoined his companions, he led the company on a difficult journey to the dark city of Rak Cthol, which was built atop a mountain in the desert of Murgos. They accomplished the difficult climb to confront Ctuchik, who knew of their coming and awaited with the child and the Orb. Then Belgarath engaged Ctuchik in a duel of sorcery. But Ctuchik, hard-pressed, tried a forbidden spell, and it rebounded on him, destroying him so utterly that no trace of him remained.

The shock of his destruction tumbled Rak Cthol from its mountaintop. While the city of the Gromlims shuddered into rubble, Garion snatched up the trusting child who bore the Orb and carried him to safety. They fled, with the hordes of Taur Urgas, King of the Murgos, pursuing them. But when they crossed into the lands of Algaria, the Algarians came against the Murgos and defeated them. Then at last, Belgarath could turn toward the Isle of the Winds to restore the Orb to its rightful place.

There in the Hall of the Rivan King at Erastide, the child whom they called Errand placed the Orb of Aldur into Garion's hand, and Garion stood on the throne to set it in its accustomed place on the pommel of the great Sword of the Rivan King. As he did so, the Orb leaped into flame, and the sword blazed with cold blue fire. By these signs, all knew that Garion was indeed the true heir to the throne of Riva and they acclaimed him King of Riva, Overlord of the West, and the Keeper of the Orb.

Soon, in keeping with the Accords signed after the Battle of Vo Mimbre, the boy who had come from a humble farm in Sendaria to become the Rivan King was betrothed to the Princess Ce'Nedra. But before the wedding could take place, the voice of prophecy that was within his head urged him to go to the room of documents and there take down the copy of the Mrin Codex.

In that ancient prophecy, he discovered that he was destined to take up Riva's sword and go with it to confront the maimed God Torak and to slay or be slain, thereby to decide the fate of the world. For Torak had begun to end his long slumber with the crowning of Garion, and in this meeting must be determined which of the two opposing Necessities or prophecies would prevail.

Garion knew that he could marshal an army to invade the East with him. But though his heart was filled with fear, he determined that he alone should accept the danger. Only Belgarath and Silk accompanied him. In the early morning, they crept out of the Citadel of Riva and set out on the long northern journey to the dark ruins of the City of Night where Torak lay.

But the Princess Ce'Nedra went to the Kings of the West and persuaded them to join her in an effort to distract the forces of the Angaraks, so that Garion might win through safely. With the help of Polgara, she marched through Sendaria, Arendia, and Tolnedra, raising a mighty army to follow her and to engage the hosts of the East. They met on the plain surrounding the city of Thull Mardu. Caught between the forces of Emperor 'Zakath of Mallorea and those of the mad King of the Murgos, Taur Urgas, Ce'Nedra's army faced annihilation. But Cho-Hag, Chief of the Clan-Chiefs of Algaria, slew Taur Urgas; and the Nadrak King Drosta lek Thun changed sides, giving her forces time to withdraw.

Ce'Nedra, Polgara, Durnik, and the child Errand, however, were captured and sent to 'Zakath, who sent them on to the ruined city of Cthol Mishrak for Zedar to judge. Zedar slew Durnik, and it was to see Polgara weeping over his body that Garion arrived.

In a duel of sorcery, Belgarath sealed Zedar into the rocks far below the surface. But by then Torak had awakened fully. The two destinies which had opposed each other since time began thus faced each other in the ruined City of Night. And there in the darkness, Garion, the Child of Light, slew Torak, the Child of Dark, with the flaming sword of the Rivan King, and the dark prophecy fled wailing into the void.

UL and the six living Gods came for the boy of Torak. And Polgara importuned them to bring Durnik back to life. Reluctantly they consented. But since it would not be mete for her so far to exceed Durnik's abilities, they gave to him the gift of sorcery.

Then all returned to the city of Riva. Belgarion married Ce'Nedra, and Polgara took Durnik as her husband. The Orb was again in its rightful place to protect the West. And the war of Gods, kings, and men, which had endured for seven thousand years, was at an end.

Or so men thought.

Part One

THE VALE OF ALDUR

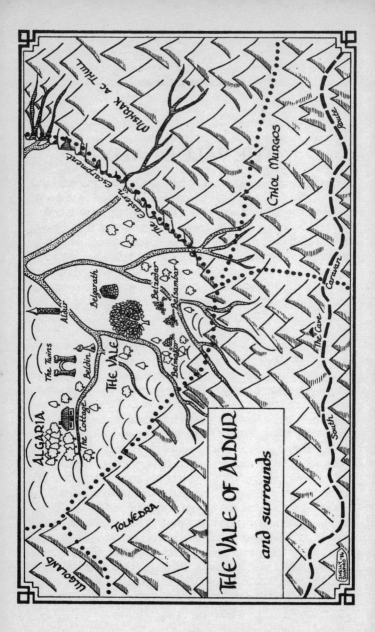

THE VALE OF ALDUR
and surrounds

Chapter One

It was late spring. The rains had come and passed, and the frost had gone out of the ground. Warmed by the soft touch of the sun, damp brown fields lay open to the sky, covered only by a faint green blush as the first tender shoots emerged from their winter's sleep. Quite early one fine morning, when the air was still cool, but the sky gave promise of a golden day, the boy Errand, along with his family, left an inn lying in one of the quieter districts of the bustling port city of Camaar on the south coast of the kingdom of Sendaria. Errand had never had a family before, and the sense of belonging was new to him. Everything around him seemed colored, overshadowed almost, by the fact that he was now included in a small, tightly knit group of people bound together by love. The purpose of the journey upon which they set out that spring morning was at once simple and very profound. They were going home. Just as he had not had a family before, Errand had never had a home; and, though he had never seen the cottage in the Vale of Aldur which was their destination, he nonetheless yearned toward that place as if its every stone and tree and bush had been imprinted upon his memory and imagination since the day he was born.

A brief rain squall had swept in off the Sea of the Winds about midnight and then had passed as quickly as it had come, leaving the gray, cobbled streets and tall, tile-roofed buildings of Cammar washed clean to greet the morning sun. As they rolled slowly through the streets in the sturdy wagon which Durnik the smith, after much careful inspection, had bought two days earlier, Errand, riding

17

burrowed amongst the bags of food and equipment which filled the wagon bed, could smell the faint, salt tang of the harbor and see the bluish morning cast in the shadows of the red-roofed buildings they passed. Durnik, of course, drove the wagon, his strong brown hands holding the reins in that competent way with which he did everything, transmitting somehow along those leather straps to the wagon team the comforting knowledge that he was completely in control and knew exactly what he was doing.

The stout, placid mare upon which Belgarath the Sorcerer rode, however, quite obviously did not share the comfortable security felt by the wagon horses. Belgarath, as he sometimes did, had stayed late in the taproom of the inn the previous night and he rode this morning slumped in the saddle, paying little or no heed to where he was going. The mare, also recently purchased, had not yet had the time to accustom herself to her new owner's peculiarities, and his almost aggressive inattention made her nervous. She rolled her eyes often, as if trying to determine if this immobile lump mounted on her back really intended for her to go along with the wagon or not.

Belgarath's daughter, known to the entire world as Polgara the Sorceress, viewed her father's semicomatose progress through the streets of Camaar with a steady gaze, reserving her comments for later. She sat beside Durnik, her husband of only a few weeks, wearing a hooded cape and a plain gray woolen dress. She had put aside the blue velvet gowns and jewels and rich, fur-trimmed capes which she had customarily worn while they had been at Riva and had assumed this simpler mode of dress as if almost with relief. Polgara was not averse to wearing finery when the occasion demanded it; and when so dressed, she appeared more regal than any queen in all the world. She had, however, an exquisite sense of the appropriate and she had dressed herself in these plain garments almost with delight, since they were appropriate to something she had wanted to do for uncounted centuries.

Unlike his daughter, Belgarath dressed entirely for comfort. The fact that his boots were mismatched was neither an indication of poverty nor of carelessness. It stemmed rather from conscious choice, since the left boot of one pair was comfortable upon his left foot and its mate pinched his toes, whereas his right boot—from another pair—was most satisfactory, while its companion chafed his heel. It was much the same with the rest of his clothing. He was indifferent to the patches on the knees of his hose, unconcerned by the fact that he was one of the few men in the world who used a length of soft rope for a belt, and quite content to wear a tunic so wrinkled and gravy-spotted that persons of only moderate fastidiousness would not even have considered using it for a scrub-rag.

The great oaken gates of Camaar stood open, for the war that had raged on the plains of Mishrak ac Thull, hundreds of leagues to the east, was over. The vast armies that had been raised by the Princess Ce'Nedra to fight that war had returned to their homes, and there was peace once more in the Kingdoms of the West. Belgarion, King of Riva and Overlord of the West, sat upon the throne in the Hall of the Rivan King with the Orb of Aldur once again in its proper place above his throne. The maimed God of Angarak was dead, and his eons-old threat to the West was gone forever.

The guards at the city gate paid scant attention to Errand's family as they passed, and so they left Camaar and set out upon the broad, straight imperial highway that stretched east towards Muros and the snow-topped mountains that separated Sendaria from the lands of the horse clans of Algaria.

Flights of birds wheeled and darted in the luminous air as the wagon team and the patient mare plodded up the long hill outside Camaar. The birds sang and trilled almost as if in greeting and hovered strangely on stuttering wings above the wagon. Polgara raised her flawless face in the clear, bright light to listen.

'What are they saying?' Durnik asked.

She smiled gently. 'They're babbling,' she replied in her rich voice. 'Birds do that a great deal. In general they're happy that it's morning and that the sun is shining and that their nests have been built. Most of them want to talk about their eggs. Birds always want to talk about their eggs.'

'And of course they're glad to see you, aren't they?'

'I suppose they are.'

'Someday do you suppose you could teach me to understand what they're saying?'

She smiled at him. 'If you wish. It's not a very practical thing to know, however.'

'It probably doesn't hurt to know a *few* things that aren't practical,' he replied with an absolutely straight face.

'Oh, my Durnik.' She laughed, fondly putting her hand over his. 'You're an absolute joy, do you know that?'

Errand, riding just behind them among the bags and boxes and the tools Durnik had so carefully selected in Camaar, smiled, feeling that he was included in the deep, warm affection they shared. Errand was not used to affection. He had been raised, if that is the proper term, by Zedar the Apostate, a man who had looked much like Belgarath. Zedar had simply come across the little boy in a narrow alleyway in some forgotten city and had taken him along for a specific purpose. The boy had been fed and clothed, nothing more, and the only words his bleak-faced guardian had ever spoken to him were, 'I have an errand for you, boy.' Because those were the only words he had heard, the only word the child spoke when he had been found by these others was 'Errand.' And since they did not know what else to call him, that had become his name.

When they reached the top of the long hill, they paused for a few moments to allow the wagon horses to catch their breath. From his comfortable perch in the wagon, Errand looked out over the broad expanse of neatly walled fields lying pale green in the long, slanting rays of the morning sun. Then he turned and looked back toward Camaar with its red roofs and its sparkling blue-green harbor filled with the ships of a half-dozen kingdoms.

'Are you warm enough?' Polgara asked him.

Errand nodded. 'Yes,' he said, 'thank you.' The words were coming more easily to him now, though he still spoke but rarely.

Belgarath lounged in his saddle, absently rubbing at his short white beard. His eyes were slightly bleary, and he squinted as if the morning sunlight was painful to him. 'I sort of like to start out a journey in the sunshine,' he said. 'It always seems to bode well for the rest of the trip.' Then he grimaced. 'I don't know that it needs to be *this* bright, however.'

'Are we feeling a bit delicate this morning, father?' Polgara asked him archly.

He turned to regard his daughter, his face set. 'Why don't you go ahead and say it, Pol? I'm sure you won't be happy until you do.'

'Why, father,' she said, her glorious eyes wide with feigned innocence, 'what makes you think I was going to say anything?'

He grunted.

'I'm sure you realize by now all by yourself that you drank a bit too much ale last night,' she continued. 'You don't need *me* to tell you that, do you?'

'I'm not really in the mood for any of this, Polgara,' he told her shortly.

'Oh, poor old dear,' she said in mock commiseration. 'Would you like to have me stir something up to make you feel better?'

'Thank you, but no,' he replied. 'The aftertaste of your concoctions lingers for days. I think I prefer the headache.'

'If a medicine doesn't taste bad, it isn't working,' she told him. She pushed back the hood of the cape she wore. Her hair was long, very dark, and touched just over her left brow with a single lock of snowy white. 'I *did* warn you, father,' she said relentlessly.

'Polgara,' he said, wincing, 'do you suppose we could skip the "I told you so's?"

'You heard me warn him, didn't you, Durnik?' Polgara asked her husband.

Durnik was obviously trying not to laugh.

The old man sighed, then reached inside his tunic and took out a small flagon. He uncorked it with his teeth and took a long drink.

'Oh, father,' Polgara said disgustedly, 'didn't you get enough last night?'

'Not if this conversation is going to linger on this particular subject, no.' He held out the flagon to his daughter's husband. 'Durnik?' he offered.

'Thanks all the same, Belgarath,' Durnik replied, 'but it's a bit early for me.'

'Pol?' Belgarath said then, offering a drink to his daughter.

'Don't be absurd.'

'As you wish.' Belgarath shrugged, recorking the bottle and tucking it away again. 'Shall we move along then?' he suggested. 'It's a very long way to the Vale of Aldur.' And he nudged his horse into a walk.

Just before the wagon rolled down on the far side of the hill, Errand looked back toward Camaar and saw a detachment of mounted men coming out through the gate. Glints and flashes of reflected sunlight said quite clearly that at least some of the garments the men wore were made of polished steel. Errand considered mentioning the fact, but decided not to. He settled back again and looked up at the deep blue sky dotted with puffy white clouds. Errand liked mornings. In the morning a day was always full of promise. The disappointments usually did not start until later.

The soldiers who had ridden out of Camaar caught up with them before they had gone another mile. The commander of the detachment was a sober-faced Sendarian officer with only one arm. As his troops fell in behind the wagon, he rode up alongside. 'Your Grace,' he greeted Polgara formally with a stiff little bow from his saddle.

'General Brendig,' she replied with a brief nod of acknowledgement. 'You're up early.'

'Soldiers are almost always up early, your Grace.'

'Brendig,' Belgarath said rather irritably, 'is this some kind of coincidence, or are you following us on purpose?'

'Sendaria is a very orderly kingdom, Ancient One,' Brendig answered blandly. 'We try to arrange things so that coincidences don't happen.'

'I thought so,' Belgarath said sourly. 'What's Fulrach up to now?'

'His Majesty merely felt that an escort might be appropriate.'

'I know the way, Brendig. I've made the trip a few times before, after all.'

'I'm sure of it, Ancient Belgarath,' Brendig agreed politely. 'The escort has to do with friendship and respect.'

'I take it then that you're going to insist?'

'Orders are orders, Ancient One.'

'Could we skip the "Ancient"?' Belgarath asked plaintively.

'My father's feeling his years this morning, General.' Polgara smiled, 'All seven thousand of them.'

Brendig almost smiled. 'Of course, your Grace.'

'Just why are we being so formal this morning, my Lord Brendig?' she asked him. 'I'm sure we know each other well enough to skip all that nonsense.'

Brendig looked at her quizzically. 'You remember when we first met?' he asked.

'As I recall, that was when you were arresting us, wasn't it?' Durnik asked with a slight grin.

'Well —' Brendig coughed uncomfortably. '—not exactly, Goodman Durnik. I was really just conveying his Majesty's invitation to you to visit him at the palace. At any rate, Lady Polgara—your esteemed wife—was posing as the Duchess of Erat, you may remember.'

Durnik nodded. 'I believe she was, yes.'

'I had occasion recently to look into some old books of heraldry and I discovered something rather remarkable. Were you aware, Goodman Durnik, that your wife really *is* the Duchess of Erat?'

Durnik blinked. 'Pol?' he said incredulously.

Polgara shrugged. 'I'd almost forgotten,' she said. 'It was a very long time ago.'

'Your title, nonetheless, is still valid, your Grace,' Brendig assured her. 'Every landholder in the District of Erat pays a small tithe each year into an account that's being held in Sendar for you.'

'How tiresome,' she said.

'Wait a minute, Pol,' Belgarath said sharply, his eyes suddenly very alert. 'Brendig, just how big is this account of my daughter's—in round figures?'

'Several million, as I understand it,' Brendig replied.

'Well,' Belgarath said, his eyes going wide. 'Well, well, well.'

Polgara gave him a level gaze. 'What have you got in your mind, father?' she asked him pointedly.

'It's just that I'm pleased for you, Pol,' he said expansively. 'Any father would be happy to know that his child has done so well.' He turned back to Brendig. 'Tell me, General, just who's managing my daughter's fortune?'

'It's supervised by the crown, Belgarath,' Brendig replied.

"That's an awful burden to lay on poor Fulrach," Belgarath said thoughtfully, 'considering all his other responsibilities. Perhaps I ought to—'

'Never mind, Old Wolf,' Polgara said firmly.

'I just thought—'

'Yes, father. I know what you thought. The money's fine right where it is.'

Belgarath sighed. 'I've never been rich before,' he said wistfully.

'Then you won't really miss it, will you?'

'You're a hard woman, Polgara—to leave your poor old father sunk in deprivation like this.'

'You've lived without money or possessions for thousands of years, father. Somehow I'm almost positive that you'll survive.'

'How did you get to be the Duchess of Erat?' Durnik asked his wife.

'I did the Duke of Vo Wacune a favor,' she replied. 'It was something that no one else could do. He was very grateful.'

Durnik looked stunned. 'But Vo Wacune was destroyed thousands of years ago,' he protested.

'Yes. I know.'

'I think I'm going to have trouble getting used to all this.'

'You knew that I wasn't like other women,' she said.

'Yes, but—'

'Does it really matter to you how old I am? Does it change anything?'

'No,' he said immediately, 'not a thing.'

'Then don't worry about it.'

They moved in easy stages across southern Sendaria, stopping each night at the solid, comfortable hostels operated by the Tolnedran legionnaires who patrolled and maintained the imperial highway and arriving in Muros on the afternoon of the third day after their departure from Camaar. Vast cattle herds from Algaria were already filling the acre upon acre of pens lying to the east of the city, and the cloud of dust raised by their milling hooves blotted out the sky. Muros was not a comfortable town during the season of the cattle drives. It was hot, dirty, and noisy. Belgarath suggested that they pass it up and stop for the night in the mountains where the air would be less dust-clogged and the neighbors less rowdy.

'Are you planning to accompany us all the way to the Vale?' he asked General Brendig after they had passed the cattle pens and were moving along the Great North Road toward the mountains.

'Ah—no, actually, Belgarath,' Brendig replied, peering ahead at a band of Algar horsemen approaching along the highway. 'As a matter of fact, I'll be turning back about now.'

The leader of the Algar riders was a tall, hawk-faced man in leather clothing, with a raven-black scalplock flowing behind him. When he reached the wagon, he reined in his horse. 'General Brendig,' he said in a quiet voice, nodding to the Sendarian officer.

'My Lord Hettar,' Brendig replied pleasantly.

'What are you doing here, Hettar?' Belgarath demanded.

Hettar's eyes went very wide. 'I just brought a cattle herd across the mountains, Belgarath,' he said innocently. 'I'll be going back now and I thought you might like some company.'

'How strange that you just happen to be here at this particular time.'

'Isn't it, though?' Hettar looked at Brendig and winked.

'Are we playing games?' Belgarath asked the pair of them. 'I don't need supervision and I definitely don't need a military escort every place I go. I'm perfectly capable of taking care of myself.'

'We all know that, Belgarath,' Hetter said placatingly. He looked at the wagon. 'It's nice to see you again, Polgara,' he said pleasantly. Then he gave Durnik a rather sly look. 'Married life agrees with you, my friend,' he added. 'I think you've put on a few pounds.'

'I'd say that *your* wife has been adding a few extra spoonfuls to your plate as well.' Durnik grinned at his friend.

'Is it starting to show?' Hettar asked.

Durnik nodded gravely. 'Just a bit,' he said.

Hettar made a rueful face and then gave Errand a peculiar little wink. Errand and Hettar had always got on well together, probably because neither of them felt any pressing need to fill up the silence with random conversation.

'I'll be leaving you now,' Brendig said. 'It's been a pleasant journey.' He bowed to Polgara and nodded to Hettar. And then, with his detachment of troops jingling along behind him, he rode back toward Muros.

'I'm going to have words with Fulrach about this,' Belgarath said darkly to Hettar, 'and with your father, too.'

'It's one of the prices of immortality, Belgarath,' Hettar said blandly. 'People tend to respect you—even when you'd rather they didn't. Shall we go?'

The mountains of eastern Sendaria were not so high as

to make travel across them unpleasant. With the fierce-looking Algar clansmen riding both to the front and to the rear of the wagon, they traveled at an easy pace along the Great North Road through the deep green forests and beside tumbling mountain streams. At one point, when they had stopped to rest their horses, Durnik stepped down from the wagon and walked to the edge of the road to gaze speculatively at a deep pool at the foot of a small, churning waterfall.

'Are we in any particular hurry?' he asked Belgarath.

'Not really. Why?'

'I just thought that this might be a pleasant place to stop for our noon meal,' the smith said artlessly.

Belgarath looked around. 'If you want, I suppose it's all right.'

'Good.' With that same slightly absent look on his face, Durnik went to the wagon and took a coil of thin, waxed cord from one of the bags. He carefully tied a hook decorated with some brightly colored yarn to one end of the cord and began looking about for a slender, springy sapling. Five minutes later he was standing on a boulder that jutted out into the pool, making long casts into the turbulent water just at the foot of the falls.

Errand drifted down to the edge of the stream to watch. Durnik was casting into the center of the main flow of the current so that the swiftly moving green water pulled his lure down deep into the pool.

After about a half an hour, Polgara called to them. 'Errand, Durnik, your lunch is ready.'

'Yes, dear,' Durnik replied absently. 'In a moment.'

Errand obediently went back up to the wagon, though his eyes yearned back toward the rushing water. Polgara gave him one brief, understanding look, then laid the meat and cheese she had sliced for him on a piece of bread so that he could carry his lunch back to the stream bank.

'Thank you,' he said simply.

Durnik continued his fishing, his face still intent. Polgara came down to the water's edge. 'Durnik,' she called. 'Lunch.'

'Yes,' he replied, not taking his eyes off the water. 'I'm coming.' He made another cast.

Polgara sighed. 'Oh, well,' she said. 'I suppose every man needs at least one vice.'

After about another half-hour, Durnik looked baffled. He jumped from his boulder to the stream bank and stood scratching his head and staring in perplexity at the swirling water. 'I *know* they're in there,' he said to Errand. 'I can almost feel them.'

'Here,' Errand said, pointing down at the deep, slow-moving eddy near the bank.

'I think they'd be farther out, Errand,' Durnik replied doubtfully.

'Here,' Errand repeated, pointing again.

Durnik shrugged. 'If you say so,' he said dubiously, flipping his lure out into the eddy. 'I still think they'd be out in the main current, though.'

And then his pole bent sharply into a tense, quivering bow. He caught four trout in rapid succession, thick, heavy-bodied trout with silvery, speckled sides and curved jaws filled with needlelike teeth.

'Why did it take you so long to find the right spot?' Belgarath asked later that afternoon when they were back on the highway.

'You have to work that kind of pool methodically, Belgarath,' Durnik explained. 'You start at one side and work your way across, cast by cast.'

'I see.'

'It's the only way to be really sure you've covered it all.'

'Of course.'

'I was fairly sure where they were lying, though.'

'Naturally.'

'It was just that I wanted to do it the right way. I'm sure you understand.'

'Perfectly,' Belgarath said gravely.

After they had passed through the mountains, they turned south, riding through the vast grasslands of the Algarian plain where herds of cattle and horses grazed in that huge green sea of grass that rippled and swayed under the steady easterly breeze. Although Hettar strongly urged them to stop by the Stronghold of the Algar clans, Polgara declined. 'Tell Cho-Hag and Silar that we may visit later,' she said, 'but we really should get to the Vale. It's probably going to take most of the summer to make my mother's house habitable again.'

Hettar nodded gravely and then waved a brief salute as he and his clansmen turned eastward and rode off across the rolling grasslands toward the mountainlike Stronghold of his father, Cho-Hag, Chief of the Clan-Chiefs of Algaria.

The cottage that had belonged to Polgara's mother lay in a valley among the rolling hills marking the northern edge of the Vale of Aldur. A sparkling stream flowed through the sheltered hollow, and there were woods, birch inter-mixed with cedar, stretching along the valley floor. The cottage was constructed of fieldstone, gray, russet, and earthy-brown, all neatly fitted together. It was a broad, low building, considerably larger than the word 'cottage' suggested. It had not been occupied for well over three thousand years, and the thatching and the doors and window frames had long since surrendered to the elements, leaving the shell of the house standing, bramble-filled and unroofed to the sky. There was, nonetheless, a peculiar sense of waiting about it, as if Poledra, the woman who had lived here, had instilled in the very stones the knowledge that one day her daughter would return.

They arrived in the middle of a golden afternoon, and Errand, lulled by a creaking wheel, had drifted into a doze. When the wagon stopped, Polgara shook him gently awake. 'Errand,' she said, 'we're here.' He opened his eyes and looked for the first time at the place he would forever call home. He saw the weathered shell of the cottage nestled in the tall green grass. He saw the woods beyond, with the white trunks of the birch trees standing out among the dark green cedars, and he saw the stream. The place had enormous possibilities. He realized that at once. The stream, of course, was perfect for sailing toy boats, for skipping stones, and, in the event of failing inspiration, for falling into. Several of the trees appeared to have been specifically designed for climbing, and one huge, white old birch overhanging the stream promised the exhilarating combination of climbing a tree and falling into the water, all at one time.

The land upon which their wagon had stopped was a long hill sloping gently down toward the cottage. It was the kind of a hill down which a boy could run on a day when the sky was a deep blue dotted with dandelion-puff clouds racing in the breeze. The knee-high grass would be lush in the sun, and the turf damply firm underfoot; the rush of sweet-smelling air as one ran down that long slope would be intoxicating.

And then he felt quite keenly a sense of deep sorrow, a sorrow which had endured unchanged for century upon century, and he turned to look at Belgarath's weathered face and the single tear coursing down the old man's furrowed cheek, to disappear in his close-cropped white beard.

In spite of Belgarath's sorrow for his lost wife, Errand looked out at this small, green valley with its trees and its stream and its lush meadow with a deep and abiding contentment. He smiled and said, 'Home,' trying the word and liking the sound of it.

Polgara looked gravely into his face. Her eyes were very large and luminous, and their color changed with her mood, ranging from a light blue so pale as to be virtually gray to a deep lavender. 'Yes, Errand,' she replied in her vibrant voice. 'Home.' Then she put her arms about him to hold him softly, and there was in that gentle embrace all the yearning toward this place which had filled her down through the weary centuries that she and her father had labored at their endless task.

Durnik the smith looked thoughtfully at the hollow spread out below in the warm sunshine, considering, planning, arranging, and rearranging things in his mind. 'It's going to take a while to get everything the way we want it, Pol,' he said to his bride.

'We have all the time in the world, Durnik,' Polgara replied with a gentle smile.

'I'll help you unload the wagon and set up your tents,' Belgarath said, scratching absently at his beard. 'Then tomorrow I suppose I ought to go on down into the Vale —have a talk with Beldin and the twins, look in on my tower—that sort of thing.'

Polgara gave him a long, steady look. 'Don't be in such a hurry to leave, father,' she told him. 'You talked with Beldin just last month at Riva and on any number of occasions you've gone for decades without visiting your tower. I've noticed that every time there's work to be done, you suddenly have pressing business someplace else.'

Belgarath's face assumed an expression of injured innocence. 'Why, Polgara—' he started to protest.

'That won't work either, father,' she told him crisply. 'A few weeks—or a month or two—of helping Durnik isn't going to injure you permanently. Or did you plan to leave us abandoned to the winter snows?'

Belgarath looked with some distaste at the shell of the house standing at the foot of the hill, with the hours of toil it was going to take to make it livable stamped all over it. 'Why, of course, Pol,' he said somewhat too quickly. 'I'd be happy to stay and lend a hand.'

'I knew we could depend on you, father,' she said sweetly.

Belgarath looked critically at Durnik, trying to assess the strength of the smith's convictions. 'I hope you weren't intending to do everything by hand,' he said tentatively. 'What I mean is—well, we *do* have certain alternatives available to us, you know.'

Durnik looked a little uncomfortable, his plain, honest face touched with the faintest hint of a disapproving expression. 'I—uh—I really don't know, Belgarath,' he said dubiously. 'I don't believe that I'd really feel right about that. If I do it by hand, then I'll know that it's been done properly. I'm not all that comfortable with this other

31

way of doing things yet. Somehow it seems like cheating —if you get what I mean.'

Belgarath sighed. 'Somehow I was afraid you might look at it that way.' He shook his head and squared his shoulders. 'All right, let's go on down there and get started.'

It took about a month to dig the accumulated debris of three eons out of the corners of the house, to reframe the doors and windows and to re-beam and thatch the roof. It would have taken twice as long had Belgarath not cheated outrageously each time Durnik's back was turned. All manner of tedious tasks somehow performed themselves whenever the smith was not around. Once, for example, Durnik took out the wagon to bring in more timbers; as soon as he was out of sight, Belgarath tossed aside the adze with which he had been laboriously squaring off a beam, looked gravely at Errand, and reached inside his jerkin for the earthenware jar of ale he had filched from Polgara's stores. He took a long drink and then he directed the force of his will at the stubborn beam and released it with a single muttered word. An absolute blizzard of white wood chips went flying in all directions. When the beam was neatly squared, the old man looked at Errand with a self-satisfied smirk and winked impishly. With a perfectly straight face, Errand winked back.

The boy had seen sorcery performed before. Zedar the Apostate had been a sorcerer, and so had Ctuchik. Indeed, throughout almost his entire life the boy had been in the care of people with that peculiar gift. Not one of the others, however, had that air of casual competence, that verve, with which Belgarath performed his art. The old man's offhand way of making the impossible seem so easy that it was hardly worth mentioning was the mark of the true virtuoso. Errand knew how it was done, of course. No one can possibly spend that much time with assorted sorcerers without picking up the theory, at least. The ease with which Belgarath made things happen almost tempted him to try it himself; but whenever he considered the idea, he realized that there wasn't really anything he wanted to do that badly.

The things the boy learned from Durnik, while more commonplace, were nonetheless very nearly as profound. Errand saw almost immediately that there was virtually nothing the smith could not do with his hands. He was familiar with almost every known tool. He could work in wood and stone as readily as in iron and brass. He could build a house or a chair or a bed with equal facility. As Errand watched closely, he picked up the hundreds of little tricks and knacks that separated the craftsman from the bumbling amateur.

Polgara dealt with all domestic matters. The tents in which they slept while the cottage was being readied were as neatly kept as any house. The bedding was aired daily, meals were prepared, and laundry was hung out to dry. On one occasion Belgarath, who had come to beg or steal more ale, looked critically at his daughter, who was humming contentedly to herself as she cut up some recently cooked-down soap. 'Pol,' he said acidly, 'you're the most powerful woman in the world. You've got more titles than you can count, and there's not a king in the world who doesn't bow to you automatically. Can you tell me exactly *why* you find it necessary to make soap that way? It's hard, hot work, and the smell is awful.'

She looked calmly at her father. 'I've spent thousands of years being the most powerful woman in the world, Old Wolf,' she replied. 'Kings have been bowing to me for centuries, and I've lost track of all the titles. This *is*, however, the very first time I've ever been married. You and I were always too busy for that. I've *wanted* to be married, though, and I've spent my whole life practicing. I know everything a good wife needs to know and I can do everything a good wife needs to do. Please don't criticize me, father, and please don't interfere. I've never been so happy in my life.'

'Making soap?'

'That's part of it, yes.'

'It's such a waste of time,' he said. He gestured negligently, and a cake of soap that had not been there before joined the ones she had already made.

'Father!' she said, stamping her foot. 'You stop that this minute!'

He picked up two cakes of soap, one his and one hers. 'Can you really tell me the difference between them, Pol?'

'Mine was made with love; yours is just a trick.'

'It's still going to get clothes just as clean.'

'Not mine, it won't,' she said, taking the cake of soap out of his hand. She held it up, balanced neatly on her palm. Then she blew on it with a slight puff, and it instantly vanished.

'That's a little silly, Pol,' he told her.

'Being silly at times runs in my family, I think,' she replied calmly. 'Just go back to your own work, father, and leave me to mine.'

'You're almost as bad as Durnik is,' he accused her.

She nodded with a contented smile. 'I know. That's probably why I married him.'

'Come along, Errand,' Belgarath said to the boy as he turned to leave. 'This sort of thing might be contagious, and I wouldn't want you to catch it.'

'Oh,' she said. 'One other thing, father. Stay out of my stores. If you want a jar of ale, ask me.'

Assuming a lofty expression, Belgarath strode away without answering. As soon as they were around the corner, however, Errand pulled a brown jar from inside his tunic and wordlessly gave it to the old man.

'Excellent, my boy.' Belgarath grinned. 'You see how easy it is, once you get the hang of it?'

Throughout that summer and well into the long, golden autumn which followed it, the four of them worked to make the cottage habitable and weathertight for the winter. Errand did what he could to help, though more often than not his help consisted primarily of providing company while keeping out from underfoot.

When the snows came, the entire world seemed somehow to change. More than ever before, the isolated cottage became a warm, safe haven. The central room, where they took their meals and where they all sat in the long evenings, faced a huge stone fireplace that provided both warmth and light. Errand, whose time was spent out of doors on all but the most bitterly cold days, was usually drowsy during those golden, firelit hours between supper and bedtime and he often lay on a fur rug before the fire and gazed into the dancing flames until his eyes slowly closed. And later he waked in the cool darkness of his own room with warm, down-filled coverlets tucked up under his chin and he knew that Polgara had quietly carried him in and put him to bed. And he sighed happily and went back to sleep.

Durnik made him a sled, of course, and the long hill which ran down into the valley was perfect for sledding. The snow was not deep enough to make the runners of the sled bog down, and Errand was able to coast amazing distances across the meadow at the bottom of the hill because of the terrific momentum built up as he slid down the slope.

The absolute cap of the entire sledding season came late one bitingly cold afternoon, just after the sun had dropped into a bank of purple clouds on the western horizon and the sky had turned to a pale, icy turquoise. Errand trudged up the hill through the frozen snow, pulling his sled behind him. When he reached the top, he stopped for a moment to catch his breath. The thatched cottage below nestled in the surrounding snowbanks with the light from its windows golden and the column of pale blue smoke rising from its chimney as straight as an arrow into the dead calm air.

Errand smiled, lay down on his sled, and pushed off. The combination of circumstances was perfect for sledding. There was not even a breeze to impede his rapid descent, and he gathered astounding speed on his way down the hill. He flew across the meadow and in among the trees. The white-barked birches and dark, shadowy cedars flashed by as he sped through the woods. He might have gone even farther had the stream not been in his way. And even that conclusion to the ride was fairly exciting, since the bank of the stream was several feet high and Errand and his sled sailed out over the dark water in a long, graceful arc which ended abruptly in a spectacular, icy splash.

Polgara spoke to him at some length when he arrived home, shivering and with ice beginning to form up on his clothing and in his hair. Polgara, he noticed, tended to overdramatize things—particularly when an opportunity presented itself for her to speak to someone about his shortcomings. She took one long look at him and immediately fetched a vile-tasting medicine, which she spooned into him liberally. Then she began to pull off his frozen clothing, commenting extensively as she did so. She had an excellent speaking voice and a fine command of language. Her intonations and inflections added whole volumes of meaning to her commentary. On the whole, however, Errand would have preferred a shorter, somewhat less exhaustive discussion of his most recent misadventure—particularly in view of the fact that Belgarath and Durnik were both trying without much success to conceal broad grins as Polgara spoke to him while simultaneously rubbing him down with a large, rough towel.

'Well,' Durnik observed, 'at least he won't need a bath this week.'

Polgara stopped drying the boy and slowly turned to gaze at her husband. There was nothing really threatening in her expression, but her eyes were frosty. 'You said something?' she asked him.

'Uh—no, dear,' he hastily assured her. 'Not really.' He looked at Belgarath a bit uncomfortably, then he rose to his feet. 'Perhaps I'd better bring in some more firewood,' he said.

One of Polgara's eyebrows went up, and her gaze moved on to her father. 'Well?' she said.

He blinked, his face a study in total innocence.

Her expression did not change, but the silence became ominous, oppressive.

'Why don't I give you a hand, Durnik?' the old man

suggested finally, also getting up. Then the two of them went outside, leaving Errand alone with Polgara.

She turned back to him. 'You slid all the way down the hill,' she asked quite calmly, 'and clear across the meadow?'

He nodded.

'And then through the woods?'

He nodded again.

'And then off the bank and into the stream?'

'Yes, ma'am,' he admitted.

'I don't suppose it occurred to you to roll off the sled *before* it went over the edge and into the water?'

Errand was not really a very talkative boy, but he felt that his position in this affair needed a bit of explanation. 'Well,' he began, 'I didn't really think of rolling off—but I don't think I would have, even if I *had* thought of it.'

'I'm sure there's an explanation for that.'

He looked at her earnestly. 'Everything had gone so splendidly up until then that—well, it just wouldn't have seemed right to get off, just because a few things started to go wrong.'

There was a long pause. 'I see,' she said at last, her expression grave. 'Then it was in the nature of a moral decision—this riding the sled all the way into the stream?'

'I suppose you might say that, yes.'

She looked at him steadily for a moment and then slowly sank her face into her hands. 'I'm not entirely certain that I have the strength to go through all of this again,' she said in a tragic voice.

'Through what?' he asked, slightly alarmed.

'Raising Garion was almost more than I could bear,' she replied, 'but not even *he* could have come up with a more illogical reason for doing something.' Then she looked at him, laughed fondly, and put her arms about him. 'Oh, Errand,' she said, pulling him tightly to her, and everything was all right again.

Chapter Two

Belgarath the Sorcerer was a man with many flaws in his character. He had never been fond of physical labor and he was perhaps a bit *too* fond of dark brown ale. He was occasionally careless about the truth and had a certain grand indifference to some of the finer points of property ownership. The company of ladies of questionable reputation did not particularly offend his sensibilities, and his choice of language very frequently left much to be desired.

Polgara the Sorceress was a woman of almost inhuman determination and she had spent several thousand years trying to reform her vagrant father, but without much notable success. She persevered, however, in the face of overwhelming odds. Down through the centuries she had fought a valiant rearguard action against his bad habits. She had regretfully surrendered on the points of indolence and shabbiness. She grudgingly gave ground on swearing and lying. She remained adamant, however, even despite repeated defeats, on the points of drunkenness, thievery, and wenching. She felt for some peculiar reason that it was her duty to fight on those issues to the very death.

Since Belgarath put off his return to his tower in the Vale of Aldur until the following spring, Errand was able to witness at close hand those endless and unbelievably involuted skirmishes between father and daughter with which they filled the periodic quiet spaces in their lives. Polgara's comments about the lazy old man's lounging about in her kitchen, soaking up the heat from her fireplace and the well-chilled ale from her stores with almost equal facility, were pointed, and Belgarath's smooth evasions revealed centuries of highly polished skill. Errand, however, saw past those waspish remarks and blandly flippant replies. The bonds between Belgarath and his daughter were so profound that they went far beyond what others might conceivably understand, and so, over the endless years, they had found it necessary to conceal their boundless love for each other behind this endless façade of contention. This is not to say that Polgara might not have preferred a more upstanding father, but she was not *quite* as disappointed in him as her observations sometimes indicated.

They both knew why Belgarath sat out the winter in Poledra's cottage with his daughter and her husband. Though not one word of the matter had ever passed between them, they knew that the memories the old man had of this house needed to be changed—not erased certainly, for no power on earth could erase Belgarath's memories of his wife, but rather they needed to be altered slightly so that this thatched cottage might also remind the old man of happy hours spent here, as well as that bleak and terrible day when he had returned to find that his beloved Poledra had died.

After the snow had been cut away by a week of warm spring rains and the sky had turned blue once again, Belgarath at last decided that it was time to take up his interrupted journey. 'I don't really have anything pressing,' he admitted, 'but I'd like to look in on Beldin and the twins, and it might be a good time to tidy up my tower. I've sort of let that slide over the past few hundred years.'

'If you'd like, we could go along,' Polgara offered. 'After all, you *did* help with the cottage—not enthusiastically, perhaps, but you did help. It only seems right that we help you with cleaning your tower.'

'Thanks all the same, Pol,' he declined firmly, 'but your idea of cleaning tends to be a bit too drastic for my taste. Things that might be important later on have a way of winding up on the dust heap when you clean. As long as there's a clear space somewhere in the center, a room is clean enough for me.'

'Oh, father,' she said, laughing, 'you never change.'

'Of course not,' he replied. He looked thoughtfully over at Errand, who was quietly eating his breakfast. 'If it's all right, though,' he said, 'I'll take the boy with me.'

She gave him a quick look.

Belgarath shrugged. 'He's company and he might enjoy a change of scenery. Besides, you and Durnik haven't really had a chance to be alone since your wedding day. Call it a belated present if you want.'

She looked at him. 'Thank you, father,' she said simply, and her eyes were suddenly very warm and filled with affection.

Belgarath looked away, almost as if her look embarrassed him. 'Did you want your things? From the tower, I mean. You've left quite a few trunks and boxes there at one time or another over the years.'

'Why, that's very nice of you, father.'

'I need the space they're taking up,' he said. Then he grinned at her.

'You *will* watch the boy, won't you? I know your mind sometimes wanders when you start puttering around in your tower.'

'He'll be fine with me, Pol,' the old man assured her.

And so the following morning Belgarath mounted his horse, and Durnik boosted Errand up behind him. 'I'll bring him home in a few weeks,' Belgarath said. 'Or at least by midsummer.' He leaned down, shook Durnik's hand, and then turned his mount toward the south.

The air was still cool, although the early spring sunshine was very bright. The scents of stirring growth were in the air, and Errand, riding easily behind Belgarath, could feel Aldur's presence as they pressed deeper into the Vale. He felt it as a calm and gentle kind of awareness, and it was dominated by an overpowering desire to know. The presence of the God Aldur here in the Vale was not some vague spiritual permeation, but rather was quite sharp, on the very edge of being palpable.

They moved on down into the Vale, riding at an easy pace through the tall, winter-browned grass. Broad trees dotted the open expanse, lifting their crowns to the sky, holding the tips of their branches, swollen with the urgency of budding leaves, up to receive the gentle kiss of sun-warmed air.

'Well, boy?' Belgarath said after they had ridden a league or more.

'Where are the towers?' Errand asked politely.

'A bit farther. How did you know about the towers?'

'You and Polgara spoke of them.'

'Eavesdropping is a very bad habit, Errand.'

'Was it a private conversation?'

'No, I suppose not.'

'Then it wasn't eavesdropping, was it?'

Belgarath turned sharply, looking over his shoulder at the boy riding behind him. 'That's a pretty fine distinction for somebody as young as you are. How did you arrive at it?'

Errand shrugged. 'It just came to me. Do they always graze here like that?' He pointed at a dozen or so reddish-brown deer feeding calmly nearby.

'They have done so ever since I can remember. There's something about Aldur's presence that keeps animals from molesting each other.'

They passed a pair of graceful towers linked by a peculiar, almost airy bridge arching between them, and Belgarath told him that they belonged to Beltira and Belkira, the twin sorcerers whose minds were so closely linked that they inevitably completed each others' sentences. A short while later they rode by a tower so delicately constructed of rose quartz that it seemed almost to float like a pink jewel in the lambent air. This tower, Belgarath told him, belonged to the hunchbacked Beldin, who had surrounded his own ugliness with a beauty so exquisite that it snatched one's breath away.

At last they reached Belgarath's own squat, functional tower and dismounted. 'Well,' the old man said, 'here we are. Let's go up.'

The room at the top of the tower was large, round, and incredibly cluttered. As he looked around at it, Belgarath's eyes took on a defeated look. 'This is going to take weeks,' he muttered.

A great many things in the room attracted Errand's eye, but he knew that, in Belgarath's present mood, the old man would not be inclined to show him or explain to him much of anything. He located the fireplace, found a tarnished brass scoop and a short-handled broom, and knelt in front of the cavernous, soot-darkened opening.

'What are you doing?' Belgarath asked.

'Durnik says that the first thing you should do in a new place is get a spot ready for your fire.'

'Oh, he does, does he?'

'It's not usually a very big chore, but it gets you started —and once you get started, the rest of the job doesn't look so big. Durnik's very wise about things like that. Do you have a pail or a dust bin of some kind?'

'You're going to insist on cleaning the fireplace?'

'Well—if you don't mind too much. It *is* pretty dirty, don't you think?'

Belgarath sighed. 'Pol and Durnik have corrupted you already, boy,' he said. 'I tried to save you, but a bad influence like that always wins out in the end.'

'I suppose you're right,' Errand agreed. 'Where did you say that pail was?'

By evening they had cleared a semicircular area around the fireplace, finding in the process a couple of couches, several chairs, and a sturdy table.

'I don't suppose you have anything to eat stored any-place?' Errand said wistfully. His stomach told him that it was definitely moving on toward suppertime.

Belgarath looked up from a parchment scroll he had just fished out from under one of the couches. 'What?' he asked. 'Oh yes. I'd almost forgotten. We'll go visit the twins. They're bound to have something on the fire.'

'Do they know we're coming?'

Belgarath shrugged. 'That doesn't really matter, Errand. You must learn that that's what friends and family are for—to be imposed upon. One of the cardinal rules, if you want to get through life without overexerting yourself, is that, when all else fails, fall back on friends and relations.'

The twin sorcerers, Beltira and Belkira, were overjoyed to see them, and the 'something on the fire' turned out to be a savory stew that was at least as good as one that might have emerged from Polgara's kitchen. When Errand commented on that, Belgarath looked amused. 'Who do you think taught her how to cook?' he asked.

It was not until several days later, when the cleaning of Belgarath's tower had progressed to the point where the floor was receiving its first scrubbing in a dozen or more centuries, that Beldin finally stopped by.

'What are you doing, Belgarath?' the filthy, misshapen hunchback demanded. Beldin was very short, dressed in battered rags, and he was gnarled like an old oak stump. His hair and beard were matted, and twigs and bits of straw clung to him in various places.

'Just a little cleaning,' Belgarath replied, looking almost embarrassed.

'What for?' Beldin asked. 'It's just going to get dirty again.' He looked at a number of very old bones lying along the curved wall. 'What you really ought to do is render down your floor for soup stock.'

'Did you come by to visit or just to be disagreeable?'

'I saw the smoke from your chimney. I wanted to see if anybody was here or if all this litter had just taken fire spontaneously.'

Errand knew that Belgarath and Beldin were genuinely fond of each other and that this banter between them was one of their favorite forms of entertainment. He continued with the work he was doing even as he listened.

'Would you like some ale?' Belgarath asked.

'Not if *you* brewed it,' Beldin replied ungraciously. 'You'd think that a man who drinks as much as you do would have learned how to make decent ale by now.'

'That last batch wasn't so bad,' Belgarath protested.

'I've run across stump water that tasted better.'

'Quit worrying. I borrowed this keg from the twins.'

'Did they know you were borrowing it?'

'What difference does that make? We all share everything anyway.'

One of Beldin's shaggy eyebrows raised. 'They share their food and drink, and you share your appetite and thirst. I suppose that works out.'

'Of course it does.' Belgarath turned with a slightly pained look. 'Errand,' he said, 'do you *have* to do that?'

Errand looked up from the flagstones he was industriously scrubbing. 'Does it bother you?' he asked.

'Of course it bothers me. Don't you know that it's terribly impolite to keep working like that when I'm resting?'

'I'll try to remember that. How long do you expect that you'll be resting?'

'Just put the brush down, Errand,' Belgarath told him. 'That patch of floor has been dirty for a dozen centuries at least. Another day or so isn't going to matter all that much.'

'He's a great deal like Belgarion was, isn't he?' Beldin said, sprawling in one of the chairs near the fire.

'It probably has something to do with Polgara's influence,' Belgarath agreed, drawing two tankards of ale from the keg. 'She leaves marks on every boy she meets. I try to moderate the effects of her prejudices as much as possible, though.' He looked gravely at Errand. 'I think this one is smarter than Garion was, but he doesn't seem to have Garion's sense of adventure—and he's just a bit too well behaved.'

'I'm sure you'll be able to work on that.'

Belgarath settled himself into another chair and pushed his feet out toward the fire. 'What have you been up to?' he asked the hunchback. 'I haven't seen you since Garion's wedding.'

'I thought that somebody ought to keep an eye on the Angaraks,' Beldin replied, scratching vigorously at one armpit.

'And?'

'And what?'

'That's an irritating habit you've picked up somewhere. What are the Angaraks doing?'

'The Murgos are still all in little pieces about the death of Taur Urgas.' Beldin laughed. 'He was completely mad, but he kept them unified—until Cho-Hag ran his sabre through him. His son Urgit isn't much of a king. He's barely able to get their attention. The western Grolims can't even function any more. Ctuchik's dead, and Torak's dead, and about all the Grolims can do now is stare at the walls and count their fingers. My guess is that Murgo society is right on the verge of collapsing entirely.'

'Good. Getting rid of the Murgos has been one of my main goals in life.'

'I wouldn't start gloating just yet,' Beldin said sourly. 'After word reached 'Zakath that Belgarion had killed Torak, he threw off all pretenses about the fiction of Angarak unity and marched his Malloreans on Rak Goska. He didn't leave much of it standing.'

Belgarath shrugged. 'It wasn't a very attractive city anyway.'

'It's a lot less attractive now. 'Zakath seems to think that crucifixions and impalings are educational. He decorated what was left of the walls of Rak Goska with object lessons. Every time he goes any place in Cthol Murgos, he leaves a trail of occupied crosses and stakes behind him.'

'I find that I can bear the misfortunes of the Murgos with great fortitude,' Belgarath replied piously.

'I think you'd better take a more realistic look at things, Belgarath,' the hunchback growled. 'We could probably match Murgo numbers if we really had to, but people don't talk about "the uncountable hordes of boundless Mallorea" for nothing. 'Zakath has a *very* big army, and he commands most of the seaports on the east coast, so he can ship in as many more troops as he wants. If he succeeds in obliterating the Murgos, he's going to be camped on our southern doorstep with a lot of bored soldiers on his hands. Certain ideas are bound to occur to him at about that time.'

Belgarath grunted. 'I'll worry about that when the time comes.'

'Oh, by the way,' Beldin said suddenly with an ironic grin, 'I found out what that apostrophe is doing in his name.'

'Whose name?'

''Zakath's. Would you believe that it indicates the word "Kal"?'

'*Kal Zakath?*' Belgarath stared at him incredulously.

'Isn't that outrageous?' Beldin chortled. 'I guess that the Mallorean emperors have been secretly yearning to take that title since just after the battle of Vo Mimbre, but they were always afraid that Torak might wake up and take offense at their presumption. Now that he's dead, a fair number of Malloreans have begun to call their ruler "Kal Zakath"—the ones who want to keep their heads do, at any rate.'

'What does "Kal" mean?' Errand asked.

'It's an Angarak word that means King and God,' Belgarath explained. 'Five hundred years ago, Torak set aside the Mallorean emperor and personally led his hordes against the west. The Angaraks—all of them; Murgos, Nadraks, and Thulls, as well as the Malloreans—called him Kal Torak.'

'What happened?' Errand asked curiously. 'When Kal Torak invaded the West, I mean?'

Belgarath shrugged. 'It's a very old story.'

'Not until you've heard it,' Errand told him.

Beldin gave Belgarath a sharp look. 'He *is* quick, isn't he?'

Belgarath looked at Errand thoughtfully. 'All right,' he said. 'Putting it very briefly, Kal Torak smashed Drasnia, laid siege to the Algarian Stronghold for eight years, and then crossed Ulgoland to the plains of Arendia. The Kingdoms of the West met him at Vo Mimbre, and he was struck down in a duel with the Rivan Warder.'

'But not killed.'

'No. Not killed. The Rivan Warder struck him straight through the head with his sword, but Torak wasn't killed. He was only bound in slumber until a king sat once again on the throne of Riva.'

'Belgarion,' Errand said.

'Right. You know what happened then. You were there, after all.'

Errand sighed. 'Yes,' he said sadly.

Belgarath turned back to Beldin. 'All right,' he said, 'what's going on in Mallorea?'

'Things are about the same as always,' Beldin replied, taking a drink of ale and belching thunderously. 'The bureaucracy is still the glue that holds everything together. There are still plots and intrigues in Melcene and Mal Zeth. Karanda and Darshiva and Gandahar are on the verge of open rebellion, and the Grolims are still afraid to go near Kell.'

'The Mallorean Grolims are still a functioning church then?' Belgarath seemed a little surprised. 'I thought that the citizenry might have taken steps—the way they did in Mishrak ac Thull. I understand that the Thulls started building bonfires with Grolims.'

'Kal Zakath sent a few orders back to Mal Zeth,' Beldin told him, 'and the army stepped in to stop the slaughter. After all, if you plan to be King *and* God, you're going to need yourself a church. Zakath seems to think that it might be easier to use one that's already established.'

'What does Urvon think of that idea?'

'He's not making much of an issue of it right now. Before the army moved in, the people of Mallorea were finding a great deal of entertainment in hanging Grolims up on iron hooks. Urvon is staying in Mal Yaska and keeping very quiet. I think he believes that the fact that he's still alive might just be an oversight on the part of his exalted Majesty, Kal Zakath. Urvon is a slimy snake, but he's no fool.'

'I've never met him.'

'You haven't missed a thing,' Beldin said sourly. He held out his tankard. 'You want to fill this?'

'You're drinking up all of my ale, Beldin.'

'You can always steal more. The twins never lock their doors. Anyway, Urvon was a disciple of Torak, the same as Ctuchik and Zedar. He doesn't have any of their good qualities, however.'

'They didn't *have* any good qualities,' Belgarath said, handing him back the refilled tankard.

'Compared to Urvon, they did. He's a natural-born bootlicker, a fawning, contemptible sneak. Even Torak despised him. But, like all people with those charming traits, as soon as he got the least little bit of power, he went absolutely berserk with it. He's not satisfied with bows as a sign of respect; he wants people to grovel before him.'

'You seem moderately unfond of him,' Belgarath noted.

'I *loathe* that piebald back stabber.'

'Piebald?'

'He's got patches of skin on his face and hands with no color at all, so he looks all splotchy—as if he had some gruesome disease. I'm viewed in some quarters as passing ugly, but Urvon could scare a troll into fits. Anyway, if Kal Zakath wants to turn the Grolim church into a state religion with *his* face on the altars instead of Torak's, he's going to have to deal with Urvon first, and Urvon always stays holed up in Mal Yaska, completely surrounded by Grolim sorcerers. Zakath won't be able to get near him. *I* can't even get near him. I give it a try every hundred years or so, hoping that somebody might get careless or that I might get lucky enough to get a large, sharp hook into his guts. What I'd really like to do, though, is drag him face down over red-hot coals for a few weeks.'

Belgarath looked a little surprised at the little man's vehemence. 'That's all he's doing then? Staying under cover in Mal Yaska?'

'Not hardly! Urvon plots and schemes even in his sleep. In the last year and a half—ever since Belgarion ran his sword through Torak—Urvon's been scrambling around, trying to preserve what's left of his church. There are some old, moth-eaten prophecies—the Grolims call them

Oracles—from a place called Ashaba in the Karandese Mountains. Urvon dusted them off and he's been twisting them around so that they seem to say that Torak will return—that he's not dead, or that he'll be resurrected or possibly reborn.'

Belgarath snorted. 'What nonsense!'

'Of course it is, but he had to do something. The Grolim church was convulsing like a headless snake, and Zakath was right on the verge of putting his fist around everybody's throat to make sure that every time any Angarak bowed, it would be to *him*. Urvon made sure that there were very few copies of these Ashabine Oracles left lying about and he's been inventing all sorts of things and claiming that he found them in the prophecies. That's about the only thing holding Zakath off right now and probably *that* wouldn't even work, if the emperor weren't so busy trying to decorate every tree he comes across with a Murgo or two.'

'Did you have any trouble moving around in Mallorea?'

Beldin snorted a crude obscenity. 'Of course not. Nobody even notices the face of a deformed man. Most people couldn't tell you if I'm an Alorn or a Marag. They can't see past the hump on my back.' He rose from his chair, went to the cask, and refilled his tankard again. 'Belgarath,' he said very seriously, 'does the name Cthrag Sardius mean anything to you?'

'Sardius? Sardonyx, you mean?'

Beldin shrugged. 'The Mallorean Grolims call it Cthrag Sardius. What's the difference?'

'Sardonyx is a gemstone—sort of orange colored with milky-white stripes. It's not really very rare—or very attractive.'

'That doesn't quite match up with the way I heard the Malloreans talk about it.' Beldin frowned. 'From the way they use the name Cthrag Sardius, I gather that it's a single stone—and that it's got a certain kind of importance.'

'What sort of importance?'

'I can't say for sure. About all I could gather was that

just about every Grolim in Mallorea would trade his soul for the chance to get his hands on it.'

'It could just be some kind of internal symbol—something to do with the power struggle that's going on over there.'

'That's possible, I suppose, but why would its name be Cthrag Sardius then? They called the Orb of Aldur "Cthrag Yaska," remember? There'd almost have to be a connection between Cthrag Sardius and Cthrag Yaska, wouldn't there? And if there is, maybe we ought to have a look into it.'

Belgarath gave him a long look and then sighed. 'I thought that, once Torak was dead, we might get a chance to rest.'

'You've had a year or so.' Beldin shrugged. 'Much more than that and you start to get flabby.'

'You're a very disagreeable fellow, do you know that?'

Beldin gave him a tight, ugly grin. 'Yes,' he agreed. 'I thought you might have noticed that.'

The next morning Belgarath began meticulously sorting through a mountainous heap of crackling parchments, trying to impose some kind of order upon centuries of chaos. Errand watched the old man quietly for a time, then drifted over to the window to look out at the sun-warmed meadows of the Vale. Perhaps a mile away, there was another tower, a tall, slender structure that looked somehow very serene.

'Do you mind if I go outside?' he asked Belgarath.

'What? No, that's all right. Just don't wander too far away.'

'I won't,' Errand promised, going to the top of the stairway that spiraled down into the cool dimness below.

The early morning sunlight slanted across the dew-drenched meadow; and skylarks sang and spun through the sweet-smelling air. A brown rabbit hopped out of the tall grass and regarded Errand quite calmly. Then it sat on its haunches and began vigorously to scratch its long ears with a busy hind foot.

Errand had not come out of the tower for random play,

however, nor to watch rabbits. He had someplace to go and he set out across the dewy green meadow in the direction of the tower he had seen from Belgarath's window.

He hadn't really counted on the dew, and his feet were uncomfortably wet by the time he reached the solitary tower. He walked around the base of the stone structure several times, his feet squelching in their sodden boots.

'I wondered how long it would take before you came by,' a very calm voice said to him. 'I was busy helping Belgarath,' Errand apologized.

'Did he really need help?'

'He was having a little trouble getting started.'

'Would you like to come up?'

'If it's all right.'

'The door's on the far side.'

Errand went around the tower and found a large stone that had been turned to reveal a doorway. He went into the tower and on up the stairs.

One tower room was much like another, but there were certain differences between this one and Belgarath's. As in Belgarath's tower, there was a fireplace here with a fire burning in it, but there appeared to be nothing in the flames here for them to feed upon. The room itself was strangely uncluttered, for the owner of *this* tower stored his parchment scrolls, tools, and implements in some unimaginable place, to be summoned as he required them.

The owner of the tower sat beside the fire. His hair and beard were white, and he wore a blue, loose-fitting robe. 'Come over to the fire and dry your feet, boy,' he said in his gentle voice.

'Thank you,' Errand replied.

'How is Polgara?'

'Very well,' Errand said, 'And happy. She likes being married, I think.' He lifted one foot and held it close to the fire.

'Don't burn your shoes.'

'I'll be careful.'

'Would you like some breakfast?'

'That would be nice. Belgarath forgets things like that sometimes.'

'On the table there.'

Errand looked at the table and saw a steaming bowl of porridge that had not been there before.

'Thank you,' he said politely, going to the table and pulling up a chair.

'Was there something special you wanted to talk about?'

'Not really,' Errand replied, picking up a spoon and starting on the porridge. 'I just thought I should come by. The Vale *is* yours, after all.'

'Polgara's been teaching you manners, I see.'

Errand smiled. 'And other things, too.'

'Are you happy with her, Errand?' the owner of the tower asked.

'Yes, Aldur, I really am,' Errand replied and continued to eat his porridge.

Chapter Three

As the summer progressed, Errand found himself rather naturally more and more in the company of Durnik. The smith, he soon discovered, was an extraordinarily patient man who did things the old way, not so much because of some moral bias against what Belgarath called 'the alternative we have available to us,' but rather because he took a deep satisfaction in working with his hands. This was not to say that Durnik did not occasionally take short cuts. Errand noticed a certain pattern to the smith's evasions. Durnik absolutely would not cheat on any project involving making something for Polgara or for their home. No matter how laborious or tedious those projects might be, Durnik completed them with his hands and his muscles.

Certain outside activities, however, were not quite so closely tied up with Durnik's sense of ethics. Two hundred yards of rail fence, for example, appeared rather quickly one morning. The fence needed to be there; there was no question of that, since a nearby herd of Algar cattle had to be diverted from plodding with bovine stubbornness across Polgara's garden on their way to water. As a matter of fact, the fence actually began to appear instantly just in front of the startled cows. They regarded the first fifty feet or so in bafflement; then, after considering the problem for several minutes, they moved to go around the obstruction. Another fifty feet of fence appeared in their path. In time, the cows grew surly about the whole thing and even tried running, perhaps thinking in their sluggish way that they might be able to outrace this phantom fence builder. Durnik, however, sat planted on a stump, his eyes intent and his face determined, extending his fence section by section in front of the increasingly irritable cows.

One dark brown bull, finally goaded into a fury of frustration, lowered his head, pawed the earth a few times, and charged the fence with a great bellow. Durnik made a peculiar twisting gesture with one hand, and the bull was suddenly charging *away* from the fence, turned around somehow in midstride without even knowing it. He ran for several hundred yards before it occurred to him that his horns had not yet encountered anything substantial. He slowed and raised his head in astonishment. He looked dubiously back over his shoulder at the fence, then turned around and gave it another try. Once again Durnik turned him, and once again he charged ferociously off in the wrong direction. The third time he tried it, he charged over the top of the hill and disappeared on the other side. He did not come back.

Durnik looked gravely at Errand and then he winked. Polgara came out of the cottage, drying her hands on her apron, and noted the fence which had somehow constructed itself while she had been washing the breakfast dishes. She gave her husband a quizzical look, and Durnik seemed a bit abashed at having been caught using sorcery rather than an axe.

'Very nice fence, dear,' she said encouragingly to him.

'We kind of needed one there,' he said apologetically. 'Those cows—well, I had to do it in a hurry.'

'Durnik,' she said gently, 'there's nothing morally reprehensible about using your talent for this sort of thing—and you *should* practice every so often.' She looked at the zig-zag pattern of the interlocking rail fence, and then her expression became concentrated. One after another, each of the junctures of the rails was suddenly bound tightly together with stout rosebushes in full bloom. 'There,' she said contentedly, patted her husband's shoulder, and went back inside.

'She's a remarkable woman, do you know that?' Durnik said to Errand.

'Yes,' Errand agreed.

Polgara was not *always* pleased with her husband's ventures into this new field, however. On one occasion toward the hot, dusty end of summer when the vegetables in her garden were beginning to wilt, Polgara devoted the bulk of one morning to locating a small, black rain cloud over the mountains in Ulgoland and gently herding its sodden puffiness toward the Vale of Aldur and, more specifically, toward her thirsty garden.

Errand was playing along the fence when the cloud came in low over the hill to the west and then stopped directly over the cottage and the waiting garden. Durnik glanced up from the harness he was mending, saw the blond-haired boy at play and the ominous black cloud directly over his head, and rather negligently pulled in his will. He made a small flipping gesture with one hand. 'Shoo,' he said to the cloud.

The cloud gave a peculiar sort of twitch, almost like a hiccup, then slowly flowed on eastward. When it was several hundred yards beyond Polgara's parched garden, it began to rain—a nice, steady, soaking downpour that very satisfactorily watered several acres of empty grassland.

Durnik was not at all prepared for his wife's reaction. The door to the cottage banged open, and Polgara emerged with her eyes flashing. She gave the happily raining cloud a hard stare, and the soggy-looking thing gave another of those peculiar hiccups and actually managed to look guilty.

Then Polgara turned and looked directly at her husband, her eyes a bit wild. 'Did you do that?' she demanded, pointing at the cloud.

'Why—yes,' he replied. 'I suppose I did, Pol.'

'*Why* did you do that?'

'Errand was out there playing,' Durnik said, still concentrating most of his attention on the harness. 'I didn't think you'd want him to get wet.'

Polgara looked at the cloud wasting all of its rain on grass so deeply rooted that it could have easily survived a ten-month drought. Then she looked at her garden and its drooping turnip tops and pathetic beans. She clenched her teeth tightly together to keep in certain words and phrases which she knew might shock her strait-laced and proper husband. She raised her face to the sky and lifted her arms in supplication. 'Why me?' she demanded in a loud, tragic voice. 'Why me?'

'Why, dear,' Durnik said mildly, 'whatever is wrong?'

Polgara told him what was wrong—at some length.

Durnik spent the next week putting in an irrigation system leading from the upper end of their valley to Polgara's garden, and she forgave him for his mistake almost as soon as he had finished it.

The winter came late that year, and autumn lingered in the Vale. The twins, Beltira and Belkira, came by just before the snows set in and told them that, after several weeks of discussion, both Belgarath and Beldin had left the Vale, and that each of them had gone away with that serious expression on his face that mean that there was trouble somewhere.

Errand missed Belgarath's company that winter. To be sure, the old sorcerer had, more often than not, managed to get him in trouble with Polgara, but Errand felt somehow that he shouldn't really be expected to devote *every* waking moment to staying out of trouble. When the snow came, he took up sledding again. After she had watched him come flying down the hill and across the meadow a few times, Polgara prudently asked Durnik to erect a barrier at the stream bank to prevent a recurrence of the previous winter's mishap. It was while the smith was erecting a woven wattle fence to keep Errand on dry land that he happened to glance down into the water. Because the often muddy little rills that emptied into their stream were all locked in ice now, the water was low and as clear as crystal. Durnik could very clearly see the long, narrow shapes hovering like shadows in the current above the beds of gravel that formed the bottom.

'What a curious thing,' he murmured, his eyes taking

on that peculiarly abstracted look. 'I've never noticed them there before.'

'I've seen them jumping,' Errand said. 'But most of the time, the water's too cloudy to see them when they're lying underwater.'

'I imagine that's the reason for it, all right,' Durnik agreed. He tied the end of the wattle fence to a tree and thoughtfully walked through the snow toward the shed he had built at the back of the cottage. A moment or so later he emerged with the skein of waxed cord in his hand; five minutes later he was fishing. Errand smiled and turned to trudge back up the long hill, towing his sled behind him. When he reached the top of the hill, a strange, hooded young woman awaited him.

'Can I help you?' he asked politely.

The young woman pushed back her hood to reveal the fact that a dark cloth was tightly bound across her eyes. 'Thou art the one they call Errand?' she asked. Her voice was low and musical, and there was a peculiar lilt to her archaic speech.

'Yes,' Errand replied, 'I am. Did you hurt your eyes?'

'Nay, gentle child,' she replied. 'I must needs look upon the world by a light other than that of the mundane sun.'

'Would you like to come down to our cottage?' Errand asked her. 'You could warm yourself by our fire, and Polgara would welcome company.'

'Though I revere the Lady Polgara, the time has not yet arrived for us to meet,' the young woman said, 'and it is not cold where I am.' She paused and bent forward slightly as if she were in fact peering at him, though the cloth over her eyes was quite thick. 'It *is* true then,' she murmured softly. 'We could not be certain at such great distance, but now that I am face to face with thee, I know that there can be no mistake.' She straightened then. 'We will meet again,' she told him.

'As you wish, ma'am,' Errand replied, remembering his manners.

She smiled, and her smile was so radiant that it seemed almost to bring sunlight to the murky winter afternoon.

'I am Cyradis,' she said, 'and I bear thee friendship, gentle Errand, even though the time may come when I must needs decide against thee.' And then she vanished, disappearing so suddenly that she was there and then gone in the space of a single heart beat.

Startled a bit, Errand glanced at the snow where she had stood and saw that there were no marks or footprints. He sat down on his sled to think about it. Nothing that the strange young woman had said really seemed to make much sense, but he was fairly sure that a time would come when it *would*. After a bit of thought he concluded that this peculiar visit would upset Polgara if she heard about it. Since he was certain that this Cyradis posed no threat and meant him no harm, he decided that he would not mention the incident.

Then, because it was growing quite chilly atop the hill, he pushed his sled into motion and coasted down the long slope and across the meadow and to within a few dozen yards of where Durnik was fishing with such total concentration that he was oblivious of all that was going on around him.

Polgara was tolerant about Durnik's pastime. She was always suitably impressed at the length, weight, and silvery color of the prizes he brought home and she drew upon all her vast knowledge to find new and interesting ways to fry, bake, broil, roast, and even poach fish. She adamantly insisted, however, that *he* clean them.

When spring returned once again, Belgarath came by, mounted on a spirited roan stallion.

'What happened to your mare?' Durnik asked the old man as he dismounted in the dooryard of the cottage.

Belgarath made a sour face. 'I was halfway to Drasnia when I discovered that she was pregnant. I traded her for *this* enthusiast.' He gave the prancing roan a hard look.

'It looks as if you might have gotten the best of the bargain,' Durnik mused, looking Belgarath's horse over.

'The mare was sedate and sensible,' the old man disagreed. 'This one doesn't have a brain in his head. All he wants to do is show off—running, jumping, rearing, and pawing the air with his hooves.' He shook his head in disgust.

'Put him in the barn, father,' Polgara suggested, 'and wash up. You're just in time for supper. You can have a baked fish. As a matter of fact, you can have several baked fish if you'd like.'

After they had eaten, Belgarath turned his chair around, leaned back, and pushed his feet out toward the fire. He looked around with a contented smile at the polished flagstone floor, the limed white walls with polished pots and kettles hanging on pegs, and at the dancing light and shadow coming from the arched fireplace. 'It's good to relax a bit,' he said. 'I don't think I've stopped moving since I left here last autumn.'

'What is it that's so pressing, father?' Polgara asked him as she cleared away the supper dishes.

'Beldin and I had quite a long talk,' the old man replied. 'There are some things going on in Mallorea that I don't quite like.'

'What earthly difference can it make now, father? Our interest in Mallorea ended at Cthol Mishrak when Torak died. You were not appointed caretaker of the world, you know.'

'I wish it were that easy, Pol,' he said. 'Does the name "the Sardion" mean anything to you? Or "Cthrag Sardius" perhaps?'

She was pouring hot water from a kettle into the large pan in which she customarily washed the dishes, but she stopped, frowning slightly. 'I think I heard a Grolim say something about "Cthrag Sardius" once. He was delirious and babbling in old Angarak.'

'Can you remember what he was saying?' Belgarath asked intently.

'I'm sorry, father, but I don't *speak* old Angarak. You never got around to teaching me, remember?' She looked at Errand and crooked one finger at him.

Errand sighed disconsolately, got up, and fetched a dish towel.

'Don't make faces, Errand,' she told. 'It doesn't hurt

59

you to help clean up after supper.' She looked back at Belgarath as she started to wash the dishes. 'What's the significance of the "Sardion" or whatever you call it?'

'I don't know,' Belgarath replied, scratching at his beard in perplexity. 'As Beldin pointed out, though, Torak called our Master's Orb "Cthrag Yaska." It's possible, I suppose, that "Cthrag Sardius" might be connected in some way.'

'I picked up a lot of "possibles" and "supposes" and "mights" in there, father,' she said. 'I wonder if you aren't chasing after shadows out of habit—or just to keep busy.'

'You know me well enough to know that I'm not all *that* enthusiastic about keeping busy, Pol,' he said wryly.

'So I've noticed. Is anything else happening in the world?'

'Let's see,' Belgarath leaned back and stared speculatively at the low-beamed ceiling. 'The Grand Duke Noragon ate something that definitely didn't agree with him.'

'Who is the Grand Duke Noragon? And why are we interested in his digestion?' Polgara asked.

'The Grand Duke Noragon *was* the candidate of the Honeth family to succeed Ran Borune on the Imperial Throne of Tolnedra,' Belgarath smirked. 'He was a complete and total jackass, and his ascension to the throne would have been an unmitigated disaster.'

'You said *was*,' Durnik noted.

'Right. Noragon's indigestion proved fatal. It is widely suspected that some splendid Horbite sympathizer used certain exotic condiments that come from the jungles of Nyissa to season the Grand Duke's last lunch. The symptoms, I understand, were quite spectacular. The Honeths are in total disarray, and the other families are gloating outrageously.'

'Tolnedran politics are disgusting,' Polgara declared.

'Our Prince Kheldar appears to be well on his way toward becoming the wealthiest man in the world,' Belgarath continued.

'Silk?' Durnik looked a bit amazed. 'Has he managed to steal *that* much already?'

'I gather that what he's doing is sort of legitimate this

time,' Belgarath said. 'He and that rascal Yarblek have somehow managed to gain control of the entire Nadrak fur harvest. I wasn't able to get all the details, but the screams of anguish coming from the major commercial houses in Boktor would seem to indicate that our friends are doing rather well.'

'I'm pleased to hear that,' Durnik said.

'That's probably because you haven't been in the market for a fur cape lately.' Belgarath chuckled. 'The price has taken quite a jump, I understand.' The old man rocked back in his chair. 'In Cthol Murgos, your friend Kal Zakath is methodically butchering his way down the east coast. He's added Rak Cthan and Rak Hagga to the list of cities he's captured and depopulated. I'm not too fond of Murgos, but it's just possible that Zakath is going a little too far.'

'Kal Zakath?' Polgara asked with one eyebrow slightly raised.

'An affectation.' Belgarath shrugged.

'More likely a symptom,' she observed. 'Angarak rulers always seem to be unstable in one way or another.' She turned to look at her father. 'Well?'

'Well what?'

'Have you heard anything from Riva? How are Garion and Ce'Nedra doing?'

'I haven't heard a sound—oh, a few official things. "The Rivan King is pleased to announce the appointment of Earl what's-his-name as Rivan ambassador to the Kingdom of Drasnia." That sort of thing, but nothing in the least bit personal.'

'We *are* sure that he knows how to write, aren't we?' she demanded exasperatedly. 'I'm sure that he's not so busy that he hasn't had the time to write at least *one* letter in the last two years.'

'He did,' Errand said quietly. He might not have mentioned the letter, but it seemed very important to Polgara.

She looked at him sharply. 'What did you say?' she asked.

'Belgarion wrote to you last winter,' Errand said. 'The

61

letter got lost, though, when the ship his messenger was aboard sank.'

'If the ship sank, then how do you—'

'Pol,' Belgarath said in a tone that seemed uncharacteristically firm, 'why don't you let me handle this?' He turned to Errand. 'You say that Garion wrote a letter to Polgara last winter?'

'Yes,' Errand said.

'But that the letter was lost when the messenger's ship sank?'

Errand nodded.

'Why didn't he write another one then?'

'He doesn't know that the ship sank.'

'But you do?'

Errand nodded again.

'Do you by any chance know what the letter said?'

'Yes.'

'Do you suppose you could recite it for us?'

'I guess I could, if you want. Belgarion's going to write another one in a week or so, though.'

Belgarath gave him a strange look. 'Why don't you tell us what the first one said? That way we won't miss anything.'

'All right,' Errand agreed. He frowned, concentrating very hard. 'He started out by saying, "Dear Aunt Pol and Durnik." I think that's sort of nice, don't you?'

'Just recite the letter, Errand,' Belgarath said patiently. 'Save the comments for later.'

'All right.' Errand stared thoughtfully into the fire. '"I'm sorry I haven't written earlier,"' he recited, '"but I've been terribly busy learning how to be a good king. It's easy enough to be King—all you need is to be born into the right family. To be a good king is harder, though. Brand helps me as much as he can, but I still have to make a lot of decisions about things that I don't really understand.

'"Ce'Nedra is well—at least I think so. We're hardly talking to each other any more, so it's kind of hard to say for sure. Brand is a bit concerned that we haven't had any children yet, but I don't think he needs to worry. So far as I can tell, we're never going to have any children, and maybe it's just as well. I really think we should have gotten to know each other a little better before we got married. I'm sure that there's some way that we could have called it off. Now it's too late. We'll just have to make the best of it. If we don't see each other too much, we can usually manage to be civil to each other—at least civil enough to keep up appearances.

'"Barak came by in that big war boat of his last summer, and we had a very good visit. He told me all about —"'

'Just a moment, Errand.' Polgara stopped the recitation. 'Does he say any more about the trouble he's having with Ce'Nedra?'

'No, ma'am,' Errand replied after a moment during which he quickly ran through the rest of the letter in his mind. 'He wrote about Barak's visit and some news he got from King Anheg and a letter from Mandorallen. That's about all. He said that he loves you and misses you very much. That's how he ended it.'

Polgar and Belgarath exchanged a very long look. Errand could feel their perplexity, but he was not sure exactly how to set their minds at rest about the matter.

'You're sure that's the way the letter went?' Belgarath asked him.

Errand nodded. 'That's what he wrote.'

'And you knew what was in the letter as soon as he wrote it?'

Errand hesitated. 'I don't know if it was like that exactly. It doesn't really work that way, you know. You have to sort of think about it, and I didn't really think about it until the subject came up—when Polgara was talking about it just now.'

'Does it matter how far away the other person is?' Belgarath asked curiously.

'No,' Errand replied, 'I don't think so. It just seems to be there when I want it to be.'

'No one can do that, father,' Polgara said to the old man. 'No one has *ever* been able to do that.'

'Apparently the rules have changed,' Belgarath said thoughtfully. 'I think we'll have to accept it as genuine, don't you?'

She nodded. 'He doesn't have any reason to make it up.'

'I think you and I are going to have to have some very long talks together, Errand,' the old man said.

'Perhaps,' Polgara said, 'but not just yet.' She turned back to the boy. 'Could you repeat what Garion said about Ce'Nedra for me?'

Errand nodded. '"Ce'Nedra is well—at least I think so. We're hardly talking to each other any more, so it's kind of hard to say for sure. Brand is a bit concerned that—"'

'That's fine, Errand,' she said, raising one hand slightly. Then she looked into the boy's face. After a moment, one of her eyebrows shot up. 'Tell me,' she said, very carefully choosing her words, 'do you know what's wrong between Garion and Ce'Nedra?'

'Yes,' Errand replied.

'Would you tell me?'

'If you want. Ce'Nedra did something that made Garion *very* angry, and then he did something that embarrassed her in public, and that made *her* angry. She thinks that he doesn't pay enough attention to her and that he spends all his time on his work so that he won't have to spend any with her. He thinks that she's selfish and spoiled and doesn't think about anybody but herself. They're both wrong, but they've had a lot of arguments about it and they've hurt each other so much with some of the things they've said that they've both given up on being married to each other. They're terribly unhappy.'

'Thank you, Errand,' she said. Then she turned to Durnik. 'We'll need to pack a few things,' she said.

'Oh?' He looked a bit surprised.

'We're going to Riva,' she said quite firmly.

64

Chapter Four

At Camaar, Belgarath ran across an old friend in a tavern near the harbor. When he brought the bearded, fur-clad Cherek to the inn where they were staying, Polgara gave the swaying sailor a penetrating look. 'How long have you been drunk, Captain Greldik?' she asked bluntly.

'What day is it?' His reply was vague.

She told him.

'Astonishing.' He belched. 'Par'n me,' he apologized. 'I appear to have lost track of several days somewhere. Do you know by any chance what *week* it is?'

'Greldik,' she said, 'do you absolutely *have* to get drunk every time you're in port?'

Greldik looked thoughtfully at the ceiling, scratching at his beard. 'Now that you mention it, Polgara, I believe I do. I hadn't really thought about it that way before, but now that you suggest it—'

She gave him a hard stare, but the look he returned was deliberately impudent. 'Don't waste your time, Polgara,' he suggested. 'I'm not married; I've never *been* married; and I'm not ever going to *get* married. I'm not ruining any woman's life by the way I behave, and it's absolutely certain that no woman is ever going to ruin mine. Now, Belgarath says that you want to go to Riva. I'll round up my crew, and we'll leave on the morning tide.'

'Will your crew be sober enough to find their way out of the harbor?'

He shrugged. 'We might bump into a Tolnedran merchantman or two on the way out, but we'll find our way to the open sea eventually. Drunk or sober, my crew is

65

the best afloat. We'll put you on the quay at Riva by midafternoon on the day after tomorrow—unless the sea freezes solid between now and then, in which case it might take a couple hours longer.' He belched again. 'Par'm me,' he said, swaying back and forth and peering at her with his bleary eyes.

'Greldik,' Belgarath said admiringly, 'you're the bravest man alive.'

'The sea doesn't frighten me,' Greldik replied.

'I wasn't talking about the sea.'

About noon of the following day, Greldik's ship was running before a freshening breeze through foaming whitecaps. A few of the less indisposed members of his crew lurched about the deck tending the lines and keeping a more or less alert eye on the stern where Greldik, puffy-eyed and obviously suffering, clung to the tiller.

'Aren't you going to shorten your sail?' Belgarath asked him.

'What for?'

'Because if you leave full sail up in this kind of wind, you'll uproot your mast.'

'You stick to your sorcery, Belgarath,' Greldik told him, 'and leave the sailing to me. We're making good time, and the deck-planking starts to buckle up long before the mast is in any danger.'

'How long before?'

Greldik shrugged. 'Almost a minute or so—most of the time.'

Belgarath stared at him. 'I think I'll go below,' he said at last.

'That's a good idea.'

By evening the wind had abated, and Greldik's ship continued across a quieter sea as night fell. There were only occasional glimpses of the stars, but they were sufficient; when the sun rose the next morning, it was, as the wayward captain had predicted, dead astern. By midmorning, the dark, rocky crags and jagged peaks that formed the crest of the Isle of the Winds were poked above the western horizon, and their ship was once again plunging like a spirited horse through the whitecaps under a crisp blue sky. A broad grin split Greldik's bearded face as his ship swooped and lurched and shuddered her way through the hammering seas, throwing out great sheets of sparkling spray each time she knifed into a wave.

'That's a *very* unreliable man,' Polgara said, giving the captain a disapproving stare.

'He really seems to be a very good sailor, Pol,' Durnik said mildly.

'That's not what I was talking about, Durnik.'

'Oh.'

The ship tacked smoothly between two rocky headlands and into the sheltered harbor of the city of Riva. The gray stone buildings mounted steeply upward toward the grim, menacing battlements of the Citadel which brooded over the city and the harbor below.

'This place always looks so bleak,' Durnik noted. 'Bleak and uninviting.'

'That was sort of the idea when they built it, Durnik,' Belgarath replied. 'They didn't really want many visitors.'

Then, at the end of a starboard tack, Greldik swung his tiller hard over, and his ship, her prow knifing through the dark water, ran directly at the stone quay jutting out from the foot of the city. At the last possible moment he swung his tiller again. To the flapping of her patched sails, the ship coasted the last few yards and bumped gently against the salt-crusted stones of the quay.

'Do you think anybody saw us coming and told Garion?' Durnik asked.

'Evidently so,' Belgarath replied, pointing toward the arched gate that had just swung open to reveal the broad flight of stone stairs mounting upward within the thick, high walls protecting the seaward side of Riva. A number of official-looking men were coming through the gate; in the center of the group strode a tall young man with sandy-colored hair and a serious expression on his face.

'Let's step over to the other side of the ship,' Belgarath suggested to Durnik and Errand. 'I want to surprise him.'

'Welcome to Riva, Captain Greldik.' Errand recognized

Garion's voice, even though it sounded older, more sure now.

Greldik squinted appraisingly over the rail. 'You've grown, boy,' he said to the King of Riva. A man as free as Greldik almost never felt the need for using customary terms of respect.

'It's been going around lately,' Garion replied drily. 'Almost everybody my age has come down with it.'

'I've brought you some visitors,' Greldik told him.

Grinning, Belgarath moved across the deck to the quay-side railing with Durnik and Errand close behind him.

'Grandfather?' Garion's face was completely astonished. 'What are you doing here? And Durnik—and Errand?'

'Actually it was your aunt's idea,' Belgarath told him.

'Is Aunt Pol here, too?'

'Of course I am,' Polgara replied calmly, emerging from the low-roofed cabin under the stern.

'Aunt Pol!' Garion exclaimed, looking dumbfounded.

'Don't stare, Garion,' she told him, adjusting the collar of her blue cloak. 'It's impolite.'

'But, why didn't you let me know you were coming? What are you all doing here?'

'Visiting, dear. People do that from time to time.'

When they joined the young king on the quay, there were the usual embraces and handshakes and the long looks into each others' faces that go with reunions. Errand, however, was much more interested in something else. As they started the climb up through the gray city toward the Citadel brooding above it, he tugged once at Garion's sleeve. 'Horse?' he asked.

Garion looked at him. 'He's in the stables, Errand. He'll be happy to see you.'

Errand smiled and nodded.

'Does he still talk that way?' Garion asked Durnik. 'Just one word at a time like that? I thought—well—'

'Most of the time he speaks normally—for his age,' Durnik replied, 'but he's been thinking about the colt ever

68

since we left the Vale and sometimes, when he gets excited, he slips back to the old way.'

'He listens, though,' Polgara added, 'which is more than I can say about another boy when he was that age.'

Garion laughed. 'Was I really that difficult, Aunt Pol?'

'Not difficult, dear. You just didn't listen.'

When they arrived at the Citadel, the Rivan Queen greeted them under the high, thick-walled arch of the front gate. Ce'Nedra was as exquisite as Errand remembered her. Her coppery-colored hair was caught at the back of her head by a pair of golden combs, and the ringlets tumbled down her back in a flaming cascade. Her green eyes were large. She was tiny, not much taller than Errand, but she was every inch a queen. She greeted them all regally, embracing Belgarth and Durnik and lightly kissing Polgara's cheek.

Then she held out both hands to Errand, and he took them in his and looked into her eyes. There was a barrier there, the faintest hint of the defensive tightening with which she kept the hurt away. She drew him to her and kissed him; even in that gesture, he could feel the unhappy tenseness that she was probably no longer even aware of. As she removed her soft lips from his cheek, Errand once again looked deeply into her eyes, letting all the love and hope and compassion he felt for her flow into his gaze. Then, without thinking, he reached out his hand and gently touched her cheek. Her eyes went very wide, and her lip began to tremble. That faint touch of agate-hard defensiveness about her face began to crumble. Two great tears welled up in her eyes; then, with a brokenhearted wail, she turned and stumbled blindly, her arms outstretched. 'Oh, Lady Polgara!' she cried.

Polgara calmly took the sobbing little queen in her arms and held her. She looked directly into Errand's face, however, and one of her eyebrows was raised questioningly. Errand returned her look and gave her a calm, answering nod.

'Well,' Belgarath said, slightly embarrassed by Ce'Nedra's sudden weeping. He scratched at his beard

69

and looked around the inner courtyard of the Citadel and the broad granite steps leading up to the massive door. 'Have you got anything to drink handy?' he asked Garion.

Polgara, her arms still about the weeping Ce'Nedra, gave him a level look. 'Isn't it a bit early, father?' she asked.

'Oh, I don't think so,' he replied blandly. 'A bit of ale helps to settle the stomach after a sea voyage.'

'There's always some excuse, isn't there?'

'I can usually manage to think of something.'

Errand spent the afternoon in the exercise yard at the rear of the royal stables. The chestnut-colored colt was not really a colt any more, but rather a full-grown young stallion. His dark coat was glossy, and his muscles rippled under that coat as he ran in a wide circle about the yard. The single white patch on his shoulder seemed almost incandescent in the bright sunlight.

The horse had known somehow that Errand was coming and had been restive and high-strung all morning. The stableman cautioned Errand about that. 'Be careful of him,' he said. 'He's a bit flighty today for some reason.'

'He'll be fine now,' Errand said, calmly unlatching the door to the young horse's stall.

'I wouldn't go—' the stableman started sharply, half-reaching out as if to pull the boy back, but Errand had already entered the stall with the wide-eyed animal. The horse snorted once and pranced nervously, his hooves thudding on the straw-covered floor. He stopped and stood quivering until Errand put out his hand and touched that bowed neck. Then everything was all right between them. Errand pushed the door of the stall open wider and, with the horse contentedly nuzzling at his shoulder, led the way out of the stable past the astonished groom.

For the time being, it was enough for the two of them just to be together—to share the bond which was between them and had somehow existed even before they had met and, in a peculiar way, even before either of them was born. There would be more later, but for now this was enough.

When the purple hue of evening began to creep up the eastern sky, Errand fed the horse, promised that he would come again the following day, and went back into the Citadel in search of his friends. He found them seated in a low-ceilinged dining hall. This room was smaller than the great main banquet hall and it was less formal. It was perhaps as close to being homey as any room in this bleak fortress could be.

'Did you have a pleasant afternoon?' Polgara asked him.

Errand nodded.

'And was the horse glad to see you?'

'Yes.'

'And now you're hungry, I suppose?'

'Well—a little.' He looked around the room, noting that the Rivan Queen was not present. 'Where's Ce'Nedra?' he asked.

'She's a little tired,' Polgara replied. 'She and I had a long talk this afternoon.'

Errand looked at her and understood. Then he looked around again. 'I really *am* sort of hungry,' he told her.

She laughed a warm, fond laugh. 'All boys are the same,' she said.

'Would you really want us to be different?' Garion asked her.

'No,' she said, 'I don't suppose I would.'

The next morning, quite early, Polgara and Errand were in front of the fire in the apartment that had always been hers. Polgara sat in a high-backed chair with a fragrant cup of tea on the small table beside her. She wore a deep blue velvet dressing gown and held a large ivory comb. Errand sat on a carpet-covered footstool directly in front of her, enduring a part of the morning ritual. The washing of the face, ears, and neck did not take all that much time, but for some reason the combing of his hair always seemed to fill up the better part of a quarter hour. Errand's personal tastes in the arrangement of his hair were fairly elemental. As long as it was out of his eyes, it was satisfactory. Polgara, however, seemed to find a great deal of entertainment in pulling a comb through his soft, pale-blond curls. Now and then at odd times of the day, he would see that peculiar softness come into her eyes and see her fingers twitching almost of their own will toward a comb and he would know that, if he did not immediately become very busy with something, he would be wordlessly seated in a chair to have his hair attended to.

There was a respectful tap on the door.

'Yes, Garion?' she replied.

'I hope I'm not too early, Aunt Pol. May I come in?'

'Of course, dear.'

Garion wore a blue doublet and hose and soft leather shoes. Errand had noticed that if he had any choice in the matter, the young King of Riva almost always wore blue.

'Good morning, dear,' Polgara said, her fingers still busy with the comb.

'Good morning, Aunt Pol,' Garion said. And then he looked at the boy who sat fidgeting slightly on the stool in front of Polgara's chair. 'Good morning, Errand,' he said gravely.

'Belgarion,' Errand said, nodding.

'Hold your head still, Errand,' Polgara said calmly. 'Would you like some tea?' she asked Garion.

'No, thank you.' He drew up another chair and sat down across from her. 'Where's Durnik?' he asked.

'He's taking a walk around the parapet,' Polgara told him. 'Durnik likes to be outside when the sun comes up.'

'Yes,' Garion smiled. 'I seem to remember that from Faldor's farm. Is everything all right? With the rooms, I mean?'

'I'm always very comfortable here,' she said. 'In some ways it always was the closest thing I had to a permanent home—at least until now.' She looked around with satisfaction at the deep crimson velvet drapes and the dark leather upholstery of her chairs and sighed contentedly.

'These have been your rooms for a long time, haven't they?'

'Yes. Beldaran set them aside for me after she and Iron-grip were married.'

'What was he like?'

'Iron-grip? Very tall—almost as tall as his father—and immensely strong.' She turned her attention back to Errand's hair.

'Was he as tall as Barak?'

'Taller, but not quite so thick-bodied. King Cherek himself was seven feet tall, and all of his sons were very big men. Dras Bull-neck was like a tree trunk. He blotted out the sky. Iron-grip was leaner and he had a fierce black beard and piercing blue eyes. By the time he and Beldaran were married, there were touches of gray in his hair and beard; but even so, there was a kind of innocence about him that we could all sense. It was very much like the innocence we all feel in Errand here.'

'You seem to remember him very well. For me, he's always been just somebody in a legend. Everybody knows about the things he did, but we don't know anything about him as a real man.'

'I'd remember him a bit more acutely, Garion. After all, there *had* been the possibility that I might have married him.'

'Iron-grip?'

'Aldur told father to send one of his daughters to the Rivan King to be his wife. Father had to choose between Beldaran and me. I think the old wolf made the right choice, but I still looked at Iron-grip in a rather special way.' She sighed and then smiled a bit ruefully. 'I don't think I'd have made him a good wife,' she said. 'My sister Beldaran was sweet and gentle and very beautiful. I was neither gentle nor very attractive.'

'But you're the most beautiful woman in the world, Aunt Pol,' Garion objected quickly.

'It's nice of you to say that, Garion, but when I was sixteen, I wasn't what most people would call pretty. I was tall and gangly. My knees were always skinned, and my face was usually dirty. Your grandfather was never very conscientious about looking after the appearance

73

of his daughters. Sometimes whole weeks would go by without a comb ever touching my hair. I didn't like my hair very much, anyway. Beldaran's was soft and golden, but mine was like a horse's mane, and there was this ugly white streak.' She absently touched the white lock at her left brow with the comb.

'What caused that?' he asked curiously.

'Your grandfather touched me there with his hand the first time he saw me—when I was just a baby. The lock turned white instantly. We're all marked in one way or another, you know. You have the mark on your palm; I have this white lock; your grandfather has a mark just over his heart. It's in different places on each of us, but it means the same thing.'

'What does it mean?'

'It has to do with what we are, dear.' She turned Errand around and looked at him, her lips pursed. Then she gently touched the curls just over his ears. 'Anyway, as I was saying, I was wild and willful and not at all pretty when I was young. The Vale of Aldur isn't really a very good place for a girl to grow up, and a group of crotchety old sorcerers is not really a very good substitute for a mother. They tend to forget that you're around. You remember that huge, ancient tree in the middle of the Vale?'

He nodded.

'I climbed up into that tree once and stayed there for two weeks before anyone noticed that I hadn't been underfoot lately. That sort of thing can make a girl feel neglected and unloved.'

'How did you finally find out—that you're really beautiful, I mean?'

She smiled. 'That's another story, dear.' She looked at him rather directly. 'Do you suppose we can stop tiptoeing around the subject now?'

'What?'

'That business in your letter about you and Ce'Nedra.'

'Oh, that. I probably shouldn't have bothered you with it, Aunt Pol. It's my problem, after all.' He looked away uncomfortably.

74

'Garion,' she said firmly, 'in our particular family there's no such thing as a private problem. I thought you knew that by now. Exactly what *is* the difficulty with Ce'Nedra?'

'It's just not working, Aunt Pol,' he said disconsolately. 'There are things that I absolutely *have* to see to by myself, and she wants me to spend every waking minute with her —well, at least she *used* to. Now we go for days without seeing each other at all. We don't sleep in the same bed any more, and—' He looked suddenly at Errand and coughed uncomfortably.

'There,' Polgara said to Errand as if nothing had happened. 'I guess you're presentable now. Why don't you put on that brown wool cape and go find Durnik? Then the two of you can go down to the stables and visit the horse.'

'All right, Polgara,' Errand agreed, slipping down off the stool and going to fetch the cape.

'He's a very good little boy, isn't he?' Garion said to Polgara.

'Most of the time,' she replied. 'If we can keep him out of the river behind my mother's house. For some reason, he seems to feel incomplete if he can't fall into the water once or twice a month.'

Errand kissed Polgara and started toward the door.

'Tell Durnik that I said the two of you can enjoy yourselves this morning,' she told him. She gave Garion a direct look. 'I think I'm going to be busy here for a few hours.'

'All right,' Errand said, and went out into the corridor. He gave only the briefest of thoughts to the problem which had made Garion and Ce'Nedra so unhappy. Polgara had already taken the matter in hand, and Errand knew that she would fix things. The problem itself was not a large one, but it had somehow been exploded into something of monstrous proportions by the arguments it had caused. The smallest misunderstanding, Errand realized, could sometimes fester like a hidden wound, if words spoken in haste and in heat were allowed to stand without apology or forgiveness. He also realized that Garion and Ce'Nedra loved each other so much that they were both extremely vulnerable to those hasty and heated words. Each had an enormous power to hurt the other. Once they were both made fully aware of that, the whole business could be allowed to blow over.

The corridors of the Citadel of Riva were lighted by torches held in iron rings protruding from the stone walls. Errand walked down a broad hallway leading to the east side of the fortress and the steps leading to the parapet and the battlements above. When he reached the thick east wall, he paused to look out one of the narrow windows that admitted a slender band of steel-gray light from the dawn sky. The Citadel was high above the city, and the gray stone buildings and narrow, cobblestone streets below were still lost in shadows and morning mist. Here and there, lighted windows gleamed in the houses of early risers. The clean salt smell of the sea, carried by an onshore breeze, wafted over the island kingdom. Contained within the ancient stones of the Citadel itself was the sense of desolation the people of Riva Iron-grip had felt when they had first glimpsed this rocky isle rising grim and storm-lashed out of a leaden sea. Also within those stones was that stern sense of duty that had made the Rivans wrest their fortress and their city directly from the rock itself, to stand forever in defense of the Orb of Aldur.

Errand climbed the flight of stone stairs and found Durnik standing at the battlements, looking out over the Sea of the Winds that was rolling endlessly in to crash in long, muted combers against the rocky shore.

'She finished with your hair, I see,' Durnik noted.

Errand nodded. 'Finally,' he said wryly.

Durnik laughed. 'We can both put up with a few things if they please her, can't we?' he said.

'Yes,' Errand agreed. 'She's talking with Belgarion right now. I think she wants us to stay away until they've talked it all out.'

Durnik nodded. 'That's the best way, really. Pol and Garion are very close. He'll tell her things when they're alone that he wouldn't say if we were around. I hope she can things straightened out between him and Ce'Nedra.'

'Polgara will fix it,' Errand assured him.

From somewhere in a meadow high above them where the morning sun had already touched the emerald grass, a shepherdess lifted her voice to sing to her flock. She sang of love in a pure, unschooled voice that rose like bird song.

'That's the way love should be,' Durnik said. 'Simple and uncomplicated and clear—just like that girl's voice.'

'I know,' Errand said. 'Polgara said we could go visit the horse—whenever you're finished up here.'

'Of course,' Durnik said, 'and we could probably stop by the kitchen and pick up some breakfast along the way.'

'That's an awfully good idea, too,' Errand said.

The day went very well. The sun was warm and bright, and the horse frolicked in the exercise yard almost like a puppy.

'The king won't let us break him,' one of the grooms told Durnik. 'He hasn't even been trained to a halter yet. His Majesty said something about this being a very special horse—which I don't understand at all. A horse is a horse, isn't it?'

'It has to do with something that happened when he was born,' Durnik explained.

'They're all born the same,' the groom said.

'You had to have been there,' Durnik told him.

At supper that evening, Garion and Ce'Nedra were looking rather tentatively across the table at each other, and Polgara had a mysterious little smile playing across her lips.

When they had all finished eating, Garion stretched and yawned somewhat theatrically. 'For some reason I'm feeling very tired tonight,' he said. 'The rest of you can sit up and talk if you'd like, but I think I'll go to bed.'

'That might not be a bad idea, Garion,' Polgara told him.

He got to his feet, and Errand could feel his trembling nervousness. With an almost agonizing casualness he turned to Ce'Nedra. 'Coming, dear?' he asked, putting an entire peace proposal into those two words.

Ce'Nedra looked at him, and her heart was in her eyes. 'Why—uh—yes, Garion,' she said with a rosy little blush, 'I believe I will. I seem to be very tired, too.'

'Good night, children,' Polgara said to them in tones of warm affection. 'Sleep well.'

'What did you say to them?' Belgarath asked his daughter when the royal couple had left the room hand in hand.

'A great many things, father,' she replied smugly.

'One of them must have done the trick,' he said. 'Durnik, be a good fellow and top this off for me. He passed his empty tankard to Durnik, who sat beside the ale barrel.

Polgara was so pleased with her success that she did not even comment on that.

It was well after midnight when Errand awoke with a slight start.

'*You're a very sound sleeper,*' a voice that seemed to be inside his mind said to him.

'I was dreaming,' Errand replied.

'*I noticed that,*' the voice said drily. '*Pull on some clothes. I need you in the throne room.*'

Errand obediently got out of bed and pulled on his tunic and his short, soft Sendarian boots.

'*Be quiet,*' the voice told him. '*Let's not wake up Polgara and Durnik.*'

Quietly they left the apartment and went down the long, deserted corridors to the Hall of the Rivan King, the vast throne room where, three years before, Errand had placed the Orb of Aldur in Garion's hand and had forever changed the young man's life.

The huge door creaked slightly as Errand pulled it open, and he heard a voice inside call out, 'Who's there?'

'It's only me, Belgarion,' Errand told him.

The great Hall was illuminated by the soft blue radiance of the Orb of Aldur, standing on the pommel of the huge sword of Riva, hanging point downward above the throne.

'What are you doing wandering around so late, Errand?'

Garion asked him. The Rivan King was sprawled on his throne with his leg cocked up over one of the arms.

'I was told to come here,' Errand replied.

Garion looked at him strangely. 'Told? *Who* told you?'

'You know,' Errand said, stepping inside the Hall and closing the door. 'Him!'

Garion blinked. 'Does he talk to *you*, too?'

'This is the first time. I've known about him, though.'

'If he's never—' Garion broke off and looked sharply up at the Orb, his eyes startled. The soft blue light of the stone had suddenly changed to a deep, angry red. Errand could very clearly hear a strange sound. For all of the time he had carried the Orb, his ears had been filled with the crystalline shimmer of its song, but now that shimmer seemed to have taken on an ugly iron overtone, as if the stone had encountered something or someone that filled it with a raging anger.

'*Beware!*' that voice which they both heard quite clearly said to them in tones which could not be ignored. '*Beware Zandramas!*'

Chapter Five

As soon as it was daylight, the two of them went in search of Belgarath. Errand could sense that Garion was troubled and he himself felt that the warning they had received concerned a matter of such importance that everything else must be set aside in the face of it. They had not really spoken much about it during those dark, silent hours while they sat together in the Hall of the Rivan King, waiting for the first light to touch the eastern horizon. Instead, they had both watched the Orb of Aldur closely, but the stone, after that one strange moment of crimson anger, had returned to its customary azure glow.

They found Belgarath seated before a recently rekindled fire in a low-beamed hall close to the royal kitchens. On the table not far from where he sat lay a large chunk of bread and a generous slab of cheese. Errand looked at the bread and cheese, realizing suddenly that he was hungry and wondering if Belgarath might be willing to share some of his breakfast. The old sorcerer seemed lost in thought as he gazed into the dancing flames, and his stout gray cloak was drawn about his shoulders, though the hall was not cold. 'You two are up early,' he noted as Garion and Errand entered and came to join him by the fiireside.

'So are you, Grandfather,' Garion said.

'I had a peculiar dream,' the old man replied. 'I've been trying to shake it off for several hours now. For some reason I dreamed that the Orb had turned red.'

'It did,' Errand told him quietly.

Belgarath looked at him sharply.

'Yes. We both saw it, Grandfather,' Garion said. 'We

were in the throne room a few hours ago, and the Orb suddenly turned red. Then that voice that I've got in here—' He tapped his forehead. '—said to beware of Zandramas.'

'Zandramas?' Belgarth said with a puzzled look. 'Is that a name or a thing or what?'

'I don't really know, Grandfather,' Garion replied, 'but both Errand and I heard it, didn't we, Errand?'

Errand nodded, his eyes still on the bread and cheese . . .

'What were the two of you doing in the throne room at that hour?' Belgarath asked, his eyes very intent.

'I was asleep,' Garion answered. Then his face flushed slightly. 'Well, sort of asleep. Ce'Nedra and I talked until quite late. We haven't talked very much lately, and so we had a lot of things to say to each other. Anyway, *he* told me to get up and go to the throne room.'

Belgarath looked at Errand. 'And you?'

'He woke me up,' Errand replied, 'and he—'

'Hold it,' Belgarath said sharply. '*Who* woke you up?'

'The same one who woke Garion.'

'You know who he is?'

'Yes.'

'And you know *what* he is?'

Errand nodded.

'Has he ever spoken to you before?'

'No.'

'But you knew immediately who and what he is?'

'Yes. He told me that he needed me in the throne room, so I got dressed and went. When I got there, the Orb turned red, and the voice said to beware of Zandramas.'

Belgarath was frowning. 'You're both absolutely positive that the Orb changed color?'

'Yes, Grandfather,' Garion assured him, 'and it sounded different, too. It usually makes this kind of ringing noise —like the sound a bell makes after you strike it. This was altogether different.'

'And you're sure that it turned red? I mean it wasn't just a darker shade of blue or something?'

'No, Grandfather. It was definitely red.'

Belgarath got up out of his chair, his face suddenly grim. 'Come with me,' he said shortly and started toward the door.

'Where are we going?' Garion asked.

'To the library. I need to check on something.'

'On what?'

'Let's wait until I read it. This is important, and I want to be sure that I've got it right.'

As he passed the table, Errand picked up the piece of cheese and broke off part of it. He took a large bite as he followed Belgarath and Garion from the room. They went quickly through the dim, torchlit corridors and up a steep, echoing flight of narrow stone steps. In the past few years Belgarath's expression had become rather whimsical and touched with a sort of lazy self-indulgence. All trace of that was gone now, and his eyes were intent and very alert. When they reached the library, the old man took a pair of candles from a dusty table and lighted them from the torch hanging in an iron ring just outside the door. Then he came back inside and set one of the candles down. 'Close the door, Garion,' he said, still holding the other candle. 'We don't want to be disturbed.'

Wordlessly, Garion shut the solid oak door. Belgarath went over to the wall, lifted his candle and began to run his eyes over the row upon row of dusty, leather-bound books and the neatly stacked, silk-wrapped scrolls. 'There,' he said, pointing to the top shelf. 'Reach that scroll down for me, Garion—the one wrapped in blue silk.'

Garion stretched up on his tiptoes and took down the scroll. He looked at it curiously before handing it to his grandfather. 'Are you sure?' he asked. 'This isn't the Mrin Codex, you know.'

'No,' Belgarath told him. 'It isn't. Don't get your attention so locked onto the Mrin Codex that you ignore all the others.' He set down his candle and carefully untied the silver tassled cord binding the scroll. He stripped off the blue silk cover and began to unroll the crackling parchment, his eyes running quickly over the ancient script. 'Here it is,' he said at last. '"Behold,"' he read, '"in the day that Aldur's Orb burns hot with crimson fire shall the name of the Child of Dark be revealed."'

'But Torak was the Child of Dark,' Garion protested. 'What is that scroll?'

'The Darine Codex,' Belgarath told him. 'It's not always as reliable as the Mrin, but it's the only one that mentions this particular event.'

'What does it mean?' Garion asked him, looking perplexed.

'It's a bit complicated,' Belgarath replied, his lips pursed and his eyes still fixed on the passage in question. 'Rather simply put, there are two prophecies.'

'Yes, I knew that, but I thought that when Torak died, the other one just—well—'

'Not exactly. I don't think it's that simple. The two have been meeting in these confrontations since before the beginning of this world. Each time, there's a Child of Light and a Child of Dark. When you and Torak met at Cthol Mishrak, you were the Child of Light and Torak was the Child of Dark. It wasn't the first time the two had met. Apparently it was not to be the last, either.'

'You mean that it's not over yet?' Garion demanded incredulously.

'Not according to this,' Belgarath said, tapping the parchment.

'All right, if this Zandramas is the Child of Dark, who's the Child of Light?'

'As far as I know. you are.'

Me? Still?

'Until we hear something to the contrary.'

'Why me?'

'Haven't we had this conversation before?' Belgarath asked drily.

Garion's shoulders slumped. 'Now I've got *this* to worry about again—on top of everything else.'

'Oh, stop feeling sorry for yourself, Garion,' Belgarath told him bluntly. 'We're all doing what we have to do, and sniveling about it won't change a thing.'

'I wasn't sniveling.'

'Whatever you call it, stop it and get to work.'

'What am I supposed to do?' Garion's tone was just a trifle sullen.

'You can start here,' the old man said, waving one hand to indicate all the dusty books and silk-wrapped scrolls. 'This is perhaps one of the world's best collections of prophecy—western prophecy at least. It doesn't include the Oracles of the Mallorean Grolims, of course, or the collection that Ctuchik had at Rak Cthol or the secret books of those people at Kell, but it's a place to start. I want you to read your way through this—all of it—and see if you can find out anything at all about this Zandramas. Make a note of every reference to "the Child of Dark." Most of them will probably have to do with Torak, but there might be some that mean Zandramas instead.' He frowned slightly. 'While you're at it, keep an eye out for anything that has to do with something called "the Sardion" or "Cthrag Sardius."'

'What's that?'

'I don't know. Beldin ran across the term in Mallorea. It might be important—or it might not.'

Garion looked around the library, his face blanching slightly. 'Are you telling me that this is *all* prophecy?'

'Of course not. A lot of it—most if it probably—is the collected ravings of assorted madmen, all faithfully written down.'

'Why would anybody want to write down what crazy people say?'

'Because the Mrin Codex is precisely that, the ravings of a lunatic. The Mrin prophet was so crazy that he had to be chained up. A lot of very conscientious people went out after he died and wrote down the gibberish of every madman they could find on the off chance that there might be prophecy hidden in it somewhere.'

'How do I tell the difference?'

'I'm not really sure. Maybe after you've read them all, you'll be able to come up with a way to separate them. If you do, let us know. It could save us all a lot of time.'

Garion looked around the library in dismay. 'But, Grandfather,' he protested, 'this could take *years*!'

'You'd probably better get started then, hadn't you? Try to concentrate on things that are supposed to happen *after* the death of Torak. We're all fairly familiar with the things that led up to that.'

'Grandfather, I'm not really a scholar. What if I miss something?'

'Don't,' Belgarath told him firmly. 'Like it or not, Garion, you're one of us. You have the same responsibilities that the rest of us do. You might as well get used to the idea that the whole world depends on you—and you *also* might just as well forget that you ever heard the words "why me?" That's the objection of a child, and you're a man now.' Then the old man turned and looked very hard at Errand. 'And what are *you* doing mixed up in all of this?' he asked.

'I'm not sure,' Errand replied calmly. 'We'll probably have to wait and see, won't we?'

That afternoon Errand was alone with Polgara in the warm comfort of her sitting room. She sat by the fire with her favorite blue robe about her and her feet on a carpeted footstool. She held an embroidery hoop in her hands and she was humming softly as her needle flashed in the golden firelight. Errand sat in the leather-covered armchair opposite hers, nibbling on an apple and watching her as she sewed. One of the things he loved about her was her ability to radiate a kind of calm contentment when she was engaged in simple domestic tasks. At such quiet times her very presense was soothing.

The pretty Rivan girl who served as Polgara's maid tapped softly and entered the room. 'Lady Polgara,' she said with a little curtsy, 'My Lord Brand asks if he might have a word with you.'

'Of course, dear,' Polgara replied, laying aside her embroidery. 'Show him in, please.' Errand had noticed that Polgara tended to call all young people 'dear,' most of the time without even being aware that she was doing it.

The maid escorted the tall, gray-haired Rivan Warder

85

into the room, curtsied again, and then quietly withdrew.

'Polgara,' Brand greeted her in his deep voice. He was a large, bulky man with a deeply lined face and tired, sad eyes and he was the last Rivan Warder. During the centuries-long interregnum following the death of King Gorek at the hands of Queen Salmisra's assassins, the Isle of the Winds and the Rivan people had been ruled by a line of men chosen for their ability and their absolute devotion to duty. So selfless had been that devotion that each Rivan Warder had submerged his own personality and had taken the name Brand. Now that Garion had come at last to claim his throne, there was no further need for that centuries-old stewardship. So long as he lived, however, this big, sad-eyed man would be absolutely committed to the royal line—not perhaps so much to Garion himself, but rather to the concept of the line and to its perpetuation. It was with that thought uppermost in his mind that he came that quiet afternoon to thank Polgara for taking the estrangement of Garion and his queen in hand.

'How did they manage to grow so far apart?' she asked him. 'When they married, they were so close that you couldn't pry them away from each other.'

'It all started about a year ago,' Brand replied in his rumbling voice. 'There are two powerful families on the northern end of the island. They had always been friendly, but a dispute arose over a property arrangement that was involved in a wedding between a young man from one family and a girl from the other. People from one family came to the Citadel and presented their cause to Ce'Nedra, and she issued a royal decree supporting them.'

'But she neglected to consult Garion about it?' Polgara surmised.

Brand nodded. 'When he found out, he was furious. There's no question that Ce'Nedra had overstepped her authority, but Garion revoked her decree in public.'

'Oh, dear,' Polgara said. 'So *that's* what all the bitterness was about. I couldn't really get a straight answer out of either of them.'

'They were probably a little too ashamed to admit it,' Brand said. 'Each one had humiliated the other in public, and neither one was mature enough just to forgive and let it slide. They kept wrangling at each other until the whole affair got completely out of hand. There were times when I wanted to shake them both—or maybe spank them.'

'That's an interesting idea.' She laughed. 'Why didn't you write and tell me they were having problems?'

'Belgarion told me not to,' he replied helplessly.

'Sometimes we have to disobey that kind of order.'

'I'm sorry, Polgara, but *I* can't do that.'

'No, I suppose you couldn't.' She turned to look at Errand, who was closely examining an exquisite piece of blown glass, a crystal wren perched on a budding twig. 'Please don't touch it, Errand,' she cautioned. 'It's fragile and very precious.'

'Yes,' he agreed, 'I know.' And to reassure her he clasped his hands firmly behind his back.

'Well.' She turned back to Brand. 'I hope the foolishness is all past now. I think we've restored peace to the royal house of Riva.'

'I certainly hope so,' Brand said with a tired smile. 'I would definitely like to see an occupant in the royal nursery.'

'That might take a bit longer.'

'It's getting sort of important, Polgara,' he said seriously. 'We're all a bit nervous about the lack of an heir to the throne. It's not only me. Anheg and Rhodar and Cho-Hag have all written to me about it. All of Aloria is holding its breath waiting for Ce'Nedra to start having children.'

'She's only nineteen, Brand.'

'Most Alorn girls have had at least two babies by the time they're nineteen.'

'Ce'Nedra isn't an Alorn. She's not even entirely Tolnedran. Her heritage is Dryad, and there are some peculiarities about Dryads and the way they mature.'

'That's going to be a little hard to explain to other

Alorns,' Brand replied. 'There *has* to be an heir to the Rivan throne. The line *must* continue.'

'Give them a little time, Brand,' Polgara said placidly. 'They'll get around to it. The important thing was to get them back into the same bedroom.'

Perhaps a day or so later, when the sun was sparkling on the waters of the Sea of the Winds and a stiff onshore breeze was flecking the tops of the green waves with frothy whitecaps, a huge Cherek war boat maneuvered its ways ponderously between the two rocky headlands embracing the harbor at Riva. The ship's captain was also more than life-sized. With his red beard streaming in the wind, Barak, Earl of Trellheim, stood at his tiller, a look of studied concentration on his face as he worked his way through a tricky eddy just inside one of the protective headlands and then across the harbor to the stone quay. Almost before his sailors had made the ship fast, Barak was coming up the long flight of granite steps to the Citadel.

Belgarath and Errand had been on the parapet atop the walls of the fortress and had witnessed the arrival of Barak's ship. And so, when the big man reached the heavy gates, they were waiting for him.

'What are *you* doing here, Belgarath?' the burly Cherek asked. 'I thought you were at the Vale.'

Belgarath shrugged. 'We came by for a visit.'

Barak looked at Errand. 'Hello, boy,' he said. 'Are Polgara and Durnik here, too?'

'Yes,' Errand replied. 'They're all in the throne room watching Belgarion.'

'What's he doing?'

'Being king,' Belgarath said shortly. 'We saw you come into the harbor.'

'Really impressive, wasn't it?' Barak said proudly.

'Your ship steers like a pregnant whale, Barak,' Belgarath told him bluntly. 'You don't seem to have grasped the idea that bigger is not necessarily better.'

Barak's face took on an injured expression. 'I don't make jokes about *your* possessions, Belgarath.'

'I don't *have* any possessions, Barak. What brought you to Riva?'

'Anheg sent me. Is Garion going to be much longer at whatever he's doing?'

'We can go find out, I suppose.'

The Rivan King, however, had concluded the formal audience for that morning and, in the company of Ce'Nedra, Polgara, and Durnik, had gone through a dim, private passageway which led from the great Hall of the Rivan King to the royal apartments.

'Barak!' Garion exclaimed, hurrying forward to greet his old friend in the corridor outside the door to the apartment.

Barak gave him a peculiar look and bowed respectfully.

'What's that all about?' Garion asked him with a puzzled look.

'You're still wearing your crown, Garion,' Polgara reminded him, 'and your state robes. All of that makes you look rather official.'

'Oh,' Garion said, looking a bit abashed, 'I forgot. Let's go inside.' He pulled open the door and led them all into the room beyond.

With a broad grin, Barak enfolded Polgara in a vast bear hug.

'Barak,' she said a trifle breathlessly, 'you'd be much nicer at close quarters if you'd remember to wash your beard after you've been eating smoked fish.'

'I only had one,' he told her.

'That's usually enough.'

He turned then and put his bulky arms around Ce'Nedra's tiny shoulders and kissed her soundly.

The little queen laughed and caught her crown in time to keep it from sliding off her head. 'You're right, Lady Polgara,' she said, 'he definitely has a certain fragrance about him.'

'Garion,' Barak said plaintively, 'I'm absolutely dying for a drink.'

'Did all the ale barrels on your ship run dry?' Polgara asked him.

'There's no drinking aboard the *Seabird*,' Barak replied.

'Oh?'

'I want my sailors sober.'

'Astonishing,' she murmured.

'It's a matter of principle,' Barak said piously.

'They *do* need their wits about them,' Belgarath agreed. 'That big ship of his is not exactly what you'd call responsive.'

Barak gave him a hurt look.

Garion sent for ale, removed his crown and state robes with obvious relief, and invited them all to sit down.

Once Barak had quenched his most immediate thirst, his expression became serious. He looked at Garion. 'Anheg sent me to warn you that we're starting to get reports about the Bear-cult again.'

'I thought they were all killed at Thull Mardu,' Durnik said.

'Grodeg's underlings were,' Barak told him. 'Unfortunately, Grodeg wasn't the whole cult.'

'I don't exactly follow you,' Durnik said.

'It gets a little complicated. You see, the Bear-cult has always been there, really. It's a fundamental part of the religious life of the more remote parts of Cherek, Drasnia, and Algaria. Every so often, though, somebody with more ambition than good sense—like Grodeg—gains control and tries to establish the cult in the cities. The cities are where the power is, and somebody like Grodeg automatically tries to use the cult to take them over. The problem is that the Bear-cult doesn't work in the cities.'

Durnik's frown became even more confused.

'People who live in cities are always coming in contact with new people and new ideas,' Barak explained. 'Out in the countryside, though, they can go for generations without ever encountering a single new thought. The Bear-cult doesn't believe in new thoughts, so it's the natural sort of thing to attract country people.'

'New ideas aren't *always* good ones,' Durnik said stiffly, his own rural background painfully obvious.

'Granted,' Barak agreed, 'but old ones aren't necessarily

good either, and the Bear-cult's been working on the same idea for several thousand years now. About the last thing Belar said to the Alorns before the Gods departed was that they should lead the Kingdoms of the West against the people of Torak. It's that word "lead" that's caused all the problems. It can mean many things, unfortunately. Bear-cultists have always taken it to mean that their very first step in obeying Belar's instructions should be a campaign to force the other Western Kingdoms to submit to Alorn domination. A good Bear-cultist isn't thinking about fighting Angaraks, because all of his attention is fixed on subduing Sendaria, Arendia, Tolnedra, Nyissa, and Maragor.'

'Maragor doesn't even exist any more,' Durnik objected.

'That news hasn't reached the cult yet,' Barak said drily. 'After all, it's only been about three thousand years now. Anyway, that's the rather tired idea behind the Bear-cult. Their first goal is to reunite Aloria; their next is to overrun and subjugate all of the Western Kingdoms; and only *then* will they start to give some thought to attacking Murgos and Malloreans.'

'They *are* just a bit backward, aren't they?' Durnik observed.

'Some of them haven't even discovered fire yet.' Barak snorted.

'I don't really see why Anheg is so concerned, Barak,' Belgarath said. 'The Bear-cult doesn't really cause any problems out there in the countryside. They jump around bonfires on midsummer's eve and put on bearskins and shuffle around in single file in the dead of winter and recite long prayers in smoky caves, until they get so dizzy that they can't stand up. Where's the danger in that?'

'I'm getting to that,' Barak said, pulling at his beard. 'Always before, the rural Bear-cult was just a reservoir of undirected stupidity and superstition. But in the last year or so, something new has been going on.'

'Oh?' Belgarath looked at him curiously.

'There's a new leader of the cult—we don't even know

who he is. In the past, Bear-cultists from one village didn't even trust the ones from another, so they were never organized enough to be any problem. This new leader of theirs has changed all of that. For the first time in history, rural Bear-cultists are all taking orders from one man.'

Belgarath frowned. 'That *is* serious,' he admitted.

'This is very interesting, Barak,' Garion said, looking a bit perplexed, 'but why did King Anheg send you all the way here to warn *me*? From what I've been told, the Bear-cult has never been able to get a foothold here on the Isle of the Winds.'

'Anheg wanted me to warn you to take a few precautions, since this new cult's antagonism is directed primarily at *you*.'

'Me? What for?'

'You married a Tolnedran,' Barak told him. 'To a Bear-cultist, a Tolnedran is worse than a Murgo.'

'That's a novel position,' Ce'Nedra said with a toss of her curls.

'That's the way those people think,' Barak told her. 'Most of those blockheads don't even know what an Angarak *is*. They've all seen Tolnedrans though—usually merchants who deal quite sharply. For a thousand years, they've been waiting for a king to come and pick up Riva's sword and lead them on a holy war to crush all the Kingdoms of the West into subjugation, and when he *does* finally show up, the very first thing he does is marry an imperial Tolnedran Princess. The way they look at it, the next Rivan King is going to be a mongrel. They hate you like poison, my little sweetheart.'

'What an absolute absurdity!' she exclaimed.

'Of course it is,' the big Cherek agreed. 'But absurdity has always been a characteristic of the mind dominated by religion. We'd all be a lot better off if Belar had just kept his mouth shut.'

Belgarath laughed suddenly.

'What's so funny?' Barak asked.

'Asking Belar to keep his mouth shut would probably have been the most futile thing any human being could even contemplate,' the old sorcerer said, still laughing. 'I remember one time when he talked for a week and a half straight without stopping.'

'What was he saying?' Garion asked curiously.

'He was explaining to the early Alorns why it wasn't a good idea to start a trek into the far north at the beginning of winter. Sometimes in those days you really had to talk to an Alorn to get an idea through to him.'

'That hasn't really changed all that much,' Ce'Nedra said with an arch look at her husband. Then she laughed and fondly touched his hand.

The next morning dawned clear and sunny, and Errand, as he usually did, went to the window as soon as he awoke to see what the day promised. He looked out over the city of Riva and saw the bright morning sun standing over the Sea of the Winds and smiled. There was not a hint of cloud. Today would be fine. He dressed himself in the tunic and hose which Polgara had laid out for him and then went to join his family. Durnik and Polgara sat in two comfortable, leather-upholstered chairs, one on each side of the fire, talking together quietly and sipping tea. As he always did, Errand went to Polgara, put his arms about her neck and kissed her.

'You slept late,' she said, brushing his tousled hair back from his eyes.

'I was a little tired,' he replied. 'I didn't get much sleep the night before last.'

'So I heard.' Almost absently, she pulled him up into her lap and held him nestled against the soft velvet of her blue robe.

'He's growing a bit big for your lap,' Durnik noted, smiling fondly at the two of them.

'I know,' Polgara answered. 'That's why I hold him as often as I can. Very soon he'll outgrow laps and cuddling, so I need to store up as much as I can now. It's all very well for them to grow up, but I miss the charm of having a small one about.'

There was a brief tap on the door, and Belgarath entered.

'Well, good morning, father,' Polgara greeted him.

'Pol.' He nodded briefly. 'Durnik.'

'Did you manage to get Barak put to bed last night?' Durnik asked with a grin.

'We poured him in about midnight. Brand's sons helped us with him. He seems to be getting heavier as he puts on the years.'

'You're looking surprisingly well,' Polgara observed, 'considering the fact that you spent the evening at Garion's ale barrel.'

'I didn't drink all that much,' he told her, coming to the fire to warm his hands.

She looked at him with one raised eyebrow.

'I've got a lot on my mind,' he said. Then he looked directly at her. 'Is everything straightened out between Garion and Ce'Nedra?'

'I think so, yes.'

'Let's be sure. I don't want things here to fly apart again. I'm going to have to get back to the Vale, but if you think you ought to stay and keep an eye on those two, I can go on ahead.' His voice was serious, even decisive. Errand looked at the old man, noting once again that Belgarath seemed sometimes to be two different people. When there was nothing of any urgency going on, he reveled in his leisure, amusing himself with drink, deception, and petty theft. When a serious problem arose, however, he could set all that aside and devote almost unlimited concentration and energy to solving it.

Polgara quietly put Errand down and looked at her father. 'It's serious, then?'

'I don't know, Pol,' he said, 'and I don't like it when things are going on that I don't know about. If you've finished with what you came here to do, I think we'd better get back. As soon as we can get Barak on his feet, we'll have him take us to Camaar. We can pick up horses there. I need to talk with Beldin—see if *he* knows anything about this Zandramas thing.'

'We'll be ready whenever you want to leave, father,' she assured him.

Later that same morning Errand went to the stables to say good-bye to the frolicsome young horse. He was a bit sad to be leaving so soon. He was genuinely fond of Garion and Ce'Nedra. The young King of Riva was in many ways like a brother to Errand, and Ce'Nedra was delightful—when she was not going out of her way to be difficult. Most of all, however, he was going to miss the horse. Errand did not think of the horse as a beast of burden. They were both young and shared a wholehearted enthusiasm for each others' company.

The boy stood in the center of the exercise yard with the long-legged animal frisking about him in the bright morning sunlight. Then he caught a movement out of the corner of his eye, turned, and saw Durnik and Garion approaching.

'Good morning, Errand,' the Rivan King said.

'Belgarion.'

'You and the horse seem to be enjoying yourselves.'

'We're friends,' Errand said. 'We like to be together.'

Garion looked almost sadly at the chestnut-hued animal. The horse came to him and curiously nuzzled at his clothing. Garion rubbed the pointed ears and ran his hand down the smooth, glossy forehead. Then he sighed. 'Would you like to have him for your very own?' he asked Errand.

'You don't own friends, Belgarion.'

'You're right,' Garion agreed, 'but would you like it if he went back to the Vale with you?'

'But he likes you, too.'

'I can always come and visit,' the Rivan King said. 'There isn't really much room for him to run here, and I'm always so busy that I don't have the time to spend with him the way I should. I think it would be best for him if he went with you. What do you think?'

Errand considered that, trying to think only of the well-being of the young animal and not of his own personal preferences. He looked at Garion and saw how much this generous offer had cost his friend. When he finally answered, his voice was quiet and very serious. 'I think you're right, Belgarion. The Vale *would* be better for him. He wouldn't have to be penned up there.'

'You'll have to train him,' Garion said. 'He's never been ridden.'

'He and I can work on that,' Errand assured him.

'He'll go with you, then,' Garion decided.

'Thank you,' Errand said simply.

'You're welcome, Errand.'

'*And done!*' Errand could hear the voice as clearly as if it had spoken in his own mind.

'*What?*' Garion's silent reply was startled.

'*Excellently done, Garion. I want these two to be together. They have things to do that need the both of them.*' Then the voice was gone.

Chapter Six

'The best way to begin is to lay a tunic or a coat across his back,' Hettar said in his quiet voice. The tall Algar wore his usual black leather and he stood with Errand in the pasture lying to the west of Poledra's cottage. 'Be sure that it's something that has your scent on it. You want him to get used to your smell and the idea that it's all right if something that smells like you is on his back.'

'He already knows what I smell like, doesn't he?' Errand asked.

'This is just a little different,' Hettar told him. 'You have to go at these things slowly. You don't want to frighten him. If he's frightened, he'll try to throw you off his back.'

'We're friends,' Errand tried to explain. 'He knows I won't do anything to hurt him, so why should he try to do something to hurt me?'

Hettar shook his head and looked out over the rolling grassland. 'Just do it the way I explained, Errand,' he said patiently. 'Believe me, I know what I'm talking about.'

'If you really want me to,' Errand replied, 'but I think it's an awful waste of time.'

'Trust me.'

Errand obediently laid one of his old tunics across the horse's back several times while the horse looked at him curiously, quite obviously wondering what he was doing. Errand wished that he could make Hettar understand. They had already wasted a good part of the morning on the hawk-faced Algar warrior's cautious approach to horse training. If they had just got right on with it, Errand

97

knew that he and the horse could be galloping together across the free open expanse of hills and valleys stretched out before them.

'Is that enough?' Errand asked after he had put the tunic on the horse's back several times. 'Can I get on him now?'

Hettar sighed. 'It looks as if you're going to have to learn the hard way,' he said. 'Go ahead and climb on, if you want. Try to find a soft place to land when he throws you off, though.'

'He wouldn't do that,' Errand replied confidently. He put his hand on the chestnut's neck and gently led him over to where a white boulder stuck up out of the turf.

'Don't you think you ought to bridle him first?' Hettar asked him. 'At least that gives you something to hang on to.'

'I don't think so,' Errand replied. 'I don't believe he'd like that bridle.'

'It's up to you,' Hettar said. 'Do it any way you like. Just try not to break anything when you fall.'

'Oh, I don't think I'll fall.'

'Tell me, do you know what the word "wager" means?'

Errand laughed and climbed up on the boulder. 'Well,' he said, 'here we go.' He threw his leg over the horse's back.

The colt flinched slightly and stood trembling.

'It's all right,' Errand assured him in a calm voice.

The horse turned and looked at him with soft astonishment in his large, liquid eyes.

'You'd better hang on,' Hettar warned, but his eyes had an oddly puzzled look, and his voice was not quite as certain as the words.

'He's fine.' Errand flexed his legs, not actually even bringing his heels in contact with the chestnut's flanks. The horse took a tentative step forward and then looked back enquiringly.

'That's the idea,' Errand encouraged him.

The horse took several more steps, then stopped to look back over his shoulder again.

'Good,' Errand said, patting his neck. 'Very, very good.' The horse pranced about enthusiastically.

'Watch out!' Hettar said sharply.

Errand leaned forward and pointed toward a grassy knoll several hundred yards off to the southwest. 'Let's go up there,' he said into the sharply upstanding ear.

The horse gave a sort of delighted shudder, bunched himself, and ran for the hilltop as hard as he could. When, moments later, they crested the knoll, he slowed and pranced about proudly.

'All right,' Errand said, laughing with sheer delight. 'Now, why don't we go to that tree way over there on that other hillside?'

'It was unnatural,' Hettar said moodily that evening as they all sat at the table in Poledra's cottage, bathed in the golden firelight.

'They seem to be doing all right,' Durnik said mildly.

'But he's doing everything wrong,' Hettar protested. 'That horse should have gone absolutely wild when Errand just got on him like that without any warning. And you don't *tell* a horse where you want him to go. You have to steer him. That's what the reins are for.'

'Errand's an unusual boy,' Belgarath told him, 'and the horse is an unusual horse. As long as they get along and understand each other, what difference does it make?'

'It's unnatural,' Hettar said again with a baffled look. 'I kept waiting for the horse to panic, but his mind stayed absolutely calm. I know what a horse is thinking, and about the only thing that colt was feeling when Errand got on his back was curiosity. *Curiosity!* He didn't do or think anything the way he should.' He shook his head darkly, and his long black scalplock swung back and forth as if in emphasis. 'It's unnatural,' he growled as if that were the only word he could think of to sum up the situation.

'I think you've already said that several times, Hettar,' Polgara told him. 'Why don't we just drop the subject— since it seems to bother you so much—and you can tell me about Adara's baby instead.'

An expression of fatuous pleasure came over Hettar's fierce, hawk-like face. 'He's a boy,' he said with the overwhelming pride of a new father.

'We gathered that,' Polgara said calmly. 'How big was he when he was born?'

'Oh—' Hettar looked perplexed. 'About so big, I'd say.' He held his hands half a yard apart.

'No one took the trouble to measure him?'

'They might have done that, I suppose. My mother and the other ladies were doing all sorts of things right after he came.'

'And would you care to estimate his weight?'

'Probably about as much as a full-grown hare, I suppose —a fairly good-sized one—or perhaps the weight of one of those red Sendarian cheeses.'

'I see. Perhaps a foot and a half long and eight or nine pounds—is that what you're trying to say?' Her look was steady.

'About that, I suppose.'

'Why didn't you say so, then?' she demanded in exasperation.

He looked at her, startled. 'Is it really *that* important?'

'Yes, Hettar, it really *is* that important. Women like to know these things.'

'I'll have to remember that. About all I was really interested in was whether he had the usual number of arms, legs, ears, and noses—things like that—that and making sure that his very first food was mare's milk, of course.'

'Of course,' she said acidly.

'It's very important, Polgara,' he assured her. 'Every Algar's first drink is mare's milk.'

'That makes him part horse, I suppose.'

He blinked. 'No, of course not, but it establishes a sort of bond.'

'Did you milk the mare for him? Or did you make him crawl out and find one for himself?'

'You're taking all this very oddly, Polgara.'

'Blame it on my age,' she said in a dangerous voice.

He caught that tone almost immediately. 'No, I don't think I'd want to do that.'

'Wise decision,' Durnik murmured. 'You said that you were going up into the mountains of Ulgoland.'

Hettar nodded. 'You remember the Hrulgin?'

'The flesh-eating horses?'

'I have a sort of an idea I want to try out. A full-grown Hrulga can't be tamed, of course, but maybe if I can capture some of their colts—'

'That's very dangerous, Hettar,' Belgarath warned. 'The whole herd will defend the young.'

'There are some ways to separate the colts from the rest of the herd.'

Polgara looked at him disapprovingly. 'Even if you succeed, what do you plan to do with the beasts?'

'Tame them,' Hettar replied simply.

'They can't be tamed.'

'Nobody's ever tried it. And even if I can't tame them, perhaps I can breed them with ordinary horses.'

Durnik looked puzzled. 'Why would you want horses with fangs and claws?'

Hettar looked thoughtfully into the fire. 'They're faster and stronger than ordinary horses,' he replied. 'They can jump much farther, and—' His voice drifted off into silence.

'And because you can't stand the idea of anything that looks like a horse that you can't ride,' Belgarath finished for him.

'That might be a part of it,' Hettar admitted. 'They'd give a man a tremendous advantage in a battle, though.'

'Hettar,' Durnik said, 'the most important thing in Algaria is the cattle, right?'

'Yes.'

'Do you really want to start raising a breed of horses that would probably look at a cow as something to eat?'

Hettar frowned and scratched at his chin. 'I hadn't thought about that,' he admitted.

Now that he had the horse, Errand's range increased enormously. The young stallion's stamina was virtually inexhaustible, and he could run for most of the day without tiring. Because Errand was still only a boy, his weight was not enough to burden the enthusiastic animal, and they ran freely over the rolling, grass-covered hills of southern Algaria and down into the tree-dotted expanse of the Vale of Aldur.

The boy rose early each morning and ate his breakfast impatiently, knowing that the chestnut stallion was waiting just outside the cottage and that, as soon as breakfast was over, the two of them could gallop out through the dew-drenched grass glistening green and lush in the slanting, golden rays of the morning sun and pound up the long slopes of the hills lying before them with the cool, sweet morning air rushing past them. Polgara, who seemed to know instinctively why they both had this need to run, said nothing as Errand wolfed down his food, sitting on the very edge of his chair so that at the very instant his plate was clean he could bolt for the door and the day which lay before him. Her eyes were gentle as she watched him, and the smile she gave him when he asked to be excused was understanding.

On a dewy, sun-filled morning in late summer when the tall grass was golden and heavy with ripe seeds, Errand came out of the door of the cottage and touched the bowed neck of his waiting friend with a gentle, caressing hand. The horse quivered with pleasure and took a few prancing steps, eager to be off. Errand laughed, took a handful of the stallion's mane, swung his leg and flowed up onto the strong, glossy back in a single, fluid move. The horse was running almost before the boy was in place. They galloped up the long hill, paused to look out over the sun-touched grassland lying open before them, and then circled the small valley where the thatched stone cottage lay and headed south, down into the Vale.

This day's ride was not, as so many of the others had been, a random excursion with no particular goal or purpose. For several days now, Errand had felt the presence of a strange, subtle awareness emanating from the Vale that seemed to be calling to him and, as he had emerged from the cottage door, he had suddenly resolved to find out exactly what it was that seemed to summon him so quietly.

As they moved down into the quiet Vale, past placidly grazing deer and curious rabbits, Errand could feel that awareness growing stronger. It was a peculiar kind of consciousness, dominated more than anything by an incredible patience—an ability, it seemed, to wait for eons for a response to these occasional quiet calls.

As they crested a tall, rounded hill a few leagues to the west of Belgarath's tower, a brief shadow flickered across the bending grass. Errand glanced up and saw a blue-banded hawk circling on motionless wings on a rising column of sun-warmed air. Even as the boy watched, the hawk tilted, sideslipped, and then spiraled down in long, graceful circles. When it was no more than inches above the golden tassels of the ripe grass, it flared its wings, thrust down with its taloned feet and seemed somehow to shimmer in the morning air. When the momentary shimmer faded, the hawk was gone and the hunchbacked Beldin stood waist-deep in the tall grass, with one eyebrow cocked curiously. 'What are you doing all the way down here, boy?' he asked without any kind of preamble.

'Good morning, Beldin,' Errand said calmly, leaning back to let the horse know that he wanted to stop for a few minutes.

'Does Pol know how far from home you've been going?' the ugly man demanded, ignoring Errand's gesture toward politeness.

'Probably not entirely,' Errand admitted. 'She knows that I'm out riding, but she might not know how much ground we can cover.'

'I've got better things to do than spend every day watching over you, you know,' the irascible old man growled.

'You don't have to do that.'

'Yes, as a matter of fact, I do. It's my month for it.'

Errand looked at him, puzzled.

'Didn't you know that one of us watches you every time you leave the cottage?'

'Why would you want to do that?'

'You *do* remember Zedar, don't you?'

Errand sighed sadly. 'Yes,' he said.

'Don't waste your sympathy on him,' Beldin said. 'he got exactly what he deserved.'

'Nobody deserves that.'

Beldin gave a snort of ugly laughter. 'He's lucky that it was Belgarath who caught up with him. If it had been me, I'd have done a lot more than just seal him up inside solid rock. But that's beside the point. You remember *why* Zedar found you and took you with him?'

'To steal the Orb of Aldur.'

'Right. So far as we know, you're the only person beside Belgarion who can touch the Orb and keep on living. Other people know that, too, so you might as well get used to the idea of being watched. We are *not* going to let you wander around alone where somebody might get his hands on you. Now, you didn't answer my question.'

'Which question?'

'What are you doing all the way down in this part of the Vale?'

'There's something I need to see.'

'What's that?'

'I don't know. It's up ahead somewhere. What is it that's off in that direction?'

'There's nothing out there but the tree.'

'That must be it, then. It wants to see me.'

'See?'

'Maybe that's the wrong word.'

Beldin scowled at him. 'Are you sure it's the tree?'

'No. Not really. All I know is that something in that direction has been—' Errand hesitated. 'I want to say *inviting* me to come by. Would that be the proper word?'

'It's talking to you, not me. Pick any word you like. All right, let's go then.'

'Would you like to ride?' Errand offered. 'Horse can carry us both.'

'Haven't you given him a name yet?'

'Horse is good enough. He doesn't seem to feel that he needs one. Would you like to ride?'

'Why would I want to ride when I can fly?'

Errand felt a sudden curiosity. 'What's it like?' he asked. 'Flying, I mean?'

Beldin's eyes suddenly changed, to become distant and almost soft. 'You couldn't even begin to imagine,' he said. 'Just keep your eyes on me. When I get over the tree, I'll circle to show you where it is.' He stooped in the tall grass, curved out his arms, and gave a strong leap. As he rose into the air, he shimmered into feathers and swooped away.

The tree stood in solitary immensity in the middle of a broad meadow, its trunk larger than a house, its widespread branches shading entire acres, and its crown rising hundreds of feet into the air. It was incredibly ancient. Its roots reached down almost into the very heart of the world; and its branches touched the sky. It stood alone and silent, as if forming a link between earth and sky, a link whose purpose was beyond the understanding of man.

As Errand rode up to the vast shaded area beneath the tree's shelter, Beldin swooped in, hovered, and dropped, almost seeming to stumble into his natural form. 'All right,' he growled, 'there it is. Now what?'

'I'm not sure.' Errand slid down off the horse's back and walked across the soft, springy turf toward the immense trunk. The sense of the tree's awareness was very strong now, and Errand approached it curiously, still unable to determine exactly what it wanted with him.

Then he put out his hand and touched the rough bark; in the instant that he touched it, he understood. He quite suddenly knew the whole of the tree's existence. He found that he could look back over a million million mornings to the time when the world had just emerged out of the elemental chaos from which the Gods had formed it. All at once, he knew of the incredible length of time that the earth had rolled in silence, awaiting the coming of man. He saw the endless turning of the seasons and felt the footsteps of the Gods upon the earth. And even as the tree knew, Errand came to know the fallacy which lay behind man's conception of the nature of time. Man needed to compartmentalize time, to break it into manageable pieces —eons, centuries, years, and hours. This eternal tree, however, understood that time was all one piece—that it was not merely an endless repetition of the same events, but rather that it moved from its beginning toward a final goal. All of that convenient segmenting which men used to make time more manageable had no real meaning. It was to tell him this simple truth that the tree had summoned him here. As he grasped that fact, the tree acknowledged him in friendship and affection.

Slowly Errand let his fingertips slide from the bark, then turned, and walked back to where Beldin stood.

'That's it?' the hunchbacked sorcerer asked. 'That's all it wanted?'

'Yes. That's all. We can go back now.'

Beldin gave him a penetrating look. 'What did it say?'

'It's not the kind of thing you can put into words.'

'Try.'

'Well—it was sort of saying that we pay too much attention to years.'

'That's enormously helpful, Errand.'

Errand struggled with it, trying to formulate words that would express what he had just learned. 'Things happen in their own time,' he said finally. 'It doesn't make any difference how many—or few—of what we call years come between things.'

'What things are we talking about?'

'The important ones. Do you really have to follow me all the way home?'

'I need to keep an eye on you. That's about all. Are you going back now?'

'Yes.'

'I'll be up there.' Beldin made a gesture toward the arching blue dome of the sky. He shuddered into the form of a hawk and drove himself into the air with strong thrusts of his wings.

Errand pulled himself up onto the chestnut stallion's back. His pensive mood was somehow communicated to the animal; instead of a gallop, the horse turned and walked north, back toward the cottage nestling in its valley.

The boy considered the message of the eternal tree as he rode slowly through the golden, sun-drenched grass and, all lost in thought, he paid but little attention to his surroundings. It was thus that he was not actually aware of the robed and hooded figure standing beneath a broad-spread pine until he was almost on top of it. It was the horse that warned him with a startled snort as the figure made a slight move.

'And so *thou* art the one,' it snarled in a voice which seemed scarcely human.

Errand calmed the horse with a reassuring hand on its quivering neck and looked at the dark figure before him. He could feel the waves of hatred emanating from that shadowy shape and he knew that, of all the things he had ever encountered, *this* was the thing he should most fear. Yet, surprising even himself, he remained calm and un-afraid.

The shape laughed, an ugly, dusty kind of sound. 'Thou art a fool, boy,' it said. 'Fear me, for the day will come when I shall surely destroy thee.'

'Not surely,' Errand replied calmly. He peered closely at the shadow-shrouded form and saw at once that—like the figure of Cyradis he had met on the snowy hilltop— this seemingly substantial shape was not really *here*, but somewhere else, sending its malevolent hatred across the empty miles. 'Besides,' he added, 'I'm old enough now not to be afraid of shadows.'

'We will meet in the flesh, boy,' the shadow snarled, 'and in that meeting shalt thou die.'

'That hasn't been decided yet, has it?' Errand said. 'That's why we have to meet—to decide which of us will stay and which must go.'

The dark-robed shape drew in its breath with a sharp hiss. 'Enjoy thy youth, boy,' it snarled, 'for it is all the life thou wilt have. I *will* prevail.' Then the dark shape vanished.

Errand drew in a deep breath and glanced skyward at the circling Beldin. He realized that not even the hawk's sharp eyes could have penetrated the spreading tree limbs to where that strange, cowled figure had stood. Beldin could not know of the meeting. Errand nudged the stallion's flanks, and they moved away from the solitary tree at a flowing canter, riding in the golden sunlight toward home.

Chapter Seven

The years that followed were quiet years at the cottage. Belgarath and Beldin were often away for long periods of time, and when they returned, travel-stained and weary, their faces usually wore the frustrated look of men who have not found what they were looking for. Although Durnik was often on the stream bank, bending all of his attention to the problem of convincing some wary trout that a thumbnail-sized bit of polished metal with a few strands of red yarn trailing behind it in the current was not merely edible but irresistibly delicious, he nonetheless maintained the cottage and its immediate surroundings in that scrupulously tidy condition which announced louder than words that the proprietor of any given farmstead was a Sendar. Although rail fences, by their very nature, zigzagged and tended to meander with the lay of the ground, Durnik firmly insisted that *his* fence lines be absolutely straight. He was quite obviously constitutionally incapable of going *around* any obstacle. Thus, if a large rock happened to intrude itself in the path of one of his fences, he immediately stopped being a fence builder and became an excavator.

Polgara immersed herself in domesticity. The interior of her cottage was immaculate. Her doorstep was not merely swept but frequently scrubbed. The rows of beans, turnips, and cabbages in her garden were as straight as any of Durnik's fences, and weeds were absolutely forbidden. Her expression as she toiled at these seemingly endless tasks was one of dreamy contentment, and she hummed or sang very old songs as she worked.

The boy, Errand, however, tended on occasion toward vagrancy. This was not to say that the was indolent, but many of the chores around a rural farmstead were tedious, involving repeating the same series of actions over and over again. Stacking firewood was not one of Errand's favorite pastimes. Weeding the garden seemed somehow futile, since the weeds grew back overnight. Drying the dishes seemed an act of utter folly, since, left alone, the dishes would dry themselves without any assistance whatsoever. He made some effort to sway Polgara to his point of view in this particular matter. She listened gravely to his impeccable logic, nodding her agreement as he demonstrated with all the eloquence at his command that the dishes did not really *need* to be dried. And when he had finished, summing up all his arguments with a dazzling display of sheer brilliance, she smiled and said, 'Yes, dear,' and implacably handed him the dishtowel.

Errand was hardly overburdened with unremitting toil, however. In point of fact, not a day went by when he did not spend several hours on the back of the chestnut stallion, roaming the grasslands surrounding the cottage as freely as the wind.

Beyond the timeless, golden doze of the Vale, the world moved on. Although the cottage was remote, visitors were not uncommon. Hettar, of course, rode by often and sometimes he was accompanied by Adara, his tall, lovely wife, and their infant son. Like her husband, Adara was an Algar to her fingertips, as much at home in the saddle as she was on her feet. Errand was very fond of her. Though her face always seemed serious, even grave, there lurked just beneath that calm exterior an ironic, penetrating wit that absolutely delighted him. It was more than that, however. The tall, dark-haired girl, with her flawless features and alabaster skin, carried about her a light delicate fragrance that always seemed to tug at the outer edges of his consciousness. There was something elusive yet strangely compelling about that scent. Once, when Polgara was playing with the baby, Adara rode with

Errand to the top of a nearby hill and there she told him about how the perfume she wore originated.

'You did know that Garion is my cousin?' she asked him.

'Yes.'

'We had ridden out from the Stronghold once—it was in the winter when everything was locked in frost. The grass was brown and lifeless, and all the leaves had fallen from the bushes. I asked him about sorcery—what it was and what he could do with it. I didn't really believe in sorcery—I wanted to, but I just couldn't bring myself to believe. He took up a twig and wrapped some dry grass around it; then he turned it into a flower right in front of my eyes.'

Errand nodded. 'Yes, that's the kind of thing Garion would do. Did it help you to believe?'

She smiled. 'Not right away—at least not altogether. There was something else I wanted him to do, but he said that he couldn't.'

'What was that?'

She blushed rosily and then laughed. 'It still embarrasses me,' she said. 'I wanted him to use his power to make Hettar love me.'

'But he didn't have to do that,' Errand said. 'Hettar loved you already, didn't he?'

'Well—he needed a little help to make him realize it. But I was feeling very sorry for myself that day. When we rode back to the Stronghold, I forgot the flower and left it behind on the sheltered side of a hill. A year or so later, the whole hillside was covered with low bushes and these beautiful little lavender flowers. Ce'Nedra calls the flower "Adara's rose," and Ariana thought it might have some medicinal value, even though we've never been able to find anything it cures. I like the fragrance of the flower, and it *is* mine in a sort of special way, so I sprinkle petals in the chests where I keep my clothes.' She laughed a wicked sort of little laugh. 'It makes Hettar *very* affectionate,' she added.

'I don't think that's entirely caused by the flower,' Errand said.

'Perhaps, but I'm not going to take any chances with that. If the scent gives me an advantage, I'm certainly going to use it.'

'That makes sense, I suppose.'

'Oh, Errand,' she laughed, 'you're an absolutely delightful boy.'

The visits of Hettar and Adara were not entirely social in nature. Hettar's father was King Cho-Hag, Chief of the Clan-Chiefs of Algaria, and Cho-Hag, the nearest of the Alorn monarchs, felt that it was his responsibility to keep Polgara advised of the events which were taking place in the world beyond the boundaries of the Vale. From time to time he sent reports of the progress of the bloody, endless war in southern Cthol Murgos, where Kal Zakath, emperor of Mallorea, continued his implacable march across the plains of Hagga and into the great southern forest in Gorut. The Kings of the West were at a loss to explain Zakath's seemingly unreasoning hatred of his Murgo cousins. There were rumors of a personal affront at some time in the past, but that had involved Taur Urgas, and Taur Urgas had died at the Battle of Thull Mardu. Zakath's enmity for the Murgos, however, had not died with the madman who ruled them, and he now led his Malloreans in a savage campaign, evidently designed to exterminate all of Murgodom and to erase from human memory all traces of the fact that the Murgos had ever even existed.

In Tolnedra, Emperor Ran Borune XXIII, the father of Queen Ce'Nedra of Riva, was in failing health; and because he had no son to succeed him on the Imperial Throne at Tol Honeth, the great families of the Empire were engaged in a vicious struggle over the succession. Enormous bribes changed hands, and assassins crept through the streets of Tol Honeth by night with sharpened daggers and vials of those deadly poisons purchased in secret from the snake-people of Nyissa. The wily Ran Borune, however, much to the chagrin and outrage of the Honeths, the Vordues, and the Horbites, had appointed General Varana, the Duke of Anadile, as his regent; and Varana, whose control of the legions was very nearly absolute, took firm steps to curb the excesses of the great houses in their scramble for the throne.

The internecine wars of the Angaraks and the only slightly less savage struggles of the Grand Dukes of the Tolnedran Empire, however, were of only passing interest to the Alorn Kings. The monarchs of the north were far more concerned with the troublesome resurgence of the Bear-cult and with the sad but undeniable fact that King Rhodar of Drasnia was quite obviously declining rapidly. Rhodar, despite his vast bulk, had demonstrated an astonishing military genius during the campaign which had culminated at the Battle of Thull Mardu, but Cho-Hag sadly reported that the corpulent Drasnian monarch had grown forgetful and in some ways even childish in the past few years. Because of his huge weight, he could no longer stand unaided and he frequently fell asleep, even during the most important state functions. His lovely young queen, Porenn, did as much as she possible could to relieve the burdens imposed upon him by his crown, but it was quite obvious to all who knew him that King Rhodar would be unable to reign much longer.

At last, toward the end of a severe winter that had locked the north in snow and ice deeper than anyone could remember, Queen Porenn sent a messenger to the Vale to entreat Polgara to come to Boktor to try her healing arts on the Drasnian king. The messenger arrived late one bitter afternoon as the wan sun sank almost wearily into a bed of purple cloud lying heavy over the mountains of Ulgo. He was thickly wrapped in rich sable fur, but his long, pointed nose protruded from the warm interior of his deep cowl and immediately identified him.

'Silk!' Durnik exclaimed as the little Drasnian dismounted in the snowy dooryard. 'What are you doing all the way down here?'

'Freezing, actually,' Silk replied. 'I hope you've got a good fire going.'

'Pol, look who's here,' Durnik called, and Polgara opened the door to look out at their visitor.

'Well, Prince Kheldar,' she said, smiling at the rat-faced

little man, 'have you so completely plundered Gar og Nadrak that you've come in search of a new theater for your depredations?'

'No,' Silk told her, stamping his half-frozen feet on the ground. 'I made the mistake of passing through Boktor on my way to Val Alorn. Porenn dragooned me into making a side trip.'

'Go inside,' Durnik told him. 'I'll tend to your horse.'

After Silk had removed his sable cloak, he stood shivering in front of the arched fireplace with his hands extended toward the flames. 'I've been cold for the last week,' he grumbled. 'Where's Belgarath?'

'He and Beldin are off in the East somewhere,' Polgara replied, mixing the half-frozen man a cup of spiced wine to help warm him.

'No matter, I suppose. Actually I came to see you. You've heard that my uncle isn't well?'

She nodded, picking up a glowing-hot poker and plunging it into the wine with a bubbling hiss. 'Hettar brought us some news about that last fall. Have his physicians put a name to his illness yet?'

'Old age.' Silk shrugged, gratefully taking the cup from her.

'Rhodar isn't really that old.'

'He's carrying a lot of extra weight. That tires a man out after a while. Porenn is desperate. She sent me to ask you—no, to *beg* you—to come to Boktor and see what *you* can do. She says to tell you that Rhodar won't see the geese come north if you don't come.'

'Is it really that bad?'

'I'm not a physician,' Silk replied, 'but he doesn't look very good, and his mind seems to be slipping. He's even starting to lose his appetite, and that's a bad sign in a man who always ate seven big meals a day.'

'Of course we'll come,' Polgara said quickly.

'Just let me get warm first,' Silk said in a plaintive tone.

They were delayed for several days just south of Aldurford by a savage blizzard that swept out of the mountains of Sendaria to howl across the open plains of northern

Algaria. As luck had it, they reached the encampment of a nomadic band of roving herdsmen just as the storm broke and sat out the days of shrieking wind and driving snow in the comfortable wagons of the hospitable Algars. When the weather cleared at last, they pressed on to Aldurford, crossed the river, and reached the broad causeway that stretched across the snow-choked fens to Boktor.

Queen Porenn, still lovely despite the dark circles under her eyes that spoke so eloquently of her sleepless concern, greeted them at the gates of King Rhodar's palace. 'Oh, Polgara,' she said, overwhelmed with gratitude and relief as she embraced the sorceress.

'Dear Porenn,' Polgara said, enfolding the careworn little Drasnian Queen in her arms. 'We'd have been here sooner, but we encountered bad weather. How's Rhodar?'

'A little weaker every day,' Porenn replied with a kind of hopelessness in her voice. 'Even Kheva tires him now.'

'Your son?'

Porenn nodded. 'The next king of Drasnia. He's only six—much too young to ascend the throne.'

'Well, let's see what we can do to delay that.'

King Rhodar, however, looked even worse than Silk's assessment of his condition had led them to believe. Errand remembered the King of Drasnia as a fat, jolly man with a quick wit and seemingly inexhaustible energy. Now he was listless, and his gray-hued skin hung on him in folds. He could not rise; perhaps even more serious was the fact that he could not lie down without his breath coming in painful, choking gasps. His voice, which had once been powerful enough to wake a sleeping army, had become a puny, querulous wheeze. He smiled a tired little smile of greeting when they entered, but after only a few minutes of conversation, he dozed off again.

'I think I need to be alone with him,' Polgara told the rest of them in a crisp, efficient voice, but the quick look she exchanged with Silk carried little hope for the ailing monarch's recovery.

When she emerged from Rhodar's room, her expression wa' grave.

'Well?' Porenn asked, her eyes fearful.

'I'll speak frankly,' Polgara said. 'We've known each other too long for me to hide the truth from you. I can make his breathing a bit easier and relieve some of his discomfort. There are some things that will make him more alert—for short periods of time—but we have to use those sparingly, probably only when there are some major decisions to be made.'

'But you cannot cure him.' Porenn's quiet voice hovered on the very edge of tears.

'It's not a condition that's subject to cure, Porenn. His body is just worn out. I've told him for years that he was eating himself to death. He's as heavy as three normal men. A man's heart was simply not designed to carry that kind of weight. He hasn't had any real exercise in the past several years, and his diet is absolutely the worst he could possibly have come up with.'

'Could you use sorcery?' the Drasnian Queen asked desperately.

'Porenn, I'd have to rebuild him from the ground up. Nothing he has really functions right any more. Sorcery simply wouldn't work. I'm sorry.'

Two great tears welled up in Queen Porenn's eyes. 'How long?' she asked in a voice scarcely more than a whisper.

'A few months—six at the most.'

Porenn nodded, and then, despite her tear-filled eyes, she lifted her chin bravely. 'When you think he's strong enough, I'd like to have you give him those potions that will clear his mind. He and I will have to talk. There are arrangements that are going to have to be made—for the sake of our son, and for Drasnia.'

'Of course, Porenn.'

The bitter cold of that long, cruel winter broke quite suddenly a couple of days later. A warm wind blew in off of the Gulf of Cherek during the night, bringing with it a gusty rainstorm that turned the drifts clogging the broad avenues of Boktor into sodden brown slush. Errand and Prince Kheva, the heir to the Drasnian throne, found themselves confined to the palace by the sudden change in the weather. Crown Prince Kheva was a sturdy little boy with dark hair and a serious expression. Like his father, the ailing King Rhodar, Kheva had a marked preference for the color red and he customarily wore a velvet doublet and hose in that hue. Though Errand was perhaps five years or so older than the prince, the two of them became friends almost immediately. Together they discovered the enormous entertainment to be found in rolling a brightly colored wooden ball down a long flight of stone stairs. After the bouncing ball knocked a silver tray from the hands of the chief butler, however, they were asked quite firmly to find other amusements.

They wandered for a time through the echoing marble halls of the palace, Kheva in his bright red velvet and Errand in sturdy peasant brown, until they came at last to the grand ballroom. At one end of the enormous hall, a broad marble staircase with a crimson carpet down the center descended from the upper floors of the palace, and along each side of that imposing stair was a smooth marble balustrade. The two boys looked speculatively at those twin bannisters, both of them immediately recognizing the tremendous potential of all that slippery marble. There were polished chairs along each side of the ballroom, and each chair was padded with a red velvet cushion. The boys looked at the balustrades. Then they looked at the cushions. Then they both turned to be sure that no guard or palace functionary was in the vicinity of the large, double doors at the back of the ballroom.

Errand prudently closed the doors; then he and Prince Kheva went to work. There were many chairs and many red velvet cushions. When those cushions were all piled in two heaps at the bottom of the marble stair railings, they made a pair of quite imposing mountains.

'Well?' Kheva said when all was in readiness.

'I guess we might as well,' Errand replied.

Together they climbed the stairs and then each of them mounted one of the smooth, cool bannisters descending grandly toward the white marble floor of the ballroom far below.

'Go!' Kheva shouted, and the two of them slid down, gaining tremendous speed as they went and landing with soft thumps in the heaps of cushions awaiting them.

Laughing with delight, the two boys ran back up the stairs again and once again they slid down. All in all, the afternoon went very well, until at last one of the cushions burst its seams and filled the quiet air of the grand ballroom with softly drifting goose down. It was, quite naturally, at that precise moment that Polgara came looking for them. Somehow it always happened that way. The moment anything was broken, spilled, or tipped over, someone in authority would appear. There was never an opportunity to tidy up, and so such situations always presented themselves in the worst possible light.

The double doors at the far end of the ballroom opened, and Polgara, regally beautiful in blue velvet, stepped inside. Her face was grave as she regarded the guilty-looking pair lying at the foot of the stairs in their piles of cushions, with a positive blizzard of goose down swirling around them.

Errand winced and held his breath.

Very softly, she closed the doors behind her and walked slowly toward them, her heels sounding ominously loud on the marble floor. She looked at the denuded chairs lining each side of the ballroom. She looked at the marble balustrades. She looked at the two boys with feathers settling on them. And then, without any warning whatsoever, she began to laugh, a rich, warm, vibrant laugh that absolutely filled the empty hall.

Errand felt somehow betrayed by her reaction. He and Kheva had gone out of their way to get themselves into trouble, and all she did was laugh about it. There was no scolding, no acid commentary, nothing but laughter. He definitely felt that this levity was out of place, an indication that she was not taking this thing as seriously as she ought. He felt a trifle bitter about the whole thing. He had *earned* the scolding she was denying him.

'You boys *will* clean it up, won't you?' she asked them.

'Of course, Lady Polgara,' Kheva assured her quickly. 'We were just about to do that.'

'Splendid, your Highness,' she said, the corners of her mouth still twitching. 'Do try to gather up *all* of the feathers.' And she turned and walked out of the ballroom, leaving the faint echo of her laughter hovering in the air behind her.

After that, the boys were watched rather closely. There was nothing really obvious about it; it was just that there always seemed to be someone around to call a halt before things got completely out of hand.

About a week later, when the rains had passed and the slush had mostly melted off the streets, Errand and Kheva were sitting on the floor of a carpeted room, building a fortress out of wooden blocks. At a table near the window Silk, splendidly dressed in rich black velvet, was carefully reading a dispatch he had received that morning from his partner, Yarblek, who had remained in Gar og Nadrak to tend the business. About midmorning, a servant came into the room and spoke briefly with the rat-faced little man. Silk nodded, rose, and came over to where the boys were playing. 'What would you gentlemen say to a breath of fresh air?' he asked them.

'Of course,' Errand replied, getting to his feet.

'And you, cousin?' Silk asked Kheva.

'Certainly, your Highness,' Kheva said.

Silk laughed. 'Must we be so formal, Kheva?'

'Mother says I should always use the proper forms of address,' Kheva told him seriously. 'I guess it's to help me keep in practice or something.'

'Your mother isn't here,' Silk told him slyly, 'so it's all right to cheat a little.'

Kheva looked around nervously. 'Do you really think we should?' he whispered.

'I'm sure of it,' Silk replied. 'Cheating is good for you. It helps you to keep your perspective.'

'Do *you* cheat often?'

'Me?' Silk was still laughing. 'All the time, cousin. All the time. Let's fetch cloaks and take a turn about the city. I have to go by the headquarters of the intelligence service;

and since I've been appointed your keeper for the day, the two of you had better come along.'

The air outside was cool and damp, and the wind was brisk enough to whip their cloaks about their legs as they passed along the cobbled streets of Boktor. The Drasnian capital was one of the major commercial centers of the world, and the streets teemed with men of all races. Richly mantled Tolnedrans spoke on street corners with sober-faced Sendars in sensible brown. Flamboyantly garbed and richly jeweled Drasnians haggled with leather-garbed Nadraks, and there were even a few black-robed Murgos striding along the blustery streets, with their broad-backed Thullish porters trailing behind them, carrying heavy packs filled with merchandise. The porters, of course, were followed at a discreet distance by the ever-present spies.

'Dear, sneaky old Boktor,' Silk declaimed extravagantly, 'where at least every other man you meet is a spy.'

'Are those men spies?' Kheva asked, looking at them with a surprised expression.

'Of course they are, your Highness.' Silk laughed again. 'Everybody in Drasnia is a spy—or wants to be. It's our national industry. Didn't you know that?'

'Well—I knew that there are quite a few spies in the palace, but I didn't think they'd be out in the streets.'

'Why should there be spies in the palace?' Errand asked him curiously.

Kheva shrugged. 'Everybody wants to know what everybody else is doing. The more important you are, the more spies you have watching you.'

'Are any of them watching you?'

'Six that I know of. There are probably a few more besides—and of course, all the spies are being spied on by other spies.'

'What a peculiar place,' Errand murmured.

Kheva laughed. 'Once, when I was about three or so, I found a hiding place under a stair and fell asleep. Eventually, all the spies in the palace joined in the search for me. You'd be amazed at how many there really are.'

This time, Silk laughed uproariously. 'That's really very

bad form, cousin,' he said. 'Members of the royal family aren't supposed to hide from the spies. It upsets them terribly. That's the building over there.' He pointed at a large stone warehouse standing on a quiet side street.

'I always thought that the headquarters was in the same building with the academy,' Kheva said.

'Those are the *official* offices, cousin. *This* is the place where the work gets done.'

They entered the warehouse and went through a cavernous room piled high with boxes and bales to a small, unobtrusive door with a bulky-looking man in a workman's smock lounging against it. The man gave Silk a quick look, bowed, and opened the door for them. Beyond that somewhat shabby-looking door lay a large, well-lighted room with a dozen or more parchment-littered tables standing along the walls. At each table sat four or five people, all poring over the documents before them.

'What are they doing?' Errand asked curiously.

'Sorting information,' Silk replied. 'There probably isn't much that happens in the world that doesn't reach this room eventually. If we really wanted to know, we could probably ask around and find out what the King of Arendia had for breakfast this morning. We want to go into that room over there.' He pointed toward a solid-looking door on the far side of the room.

The chamber beyond that door was plain, even bare. It contained a table and four chairs—nothing more. The man seated at the table in one of the chairs wore black hose and a pearl-gray doublet. He was as thin as an old bone, and even here, in the very midst of his own people, there was about him the sense of a tightly coiled spring. 'Silk,' he said with a terse nod.

'Javelin,' Silk replied. 'You wanted to see me?'

The man at the table looked at the two boys. He inclined his head briefly to Kheva. 'Your Highness,' he said.

'Margrave Khendon,' the prince responded with a polite bow.

The seated man looked at Silk, his idle-appearing fingers twitching slightly.

'Margrave,' Kheva said almost apologetically, 'my mother's been teaching me the secret language. I know what you're saying.'

The man Silk had called Javelin stopped moving his fingers with a rueful expression. 'Caught by my own cleverness, I see,' he said. He looked speculatively at Errand.

'This is Errand, the boy Polgara and Durnik are raising,' Silk told him.

'Ah,' Javelin said, 'the bearer of the Orb.'

'Kheva and I can wait outside if you want to speak privately,' Errand offered.

Javelin thought about that. 'That probably won't be necessary,' he decided. 'I think we can trust you both to be discreet. Sit down, gentlemen.' He pointed at the other three chairs.

'I'm sort of retired, Javelin,' Silk told him. 'I've got enough other things to keep me busy just now.'

'I wasn't really going to ask you to get personally involved,' Javelin replied. 'All I really want is for you to find room for a couple of new employees in one of your enterprises.'

Silk gave him a curious look.

'You're shipping goods out of Gar og Nadrak along the North Caravan Route,' Javelin continued. 'There are several villages near the border where the citizens are highly suspicious of strangers with no valid reason for passing through.'

'And you want to use *my* caravans to give your men an excuse for being in those villages,' Silk concluded.

Javelin shrugged. 'It's not an uncommon practice.'

'What's going on in eastern Drasnia that you're so interested in?'

'The same thing that's always going on in the outlying districts.'

'The Bear-cult?' Silk asked incredulously. 'You're going to waste time on *them*?'

'They've been behaving peculiarly lately. I want to find out why.'

Silk looked at him with one eyebrow raised.

'Just call it idle curiosity if you like.'

The look Silk gave him then was very hard. 'Oh, no. You're not going to catch me *that* easily, my friend.'

'Aren't *you* the least bit curious?'

'No. As a matter of fact, I'm not. No amount of clever trickery is going to lure me into neglecting my own affairs to go off on another one of your fishing expeditions. I'm too busy, Javelin.' His eyes narrowed ever so slightly. 'Why don't you send Hunter?'

'Hunter's busy someplace else, Silk, and stop trying to find out who Hunter is.'

'It was worth a try. Actually I'm not interested at all. Not in the least.' He sat back in his chair with his arms adamantly crossed. His long, pointed nose, however, was twitching. 'What do you mean by "behaving peculiarly?"' he asked after a moment.

'I thought you weren't interested.'

'I'm not,' Silk repeated hastily. 'I most definitely am *not*.' His nose, however, was twitching even more violently. Angrily he got to his feet. 'Give me the names of the men you want me to hire,' he said abruptly. 'I'll see what I can do.'

'Of course, Prince Kheldar,' Javelin said blandly. 'I appreciate your sense of loyalty to your old service.'

Errand remembered something that Silk had said in the large outer room. 'Silk says that information about almost everything is brought to this building,' he said to Javelin.

'That might be an exaggeration, but we try.'

'Then perhaps you might have heard something about Zandramas.'

Javelin looked at him blankly.

'It's something that Belgarion and I heard about,' Errand explained. 'And Belgarath is curious about it, too. I thought you might have heard about it.'

'I can't say that I have,' Javelin admitted. 'Of course we're a long way from Darshiva.'

'What's Darshiva?' Errand asked.

'It's one of the principalities of the old Melcene Empire

123

in eastern Mallorea. Zandramas is a Darshivan name. Didn't you know that?'

'No. We didn't.'

There was a light tap on the door.

'Yes?' Javelin answered.

The door opened, and a young lady of perhaps nineteen or twenty came in. Her hair was the color of honey, her eyes were a warm, golden brown, and she wore a plain-looking gray dress. Her expression was serious, but there was just the hint of a dimple in each of her cheeks. 'Uncle,' she said, and her voice had a kind of vibrancy about it that made it almost irresistibly compelling.

Javelin's hard, angular face softened noticeably. 'Yes, Liselle?' he said.

'Is this little Liselle?' Silk exclaimed.

'Not quite so little any more,' Javelin said.

'The last time I saw her, she was still in braids.'

'She combed out the braids a few years ago,' Javelin said drily, 'and look what was hiding under them.'

'I am looking,' Silk said admiringly.

'The reports you wanted, uncle,' the girl said, laying a sheaf of parchment on the table. Then she turned to Kheva and curtsied to him with incredible grace. 'Your Highness,' she greeted him.

'Margravine Liselle,' the little prince replied with a polite bow.

'And Prince Kheldar,' the girl said then.

'We weren't at all so formal when you were a child,' Silk protested.

'But then, I'm not a child any more, your Highness.'

Silk looked over at Javelin. 'When she was a little girl, she used to pull my nose.'

'But it's such a long, interesting nose,' Liselle said. And then she smiled, and the dimples suddenly sprang to life.

'Liselle is helping out here,' Javelin said. 'She'll be entering the academy in a few months.'

'You're going to be a spy?' Silk asked her incredulously.

'It's the family business, Prince Kheldar. My father and mother were both spies. My uncle here is a spy. All of my friends are spies. How could I possibly be anything else?'

Silk looked a trifle off-balance. 'It just doesn't seem appropriate, for some reason.'

'That probably means that I'll be quite successful, doesn't it? You *look* like a spy, Prince Kheldar. I don't, so I won't have nearly as many problems as you've had.'

Though the girl's answers were clever, even pert, Errand could see something in her warm, brown eyes that Silk probably could not. Despite the fact that the Margravine Liselle was obviously a grown woman, Silk just as obviously still thought of her as a little girl—one who had pulled his nose. The look she gave *him*, however, was not the look of a little girl, and Errand realized that she had been waiting for a number of years for the opportunity to meet Silk on adult terms. Errand covered his mouth with his hand to hide a smile. The wily Prince Kheldar had some *very* interesting times ahead of him.

The door opened again, and a nondescript man came in, quickly crossed to the table, and whispered something to Javelin. The man's face, Errand noticed, was pale, and his hands were trembling.

Javelin's face grew set, and he sighed. He gave no other outward sign of emotion, however. He rose to his feet and came around the table. 'Your Majesty,' he said formally to Prince Kheva, 'I believe that you should return to the palace immediately.'

Silk and Liselle both caught the changed form of address and looked sharply at the Chief of Drasnian Intelligence.

'I believe that we should all accompany the King back to the palace,' Javelin said sadly. 'We must offer our condolences to his mother and aid her in any way we can in her hour of grief.'

The King of Drasnia looked at his intelligence chief, his eyes very wide and his lip trembling.

Errand gently took the little boy's hand in his. 'We'd better go, Kheva,' he said. 'Your mother will need you very much right now.'

Chapter Eight

The Kings of Aloria gathered in Boktor for the funeral of King Rhodar and the subsequent coronation of his son, Kheva. Such a gathering, of course, was traditional. Though the nations of the north had diverged somewhat over the centuries, the Alorns nonetheless had never forgotten their origins in the single kingdom of King Cherek Bear-shoulders five thousand years in the dim past, and they came together at such times in sadness to bury a brother. Because King Rhodar had been beloved and respected by other nations as well, Anheg of Cherek, Cho-Hag of Algaria, and Belgarion of Riva were joined by Fulrach of Sendaria, Korodullin of Arendia, and even by the erratic Drosta lek Thun of Gar og Nadrak. In addition, General Varana was present as the representative of Emperor Ran Borune XXIII of Tolnedra, and Sadi, Chief Eunuch of the palace of Queen Salmissra of Nyissa, was also in attendance.

The burial of an Alorn King was a serious matter, and it involved certain ceremonies at which only the other Alorn monarchs were present. No gathering of so many kings and high-ranking functionaries, however, could ever be entirely ceremonial. Inevitably, politics were of major concern in the quiet discussions which took place in the somberly draped corridors of the palace.

Errand, soberly dressed and quiet, drifted from one small gathering to another in those days preceeding the funeral. The Kings all knew him, but they seemed for some reason to take little note of his presence, and so he heard many conversations which he might perhaps not have heard had they stopped to consider the fact that he was no longer the little boy they had known during the campaign in Mishrak ac Thull.

The Alorn Kings—Belgarion in his usual blue doublet and hose, the brutish-looking Anheg in his rumpled blue robe and dented crown, and quiet-voiced Cho-Hag in silver and black—stood together in a sable-draped embrasure in one of the broad hallways of the palace.

'Porenn is going to have to serve as regent,' Garion said. 'Kheva is only six, and somebody's going to have to run things until he's old enough to take charge himself.'

'A *woman?*' Anheg said, aghast.

'Anheg, are we going to have *that* argument again?' Cho-Hag asked mildly.

'I don't see any alternative, Anheg,' Garion said in his most persuasive manner. 'King Drosta is almost drooling at the prospect of a boy king on the throne of Drasnia. His troops will be biting off chunks of the borderlands before the rest of us get home unless we put someone in charge here.'

'But Porenn is so tiny,' Anheg objected irrationally, 'and so pretty. How can she possibly run a kingdom?'

'Probably very well,' Cho-Hag replied, shifting his weight carefully on his crippled legs. 'Rhodar confided in her completely, and she *was* behind the scheme that eliminated Grodeg, after all.'

'About the only other person in Drasnia competent enough to take charge here is the Margrave Khendon,' Garion told the King of Cherek. 'The one they call Javelin. Do you want the Chief of Drasnian Intelligence sitting behind the throne giving orders?'

Anheg shuddered. 'That's a ghastly thought. What about Prince Kheldar?'

Garion stared at him. 'You're not serious, Anheg,' he said incredulously. 'Silk? As regent?'

'You might be right,' Anheg conceded after a moment's thought. 'He *is* just a little unreliable, isn't he?'

'A *little?*' Garion laughed.

'Are we agreed, then?' Cho-Hag asked. 'It has to be Porenn, right?'

Anheg grumbled, but finally agreed.

The Algar King turned to Garion. 'You'll probably have to issue a proclamation.'

'Me? I don't have any authority in Drasnia.'

'You're the Overlord of the West,' Cho-Hag reminded him. 'Just announce that you recognize Porenn's regency and declare that anyone who argues about it or violates her borders will have to answer to *you*.'

'*That* should back Drosta off.' Anheg chuckled grossly. 'He's almost more frightened of you than he is of Zakath. He probably has nightmares about your flaming sword sliding between his ribs.'

In another corridor, Errand came upon General Varana and Sadi the Eunuch. Sadi wore the mottled, iridescent silk robe of the Nyissans, and the general was draped in a silver Tolnedran mantle with broad bands of gold-colored trim across his shoulders.

'So, it's official, then?' Sadi said in his oddly contralto voice, eyeing the general's mantle.

'What's that?' Varana asked him. The general was a blocky-looking man with iron-gray hair and a slightly amused expression.

'We had heard rumors in Sthiss Tor that Ran Borune had adopted you as his son.'

'Expediency.' Varana shrugged. 'The major families of the Empire were dismantling Tolnedra in their scramble for the throne. Ran Borune had to take steps to quiet things down.'

'You *will* take the throne when he dies, though, won't you?'

'We'll see,' Varana replied evasively. 'Let's pray that his Majesty will live for many years yet.'

'Of course,' Sadi murmured. 'The silver mantle of the crown prince *does* become you, however, my dear General.' He rubbed one long-fingered hand over his shaved scalp.

'Thank you,' Varana said with a slight bow. 'And how are affairs in Salmissra's palace?'

Sadi laughed sardonically. 'The same as they always

are. We connive and plot and scheme against each other, and every scrap of food prepared in our kitchens is tainted with poison.'

'I'd heard that was the custom,' Varana remarked. 'How does one survive in such a lethal atmosphere?'

'Nervously,' Sadi replied, making a sour face. 'We are all on a strict regimen. We routinely dose ourselves with every known antidote to every known poison. Some of the poisons are actually quite flavorful. The antidotes all taste foul, however.'

'The price of power, I suppose.'

'Truly. What was the reaction of the Grand dukes of Tolnedra when the Emperor designated you his heir?'

Varana laughed. 'You could hear the screams echoing from the wood of the Dryads to the Arendish border.'

'When the time comes, you may have to step on a few necks.'

'It's possible.'

'Of course the legions are all loyal to you.'

'The legions are a great comfort to me.'

'I think I like you, General Varana,' the shaved-headed Nyissan said. 'I'm certain that you and I will be able to come to some mutually profitable accommodations.'

'I always like to be on good terms with my neighbors, Sadi,' Varana agreed with aplomb.

In another corridor, Errand found a strangely assorted group. King Fulrach of Sendaria, dressed in sober, businesslike brown, was speaking quietly with the purple-garbed King Korodullin of Arendia and with the scabrous-looking Drosta lek Thun, who wore a richly jeweled doublet of an unwholesome-looking yellow.

'Have either of you heard anything about any decisions concerning a regency?' the emaciated Nadrak king asked in his shrill voice. Drosta's eyes bulged, seemingly almost to start out of his pock-marked face, and he fidgeted continuously.

'I would imagine that Queen Porenn will guide the young king,' Fulrach surmised.

'They surely wouldn't put a woman in charge,' Drosta

scoffed. 'I know Alorns, and they all look at women as subhuman.'

'Porenn is not exactly like other women,' the King of Sendaria noted. 'She's extraordinarily gifted.'

'How could a woman possibly defend the borders of so large a kingdom as Drasnia?'

'Thy perception is awry, your Majesty,' Korodullin told the Nadrak with uncharacteristic bluntness. 'Inevitably, the other Alorn Kings will support her, and most particularly Belgarion of Riva will defend her. Methinks no monarch alive would be so foolhardy as to counter the wishes of the Overlord of the West.'

'Riva's a long way away,' Drosta suggested, his eyes narrowing.

'Not that far, Drosta,' Fulrach told him. 'Belgarion has a very long arm.'

'What news hast thou heard from the south, your Majesty?' Korodullin asked the King of the Nadraks.

Drosta made an indelicate sound. 'Kal Zakath is wading in Murgo blood,' he said disgustedly. 'He's pushed Urgit into the western mountains and he's butchering every Murgo he can lay his hands on. I keep hoping that someone will stick an arrow into him, but you can't depend on a Murgo to do anything right.'

'Have you considered an alliance with King Gethell?' Fulrach asked.

'With the Thulls? You're not serious, Fulrach. I wouldn't saddle myself with the Thulls, even if it meant that I had to face the Malloreans alone. Gethell's so afraid of Zakath that he wets himself at the mention of his name. After the Battle of Thull Mardu, Zakath told my Thullish cousin that the very next time Gethell displeased him, he was going to have Gethell crucified. If Kal Zakath decides to come north, Gethell will probably hide himself under the nearest manure pile.'

'Zakath is not overfond of thee either, I am told,' Korodullin said.

Drosta laughed a shrill, somehow hysterical-sounding laugh. 'He wants to grill me over a slow fire,' he replied. 'And possibly use my skin to make a pair of shoes.'

'I'm amazed that you Angaraks didn't destroy each other eons ago.' Fulrach smiled.

'Torak told us not to.' Drosta shrugged. 'And he told his Grolims to gut anybody who disobeyed. We may not always have *liked* Torak, but we always did what he told us to. Only an idiot did otherwise—a dead idiot, usually.'

On the following day, Belgarath the Sorcerer arrived from the East, and King Rhodar of Drasnia was laid to rest. The small blonde Queen Porenn, dressed in deepest black, stood beside young King Kheva during the ceremony. Prince Kheldar stood directly behind the young king and his mother, and there was a strange, almost haunted look in his eyes. As Errand looked at him, he could see very plainly that the little spy had loved his uncle's tiny wife for years, but also that Porenn, though she was fond of him, did not return that love. State funerals, like all state functions, are long. Both Queen Porenn and her young son were very pale during the interminable proceedings, but at no time did either of them show any outward signs of grief.

Immediately following the funeral, Kheva's coronation took place, and the newly crowned Drasnian king announced in a piping but firm voice that his mother would guide him through the difficult years ahead.

At the conclusion of the ceremony, Belgarion, King of Riva and Overlord of the West, arose and briefly addressed the assembled notables. He welcomed Kheva to the rather exclusive fraternity of reigning monarchs, complimented him on the wisdom of the choice of the Queen Mother as regent and then advised one and all that he fully supported Queen Porenn and that anyone offering her the slightest impertinence would most surely regret it. Since he was leaning on the massive sword of Riva Iron-grip as he made that declaration, everyone in the Drasnian throne room took him very seriously.

A few days later, the visitors all departed.

Spring had come to the plains of Algaria as Polgara,

Durnik, Errand, and Belgarath rode southward in the company of King Cho-Hag and Queen Silar.

'A sad journey,' Cho-Hag said to Belgarath as they rode. 'I'm going to miss Rhodar.'

'I think we all will,' Belgarath replied. He looked ahead where a vast herd of cattle under the watchful eyes of a band of Algar clansmen was plodding slowly west toward the mountains of Sendaria and the great cattle fair at Muros. 'I'm a little surprised that Hettar agreed to go back to Riva with Garion at this time of year. He's usually at the head of the cattle herds.'

'Adara persuaded him,' Queen Silar told the old man. 'She and Ce'Nedra wanted to spend some time together, and there's almost nothing that Hettar won't do for his wife.'

Polgara smiled. 'Poor Hettar,' she said. 'With both Adara and Ce'Nedra working on him, he didn't stand a chance. That's a pair of very determined young ladies.'

'The change of scenery will do him good,' Cho-Hag noted. 'He always gets restless in the summertime and, now that all the Murgos have retreated to the south, he can't even amuse himself by hunting down their raiding parties.'

When they reached southern Algaria, Cho-Hag and Silar bade them farewell and turned eastward toward the Stronghold. The rest of the ride south to the Vale was uneventful. Belgarath stayed at the cottage for a few days and then prepared to return to his tower. Almost as an afterthought, he invited Errand to accompany him.

'We *are* a bit behind here, father,' Polgara told him. 'I need to get my garden in, and Durnik has a great deal of work ahead of him after this past winter.'

'Then it's probably best if the boy is out from underfoot, isn't it?'

She gave him a long steady look and then finally gave up. 'Oh, very well, father,' she said.

'I knew you'd see it my way, Pol,' he said.

'Just don't keep him all summer.'

'Of course not. I want to talk with the twins for a while

and see if Beldin has come back. I'll be off again in a month or so. I'll bring him home then.'

And so Errand and Belgarath went on down into the heart of the Vale again and once more took up residence in the old man's tower. Beldin had not yet returned from Mallorea, but Belgarath had much to discuss with Beltira and Belkira, and so Errand and his chestnut stallion were left largely to find their own amusements.

It was on a bright summer morning that they turned toward the western edge of the Vale to explore the foothills that marked the boundary of Ulgoland. They had ridden for several miles through those rolling, tree-clad hills and stopped in a broad, shallow ravine where a tumbling brook babbled over mossy green stones. The morning sun was very warm, and the shade of the tall, fragrant pines was pleasant.

As they sat, a she-wolf padded quietly from out of the bushes at the edge of the brook, stopped, and sat on her haunches to look at them. There was about the she-wolf a peculiar blue nimbus, a soft glow that seemed to emanate from her thick fur.

The normal reaction of a horse to the presence or even the scent of a wolf would have been blind panic, but the stallion returned the blue wolf's gaze calmly, with not even so much as a hint of a tremor.

The boy knew who the wolf was, but he was surprised to meet her here. 'Good morning,' he said politely to her. 'It's a pleasant day, isn't it?'

The wolf seemed to shimmer in the same way that Beldin shimmered as he assumed the shape of the hawk. When the air around her cleared, there stood in the animal's place a tawny-haired woman with golden eyes and a faintly amused smile on her lips. Though her gown was a plain brown such as one might see on any peasant woman, she wore it in a regal manner which any queen in jeweled brocade might envy. 'Do you always greet wolves with such courtesy?' she asked him.

'I haven't met many wolves,' he replied, 'but I was fairly certain who you were.'

'Yes, I suppose you would have been, at that.'

Errand slid down off the horse's back.

'Does *he* know where you are this morning?'

'Belgarath? Probably not. He's talking with Beltira and Belkira, so the horse and I just came out to look at someplace new.'

'It would be best perhaps if you didn't go too much farther into the Ulgo mountains,' she advised. 'There are creatures in these hills that are quite savage.'

He nodded. 'I'll keep that in mind.'

'Will you do something for me?' she asked quite directly.

'If I can.'

'Speak to my daughter.'

'Of course.'

'Tell Polgara that there is a great evil in the world and a great danger.'

'Zandramas?' Errand asked.

'Zandramas is a part of it, but the Sardion is at the center of the evil. It must be destroyed. Tell my husband and my daughter to warn Belgarion. His task is not yet finished.'

'I'll tell them,' Errand promised, 'but couldn't you just as easily tell Polgara yourself?'

The tawny-haired woman looked off down the shady ravine. 'No,' she replied sadly. 'It causes her too much pain when I appear to her.'

'Why is that?'

'It reminds her of all the lost years and brings back all the anguish of a young girl who had to grow up without her mother to guide her. All of that comes back to her each time she sees me.'

'You've never told her then? Of the sacrifice you were asked to make?'

She looked at him penetratingly. 'How is it that you know what even my husband and Polgara do not?'

'I'm not sure,' he replied. 'I *do*, though—just as I know that you did *not* die.'

'And will you tell Polgara that?'

'Not if you'd rather I didn't.'

She sighed. 'Someday, perhaps, but not yet. I think it's best if she and her father aren't aware of it. My task still lies ahead of me and it's a thing I can face best without any distractions.'

'Whatever you wish,' Errand said politely.

'We'll meet again,' she told him. 'Warn them about the Sardion. Tell them not to become so caught up in the search for Zandramas that they lose sight of that. It is from the Sardion that the evil stems. And be a trifle wary of Cyradis when next you meet her. She means you no ill, but she has her own task as well and she will do what she must to complete it.'

'I will, Poledra,' he promised.

'Oh,' she said, almost as an afterthought, 'there's someone waiting for you just ahead there.' She gestured toward the long tongue of a rock-strewn ridge thrusting out into the grassy Vale. 'He can't see you yet, but he's waiting.' Then she smiled, shimmered back into the form of the blue-tinged wolf, and loped away without a backward glance.

Curiously, Errand remounted and rode up out of the ravine and continued on southward, skirting the higher hills that rose toward the glistening white peaks of the land of the Ulgos as he rode toward the ridge. Then, as his eyes searched the rocky slope, he caught a momentary flicker of sunlight reflected from something shiny in the middle of a bushy outcrop halfway up the slope. Without hesitation, he rode in that direction.

The man who sat among the thick bushes wore a peculiar shirt of mail, constructed of overlapping metal scales. He was short but had powerful shoulders, and his eyes were veiled with a gauzey strip of cloth that was not so much a blindfold as it was a shield against the bright sunlight.

'Is that you, Errand?' the veiled man asked in a harsh-sounding voice.

'Yes,' Errand replied. 'I haven't seen you in a long time, Relg.'

'I need to talk with you,' the harsh-voiced zealot said. 'Can we get back out of the light?'

'Of course.' Errand slid down off his horse and followed the Ulgo through the rustling bushes to a cave mouth running back into the hillside. Relg stooped slightly under the overhanging rock and went inside. 'I thought I recognized you,' he said as Errand joined him in the cool dimness within the cave, 'but I couldn't be sure out there in all that light.' He untied the cloth from across his eyes and peered at the boy. 'You've grown.'

Errand smiled. 'It's been a few years. How is Taiba?'

'She has given me a son,' Relg said, almost in a kind of wonder. 'A very special son.'

'I'm glad to hear that.'

'When I was younger and filled with the notion of my own sanctity, UL spoke to me in my soul. He told me that the child who will be the new Gorim would come to Ulgo through me. In my pride I thought that he meant that I was to seek out the child and reveal him. How could I know that what he meant was a much simpler thing? It is my son that he spoke of. The mark is on my son—*my* son!' There was an awed pride in the zealot's voice.

'UL's ways are not the ways of men.'

'How truly you speak.'

'And are you happy?'

'My life is filled,' Relg said simply. 'But now I have another task. Our aged Gorim has sent me to seek out Belgarath. It is urgent that he come with me to Prolgu.'

'He's not far away,' Errand said. He looked at Relg and saw how, even in this dim cave, the zealot kept his eyes squinted almost shut to protect them from the light. 'I have a horse,' he said. 'I can go and bring him back here in a few hours, if you want. That way you won't have to go out into the sunlight.'

Relg gave him a quick, grateful look and then nodded. 'Tell him that he *must* come. The Gorim must speak with him.'

'I will,' Errand promised. Then he turned and left the cave.

'What does *he* want?' Belgarath demanded irritably when Errand told him that Relg wanted to see him.

'He wants you to go with him to Prolgu,' Errand replied. 'The Gorim wants to see you—the old one.'

'The *old* one? Is there a new one?'

Errand nodded. 'Relg's son,' he said.

Belgarath stared at Errand for a moment and then he suddenly began to laugh.

'What's so funny?'

'It appears that UL has a sense of humor,' the old man chortled. 'I wouldn't have suspected that of him.'

'I don't quite follow.'

'It's a very long story,' Belgarath said, still laughing. 'I guess that, if the Gorim wants to see me, we'd better go.'

'You want me to go along?'

'Polgara would skin me alive if I left you here alone. Let's get started.'

Errand led the old man back across the Vale to the ridge line in the foothills and the cave where Relg waited. It took a few minutes to explain to the young horse that he was supposed to go back to Belgarath's tower alone. Errand spoke with him at some length, and it finally appeared that the animal had grasped the edges, at least, of the idea.

The trip through the dark galleries to Prolgu took several days. For most of the way, Errand felt that they were groping along blindly; but for Relg, whose eyes were virtually useless in open daylight, these lightless passageways were home, and his sense of direction was unerring. And so it was that they came at last to the faintly lighted cavern with its shallow, glass-clear lake and the island rising in the center where the aged Gorim awaited them.

"*Yad ho*, Belgarath,' the saintly old man in his white robe called when they reached the shore of the subterranean lake, '*Groja UL.*'

'Gorim,' Belgarath replied with a respectful bow, '*Yad ho, Groja UL.*' Then they crossed the marble causeway to join the Gorim. Belgarath and the old man clasped each others' arms warmly. 'It's been a few years, hasn't it?' the sorcerer said. 'How are you bearing up?'

'I feel almost young.' The Gorim smiled. 'Now that Relg has found my successor, I can at last see the end of my task.'

'Found?' Belgarath asked quizzically.

'It amounts to the same thing.' The Gorim looked fondly at Relg. 'We had our disagreements, didn't we, my son?' he said. 'But as it turned out, we were all working toward the same end.'

'It took me a little longer to realize it, Holy Gorim,' Relg replied wryly. 'I'm a bit more stubborn than most men. Sometimes I'm amazed that UL didn't lose patience with me. Please excuse me, but I must go to my wife and son. I've been many days away from them.' He turned and went quickly back across the causeway.

Belgarath grinned. 'A remarkably changed man.'

'His wife is a marvel,' the Gorim agreed.

'Are you sure that their child is the chosen one?'

The Gorim nodded. 'UL has confirmed it. There were those who objected, since Taiba is a Marag rather than a daughter of Ulgo, but UL's voice silenced them.'

'I'm sure it did. UL's voice is very penetrating, I've noticed. You wanted to see me?'

The Gorim's expression became grave. He gestured toward his pyramid-shaped house. 'Let's go inside. There's a matter of urgency we need to discuss.'

Errand followed along behind the two old men as they entered the house. The room inside was dimly lighted by a glowing crystal globe hanging on a chain from the ceiling, and there was a table with low stone benches. They sat at the table, and the old Gorim looked solemnly at Belgarath. 'We are not like the people who live above in the light of the sun, my friend,' he said. 'For them, there is the sound of the wind in the trees, of rushing streams, and of birds filling the air with song. Here in our caves, however, we hear only the sounds of the earth herself.'

Belgarath nodded.

'The earth and the rocks speak to the people of Ulgo in peculiar ways,' the Gorim continued. 'A sound can come to us from half around the world. Such a sound has been muttering in the rocks for some years now, growing louder and more distinct with each passing month.'

'A fault perhaps?' Belgarath suggested. 'Some place where the stone bed of a continent is shifting?'

'I don't believe so, my friend,' the Gorim disagreed. 'The sound we hear is not the shifting of the restless earth. It is a sound caused by the awakening of a single stone.'

'I'm not sure I follow you,' Belgarath said, frowning.

'The stone we hear is alive, Belgarath.'

The old sorcerer looked at his friend. 'There's only one living stone, Gorim.'

'I had always believed so myself. I have heard the sound of Aldur's Orb as it moves about the world, and this new sound is also the sound of a living stone. It awakens, Belgarath, and it feels its power. It is evil, my friend—so evil that earth herself groans under its weight.'

'How long has this sound been coming to you?'

'It began not long after the death of accursed Torak.'

Belgarath pursed his lips. 'We've known that something has been moving around over in Mallorea,' he said. 'We didn't know it was quite this serious, however. Can you tell me anything more about this stone?'

'Only its name,' the Gorim replied. 'We hear it whispered through the caves and galleries and the fissures of earth. It is called "Sardius."'

Belgarath's head came up. '*Cthrag Sardius*? The Sardion?'

'You have heard of it?'

'Beldin ran across it in Mallorea. It was connected with something called Zandramas.'

The Gorim gasped, and his face went deathly pale. 'Balgarath!' he exclaimed in a shocked voice.

'What's the matter?'

'That's the most dreadful curse in our language.'

Belgarath stared at him. 'I thought I knew most of the words in the Ulgo tongue. How is it that I've never heard that one before?'

'No one would have repeated it to you.'

'I didn't think Ulgos even knew *how* to curse. What does it mean—in general terms?'

'It means confusion—chaos—absolute negation. It's a horrible word.'

Belgarath frowned. 'Why would an Ulgo curse word show up in Darshiva as the name of someone or something? And why in connection with the Sardion?'

'Is it possible that they are using the two words to mean the same thing?'

'I hadn't thought of that,' Belgarath admitted. 'I suppose they could be. The sense seems to be similar.'

Polgara had rather carefully instructed Errand that he must not interrupt when his elders were talking, but this seemed so important that he felt that the rule needed to be broken. 'They aren't the same,' he told the two old men.

Belgarath gave him a strange look.

'The Sardion is a stone, isn't it?'

'Yes,' the Gorim replied.

'Zandramas isn't a stone. It's a person.'

'How could you know that, my boy?'

'We've met,' Errand told him quietly. 'Not exactly face to face, but—well—' It was a difficult thing to explain. 'It was kind of like a shadow—except that the person who was casting the shadow was someplace else.'

'A projection,' Belgarath explained to the Gorim. 'It's a fairly simple trick that the Grolims are fond of.' He turned back to the boy. 'Did this shadow say anything to you?'

Errand nodded. 'It said that it was going to kill me.'

Belgarath drew in his breath sharply.'Did you tell Polgara?' he demanded.

'No. Should I?'

'Didn't you think it was fairly significant?'

'I thought it was just a threat—meant to frighten me.'

'Did it?'

'Frighten me? No, not really.'

'Aren't you being just a little blasé, Errand?' Belgarath asked. 'Do people go around threatening to kill you so often that it bores you or something?'

'No. That was the only time. It was only a shadow, though, and a shadow can't really hurt you, can it?'

'Have you run across many more of these shadows?'

'Just Cyradis.'

'And who is Cyradis?'

'I'm not really sure. She talks the way Mandorallen does—thee's and thou's and all that—and she wears a blindfold over her eyes.'

'A seeress.' Belgarath grunted. 'And what did *she* tell you?'

'She said that we were going to meet again and that she sort of liked me.'

'I'm sure that was comforting,' Belgarath said drily. 'Don't keep secrets like this, Errand. When something unusual happens, *tell* somebody.'

'I'm sorry,' Errand apologized. 'I just thought that—well—you and Polgara and Durnik had other things on your minds, that's all.'

'We don't really mind being interrupted all *that* much, boy. *Share* these little adventures with us.'

'If you want me to.'

Belgarath turned back to the Gorim. 'I think we're starting to get somewhere,' he said, 'thanks to our reticent young friend here. We know that Zandramas, if you'll pardon the word, is a person—a person that's somehow connected to this living stone that the Angaraks call Cthrag Sardius. We've had warnings about Zandramas before, so I think we'll have to assume that the Sardion is *also* a direct threat.'

'What must we do now, then?' the Gorim asked him.

'I think we're all going to have to concentrate on finding out just exactly what's going on over there in Mallorea—even if we have to take the place apart stone by stone. Up until now, I was only curious. Now it looks as if I'd better start taking this whole thing seriously. If the Sardion is a living stone, then it's like the Orb, and I don't want something with that kind of power in the hands of the wrong person—and from everything I've been able to gather, this Zandramas is most *definitely* the wrong person.' He turned then to look at Errand, his expression puzzled. 'What's *your* connection with all of this, boy?' he asked. 'Why is it that everyone and everything involved in this whole thing stops by to pay you a visit?'

'I don't know, Belgarath,' Errand replied truthfully.

'Maybe that's the place we should start. I've been promising myself that I was going to have a long talk with you one of these days. Maybe it's time we did just that.'

'If you wish,' Errand said. 'I don't know how much help I'll be, though.'

'That's what we're going to find out, Errand. That's what we're going to find out.'

Part Two

RIVA

SEA OF THE WINDS

Peat Bogos

Pasturelands

D. of Veils

Riva

THE
ISLE OF
THE WINDS

The Hook
of Arendia

SHELLY
SHAPIRO 83

Chapter Nine

Belgarion of Riva had not actually been prepared to occupy a throne. He had grown up on a farm in Sendaria, and his childhood had been that of an ordinary farm boy. When he had first come to the basalt throne in the Hall of the Rivan King, he had known much more about farm kitchens and stables than he had about throne rooms and council chambers. Statecraft had been a mystery to him, and he had known no more of diplomacy than he had of algebra.

Fortunately, the Isle of the Winds was not a difficult kingdom to rule. The Rivan people were orderly, sober, and had a strong regard for duty and civic responsibility. This had made things much easier for their tall, sandy-haired monarch during the trying early years of his reign while he was learning the difficult art of ruling well. He made mistakes, naturally, but the consequences of those early slips and miscalculations were never dire, and his subjects were pleased to note that this earnest, sincere young man who had come so startlingly to the throne never made the same mistake twice. Once he had settled in and had become accustomed to his job, it was probably safe to say that Belgarion—or Garion, as he preferred to be called—almost never encountered major problems in his capacity as King of Riva.

He had other titles, however. Some were purely honorary, others not so much so. 'Godslayer,' for example, involved certain duties which were not likely to come up very often. 'Lord of the Western Sea' caused him almost no concern whatsoever, since he had concluded quite early that the waves and tides needed little supervision and that fish, for the most part, were entirely capable of managing their own government. Most of Garion's headaches stemmed directly from the grand-sounding title, 'Overlord of the West.' He had assumed at first—since the war with the Angarakas was over—that this title, like the others, was merely something in the nature of a formality, something impressive, but largely empty, which had been tacked on to all the rest, sort of to round them out. It earned him, after all, no tax revenue; it had no special crown or throne; and there was no administrative staff to deal with day-to-day problems.

But to his chagrin, he soon discovered that one of the peculiarities of human nature was the tendency to want to take problems to the person in charge. Had there *not* been an Overlord of the West, he was quite sure that his fellow monarchs would have found ways to deal with all those perplexing difficulties by themselves. But as long as he occupied that exalted position, they all seemed to take an almost childlike delight in bringing him the more difficult, the most agonizing, and the most utterly insoluble problems and then happily sitting back with trusting smiles on their faces while he struggled and floundered with them.

As a case in point, there was the situation which arose in Arendia during the summer of Garion's twenty-third year. The year had gone fairly well up until that point. The misunderstanding which had marred his relationship with Ce'Nedra had been smoothed over, and Garion and his complicated little wife were living together in what might best be described as domestic felicity. The campaign of Emperor Kal Zakath of Mallorea, whose presence on this continent had been a great cause for concern, had bogged down in the mountains of western Cthol Murgos and showed some promise of grinding on for decades far from the borders of any of the Kingdoms of the West. General Varana, the Duke of Anadile, functioning as regent for the ailing Emperor Ran Borune XXIII, had clamped down quite firmly on the excesses of the great families of Tolnedra in their unseemly scramble for the Imperial Throne. All in all, Garion had been looking forward to a period of peace and tranquility until that warm, early summer day when the letter arrived from King Korodullin of Arendia.

Garion and Ce'Nedra had been spending a quiet afternoon together in the comfortable royal apartment, talking idly of little, unimportant things—more for the pleasure of each other's company than out of any real concern for the subjects at hand. Garion lounged in a large, blue velvet armchair by the window, and Ce'Nedra sat before a gilt-edged mirror, brushing her long, copper-colored hair. Garion was very fond of Ce'Nedra's hair. Its color was exciting. It smelled good, and there was one delightfully vagrant curl that always seemed to want to tumble appealingly down the side of her smooth, white neck. When the servant brought the letter from the King of Arendia, tastefully carried on a silver tray, Garion took his eyes off his lovely wife almost regretfully. He broke the ornately stamped wax seal and opened the crackling parchment.

'Who is it from, Garion?' Ce'Nedra asked, still pulling the brush through her hair and regarding her reflection in the mirror with a kind of dreamy contentment.

'Korodullin,' he replied and then began to read.

'To his Majesty, King Belgarion of Riva, Overlord of the West, greetings:' the letter began.

'It is our fervent hope that this finds thee and thy queen in good health and tranquil spirits. Gladly would I permit my pen the leisure to dwell fulsomely upon the regard and affection my queen and I bear thee and her Majesty, but a crisis hath arisen here in Arendia; and because it doth derive directly from the actions of certain friends of thine, I have resolved to seek thy aid in meeting it.

'To our great sorrow, our dear friend the Baron of Vo Ebor succumbed at last to those grievous wounds which he received upon the battlefield at Thull Mardu. His passing this spring hath grieved us more than I can tell thee. He was a good and faithful knight. His heir, since he and the baroness Nerina were childless, is a distant nephew, one Sir Embrig, a somewhat rash knight more interested, I fear, in the title and lands of his inheritance than in the fact that he doth intrude himself upon the tragic baroness. With airs most unbecoming to one of gentle birth, he journeyed straightway to Vo Ebor to take possession of his new estates and with him he brought diverse other knights of his acquaintance, his cronies and drinking companions. When they reached Vo Ebor, Sir Embrig and his cohorts gave themselves over to unseemly carouse, and when they were all deep in their cups, one of these rude knights expressed admiration for the person of the but recently widowed Nerina. Without pausing to think or to consider the lady's bereavement, Sir Embrig promptly promised her hand to his drunken companion. Now in Arendia, by reason of certain of our laws, Sir Embrig hath indeed this right, though no true knight would so incivilly insist on imposing his will upon a kinswoman in her time of grief.

'The news of this outrage was carried at once to Sir Mandorallen, the mighty Baron of Vo Mandor, and that great knight went immediately to horse. What transpired upon his arrival at Vo Ebor thou canst well imagine, given Sir Mandorallen's prowess and the depth of his regard for the Baroness Nerina. Sir Embrig and his cohorts rashly attempted to stand in his path, and there were, as I understand, some fatalities and a great number of grievous injuries as a result. Thy friend removed the baroness to his own keep at Vo Mandor, where he holds her in protective custody. Sir Embrig, who—regrettably perhaps—will recover from his wounds, hath declared that a state of war doth exist between Ebor and Mandor and he hath summoned to his cause diverse noblemen. Other noblemen flock to the banner of Sir Mandorallen, and southwestern Arendia doth stand on the brink of general war. I have even been informed that Lelldorin of Wildantor, ever a rash youth, hath raised an army of Asturian bowmen and at this moment doth march southward with them, intending to aid his old comrade in arms.

'Thus it doth stand. Know that I am reluctant to bring the power of the Arendish crown to bear in this matter, since, should I be compelled to make a judgment, I would be forced by our laws to decide in favor of Sir Embrig.

'I appeal to thee, King Belgarion, to come to Arendia and to use thy influence with thy former companions and dear friends to bring them back from the precipice upon which they now stand. Only thy intercession, I fear, can avert this impending disaster.

In hope and friendship,
Korodullin.'

Garion stared helplessly at the letter. 'Why me?' he demanded without even thinking.

'What does he say, dear?' Ce'Nedra asked, laying aside her brush and picking up an ivory comb.

'He says that—' Garion broke off. 'Mandorallen and Lelldorin—' he got up and began to swear. 'Here,' he said, thrusting the letter at her. 'Read it.' He began to pace up and down with his fists clenched behind his back, still muttering curse words.

Ce'Nedra read the letter as he continued pacing. 'Oh dear,' she said finally in dismay. 'Oh dear.'

'That sums it up pretty well, I'd say.' He started swearing again.

'Garion, please don't use that kind of language. It makes you sound like a pirate. What are you going to do about this?'

'I haven't the faintest idea.'

'Well, you're going to have to do *something*.'

'Why me?' he burst out. 'Why do they always bring these things to me?'

'Because they all know that you can take care of these little problems better than anybody else.'

'Thanks,' he said drily.

'Be nice,' she told him. Then she pursed her lips thoughtfully, tapping her cheek with the ivory comb. 'You'll need your crown, of course—and I think the blue and silver doublet would be nice.'

'What are you talking about?'

'You're going to have to go to Arendia to get this all straightened out, and I think you should look your very best—Arends are so conscious of appearances. Why don't you go see about a ship? I'll pack a few things for you.' She looked out the window at the golden afternoon sunlight. 'Do you think it might be too warm for you to wear your ermine?'

'I won't be wearing ermine, Ce'Nedra. I'll be wearing armor and my sword.'

'Oh, don't be so dramatic, Garion. All you have to do is go there and tell them to stop.'

'Maybe, but I have to get their attention first. This is Mandorallen we're talking about—and Lelldorin. We're not dealing with sensible people, remember?'

A little frown creased her forehead. 'That *is* true,' she admitted. But then she gave him an encouraging little smile. 'I'm sure you can fix it, though. I have every confidence in you.'

'You're as bad as all the rest,' he said a bit sullenly.

'But you *can*, Garion. Everybody says so.'

'I guess I'd better go talk to Brand,' he said glumly. 'There are some things that need to be attended to, and this is likely to take me a few weeks.'

'I'll take care of them for you, dear,' she said reassuringly, reaching up and patting his cheek. 'You just run along now. I can manage things here very well while you're gone.'

He stared at her with a sinking feeling in the pit of his stomach.

When he arrived at Vo Mandor on a cloudy morning several days later, the situation had deteriorated even further. The forces of Sir Embrig were in the field, encamped not three leagues from Mandorallen's castle, and

Mandorallen and Lelldorin had marched from the city to meet them. Garion thundered up to the gates of his friend's stout fortress on the war horse he had borrowed from an accommodating baron upon his arrival in Arendia. He wore the full suit of steel armor that had been a gift from King Korodullin, and Iron-grip's enormous sword rode in its scabbard across his back. The gates swung wide for him, and he entered the courtyard, swung awkwardly down from his saddle, and demanded to be taken immediately to the Baroness Nerina.

He found her pale-faced and dressed all in black, standing somberly on the battlements, searching the cloudy sky to the east for the telltale columns of smoke which would announce that the battle had begun. 'It doth lie upon me, King Belgarion,' she declared almost morbidly. 'Strife and discord and anguish hath derived from me since the day I first wed my dear departed lord.'

'There's no need to blame yourself,' Garion told her. 'Mandorallen can usually get himself into trouble without help from anyone. When did he and Lelldorin leave?'

'Somewhat past noon yesterday,' she replied. 'Methinks the battle will be joined 'ere long.' She looked mournfully down at the flagstones of courtyard lying far below and sighed.

'I guess I'd better go then,' he said grimly. 'Maybe if I can get there before they start, I can head this off.'

'I have just had a most excellent thought, your Majesty,' she declared, a bright little smile lighting up her pale face. 'I can make thy task much easier.'

'I hope *somebody* can,' he said. 'The way things look right now, I'm going to be in for a very bad morning.'

'Make haste then, your Majesty, to the field where rude war even now doth hover above our dear friends, and advise them that the cause of their impending battle hath departed from this sad world.'

'I'm not sure I follow that.'

'It is most simple, your Majesty. Since *I* am the cause of all this strife, it doth lie upon me to end it.'

He looked at her suspiciously. 'Just what are we talking

about here, Nerina? How do you propose to bring all those idiots to their senses?'

Her smile became actually radiant. 'I have but to hurl myself from this lofty battlement, my Lord, and join my husband in the silence of the grave to end this dreadful bloodshed before it hath begun. Go quickly, my Lord. Descend to that courtyard far below and take to horse. I will descend by this shorter, happier route and await thee upon those rude stones below. Then mayest thou carry the news of my death to the battlefield. Once I am dead, no man's blood need be spilt over me.' She put one hand on the rough stone of the parapet.

'Oh, stop that,' he said in disgust, 'and get away from there.'

'Ah, nay, your Majesty,' she said quite firmly. 'This is the best of all possible answers. At one stroke I can avert this impending battle and rid myself of this burdensome life.'

'Nerina,' he said in a flat voice, 'I'm not going to let you jump, and that's all there is to that.'

'Surely thou wouldst not be so rude as to lay hands upon my person to prevent me,' she said in a shocked tone of voice.

'I won't have to,' he said. He looked at her pale, uncomprehending face and realized that she did not have the faintest idea of what he was talking about. 'On second thought, maybe it's not such a bad idea after all. The trip down to that courtyard is likely to take you about a day and a half, so it should give you time to think this all the way through—besides, it might just possibly keep you out of mischief while I'm gone.'

Her eyes went suddenly wide as what he was saying to her seeped ever so slowly into her mind. 'Thou wouldst not use *sorcery* to foil my most excellent solution,' she gasped.

'Try me.'

She looked at him helplessly, tears coming to her eyes. 'This is most unchivalrous of thee, my Lord,' she accused him.

'I was raised on a farm in Sendaria, my lady,' he reminded her. 'I didn't have the advantages of a noble upbringing, so I have these little lapses from time to time. I'm sure you'll forgive me for not letting you kill yourself. Now, if you'll excuse me, I have to stop that nonsense out there.' He turned and clanked toward the stairs. 'Oh,' he said, looking over his shoulder at her, 'don't get any ideas about jumping as soon as my back's turned either. I have a long arm, Nerina—a very long arm.'

She stared at him, her lip trembling.

'That's better,' he said and went on down the stairs.

The servants in Mandorallen's castle took one look at Garion's stormy face as he strode into the courtyard below and prudently melted out of his path. Laboriously, he hauled himself into the saddle of the huge roan war horse upon which he had arrived, adjusted the great sword of the Rivan King in its scabbard across his back, and looked around. 'Somebody bring me a lance,' he commanded.

They brought him several, stumbling over each other in their haste to comply. He selected one and then set off at a thundering gallop.

The citizens of the town of Vo Mandor, which lay just beyond the walls of Mandorallen's keep, were as prudent as the servants within the walls had been. A wide path was opened along the cobblestone streets as the angry King of Riva passed through, and the town gates stood wide open for him.

Garion knew that he was going to have to get their attention, and Arends on the verge of battle are notoriously difficult to reach. He would need to startle them with something. As he thundered through the green Arendish countryside, past neat, thatch-roofed villages and groves of beech and maple, he cast an appraising eye toward the gray, scudding clouds overhead, and the first faint hints of a plan began to form in his mind.

When he arrived, he found the two armies drawn up on opposite sides of a broad, open meadow. As was the age-old Arendish custom, a number of personal challenges had been issued, and those matters were in the process of being settled as a sort of prelude to the grand general mêlée which would follow. Several armored knights from either side were tilting in the center of the field as the two armies looked on approvingly. Enthusiastically, the brainless, steel-clad young nobles crashed into each other, littering the turf with splinters from the shattered remains of their lances.

Garion took in the situation at a single glance, scarcely pausing before riding directly into the middle of the fray. It must be admitted that he cheated just a little during the encounter. The lance he carried *looked* the same as those with which the Mimbrate knights were attempting to kill or maim each other. About the only real difference lay in the fact that *his* lance, unlike theirs, would not break, no matter what it encountered and was, moreover, enveloped in a kind of nimbus of sheer force. Garion had no real desire to run the sharp steel tip of that lance through anybody. He merely wanted them off their horses. On his first course through the center of the startled, milling knights, he hurled three of them from their saddles in rapid succession. Then he wheeled his charger and unhorsed two more so quickly that the vast clatter they made as they fell merged into a single sound.

It needed a bit more, however, something suitably spectacular to penetrate the solid bone Arends used for heads. Almost negligently, Garion discarded his invincible lance, reached back over his shoulder and drew the mighty sword of the Rivan King. The Orb of Aldur blazed forth its dazzling blue light, and the sword itself immediately burst into flame. As always, despite its vast size, the sword in his hand had no apparent weight, and he wielded it with blinding speed. He drove directly at one startled knight, chopping the amazed man's lance into foot-long chunks as he worked his way up the weapon's shaft. When only the butt remained, Garion smashed the knight from his saddle with the flat of the burning sword. He wheeled then, chopped an upraised mace neatly in two and rode the bearer of the mace into the ground, horse and all.

Stunned by the ferocity of his attack, the wide-eyed

Mimbrate knights drew back. It was not merely his over-whelming prowess in battle, however, that made them retreat. From between clenched teeth, the King of Riva was swearing sulfurously, and his choice of oaths made strong men go pale. He looked around, his eyes ablaze, then gathered in his will. He raised his flaming sword and pointed it at the roiling sky overhead. '*NOW!*' he barked in a voice like the cracking of a whip.

The clouds shuddered, almost seeming to flinch as the full force of Belgarion's will smote them. A sizzling bolt of lightning as thick as the trunk of a mighty tree crashed to earth with a deafening thunderclap that shook the ground for miles in every direction. A great, smoking hole appeared in the turf where the bolt had struck. Again and again Garion called down the lightning. The noise of thunder ripped and rolled through the air, and the reek of burning sod and singed earth hung like a cloud over the suddenly terrified armies.

Then a great, howling gale struck; at the same time, the clouds ripped open to inundate the opposing forces in a deluge so intense that many knights were actually hurled from their saddles by the impact. Even as the gale shrieked and the driving downpour struck them, flickering bolts of lightning continued to stagger across the field which separated them, sizzling dreadfully and filling the air with steam and smoke. To cross that field was unthinkable.

Grimly, Garion sat his terrified charger in the very midst of that awful display, with the lightning dancing around him. He let it rain on the two armies for several minutes until he was certain that he had their full attention; then, with a negligent flick of his flaming sword, he turned off the downpour.

'I have had enough of this stupidity!' he announced in a voice as loud as the thunder had been. 'Lay down your weapons at once!'

They stared at him and then distrustfully at each other.

'*AT ONCE!*' Garion roared, emphasizing his command with yet another lightning bolt and a shattering thunder-clap.

The clatter of suddenly discarded weapons was enormous.

'I want to see Sir Embrig and Sir Mandorallen right *here*,' Garion said then, pointing with his sword at a spot directly in front of his horse. 'Immediately!'

Slowly, almost like reluctant schoolboys, the two steel-clad knights warily approached him.

'Just exactly what do the two of you think you're doing?' Garion demanded of them.

'Mine honor compelled me, your Majesty,' Sir Embrig declared in a faltering voice. He was a stout, florid-faced man of about forty with the purple-veined nose of one who drinks heavily. 'Sir Mandorallen hath abducted my kinswoman.'

'Thy concern for the lady extendeth only to thy authority over her person,' Mandorallen retorted hotly. 'Thou hast usurped her lands and chattels with churlish disregard for her feelings, and—'

'All right,' Garion snapped, 'that's enough. Your personal squabble has brought half of Arendia to the brink of war. Is that what you wanted? Are you such a pair of children that you're willing to destroy your homeland just to get your own way?'

'But—' Mandorallen tried to say.

'But nothing.' Garion then proceeded—at some length —to tell them exactly what he thought of them. His tone was scornful, and his choice of language wide-ranging. The two frequently went pale as he spoke. Then he saw Lelldorin drawing cautiously near to listen.

'And you!' Garion turned his attention to the young Asturian. 'What are *you* doing down here in Mimbre?'

'Me? Well—Mandorallen *is* my friend, Garion.'

'Did he ask for your help?'

'Well—'

'I didn't think so. You just took it on yourself.' He then included Lelldorin in his commentary, gesturing often with the burning sword in his right hand. The three watched that sword with a certain wide-eyed anxiety as he waved it in their faces.

'Very well, then,' Garion said after he had cleared the air, 'this is what we're going to do.' He looked belligerently at Sir Embrig. 'Do you want to fight me?' he challenged, thrusting out his jaw pugnaciously.

Sir Embrig's face went a pasty white, and his eyes started from his head. '*Me*, your Majesty?' he gasped. 'Thou wouldst have *me* take the field against the Godslayer?' He began to tremble violently.

'I didn't think so.' Garion grunted. 'Since that's the case, you'll immediately relinquish all claim of authority over the Baroness Nerina to *me*.'

'Most gladly, your Majesty.' Embrig's words tumbled over themselves as they came out.

'Mandorallen,' Garion said, 'do *you* want to fight me?'

'Thou art my friend, Garion,' Mandorallen protested. 'I would die before I raised my hand against thee.'

'Good. Then *you* will turn all territorial claims on behalf of the baroness over to me—at once. *I* am her protector now.'

'I agree to this,' Mandorallen replied gravely.

'Sir Embrig,' Garion said then, 'I bestow upon you the entirety of the Barony of Vo·Ebor—including those lands which would normally go to Nerina. Will you accept them?'

'I will, your Majesty.'

'Sir Mandorallen, I offer you the hand in marriage of my ward, Nerina of Vo Ebor. Will you accept her?'

'With all my heart, my Lord,' Mandorallen choked, with tears coming to his eyes.

'Splendid,' Lelldorin said admiringly.

'Shut up, Lelldorin,' Garion told him. 'That's it, then, gentlemen. Your war is over. Pack up your armies and go home—and if this breaks out again, I'll come back. The next time I have to come down here, I'm going to be *very* angry. Do we all understand each other?'

Mutely they nodded. That ended the war.

The Baroness Nerina, however, raised certain strenuous objections when she was informed of Garion's decisions upon the return of Mandorallen's army to Vo Mandor.

'Am I some common serf girl to be bestowed upon any man who pleases my lord?' she demanded with a fine air of high drama.

'Are you questioning my authority as your guardian?' Garion asked her directly.

'Nay, my Lord. Sir Embrig hath consented to this. Thou art my guardian now. I must do as thou commandest me.'

'Do you love Mandorallen?'

She looked quickly at the great knight and then blushed.

'Answer me!'

'I do, my Lord,' she confessed in a small voice.

'What's the problem then? You've loved him for years, but when I order you to marry him, you object.'

'My Lord,' she replied stiffly, 'there are certain proprieties to be observed. A lady may not be so churlishly disposed of.' And with that she turned her back and stormed away.

Mandorallen groaned, and a sob escaped him.

'What is it now?' Garion demanded.

'My Nerina and I will never wed, I fear,' Mandorallen declared brokenly.

'Nonsense. Lelldorin, do *you* understand what this is all about?'

Lelldorin frowned. 'I think so, Garion. There are a whole series of rather delicate negotiations and formalities that you're leaping over here. There's the question of the dowry, the formal, written consent of the guardian— that's you, of course—and probably most important, there has to be a formal proposal—with witnesses.'

'She's refusing over technicalities?' Garion asked incredulously.

'Technicalities are very important to a woman, Garion.'

Garion sighed with resignation. This was going to take longer than he had thought. 'Come with me,' he told them.

Nerina had locked her door and refused to answer Garion's polite knock. Finally he looked at the stout oak planks barring his way. 'Burst!' he said, and the door blew inward, showering the startled lady seated on the bed with splinters. 'Now,' Garion said, stepping over the wreckage, 'let's get down to business. How big a dowry do we think would be appropriate?'

Mandorallen was willing—more than willing—to accept some mere token, but Nerina stubbornly insisted upon something significant. Wincing slightly, Garion made an offer acceptable to the lady. He then called for pen and ink and scribbled—with Lelldorin's aid—a suitable document of consent. 'Very well,' he said then to Mandorallen, 'ask her.'

'Such proposal doth not customarily come with such unseemly haste, your Majesty,' Nerina protested. 'It is considered proper for the couple to have some time to acquaint themselves with each other.'

'You're already acquainted, Nerina,' he reminded her. 'Get on with it.'

Mandorallen sank to his knees before his lady, his armor clinking on the floor. 'Wilt thou have me as thy husband, Nerina?' he implored her.

She stared at him helplessly. 'I have not, my Lord, had time to frame a suitable reply.'

'Try "yes," Nerina,' Garion suggested.

'Is such thy command, my Lord?'

'If you want to put it that way.'

'I must obey, then. I will have thee, Sir Mandorallen—with all my heart.'

'Splendid,' Garion said briskly, rubbing his hands together. 'Get up, Mandorallen, and let's go down to your chapel. We'll find a priest and get this all formalized by suppertime.'

'Surely thou art not proposing such haste, my Lord,' Nerina gasped.

'As a matter of fact, I am. I have to get back to Riva and I'm not going to leave here until the two of you are safely married. Things have a way of going wrong in Arendia if somebody isn't around to watch them.'

'I am not suitably attired, your Majesty,' Nerina protested, looking down at her black dress. 'Thou wouldst not have me married in a gown of sable hue?'

'And I,' Mandorallen also objected, 'I am still under arms. A man should not approach his wedding clad in steel.'

'I don't have the slightest concern about what either of you is wearing,' Garion informed them. 'It's what's in your hearts that's important, not what's on your backs.'

'But—' Nerina faltered. 'I do not even have a veil.'

Garion gave her a long, steady look. Then he cast a quick look around the room, picked up a lace doily from a nearby table and set it neatly atop the lady's head. 'Charming,' he murmured. 'Can anyone think of anything else?'

'A ring?' Lelldorin suggested hesitantly.

Garion turned to stare at him. 'You, too?' he said.

'They really ought to have a ring, Garion,' Lelldorin said defensively.

Garion considered that for a moment, concentrated, and then forged a plain gold ring out of insubstantial air. 'Will this do?' he asked, holding it out to them.

'Might I not be attended?' Nerina asked in a small, trembling voice. 'It is unseemly for a noblewoman to be wed without the presence of some lady of suitable rank to support and encourage her.'

'Go fetch somebody' Garion said to Lelldorin.

'Whom should I select?' Lelldorin asked helplessly.

'I don't care. Just bring a lady of noble birth to the chapel—even if you have to drag her by the hair.'

Lelldorin scurried out.

'Is there anything else?' Garion asked Mandorallen and Nerina in the slightly dangerous tone that indicated that his patience was wearing very thin.

'It is customary for a bridegroom to be accompanied by a close friend, Garion,' Mandorallen reminded him.

'Lelldorin will be there,' Garion said, 'and so will I. We won't let you fall down or faint or run away.'

'Might I not have a few small flowers?' Nerina asked in a plaintive voice.

Garion looked at her. 'Certainly,' he replied in a deceptively mild tone. 'Hold out your hand.' He then began to create lilies—rapidly—popping them out of empty air and depositing them one after another in the startled lady's hand. 'Are they the right color, Nerina?' he asked her. 'I can change them if you like—purple, perhaps, or chartreuse, or maybe bright blue would suit you.'

And then he finally decided that he was not really getting anywhere. They were going to continue to raise objections for as long as they possibly could. They were both so accustomed to living in the very heart of their colossal tragedy that they were unwilling—unable even—to give up their mournful entertainment. The solution, of necessity, was going to be entirely up to him. Knowing that it was a trifle overdramatic, but considering the mental capabilities of the two involved, he drew his sword. 'We are all now going directly to the chapel,' he announced, 'and the two of you are going to get married.' He pointed at the splintered door with the sword. 'Now march!' he commanded.

And so it was that one of the great tragic love stories of all time came at last to a happy ending. Mandorallen and his Nerina were married that very afternoon, with Garion quite literally standing over them with flaming sword to ensure that no last-minute hitches could interrupt.

On the whole, Garion was rather pleased with himself and with the way he had handled things. His mood was self-congratulatory as he departed the following morning to return to Riva.

Chapter Ten

'Anyway,' Garion was saying as he and Ce'Nedra relaxed in their blue-carpeted sitting room on the evening of his return to Riva, 'when we got back to Mandorallen's castle and told Nerina that it was all right for them to get married, she raised all kinds of objections.'

'I always thought she loved him,' Ce'Nedra said.

'She does, but she's been in the very center of this great tragic situation for all these years, and she didn't really want to give that up. She hadn't got all that noble suffering out of her system yet.'

'Don't be snide, Garion.'

'Arends make my teeth ache. First she held out for a dowry—a very big one.'

'That seems reasonable.'

'Not when you consider the fact that *I* had to pay it.'

'You? Why should you have to pay it?'

'I'm her guardian, remember? For all of her thee's and thou's and vaporish airs, she haggles like a Drasnian horse trader. By the time she was done, my purse was very lean. And she had to have a formal letter of consent—and a veil, a lady to attend her, a ring, and flowers. And I was getting more irritated by the minute.'

'Aren't you forgetting something?'

'I don't think so.'

'Didn't Mandorallen propose to her?' Ce'Nedra leaned forward, her little face very intent. 'I'm certain that she would have insisted on that.'

'You're right. I almost forgot that part.'

She shook her head almost sadly. 'Oh, Garion,' she said in a disapproving tone.

'That came earlier—right after the business with the dowry. Anyway, he proposed, and I made her say yes, and then —'

'Wait a minute,' Ce'Nedra said firmly, holding up one little hand. 'Don't rush through that part. Exactly what did he say when he asked her?'

Garion scratched his ear. 'I'm not sure I remember,' he confessed.

'Try,' she urged him. 'Please.'

'Let's see,' he pondered, looking up at the ornately carved wooden beams of the ceiling. 'First she objected to having the proposal come before they had gone through all the business of "getting acquainted," as she put it. I guess she meant all the sneaking around so that they could be alone together in secluded places—and the love poems and the flowers and all those calf-eyed looks.'

Ce'Nedra gave him a hard little stare. 'You know, sometimes you can be absolutely infuriating. You've got about as much sensitivity as a block of wood.'

'What's that supposed to mean?'

'Never mind. Just tell me what happened next.'

'Well, I told her straight off that I wasn't having any of *that* nonsense. I said that they were already acquainted and to get on with it.'

'You're just full of charm, aren't you?' she said sarcastically.

'Ce'Nedra, what *is* the problem here?'

'Never mind. Just get on with the story. You always dawdle so when you're telling me about something like this.'

'Me? You're the one who keeps interrupting.'

'Just move along with it, Garion.'

He shrugged. 'There isn't much more. He asked her; she said yes; and then I marched them down to the chapel.'

'The words, Garion,' she insisted. 'The words. Exactly what did he say?'

'Nothing very earth-shaking. It went sort of like "Wilt thou have me as thy husband, Nerina?"'

'Oh,' Ce'Nedra said with a catch in her voice. He was astonished to see tears in her eyes.

'What's the matter?' he demanded.

'Never mind,' she replied, dabbing at her eyes with a wispy scrap of a handkerchief. 'What did she say then?'

'She said that she hadn't had time to work up a suitable answer, so I told her just to say "yes."'

'And?'

'She said, "I will have thee, Sir Mandorallen—with all my heart."'

'Oh,' Ce'Nedra said again, her handkerchief going once more to her brimming eyes. 'That's just lovely.'

'If you say so,' he said. 'It seemed a little drawn-out to me.'

'Sometimes you're hopeless,' she told him. Then she sighed a little forlornly. 'I never got a formal proposal,' she said.

'You most certainly did,' he said indignantly. 'Don't you remember all that ceremony when you and the Tolnedran Ambassador came into the throne room?'

'*I* did the proposing, Garion,' she reminded him with a toss of her flaming curls. 'I presented myself before your throne and asked you if you would consent to take me to wife. You agreed, and that's all there was to it. You never once asked *me*.'

He frowned and thought back. 'I *must* have.'

'Not once.'

'Well, as long as we got married anyway, it doesn't really matter all that much, does it?'

Her expression turned to ice.

He caught that look. 'Is it really that important, Ce'Nedra?' he asked her.

'Yes, Garion. It is.'

He sighed. 'All right then. I guess I'd better do it.'

'Do what?'

'Propose. Will you marry me, Ce'Nedra?'

'Is that the best you can do?'

He gave her a long, steady look. She was, he had to admit, very appealing. She was wearing a pale green dress, all frilly and touched here and there with lace, and she sat rather primly in her chair, looking pouty and discontented. He arose from his chair, crossed to where she sat, and sank extravagantly to his knees. He took her small hand in both of his and looked imploringly into her face, trying to match the look of fatuous adoration that Mandorallen had worn. 'Will her Imperial Highness consent to have me as her husband?' he asked her. 'I can offer little besides an honest, loving heart and boundless devotion.'

'Are you making fun of me?' she asked suspiciously.

'No,' he said. 'You wanted a formal proposal, so I just gave you one. Well?'

'Well what?'

'Will you consent to marry me?'

She gave him an arch look, her eyes twinkling. Then she reached out and fondly tousled his hair. 'I'll think about it,' she replied.

'What do you mean, you'll think about it?'

'Who knows?' she said with a smirk. 'I might get a better offer. Do get up, Garion. you'll make the knees of your hose all baggy if you stay down on the floor like that.'

He got to his feet. 'Women!' he said exasperatedly, throwing his arms in the air.

She gave him that tiny, wide-eyed look that at one time, before he had come to recognize it as pure deception, had always made his knees go weak. 'Don't you love me any more?' she asked in that trembling, dishonest, little-girl voice.

'Didn't we decide that we weren't going to do that to each other any more?'

'This is a special occasion, dear,' she replied. And then she laughed, sprang up from her chair, and threw her arms about his neck. 'Oh, Garion,' she said, still laughing. 'I *do* love you.'

'I certainly hope so,' he said, wrapping his arms around her shoulders and kissing her upturned lips.

The following morning Garion dressed rather informally and then tapped on the door to Ce'Nedra's private sitting-room.

'Yes?' she answered.

'It's Garion,' he said. 'May I come in?' His Sendarian good manners had been so deeply ingrained in him that even though he was the King here, he always asked permission before opening the door to someone else's room.

'Of course,' she said.

He turned the latch and entered her frilly private domain, a room all pink and pale-green flounces and with yards of rustling satin and brocade drapery. Ce'Nedra's favorite lady-in-waiting, Arell, rose in some confusion to perform the customary curtsy. Arell was Brand's niece, the daughter of his youngest sister, and she was one of several high born Rivan ladies who attended the queen. She was very nearly the archetypical Alorn woman, tall, blond and buxom, with golden braids coiled about her head, deep blue eyes and a complexion like new milk. She and Ce'Nedra were virtually inseparable, and the two spent much of their time with their heads together, whispering and giggling. For some reason, Arell always blushed rosily whenever Garion entered the room. He did not understand that at all, but privately suspected that Ce'Nedra had told her lady-in-waiting certain things that really *should* have remained private—things that brought a blush to the Rivan girl's cheeks whenever she looked at him.

'I'm going down into the city,' Garion told his wife. 'Did you want anything?'

'I prefer to do my own shopping, Garion,' Ce'Nedra replied, smoothing the front of her satin dressing gown. 'You never get things right anyway.'

He was about to reply to that, but decided against it. 'Whatever you want. I'll see you at luncheon then.'

'As my Lord commands,' Ce'Nedra said with a mocking little genuflection.

'Stop that.'

She made a face at him and then came over and kissed him.

Garion turned to Arell. 'My Lady,' he said, bowing politely.

Arell's blue eyes were filled with suppressed mirth, and there was a slightly speculative look in them as well.She blushed and curtsied again. 'Your Majesty,' she said respectfully.

As Garion left the royal apartment, he wondered idly what Ce'Nedra had told Arell to cause all those blushes and peculiar looks. He was grateful to the blond girl, however. Her presence provided Ce'Nedra with company, which left him free to attend to other matters. Since Aunt Pol had intervened and healed the estrangement that had caused them both so much anguish, Ce'Nedra had become very possessive about Garion's spare time. On the whole he felt that being married was rather nice, but sometimes Ce'Nedra tended to overdo things a bit.

In the corridor outside, Brand's second son, Kail, was waiting, holding a parchment sheet in his hand. 'I think this needs your immediate attention, Sire,' he said formally.

Although Kail was a warrior, tall and broad-shouldered like his father and his brothers, he was nonetheless a studious man, intelligent and discreet, and he knew enough about Riva and its people to be able to sort through the voluminous petitions, appeals, and proposals directed to the throne and to separate the important from the trivial. When Garion had first come to the throne, the need for someone to manage the administrative staff had been painfully clear, and Kail had been the obvious choice for that post. He was about twenty-four years old and wore a neatly trimmed brown beard. The hours he had spent in study had given him a slight squint and a permanent furrow between his eyebrows. Since he and Garion spent several hours a day together, they had soon become friends, and Garion greatly respected Kail's judgment and advice. 'Is it serious?' he asked, taking the parchment and glancing at it.

'It could be, Sire,' Kail replied. 'There's a dispute over the ownership of a certain valley. The families involved are both quite powerful, and I think we'll want to settle the matter before things go any further.'

'Is there any clear-cut evidence of ownership on either side?'

Kail shook his head. 'The two families have used the land in common for centuries. There's been some friction between them lately, however.'

'I see,' Garion said. He thought about it. 'No matter what I decide, one side or the other is going to be unhappy with me, right?'

'Very probably, your Majesty.'

'All right, then. We'll let them both be unhappy. Write up something that sounds sort of official declaring that this valley of theirs now belongs to me. We'll let them stew about that for a week or so, and then I'll divide the land right down the middle and give half to each of them. They'll be so angry with me that they'll forget that they don't like each other. I don't want this island turning into another Arendia.'

Kail laughed. 'Very practical, Belgarion,' he said.

Garion grinned at him. 'I grew up in Sendaria, remember? Oh, keep a strip of the valley—about a hundred yards wide right through the center. Call it crown land or something and forbid them to trespass on it. That should keep them from butting heads along the fence line.' He handed the parchment back to Kail and went on down the corridor, rather pleased with himself.

His mission in the city that morning took him to the shop of a young glass blower of his acquaintance, a skilled artisan named Joran. Ostensibly the visit was for the purpose of inspecting a set of crystal goblets he had commissioned as a present for Ce'Nedra. Its real purpose, however, was somewhat more serious. Because his upbringing had been humble, Garion was more aware than most monarchs that the opinions and problems of the common people seldom came to the attention of the throne. He strongly felt that he needed a pair of ears in the city—not to spy out unfavorable opinion, but rather to give him a clear, unprejudiced awareness of the real problems of his people. Joran had been his choice for that task.

After they had gone through the motions of looking at the goblets, the two of them went into a small, private room at the back of Joran's shop.

'I got your note as soon as I got back from Arendia,' Garion said. 'Is the matter really that serious?'

'I believe so, your Majesty,' Joran replied. 'The tax was poorly thought out, I think, and it's causing a great deal of unfavorable comment.'

'All directed at me, I suppose?'

'You *are* the king, after all.'

'Thanks,' Garion said drily. 'What's the main dissatisfaction with it?'

'All taxes are odious,' Joran observed, 'but they're bearable as long as everybody has to pay the same. It's the exclusion that irritates people.'

'Exclusion? What's that?'

'The nobility doesn't have to pay commercial taxes. Didn't you know that?'

'No,' Garion said. 'I didn't.'

'The theory was that nobles have other obligations—raising and supporting troops and so on. That simply doesn't hold true any more. The crown raises its own army now. If a nobleman goes into trade, though, he doesn't have to pay any commercial taxes. The only real difference between him and any other tradesman is that he happens to have a title. His shop is the same as mine, and he spends his time the same way that I do—but I have to pay the tax, and he doesn't.'

'That doesn't seem very fair,' Garion agreed.

'What makes it worse is that I have to charge higher prices in order to pay the tax, but the nobleman can cut his rates and steal my customers away from me.'

'That's going to have to be fixed,' Garion said. 'We'll eliminate that exclusion.'

'The nobles won't like it,' Joran warned.

'They don't have to like it,' Garion said flatly.

'You're a very fair king, your Majesty.'

'Fairness doesn't really have all that much to do with it,' Garion disagreed. 'How many nobles are in business here in the city?'

Joran shrugged. 'A couple dozen, I suppose.'

'And how many other businessmen are there?'

'Hundreds.'

'I'd rather have two dozen people hate me than several hundred.'

'I hadn't thought of it that way,' Joran admitted.

'I sort of have to,' Garion said wryly.

The following week a series of squalls swept in off the Sea of the Winds, raking the rocky isle with chill gales and tattered sheets of slanting rain. The weather at Riva was never really what one would call pleasant for very long, and these summer storms were so common that the Rivans accepted them as part of the natural order of things. Ce'Nedra, however, had been raised far to the south in the endless sunshine at Tol Honeth, and the damp chill which invaded the Citadel each time the sky turned gray and soggy depressed her spirits and made her irritable and out of sorts. She customarily endured these spells of bad weather by ensconcing herself in a large green velvet armchair by the fire with a warm blanket, a cup of tea, and an oversized book—usually an Arendish romance which dwelt fulsomely on impossibly splendid knights and sighing ladies perpetually on the verge of disaster. Prolonged confinement, however, almost always drove her at last from her book in search of other diversions.

One midmorning when the wind was moaning in the chimneys and the rain was slashing at the windows, she entered the study where Garion was carefully going over an exhaustive report on wool production on crown lands in the north. The little queen wore an ermine-trimmed gown of green velvet and a discontented expression. 'What are you doing?' she asked.

'Reading about wool,' he replied.

'Why?'

'I think I'm supposed to know about it. Everybody

stands round talking about wool with these sober expressions on their faces. It seems to be terribly important to them.'

'Do you really care that much about it?'

He shrugged. 'It helps to pay the bills.'

She drifted over to the window and stared out at the rain. 'Will it *never* stop?' she demanded at last.

'Eventually, I suppose.'

'I think I'll send for Arell. Maybe we can go down into the city and look around the shops.'

'It's pretty wet out there, Ce'Nedra.'

'I can wear a cloak, and a little rain won't make me melt. Would you give me some money?'

'I thought I gave you some just last week.'

'I spent it. Now I need some more.'

Garion put aside the report and went to a heavy cabinet standing against the wall. He took a key from a pocket in his doublet, unlocked the cabinet and pulled out the top drawer. Ce'Nedra came over and looked curiously into the drawer. It was about half-filled with coins, gold, silver, and copper, all jumbled together.

'Where did you get all of that?' she exclaimed.

'They give it to me from time to time,' he answered. 'I throw it in there because I don't want to have to carry it around. I thought you knew about it.'

'How would I know about it? You never tell me anything. How much have you got in there?'

He shrugged. 'I don't know.'

'Garion!' Her voice was shocked. 'Don't you even count it?'

'No. Should I?'

'You're obviously not a Tolnedran. This isn't the whole royal treasury, is it?'

'No. They keep that someplace else. This is just for personal expenses, I think.'

'It *has* to be counted, Garion.'

'I don't really have the time, Ce'Nedra.'

'Well, I do. Pull that drawer out and bring it over to the table.'

He did that, grunting slightly at the weight, and then stood smiling fondly as she sat down and happily started counting money. He had not realized just how much sheer pleasure she could take in handling and stacking coins. She actually glowed as the merry tinkle of money filled her ears. A few of the coins had become tarnished. She looked at those disapprovingly and stopped the count to polish them carefully on the hem of her gown.

'Were you going to go down into the city?' he asked, resuming his seat at the other end of the table.

'Not today, I guess.' She kept on counting. A single lock of her hair strayed down across her face, and she absently blew at it from time to time as she concentrated on the task at hand. She dug another handful of jingling coins out of the drawer and began to stack them carefully on the table in front of her. She looked so serious about it that Garion started to laugh.

She looked up sharply. 'What's so funny?' she demanded.

'Nothing, dear,' he said and went back to work to the clinking accompaniment of Ce'Nedra's counting.

As the summer wore on, the news from the southern latitudes continued to be good. King Urgit of Cthol Murgos had retreated deeper into the mountains, and the advance of the Emperor Kal Zakath of Mallorea slowed even more. The Mallorean army had suffered dreadful losses in its first efforts to pursue the Murgos into that craggy wasteland and it now moved with extreme caution. Garion received the news of the near-stalemate in the south with great satisfaction.

Toward the end of summer, word arrived from Algaria that Garion's cousin Adara had just presented Hettar with their second son. Ce'Nedra went wild with delight and dipped deeply into the drawer in Garion's study to buy suitable gifts for both mother and child.

The news which arrived in early autumn, however, was not so joyous. In a sadly worded letter, General Varana advised them that Ce'Nedra's father, Emperor Ran Borune

XXIII, was sinking fast and that they should make haste to Tol Honeth. Fortunately, the autumn sky remained clear as the ship which carried the Rivan King and his desperately worried little wife ran south before a good following breeze. They reached Tol Horb at the broad mouth of the Nedrane within a week and then began rowing upriver to the Imperial Capital at Tol Honeth.

They had gone no more than a few leagues when their ship was met by a flotilla of white and gold barges, which formed up around them to escort them to Tol Honeth. Aboard those barges was a chorus of young Tolnedran women who strewed flower petals on the broad surface of the Nedrane and caroled a formal greeting to the Imperial Princess.

Garion stood beside Ce'Nedra on the deck of their ship, frowning slightly at this choral welcome. 'Is that altogether appropriate?' he asked.

'It's the custom,' she said. 'Members of the Imperial Family are always escorted to the city.'

Garion listened to the words of the song. 'Haven't they heard about your wedding yet?' he asked. 'They're greeting the Imperial Princess, not the Rivan Queen.'

'We're a provincial people, Garion,' Ce'Nedra said. 'In Tolnedran's eyes, an Imperial Princess is much more important than the queen of some remote island.'

The singing continued as they moved on upriver. As the gleaming white city of Tol Honeth came into view, a huge brazen fanfare greeted them from the walls. A detachment of burnished legionnaires, their scarlet pennons snapping in the breeze and the plumes on their helmets tossing, awaited them on the marble quay to escort them through the broad avenues to the grounds of the Imperial palace.

General Varana, a blocky-looking professional soldier with short-cropped, curly hair and a noticeable limp, met them at the palace gate. His expression was somber.

'Are we in time, uncle?' Ce'Nedra asked with an almost frightened note in her voice.

The general nodded, then took the little queen in his

arms. 'You're going to have to be brave, Ce'Nedra,' he told her. 'Your father is very, very ill.'

'Is there any hope at all?' she asked in a small voice.

'We can always hope,' Varana replied, but his tone said otherwise.

'Can I see him now?'

'Of course.' The general looked gravely at Garion. 'Your Majesty,' he said, nodding.

'Your Highness,' Garion replied, remembering that Ce'Nedra's wily father had 'adopted' Varana several years back, and that the general was heir apparent to the Imperial Throne.

Varana led them with his limping gait through the marble corridors of the vast palace to a quiet wing and a door flanked by a towering pair of legionnaires in burnished breastplates. As they approached, the heavy door opened quietly, and Lord Morin, the brown-mantled Imperial Chamberlain emerged. Morin had aged since Garion had last seen him, and his concern for his failing Emperor was written clearly on his face.

'Dear Morin,' Ce'Nedra said, impulsively embracing her father's closest friend.

'Little Ce'Nedra,' he replied fondly. 'I'm so glad you arrived in time. He's been asking for you. I think perhaps the fact you were coming is all he's been hanging on to.'

'Is he awake?'

Morin nodded. 'He dozes a great deal, but he's still alert most of the time.'

Ce'Nedra drew herself up, squared her shoulders and carefully assumed a bright, optimistic smile. 'All right,' she said. 'Let's go in.'

Ran Borune lay in a vast canopied bed beneath a gold-colored coverlet. He had never been a large man, and his illness had wasted him down to a near-skeleton. His complexion was not so much pale as it was gray, and his beaklike nose was pinched and rose from his drawn face like the prow of a ship. His eyes were closed, and his thin chest seemed almost to flutter as he struggled to breathe.

'Father?' Ce'Nedra said so softly that her voice was hardly more than a whisper.

The Emperor opened one eye. 'Well,' he said testily, 'I see that you finally got here.'

'Nothing could have kept me away,' she told him, bending over the bed to kiss his withered cheek.

'That's hardly encouraging,' he grunted.

'Now that I'm here, we'll have to see about getting you well again.'

'Don't patronize me, Ce'Nedra. My physicians have given up entirely.'

'What do they know? We Borunes are indestructable.'

'Did someone pass that law while I wasn't looking?' The Emperor looked past his daughter's shoulder at his son-in-law. 'You're looking well, Garion,' he said. 'And please don't waste your time on platitudes by telling me how well *I* look. I look awful, don't I?'

'Moderately awful, yes,' Garion replied.

Ran Borune flashed him a quick little grin. Then he turned back to his daughter. 'Well, Ce'Nedra,' he said pleasantly, 'what shall we fight about today?'

'Fight? Who said we were going to fight?'

'We always fight. I've been looking forward to it. I haven't had a really good fight since you stole my legions that day.'

'Borrowed, father,' she corrected primly, almost in spite of herself.

'Is that what you call it?' He winked broadly at Garion. 'You should have been there,' he chuckled. 'She goaded me into a fit and then pinched my whole army while I was frothing at the mouth.'

'*Pinched!*' Ce'Nedra exclaimed.

Ran Borune began to chuckle, but his laughter turned into a tearing cough that left him gasping and so weak that he could not even raise his head. He closed his eyes then and dozed for a while as Ce'Nedra hovered anxiously over him.

After a quarter of an hour or so, Lord Morin quietly entered with a small flask and a silver spoon. 'It's time for his medicine,' he said softly to Ce'Nedra. 'I don't think it really helps very much, but we go through the motions anyway.'

'Is that you, Morin?' the Emperor asked without opening his eyes.

'Yes, Ran Borune.'

'Is there any word from Tol Rane yet?'

'Yes, your Majesty.'

'What did you say?'

'I'm afraid the season's over there, too.'

'There has to be *one* tree somewhere in the world that's still bearing fruit,' the emaciated little man in the imperial bed said exasperatedly.

'His Majesty has expressed a desire for some fresh fruit,' Morin told Ce'Nedra and Garion.

'Not just *any* fruit, Morin,' Ran Borune wheezed. 'Cherries. I want cherries. Right now I'd bestow a Grand Duchy on any man who could bring me ripe cherries.'

'Don't be so difficult, father,' Ce'Nedra chided him. 'The season for cherries was over months ago. How about a nice, ripe peach?'

'I don't *want* peaches. I want cherries!'

'Well, you can't have them.'

'You're an undutiful daughter, Ce'Nedra,' he accused her.

Garion leaned forward and spoke quietly to Ce'Nedra. 'I'll be right back,' he told her and went out of the room with Morin. In the corridor outside they met General Varana.

'How is he?' the general asked.

'Peevish,' Garion replied. 'He wants some cherries.'

'I know,' Varana said sourly. 'He's been asking for them for weeks. Trust a Borune to demand the impossible.'

'Are there any cherry trees here on the palace grounds?'

'There are a couple in his private garden. Why?'

'I thought I might have a word with them,' Garion said innocently, 'explain a few things, and give them a bit of encouragement.'

Varana gave him a look of profound disapproval.

'It's not really immoral,' Garion assured him.

Varana raised one hand and turned his face away. 'Please, Belgarion,' he said in a pained voice, 'don't try to explain it to me. I don't even want to hear about it. If you're going to do it, just do it, and get it over with, but please don't try to convince me that it's in any way natural or wholesome.'

'All right,' Garion agreed. 'Which way did you say that garden was?'

It wasn't really difficult, of course. Garion had seen Belgarath the Sorcerer do it on several occasions. It was no more than ten minutes later that he returned to the corridor outside the sickroom with a small basket of dark purple cherries.

Varana looked steadily at the basket, but said nothing. Garion quietly opened the door and went inside.

Ran Borune lay propped on his pillows, his drawn face sagging with exhaustion. 'I don't see why not,' he was saying to Ce'Nedra. 'A respectful daughter would have presented her father with a half-dozen grandchildren by now.'

'We'll get to it, father,' she replied. 'Why is everyone so worried about it?'

'Because it's important, Ce'Nedra. Not even *you* could be so silly as to—' He broke off, staring incredulously at the basket in Garion's hand. 'Where did you get those?' he demanded.

'I don't think you really want to know, Ran Borune. It's the kind of thing that seems to upset Tolnedrans for some reason.'

'You didn't just make them, did you?' the Emperor asked suspiciously.

'No. It's much harder that way. I just gave the trees in your garden a little encouragement, that's all. They were very co-operative.'

'What an absolutely splendid fellow you married, Ce'Nedra,' Ran Borune exclaimed, eying the cherries greedily. 'Put those right here, my boy.' He patted the bed at his side.

Ce'Nedra flashed her husband a grateful little smile, took the basket from him, and deposited it by her father's side. Almost absently she took one of the cherries and popped it into her mouth.

'Ce'Nedra! You stop eating my cherries!'

'Just checking to see if they're ripe, father.'

'Any idiot can see that they're ripe,' he said, clutching the basket possessively to his side. 'If you want any, go get your own.' He carefully selected one of the plump, glowing cherries and put it in his mouth. 'Marvelous,' he said, chewing happily.

'Don't spit the seeds on the floor like that, father,' Ce'Nedra reproved him.

'It's my floor,' he told her. 'Mind your own business. Spitting the seeds is part of the fun.' He ate several more cherries. 'We won't discuss how you came by these, Garion,' he said magnanimously. 'Technically, it's a violation of Tolnedran law to practice sorcery anywhere in the Empire, but we'll let it pass—just this once.'

'Thank you, Ran Borune,' Garion said. 'I appreciate that.'

After he had eaten about half of the cherries, the Emperor smiled and sighed contentedly. 'I feel better already,' he said. 'Ce'Vanne used to bring me fresh cherries in that same kind of basket.'

'My mother,' Ce'Nedra said to Garion.

Ran Borune's eyes clouded over. 'I miss her,' he said very quietly. 'She was impossible to live with, but I miss her more every day.'

'I scarcely remember her,' Ce'Nedra said wistfully.

'I remember her very well,' her father said. 'I'd give my whole Empire if I could see her face just one more time.'

Ce'Nedra took his wasted hand in hers and looked imploringly at Garion. 'Could you?' she asked, two great tears standing in her eyes.

'I'm not entirely sure,' he replied in some perplexity. 'I think I know how it's done, but I never met your mother, so I'd have to—' He broke off, still trying to work it out in his mind. 'I'm sure Aunt Pol could do it, but—' He came to the bedside. 'We can try,' he said. He took Ce'Nedra's other hand and then Ran Borune's linking the three of them together.

It was extremely difficult. Ran Borune's memory was clouded by age and his long illness, and Ce'Nedra's remembrance of her mother was so sketchy that it could hardly be said to exist at all. Garion concentrated, bending all his will upon it. Beads of perspiration stood out on his forehead as he struggled to gather all those fleeting memories into one single image.

The light coming in through the flimsy curtains at the window seemed to darken as if a cloud had passed over the sun, and there was a faint, far-off tinkling sound, as if of small, golden bells. The room was suddenly filled with a kind of woodland fragrance—a subtle smell of moss and leaves and green trees. The light faded a bit more, and the tinkling and the odor grew stronger.

And then there was a hazy, nebulous luminosity in the air at the foot of the dying Emperor's bed. The glow grew brighter, and she was there. Ce'Vanne had been a bit taller than her daughter, but Garion saw instantly why Ran Borune had always so doted on his only child. The hair was precisely the same deep auburn; the complexion was that same golden-tinged olive; and the eyes were of that exact same green. The face was willful, certainly, but the eyes were filled with love.

The figure came silently around the bed, reaching out briefly in passing to touch Ce'Nedra's face with lingering, phantom fingertips. Garion could suddenly see the source of that small bell sound. Ce'Nedra's mother wore the two golden acorn earrings of which her daughter was so fond, and the two tiny clappers inside them gave off that faint, musical tinkle whenever she moved her head. For no particular reason, Garion remembered that those same earrings lay on his wife's dressing table back at Riva.

Ce'Vanne reached out her hand to her husband. Ran Borune's face was filled with wonder, and his eyes with tears. 'Ce'Vanne,' he said in a trembling whisper, struggling to raise himself from his pillow. He pulled his shaking hand free from Garion's grasp and reached out toward her. For a moment their hands seemed to touch, and then Ran Borune gave a long, quavering sigh, sank back on his pillows, and died.

Ce'Nedra sat for a long time holding her father's hand as the faint, woodland smell and the echo of the little golden bells slowly subsided from the room and the light from the window returned. Finally she placed the wasted hand gently back on the coverlet, rose, and looked around the room with an almost casual air. 'It's going to have to be aired out, of course,' she said absently. 'Maybe some cut flowers to sweeten the air.' She smoothed the coverlet at the side of the bed and gravely looked at her father's body. Then she turned. 'Oh, Garion,' she wailed, suddenly throwing herself into his arms.

Garion held her, smoothing her hair and feeling the shaking of her tiny body against him and looking all the while at the still, peaceful face of the Emperor of Tolnedra. It may have been some trick of the light, but it almost seemed that there was a smile on Ran Borune's lips.

Chapter Eleven

The state funeral for Emperor Ran Borune XXIII of the Third Borune Dynasty took place a few days later in the Temple of Nedra, Lion God of the Empire. The temple was a huge marble building not far from the Imperial Palace. The altar was backed by a vast fan of pure, beaten gold, with the head of a lion in its center. Directly in front of the altar stood the simple marble bier of Ce'Nedra's father. The late Emperor lay in calm repose, covered from the neck down by a cloth of gold. The column-lined inner hall of the temple was filled to overflowing as the members of the great families vied with one another, not so much to pay their respects to Ran Borune, but rather to display the opulence of their clothing and the sheer weight of their personal adornment.

Garion and Ce'Nedra, both dressed in deepest mourning, sat beside General Varana at the front of the vast hall as the eulogies were delivered. Tolnedran politics dictated that a representative of each of the major houses should speak upon this sad occasion. The speeches, Garion suspected, had been prepared long in advance. They were all quite flowery and tiresome, and each one seemed to be directed at the point that, although Ran Borune was gone, the Empire lived on. Many of the speakers seemed quite smug about that.

When the eulogies had at last been completed, the white-robed High Priest of Nedra, a pudgy, sweating man with a grossly sensual mouth, arose and stepped to the front of the altar to add his own contribution. Drawing upon events in the life of Ran Borune, he delivered a lengthy homily on the advantages of having wealth and using it wisely. At first Garion was shocked by the High Priest's choice of subject matter, but the rapt faces of the throng in the temple told him that a sermon about money was very moving to a Tolnedran congregation and that the High Priest, by selecting such a topic, was able thereby to slip in any number of laudatory comments about Ce'Nedra's father.

Once all the tedius speeches were completed, the little Emperor was laid to rest beside his wife under a marble slab in the Borune section of the catacombs beneath the temple. The so-called mourners then returned to the main temple hall to express their condolences to the bereaved family. Ce'Nedra bore up well, though she was very pale. On one occasion she swayed slightly, and Garion, without thinking, reached out to support her.

'Don't touch me!' she whispered sharply under her breath, raising her chin sharply.

'What?' Garion was startled.

'We can *not* show any sign of weakness in the presence of our enemies. I will *not* break down for the entertainment of the Honeths or the Horbites or the Vordues. My father would rise from his grave in disgust if I did.'

The nobles of all the great houses continued to file past to offer their extensive and obviously counterfeit sympathy to the sable-gowned little Rivan Queen. Garion found their half-concealed smirks contemptible and their barbed jibes disgusting. His face grew more stern and disapproving as the moments passed. His threatening presence soon dampened the enjoyment of the Grand Dukes and their ladies and sycophants. The Tolnedrans were genuinely afraid of this tall, mysterious Alorn monarch who had come out of nowhere to assume Riva's throne and to shake the very earth with his footsteps. Even as they approached Ce'Nedra to deliver their poisonous observations, his cold, grim face made them falter, and many carefully prepared impertinences went unsaid.

At last, disgusted so much that even his Sendarian good manners deserted him, he placed his hand firmly on his wife's elbow. 'We will leave now,' he said to her in a voice which could be clearly heard by everyone in the vast temple. 'The air in this place has turned a trifle rancid.'

Ce'Nedra cast him one startled glance, then lifted her chin in her most regal and imperious manner, laid her hand lightly on his arm, and walked with him toward the huge bronze doors. The silence was vast as they moved with stately pace through the throng, and a wide path opened for them.

'That was very nicely done, dear,' Ce'Nedra complimented him warmly as they rode in the gold-inlaid imperial carriage back toward the palace.

'It seemed appropriate,' he replied. 'I'd reached the point where I either had to say something rather pointed or turn the whole lot of them into toads.'

'My, what an enchanting thought,' she exclaimed. 'We could go back, if you want.'

When Varana arrived back at the palace an hour or so later, he was positively gloating. 'Belgarion,' he said with a broad grin, 'you're a splendid young fellow, do you know that? With that one word you mortally offended virtually the entire nobility of northern Tolnedra.'

'Which word was that?'

'Rancid.'

'I'm sorry about that one.'

'Don't be. It perfectly describes them.'

'It is a bit coarse, though.'

'Not under the circumstances. It *did* manage to make you any number of lifelong enemies, however.'

'That's all I need,' Garion replied sourly. 'Give me just a few more years, and I'll have enemies in all parts of the world.'

'A king isn't really doing his job if he doesn't make enemies, Belgarion. Any jackass can go through life without offending people.'

'Thanks.'

There had been some uncertainty about which course Varana would follow once Ran Borune was gone. His 'adoption' by the late Emperor had clearly been a ruse with very little in the way of legality to back it up. The candidates for the throne, blinded by their own lust for the Imperial Crown, had convinced themselves that he would merely serve as a kind of caretaker until the question of the succession had been settled in the usual fashion.

The issue remained in doubt until his official coronation, which took place two days after Ran Borune's funeral. The gloating exultation among the contenders for the throne was almost audible when the general limped into the Temple of Nedra dressed in his uniform, rather than the traditional gold mantle which only the Emperor was allowed to wear. Obviously this man did not intend to take his elevation seriously. It might cost a bit to bribe him, but the way to the Imperial Palace was still open. The grins were broad as Varana, gleaming in his gold-inlaid breastplate, approached the altar.

The pudgy High Priest bent forward for a moment of whispered consultation. Varana replied, and the ecclesiast's face suddenly went deathly pale. Trembling violently, he opened the gold and crystal cask on the altar and removed the jewel-encrusted Imperial Crown. Varana's short-cropped hair was annointed with the traditional unguent, and the High Priest raised the crown with shaking hands. 'I crown thee,' he declared in a voice almost squeaky with fright. '—I crown thee Emperor Ran Borune XXIV, Lord of all Tolnedra.'

It took a moment for that to sink in. Then the temple was filled with howls of anguished protest as the Tolnedran nobility grasped the fact that by the choice of his imperial name, Varana was clearly announcing that he intended to keep the crown for himself. Those howls were cut off sharply as the Tolnedran legionnaires, who had quietly filed into place along the colonnade surrounding the main temple floor, drew their swords with a huge, steely rasp. The gleaming swords raised in salute.

'Hail Ran Borune!' the legions thundered. 'Hail Emperor of Tolnedra!'

And that was that.

That evening as Garion, Ce'Nedra, and the newly crowned Emperor sat together in a crimson-draped private chamber filled with the golden glow of dozens of candles, Varana explained. 'Surprise is as important in politics as it is in military tactics, Belgarion. If your opponent doesn't know what you're going to do, there's no way he can prepare countermeasures.' The general now openly wore the gold mantle of the Emperor.

'That makes sense,' Garion replied, sipping at a goblet of Tolnedran wine. 'Wearing your breastplate instead of the Imperial Mantle kept them guessing right up until the last minute.'

'That was for a much more practical reason.' Varana laughed. 'Many of those young nobles have had military training, and we teach our legionnaires how to throw daggers. Since my back was going to be toward them, I wanted a good, solid layer of steel covering the area between my shoulder blades.'

'Tolnedran politics are very nervous, aren't they?'

Varana nodded his agreement. 'Fun, though,' he added.

'You have a peculiar notion of fun. I've had a few daggers thrown at me and I didn't find it all that amusing.'

'We Anadiles have always had a peculiar sense of humor.'

'Borune, uncle,' Ce'Nedra corrected primly.

'What was that, dear?'

'You're a Borune now, not an Anadile—and you should start acting like one.'

'Bad-tempered, you mean? That's not really in my nature.'

'Ce'Nedra could give you lessons, if you like,' Garion offered, grinning fondly at his wife.

'*What?*' Ce'Nedra exclaimed indignantly, her voice going up an octave or so.

'I suppose she could at that,' Varana agreed blandly. 'She's always been very good at it.'

Ce'Nedra sighed mournfully, eyeing the pair of grinning monarchs. Then her expression became artfully tragic.

'What's a poor little girl to do?' she asked in a trembling voice. 'Here I am, maltreated and abused by both my husband and my brother.'

Varana blinked. 'You know, I hadn't even thought of that. You *are* my sister now, aren't you?'

'Perhaps you aren't quite as clever as I thought, brother dear,' she purred at him. 'I *know* that Garion's not quite bright, but I thought better of you.'

Garion and Varana exchanged rueful glances.

'Would you gentlemen like to play some more?' Ce'Nedra asked them, her eyes twinkling and a smug smile hovering about her lips.

There was a light tap on the door.

'Yes?' Varana said.

'Lord Morin to see you, your Majesty,' the guard outside the door announced.

'Send him in, please.'

The Imperial Chamberlain entered quietly. His face was marked by the sorrow he felt at the passing of the man he had served so long and faithfully, but he still performed his duties with the quiet efficiency that had always been his outstanding characteristic.

'Yes, Morin?' Varana said.

'Ther's someone waiting outside, your Majesty. She's rather notorious, so I thought I should speak to you privately before I presented her to you.'

'Notorious?'

'It's the courtesan Bethra, your Majesty,' Morin said with a faintly embarrassed look at Ce'Nedra. 'She's been —ah—shall we say, useful to the crown in the past. She has access to a great deal of information as a result of her professional activities and she was a longtime friend of Ran Borune's. From time to time she kept him advised of the activities of certain unfriendly nobles. He made arrangements for there to be a way by which she could enter the palace unnoticed so that they could—ah—talk, among other things.'

'Why, that sly old fox.'

'I have never known her information to be inaccurate,

your Majesty,' Morin continued. 'She says that she has something very important to tell you.'

'You'd better bring her in, then, Morin,' Varana said, 'With you permission, of course, dear sister,' he added to Ce'Nedra.

'Certainly,' Ce'Nedra agreed, her eyes afire with curiosity.

When Morin brought the woman in, she was wearing a light, hooded cloak, but when, with one smooth, round arm, she reached up and pushed the hood back, Garion started slightly. He knew her. He recalled that when he and Aunt Pol and the others had been passing through Tol Honeth during their pursuit of Zedar the Apostate and the stolen Orb, this same woman had accosted Silk for a bantering exchange. As she unfastened the neck of her cloak and let it slide almost sensuously from her creamy shoulders, he saw that she had not changed in the nearly ten years since he had last seen her. Her lustrous, blue-black hair was untouched by any hint of gray. Her startlingly beautiful face was still as smooth as a girl's, and her heavy-lidded eyes were still filled with a sultry wickedness. Her gown was of palest lavender and cut in such a way as to enhance rather than conceal the lush, almost overripe body it enclosed. It was the kind of body that was a direct challenge to every man she met. Garion stared openly at her until he caught Ce'Nedra's green eyes, agate-hard, boring into him, and he quickly looked away.

'Your Majesty,' Bethra said in a throaty contralto as she curtsied gracefully to the new Emperor, 'I would have waited a time before introducing myself, but I've heard a few things I thought you should know immediately.'

'I appreciate your friendship, Lady Bethra,' Varana replied with exquisite courtesy.

She laughed a warm, wicked laugh. 'I'm not a lady, your Majesty,' she corrected him. 'Most definitely *not* a lady.' She made a small curtsy to Ce'Nedra. 'Princess,' she murmured.

'Madame,' Ce'Nedra responded with a faint chill in her voice and a very slight inclination of her head.

'Ah,' Bethra said almost sadly. Then she turned back to Varana. 'Late this afternoon I was entertaining Count Ergon and the Baron Kelbor at my establishment.'

'A pair of powerful Honethite nobles,' Varana explained to Garion.

'The gentlemen from the house of Honeth are less than pleased with your Majesty's choice of an official name,' Bethra continued. 'They spoke hastily and in some heat, but I think that you might want to take what they said seriously. Ergon is an unmitigated ass, all bluster and pomposity, but Baron Kelbor is not the sort to be taken lightly. At any rate, they concluded that, with the legions all around the palace, it would be unlikely that an assassin could reach you; but then Kelbor said, "If you want to kill a snake, you cut off its tail—just behind the head. We can't reach Varana, but we *can* reach his son. Without an heir, Varana's line dies with him."'

'My son?' Varana said sharply.

'His life is in danger, your Majesty. I thought you should know.'

'Thank you, Bethra,' Varana replied gravely. Then he turned to Morin. 'Send a detachment of the third legion to my son's house,' he said. 'No one is to go in or out until I've had time to make other arrangements.'

'At once, your Majesty.'

'I would also like to speak with the two gentlemen from the House of Honeth. Send some troops to invite them to the palace. Have them wait in that little room adjoining the torture chamber down in the dungeons until I have the time to discuss this with them.'

'You wouldn't,' Ce'Nedra gasped.

'Probably not,' Varana admitted, 'but they don't have to know that, do they? Let's give them a nervous hour or two.'

'I'll see to it immediately, your Majesty,' Morin said. He bowed and quietly left the room.

'I'm told that you knew my father,' Ce'Nedra said to the lushly curved woman standing in the center of the room.

'Yes, Princess,' Bethra responded. 'Quite well, actually. We were friends for years.'

Ce'Nedra's eyes narrowed.

'Your father was a vigorous man, Princess,' Bethra told her calmly. 'I'm told that many people prefer not to believe that kind of thing about their parents, but it does happen now and again. I was quite fond of him and I'll miss him very much, I think.'

'I don't believe you,' Ce'Nedra said bluntly.

'That's up to you, of course.'

'My father would not have done that.'

'Whatever you say, Princess,' Bethra said with a faint smile.

'You're lying!' Ce'Nedra snapped.

A momentary glint came into Bethra's eyes. 'No, Princess. I don't lie. I might conceal the truth at times, but I never lie. Lies are too easily found out. Ran Borune and I were intimate friends and we enjoyed each other's company in many ways.' Her look became faintly amused. 'Your upbringing has sheltered you from certain facts, Princess Ce'Nedra. Tol Honeth is an extremely corrupt city, and I am fully at home here. Let's face a certain blunt truth. I'm a harlot and I make no apology for that fact. The work is easy—even pleasant at times—and the pay is very good. I'm on the best of terms with some of the richest and most powerful men in the world. We talk, and they value my conversation, but when they come to my house, it's not the talk they're interested in. The talk comes later. It was much the same when I visited your father. We *did* talk, Princess, but it was usually later.'

Ce'Nedra's face was flaming, and her eyes were wide with shock. 'No one has *ever* talked to me that way before,' she gasped.

'Then it was probably overdue,' Bethra said calmly. 'You're much wiser now—not happier, perhaps, but wiser. Now, if you'll all excuse me, I should probably leave. The Honeths have spies everywhere, and I think it might not be a good idea for them to find out about this visit.'

'I want to thank you for the information you've just brought me, Bethra,' Varana said to her. 'Let me give you something for your trouble.'

'That has never been necessary, your Majesty,' she replied with an arch little smile. 'Information is *not* what I sell. I'll go now—unless you want to talk business, of course.' She paused in the act of putting her cloak back on and gave him a very direct look.

'Ah—this might not really be the best time, Bethra,' Varana said with a faintly regretful note in his voice and a quick sidelong glance at Ce'Nedra.

'Some other time then, perhaps.' She curtsied again and quietly left the room, the musky fragrance of the scent she wore lingering in the air behind her.

Ce'Nedra was still blushing furiously, and her eyes were outraged. She spun to face Garion and Varana. 'Don't either of you *dare* say anything,' she commanded. 'Not one single word.'

The sad visit to Tol Honeth ended a few days later, and Garion and Ce'Nedra took ship again for the voyage back to the Isle of the Winds. Though Ce'Nedra seldom gave any outward hints of her grief, Garion knew her well enough to understand that her father's death had hurt her deeply. Because he loved her and was sensitive to her emotions, he treated her with a certain extra tenderness and consideration for the next several months.

In midautumn that year, the Alorn Kings and Queen Porenn, Regent of Drasnia, arrived at Riva for the traditional meeting of the Alorn Council. The meeting had none of the urgency which had marked those meetings previously. Torak was dead, the Angaraks were convulsed by war, and a king sat upon the Rivan throne. The entire affair was almost purely social, though the kings did make some pretense at holding business sessions in the blue-draped council chamber high in the south tower of the Citadel. They gravely talked about the stalemated war in southern Cthol Murgos and about the troubles Varana was having with the Vordue family of northern Tolnedra.

Warned perhaps by the failure of the Honeths in their

attempts at assassination, the Vordues decided to try secession. Shortly after Varana's coronation as Ran Borune XXIV, the Vordue family declared that their Grand Duchy was no longer a part of Tolnedra but rather was a separate, independent kingdom—although they had not yet decided which of their number was to ascend the throne.

'Varana's going to have to move the legions against them,' King Anheg declared, wiping the ale foam from his mouth with his sleeve. 'Otherwise, the other families will seeced too, and Tolnedra will fly apart like a broken spring.'

'It's not really that simple, Anheg,' Queen Porenn told him smoothly, turning back from the window out of which she had been watching the activity in the harbor far below. The Queen of Drasnia still wore deep mourning, and her black gown seemed to enhance her blonde loveliness. 'The legions will gladly fight any foreign enemy, but Varana can't ask them to attack their own people.'

Anheg shrugged. 'He could bring up legions from the south. They're all Borunes or Anadiles or Ranites. They wouldn't mind trampling over the Vordues.'

'But then the northern legions would step in to stop them. Once the legions start fighting each other, the Empire will *really* disintegrate.'

'I guess I really hadn't thought of it that way,' Anheg admitted. 'You know, Porenn, you're extremely intelligent —for a woman.'

'And you're extremely perceptive—for a man,' she replied with a sweet smile.

'That's one for her side,' King Cho-Hag said quietly.

'Were we keeping score?' Garion asked mildly.

'It helps us to keep track, sort of,' the Chief of the Clan-Chiefs of Algaria answered with a straight face.

It was not until several days later that word reached Riva concerning Varana's rather novel approach to his problem with the Vordues. A Drasnian ship sailed into the harbor one morning, and an agent of the Drasnia Intelligence Service brought a sheaf of dispatches to Queen

Porenn. After she read them, she entered the council chamber with a smug little smile. 'I believe we can set our minds at rest about Varana's abilities, gentlemen,' she told the Alorn Kings. 'He appears to have found a solution to the Vordue question.'

'Oh?' Brand rumbled. 'What is it?'

'My informants advise me that he has made a secret arrangement with King Korodullin of Arendia. This so-called Kingdom of Vordue has suddenly become absolutely infested with Arendish bandits—most of them in full armor, oddly enough.'

'Wait a minute, Porenn,' Anheg interrupted. 'If it's a secret arrangement, how is it that you know about it?'

The little blonde Queen of Drasnia lowered her eyelids demurely. 'Why, Anheg, dear, weren't you aware of the fact that I know everything?'

'Another one for her side,' King Cho-Hag said to Garion.

'I'd say so, yes,' Garion agreed.

'At any rate,' the Drasnian Queen continued, 'there are now whole battalions of brainless young Mimbrate knights in Vordue, all posing as bandits and plundering and burning at will. The Vordues don't have what you could call an army, so they've been screaming for aid from the legions. My people managed to get their hands on a copy of Varana's reply.' She unfolded a document. '"To the government of the Kingdom of Vordue,"' she read, '"Greetings: Your recent appeal for help came as a great surprise to me. Surely the esteemed gentlemen in Tol Vordue would not want me to violate the sovereignty of their newly established kingdom by sending Tolnedran legions across their borders to deal with a few Arendish brigands. The maintenance of public order is the paramount responsibility of any government, and I would not dream of intruding my forces into so fundamental an area. To do so would raise grave doubts in the minds of reasonable men the world over as to the viability of your new state. I do, however, send you my best wishes in your efforts to deal with what is, after all, a strictly internal matter."'

Anheg began to laugh, pounding his heavy fist on the table in his glee. 'I think that calls for a drink,' he chortled.

'I think it might call for several,' Garion agreed. 'We can toast the efforts of the Vordues to maintain order.'

'I trust you gentlemen will excuse me then,' Queen Porenn said. 'No mere woman could ever hope to compete with the Kings of Aloria when it comes to really serious drinking.'

'Of course, Porenn,' Anheg agreed magnanimously. 'We'll even drink your share for you.'

'You're too kind,' she murmured and withdrew.

Much of the evening that followed was lost in a hazy fog of ale fumes for Garion. He seemed to remember weaving down a corridor with Anheg on one side and Brand on the other. The three of them had their arms about one anothers' shoulders, and they staggered in a peculiar kind of unison. He also seemed to remember that they were singing. When he was sober, Garion never sang. That night, however, it seemed like the most natural and enjoyable thing in the world.

He had not been drunk before. Aunt Pol had always disapproved of drinking, and, as he did in most things, he had deferred to her opinions about the matter. Thus, he was totally unprepared for the way he felt the next morning.

Ce'Nedra was unsympathetic, to say the very least. Like every woman who had ever lived since the beginning of time, she smugly enjoyed her husband's suffering. 'I told you that you were drinking too much,' she reminded him.

'Please don't,' he said, holding his head between his hands.

'It's your own fault,' she smirked.

'Just leave me alone,' he begged. 'I'm trying to die.'

'Oh, I don't think you'll die, Garion. You might wish you could, but you won't.'

'Do you have to talk so loud?'

'We all just *loved* your singing,' she congratulated him

brightly. 'I actually think you invented notes that didn't even exist before.'

Garion groaned and once more buried his face between his trembling hands.

The Alorn Council lasted for perhaps another week. It might have continued longer had not a savage autumn storm announced with a howling gale that it was time for the assembled guests to return to the mainland while the Sea of the Winds was still navigable.

Not too many days later, Brand, the tall, aging Rivan Warder, requested a private audience with Garion. It was raining gustily outside, and sheets of water intermittently clawed at the windows of Garion's study as the two men sat down in comfortable chairs across the table from each other. 'May I speak frankly, Belgarion?' the big, sad-eyed man asked.

'You know you don't have to ask that.'

'The matter at hand is a personal one. I don't want you to be offended.'

'Say what you think needs to be said. I promise not to be offended.'

Brand glanced out the window at the gray sky and the wind-driven rain. 'Belgarion, it's been almost eight years now since you married Princess Ce'Nedra.'

Garion nodded.

'I'm not trying to intrude on your privacy, but the fact that your wife has not yet produced an heir to the throne is, after all, a state matter.'

Garion pursed his lips. 'I know that you and Anheg and the others are very concerned. I think your concern is premature, though.'

'Eight years is a long time, Belgarion. We all know how much you love your wife. We're all fond of her.' Brand smiled briefly. 'Even though she's a little difficult at times.'

'You've noticed.'

'We followed her willingly to the battlefield at Thull Mardu—and probably would again if she asked us to— but I think we'd better face the possibility that she may be barren.'

'I'm positive that she's not,' Garion said firmly.

'Then why isn't she having children?'

Garion couldn't answer that.

'Belgarion, the fate of this kingdom—and of all Aloria—hangs on your weakest breath. There's virtually no other topic of conversation in all the northern kingdoms.'

'I didn't know that,' Garion admitted.

'Grodeg and his henchmen were virtually wiped out at Thull Mardu, but there's been a resurgence of the Bear-cult in remote parts of Cherek, Drasnia, and Algaria. You knew that, didn't you?'

Garion nodded.

'And even in the cities there are those elements that sympathize with the cult's aims and beliefs. Those people were not happy that you chose a Tolnedran princess for your wife. Rumors are already abroad that Ce'Nedra's inability to have children is a sign of Belar's disapproval of your marriage to her.'

'That's superstitious nonsense,' Garion scoffed.

'Of course it is, but if that kind of thinking begins to take hold, it's ultimately going to have some unpleasant effects. Other elements in Alorn society—friendly to you—are very concerned about it. To put it bluntly, there's a rather widely held opinion that the time has come for you to divorce Ce'Nedra.'

'What?'

'You *do* have that power, you know. The way they all see it, the best solution might be for you to put aside your barren Tolnedran queen and take some nice, fertile Alorn girl, who'll present you with babies by the dozen.'

'That's absolutely out of the question,' Garion said hotly. 'I won't do it. Didn't those idiots ever hear about the Accords of Vo Mimbre? Even if I wanted to divorce Ce'Nedra, I couldn't. Our marriage was agreed upon five hundred years ago.'

'The Bear-cult feels that the arrangement was forced on the Alorns by Belgarath and Polgara,' Brand replied. 'Since those two are loyal to Aldur, the cult feels that it might have been done without Belar's approval.'

'Nonsense,' Garion snapped.

'There's a lot of nonsense in any religion, Belgarion. The point remains, however, that Ce'Nedra has few friends in any part of Alorn society. Even those who are friendly to you aren't very fond of her. Both your enemies *and* your friends would like to see you divorce her. They all know how fond of her you are, so they'll probably never approach you with the idea. They're likely to take more direct action instead.'

'Such as?'

'Since they know that you can't be persuaded to divorce her, someone may try to remove her permanently.'

'They wouldn't dare!'

'Alorns are almost as emotional as Arends are, Belgarion—and sometimes almost as thick-headed. We're all aware of it. Anheg and Cho-Hag both urged me to warn you about this possibility, and Porenn has put whole platoons of her spies to work on it so that we'll at least have some advance warning, if someone starts plotting against the queen.'

'And just where do you stand in this, Brand?' Garion asked quietly.

'Belgarion,' the big man said firmly, 'I love you as if you were my own son, and Ce'Nedra is as dear to me as the daughter I never had. Nothing in this world would make me happier than to see the floor of that nursery next to your bedroom absolutely littered with children. But it's been eight years. Things have reached the point where we must do something—if for no other reason, then to protect that tiny, brave girl we both love.'

'What can we do?' Garion asked helplessly.

'You and I are only men, Garion. How can *we* know why a woman does or does not have children? And that's the crux of the whole situation. I implore you, Garion— I beg you—send for Polgara. We need her advice and help —and we need it now.'

After the Warder had quietly left, Garion sat for a long while staring out at the rain. All in all, he decided that it might be wiser not to tell Ce'Nedra about the conversation. He did not want to frighten her with talk of assassins lurking in the dim corridors, and any hint that political expediency might compel consideration of divorce would *not* be well received. After careful thought, he concluded that the best course would be to just keep his mouth shut and send for Aunt Pol. Unfortunately, he had forgotten something rather important. When he entered the cheery, candlelit royal apartment that evening, he wore a carefully assumed smile designed to indicate that nothing untoward had happened during the day.

The frosty silence which greeted him should have warned him; even had he missed that danger sign, he certainly should have noticed the scars on the door casing and the broken shards of several vases and assorted porcelain figurines that lay in the corners where they had been missed in the hasty clean-up following an explosion of some sort. The Rivan King, however, sometimes tended to be slightly unobservant. 'Good evening, dear,' he greeted his icy little wife in a cheerful voice.

'Really?'

'How did your day go?'

She turned to regard him with a look filled with daggers. 'How can you possibly have the nerve to ask that?'

Garion blinked.

'Tell me,' she said, 'just when is it that I am to be put aside so that my Lord can marry the blonde-headed brood sow who's going to replace me in my Lord's bed and fill the entire Citadel with litters of runny-nosed Alorn brats?'

'How—?'

'My Lord appears to have forgotten the gift he chained about my neck when we were betrothed,' she said. 'My Lord also appears to have forgotten just exactly what Beldaran's amulet can do.'

'Oh,' Garion said, suddenly remembering. 'Oh, my.'

'Unfortunately, the amulet won't come off,' Ce'Nedra told him bitingly. 'You won't be able to give it to your next wife—unless you plan to have my head cut off so that you can reclaim it.'

"*Will* you stop that?"

'As my Lord commands me. Did you plan to ship me back to Tolnedra—or am I just to be shoved out the front gate into the rain and left to fend for myself?'

'You heard the discussion I had with Brand, then, I take it.'

'Obviously.'

'If you heard part of it, then I'm sure you heard it all. Brand was only reporting a danger to you caused by the absurd notions of a group of frothing fanatics.'

'You should not have even listened to him.'

'When he's trying to warn me that somebody might attempt to kill you? Ce'Nedra, be serious.'

'The thought is there now, Garion,' she said accusingly. 'Now you know that you can get rid of me any time you want. I've seen you ogling those empty-headed Alorn girls with their long blonde braids and their overdeveloped bosoms. Now's your chance, Garion. Which one will you choose?'

'Are you about finished with all of this?'

Her eyes narrowed. 'I see,' she said. 'Now I'm not merely barren, I'm also hysterical.'

'No, you're just a little silly now and then, that's all.'

'*Silly?*'

'Everybody's silly once in a while,' he added quite calmly. 'It's part of being human. I'm actually a little surprised that you aren't throwing things.'

She threw a quick, guilty glance in the direction of some of the broken fragments in the corner.

'Oh,' he said, catching the glance. 'You did that earlier, I see. I'm glad I missed that part. It's hard to try to reason with somebody when you're dodging flying crockery and the other person is shrieking curses.'

Ce'Nedra blushed slightly.

'You did *that* too?' he asked mildly. 'Sometimes I wonder where you managed to pick up all those words. How did you ever find out what they mean?'

'*You* swear all the time,' she accused.

'I know,' he admitted. 'It's terribly unfair. I'm allowed to, but you're not.'

'I'd like to know who made up *that* rule,' she started, and then her eyes narrowed. 'You're trying to change the subject,' she accused him.

'No, Ce'Nedra, I already did. We weren't getting anywhere with the other topic. You are *not* barren, and I am *not* going to divorce you, no matter how long somebody else's braids are, or how—well, never mind.'

She looked at him. 'Oh, Garion, what if I am?' she said in a small voice. 'Barren, I mean?'

'That's absurd, Ce'Nedra. We won't even discuss that.'

The lingering doubt in the eyes of the Rivan Queen, however, said quite clearly that, even if they did not discuss it, she would continue to worry about it.

Chapter Twelve

The season made the Sea of the Winds extremely hazardous, and Garion was forced to wait for a full month before he could dispatch a messenger to the Vale of Aldur. By then the late autumn snowstorms had clogged the passes in the mountains of eastern Sendaria, and the royal messenger was obliged literally to wade his way across to the plains of Algaria. With all these delays, it was very nearly Erastide by the time Aunt Pol, Durnik, and Errand arrived at the snowy quay in the harbor at Riva. Durnik admitted to Garion that it had only been a chance meeting with the wayward Captain Greldik, who feared no storm that any sea could hurl at him, that had made the trip possible at all. Polgara spoke briefly with the vagabond seaman before they began the long climb up to the Citadel, and Garion noted with some surprise that Greldik slipped his hawsers immediately and sailed back out to sea.

Polgara seemed quite unconcerned about the gravity of the problem that had impelled Garion to send for her. She spoke with him only a couple of times about it, asking a few rather direct questions that set his ears to flaming. Her discussions with Ce'Nedra were a bit more lengthy, but only slightly so. Garion received the distinct impression that she was waiting for someone or something before proceeding.

The Erastide celebration at Riva that year was somewhat subdued. Although it was very pleasant to have Polgara, Durnik, and Errand with them to join in the festivities, Garion's concern over the problem Brand had raised dampened his enjoyment of the holiday.

Several weeks afterward, Garion entered the royal apartment one snowy midafternoon to find Polgara and Ce'Nedra seated by a cozy fire sipping tea and chatting together quietly. The curiosity which had been growing in him since the arrival of his visitors finally boiled to a head.

'Aunt Pol,' he began.

'Yes dear?'

'You've been here for almost a month now.'

'Has it been that long? The time certainly passes quickly when you're with people you love.'

'There's still this little problem, you know,' he reminded her.

'Yes, Garion,' she replied patiently. 'I'm aware of that.'

'Are we doing anything about it?'

'No,' she said placidly, 'not yet, anyhow.'

'It's sort of important, Aunt Pol. I don't want to seem to be trying to rush you or anything, but—' He broke off helplessly.

Polgara rose from her chair, went to the window, and looked out at the small private garden just outside. The garden was clogged with snow, and the pair of intertwined oak trees Ce'Nedra had planted there at the time of her betrothal to Garion were bowed slightly beneath the weight on their limbs. 'One of the things you'll learn as you grow older, Garion,' she said to him, gravely looking out at the snowy garden, 'is patience. Everything has its proper season. The solution to your problem isn't all that complicated, but it's just not the proper time to come to grips with it yet.'

'I don't understand at all, Aunt Pol.'

'Then you'll just have to trust me, won't you?'

'Of course I trust you, Aunt Pol. It's just—'

'Just what, dear?'

'Nothing.'

It was late winter before Captain Greldik returned from the south. A storm had sprung one of the seams of his ship, and she was taking water as she wallowed heavily around the headland and made for the quay.

'I thought for a while there that I might have to swim,' the bearded Cherek growled as he jumped across to the quay. 'Where's the best place to beach this poor old cow of mine? I'm going to have to calk her bottom.'

'Most sailors use that inlet there,' Garion replied, pointing.

'I *hate* to beach a ship in the winter,' Greldik said bitterly. 'Is there someplace where I can get a drink?'

'Up at the Citadel,' Garion offered.

'Thanks. Oh, I brought that visitor Polgara wanted.'

'Visitor?'

Greldik stepped back, squinted at his ship to determine the location of the aft cabin, then went over and kicked the planking several times. 'We're here!' he bellowed. He turned back to Garion. 'I really hate to sail with women on board. I'm not superstitious, but sometimes I really think they *do* bring bad luck—and you've always got to watch your manners.'

'You have a woman aboard?' Garion asked curiously.

Greldik grunted sourly. 'Pretty little thing, but she seems to expect deferential treatment; and when your whole crew is busy bailing seawater out of your bilges, you don't have much time for that.'

'Hello, Garion,' a light voice said from up on deck.

'Xera?' Garion stared up into the small face of his wife's cousin. 'Is that really you?'

'Yes, Garion,' the red-haired Dryad replied calmly. She was bundled up to the ears in thick, warm furs, and her breath steamed in the frosty air. 'I got here as quickly as I could when I received Lady Polgara's summons.' She smiled sweetly down at the sour-faced Greldik. 'Captain,' she said, 'could you have some of your men bring those bales along for me?'

'Dirt,' Greldik snorted. 'I sail two thousand leagues in the dead of winter to carry one small girl, two casks of water, and four bales of dirt.'

'Loam, Captain,' Xera corrected meticulously, 'loam. There's a difference, you know.'

'I'm a sailor,' Greldik said. 'To me, dirt is dirt.'

'Whatever you wish, Captain,' Xera said winsomely. 'Now do be a dear and have the bales carried up to the Citadel for me—and I'll need the casks as well.'

Grumbling, Captain Greldik gave the orders.

Ce'Nedra was ecstatic when she learned that her cousin had arrived in Riva. The two of them flew into each other's arms and dashed off immediately to find Polgara.

'They're very fond of each other, aren't they?' Durnik observed. The smith was dressed in furs and wore a pair of well-tarred boots. Shortly after his arrival, despite the fact that it was in the dead of winter, Durnik had discovered a large, swirling pool in the river that dropped out of the mountains and ran just to the north of the city. With astounding self-restraint, he had actually stared at that ice-rimmed pool for a full ten minutes before going in search of a fishing pole. Now he happily spent most of each day probing those dark, churning waters with a waxed line and a bright lure in search of the silvery-sided salmon that lurked beneath the turbulent surface. The closest Garion had ever seen his Aunt Pol actually come to scolding her husband had been on the day when she had intercepted him on his way out of the Citadel into the very teeth of a screaming blizzard, whistling, and with his fishing pole over his shoulder.

'What am I supposed to do with all of this?' Greldik demanded, pointing at the six burly sailors who had carried Xera's bales and casks up the long stairway to the grim fortress brooding over the city.

'Oh,' Garion said, 'just have your men put them over there.' He pointed toward a corner of the antechamber they had just entered. 'I'll find out what the ladies want done with them later.'

Greldik grunted. 'Good.' Then he rubbed his hands together. 'Now, about that drink—'

Garion did not have the faintest idea what his wife and her cousin and Polgara were up to. Most of the time, their conversations broke off as soon as he entered the room. To his astonishment, the four bales of loam and the two casks of what seemed to be water were stacked rather untidily in one corner of the royal bedroom. Ce'Nedra adamantly refused to explain, but the look she gave him when he asked why they needed to be so close to the royal bed was not only mysterious, but actually faintly naughty.

It was perhaps a week or two after Xera's arrival that a sudden break in the weather brought the sun out, and the temperature soared up to almost freezing. Shortly before noon, Garion was in conference with the Drasnian ambassador when a wide-eyed servant hesitantly entered the royal study. 'Please, your Majesty,' the poor man stammered. 'Please forgive me for interrupting, but Lady Polgara told me to bring you to her at once. I tried to tell her that we don't bother you when you're busy, but she —well, she sort of insisted.'

'You'd better go see what she wants, your Majesty,' the Drasnian ambassador suggested. 'If the Lady Polgara had just summoned *me*, I'd be running toward her door already.'

'You don't really have to be afraid of her, Margrave,' Garion told him. 'She wouldn't actually hurt you.'

'That's a chance I'd prefer not to take, your Majesty. We can talk about the matter we were discussing some other time.'

Frowning slightly, Garion went down the hall to the door of Aunt Pol's apartment. He tapped gently and then went in.

'Ah, there you are,' she said crisply. 'I was about to send another servant after you.' She wore a fur-lined cloak with a deep hood pulled up until it framed her face. Ce'Nedra and Xera, similarly garbed, were standing just behind her. 'I want you to go find Durnik,' she said. 'He's probably fishing. Find him and bring him back to the Citadel. Get a shovel and a pick from someplace and then bring Durnik and the tools to that little garden just outside your apartment window.'

He stared at her.

She made a kind of flipping motion with one hand. 'Quickly, quickly, Garion,' she said. 'The day is wearing on.'

'Yes, Aunt Pol,' he said without even thinking. He turned and went back out, half-running. He was nearly to the end of the hallway before he remembered that he was the king here, and that people *probably* shouldn't order him around like that.

Durnik, of course, responded immediately to his wife's summons—well, *almost* immediately. He *did* make one last cast before carefully coiling up his fishing line and following Garion back to the Citadel. When the two of them entered the small private garden adjoining the royal apartment, Aunt Pol, Ce'Nedra, and Xera were already there, standing beneath the intertwined oak trees.

'Here's what we're going to do,' Aunt Pol said in a businesslike fashion. 'I'd like to have the area around these tree trunks opened up to a depth of about two feet.'

'Uh—Aunt Pol,' Garion interposed, 'the ground is sort of frozen. Digging is going to be a little difficult.'

'That's what the pick is for, dear,' she said patiently.

'Wouldn't it be easier to wait until the ground thaws?'

'Probably, but it needs to be done now. Dig, Garion.'

'I've got gardeners, Aunt Pol. We could send for a couple of them.' He eyed the pick and shovel uncomfortably.

'It's probably better if we keep it in the family, dear. You can start digging right here.' She pointed.

Garion sighed and took up the pick.

What followed made no sense at all. Garion and Durnik picked and spaded at the frozen ground until late afternoon, opening up the area Aunt Pol had indicated. Then they dumped the four bales of loam into the hole they had prepared, tamped down the loose earth, and watered the dark soil liberally with the water from the two casks. After that, Aunt Pol instructed them to cover everything back up again with snow.

'Did you understand any of that?' Garion asked Durnik as the two of them returned their tools to the gardeners' shed in the courtyard near the stables.

'No,' Durnik admitted, 'but I'm sure she knows what she's doing.' He glanced at the evening sky and then sighed. 'It's probably a little late to go back to that pool,' he said regretfully.

Aunt Pol and the two girls visited the garden daily, but Garion could never discover exactly what they were doing, and the following week his attention was diverted by the sudden appearance of his grandfather, Belgarath the Sorcerer. The young king was sitting in his study with Errand as the boy described in some detail the training of the horse Garion had given him a few years back when the door banged unceremoniously open and Belgarath, travel-stained and with a face like a thundercloud, strode in.

'Grandfather!' Garion exclaimed, starting to his feet. 'What are—'

'Shut up and sit down!' Belgarath shouted at him.

'What?'

'Do as I tell you. We are going to have a talk, Garion —that is, *I'm* going to talk, and *you're* going to listen.' He paused as if to get control of what appeared to be a towering anger. 'Do you have any idea of what you've done?' he demanded at last.

'Me? What are we talking about, Grandfather?' Garion asked.

'We're talking about your little display of pyrotechnics on the plains of Mimbre,' Belgarath replied icily. 'That impromptu thunderstorm of yours.'

'Grandfather,' Garion explained as mildly as possible, 'they were right on the brink of war. All Arendia would probably have gotten involved. You've said yourself that we didn't want that to happen. I had to stop them.'

'We aren't talking about your motives, Garion. We're talking about your methods. What possessed you to use a thunderstorm?'

'It seemed like the best way to get their attention.'

'You couldn't think of anything else?'

'They were already charging, Grandfather. I didn't have a lot of time to consider alternatives.'

'Haven't I told you again and again that we don't tamper with the weather?'

'Well—it was sort of an emergency.'

206

'If you thought *that* was an emergency, you should have seen the blizzard you touched off in the Vale with your foolishness— and the hurricanes it spawned in the Sea of the East—not to mention the droughts and tornados you kicked up all over the world. Don't you have any sense of responsibility at all?'

'I didn't know it was going to do that.' Garion was aghast.

'Boy, it's your business to know!' Belgarath suddenly roared at him, his face mottled with rage. 'It's taken Beldin and me six months of constant travel and the Gods only know how much effort to quiet things down. Do you realize that with that one thoughtless storm of yours you came very close to changing the weather patterns of the entire globe? And that the change would have been a universal disaster?'

'One tiny little storm?'

'Yes, one tiny little storm,' Belgarath said scathingly. 'Your one tiny little storm in the right place at the right time came very close to altering the weather for the next several eons—all over the world—you blockhead!'

'Grandfather,' Garion protested.

'Do you know what the term ice age means?'

Garion shook his head, his face blank.

'It's a time when the average temperature drops—just a bit. In the extreme north, that means that the snow doesn't melt in the summer. It keeps piling up, year after year. It forms glaciers, and the glaciers start to move farther and farther south. In just a few centuries, that little display of yours could have had a wall of ice two hundred feet high moving down across the moors of Drasnia. You'd have buried Boktor and Val Alorn under solid ice, you idiot. Is that what you wanted?'

'Of course not. Grandfather, I honestly didn't know. I wouldn't have started it if I'd known.'

'That would have been a great comfort to the millions of people you very nearly entombed in ice,' Belgarath retorted with a vast sarcasm. 'Don't *ever* do that again! Don't even *think* about putting your hands on something until you're absolutely certain you know everything there is to know about it. Even then, it's best not to gamble.'

'But—but—you and Aunt Pol called down that rain-storm in the Wood of the Dryads,' Garion pointed out defensively.

'We knew what we were doing,' Belgarath almost screamed. 'There was no danger there.' With an enormous effort the old man got control of himself. 'Don't *ever* touch the weather again, Garion—not until you've had at least a thousand years of study.'

'A thousand years!'

'At least. In your case, maybe two thousand. You seem to have this extraordinary luck. You always manage to be in the wrong place at the wrong time.'

'I won't do it again, Grandfather,' Garion promised fervently, shuddering at the thought of towering ice walls creeping inexorably across the world.

Belgarath gave him a long, hard look and then let the matter drop. Later when he had regained his composure, he lounged in a chair by the fire with a tankard of ale in one hand. Garion knew his grandfather well enough to be aware of the fact that ale mellowed the old man's disposition and he had prudently sent for some as soon as the initial explosion had subsided. 'How are your studies going, boy?' the old sorcerer asked.

'I've been a little pressed for time lately, Grandfather,' Garion replied guiltily.

Belgarath gave him a long, cold stare, and Garion could clearly see the mottling on his neck that indicated that the old man's interior temperature was rising again.

'I'm sorry Grandfather,' he apologized quickly. 'From now on, I'll *make* the time to study.'

Belgarath's eyes widened slightly. 'Don't do that,' he said quickly. 'You got into enough trouble fooling around with the weather. If you start in on time, not even the Gods could predict the outcome.'

'I didn't exactly mean it that way, Grandfather.'

'Say what you mean, then. This isn't a good area for misunderstandings, you know.' He turned his attention then to Errand. 'What are you doing here, boy?' he asked.

'Durnik and Polgara are here,' Errand replied. 'They thought I ought to come along.'

'Polgara's here?' Belgarath seemed surprised.

'I asked her to come,' Garion told him. 'There's a little bit of a problem she's fixing for me—at least I *think* she's fixing it. She's been acting sort of mysterious.'

'She overdramatizes things sometimes. Exactly what is this problem she's working on?'

'Uh—' Garion glanced at Errand, who sat watching the two of them with polite interest. Garion flushed slightly. 'It—uh—has to do with the—uh—heir to the Rivan Throne,' he explained delicately.

'What's the problem there?' Belgarath demanded obtusely. '*You're* the heir to the Rivan Throne.'

'No, I mean the next one.'

'I still don't see any problem.'

'Grandfather, there *isn't* one—not yet, at least.'

'There *isn't*? What have you been doing, boy?'

'Never mind,' Garion said, giving up.

When spring arrived at last, Polgara's attention to the two embracing oak-trees became all-consuming. She went to the garden at least a dozen times a day to examine every twig meticulously for signs of budding. When at last the twig ends began to swell, a look of strange satisfaction became apparent on her face. Once again she and the two young women, Ce'Nedra and Xera, began puttering in the garden. Garion found all these botanical pastimes baffling —even a little irritating. He had, after all, asked Aunt Pol to come to Riva to deal with a much more serious problem.

Xera returned home to the Wood of the Dryads at the first break in the weather. Not long afterward, Aunt Pol calmly announced that she and Durnik and Errand would also be leaving soon. 'We'll take father with us,' she declared, looking disapprovingly over at the old sorcerer, who was drinking ale and bantering outrageously with Brand's niece, the blushing Lady Arell.

'Aunt Pol,' Garion protested, 'what about that little— uh—difficulty Ce'Nedra and I were having?'

'What about it, dear?'

'Aren't you going to do something about it?'

'I did, Garion,' she replied blandly.

'Aunt Pol, you spent all your time out in that garden.'

'Yes, dear. I know.'

Garion brooded about the whole matter for several weeks after they had all left. He even began to wonder if he had somehow failed to explain fully the problem or if Aunt Pol had somehow misunderstood.

When spring was in full flower and the meadows rising steeply behind the city had turned bright green, touched here and there with vibrantly colored patches of wild-flowers, Ce'Nedra began behaving peculiarly. He frequently found her seated in their garden gazing with an odd, tender expression at her oak trees, and quite often she was gone from the Citadel entirely, to return at the end of the day in the company of Lady Arell all bedecked with wild flowers. Before each meal, she took a sip from a small, silver flagon and made a dreadful face.

'What's that you're drinking?' he asked her curiously one morning.

'It's a sort of a tonic,' she replied, shuddering. 'It has oak buds in it and it tastes absolutely vile.'

'Aunt Pol made it for you.'

'How did you know that?'

'Her medicines always taste awful.'

'Mmm,' she said absently. Then she gave him a long look. 'Are you going to be very busy today?'

'Not really. Why?'

'I thought that we might stop by the kitchen, pick up some meat, bread, and cheese, and then go spend a day out in the forest.'

'In the forest? What for?'

'Garion,' she said almost crossly, 'I've been cooped up in this dreary old castle all winter. I'd like some fresh air and sunshine—and the smell of trees and wildflowers around me instead of damp stone.'

'Why don't you ask Arell to go with you? I probably shouldn't really be gone all day.'

She gave him an exasperated look. 'You just said you didn't have anything important to do.'

'You never know. Something might come up.'

'It can wait,' she said from between clenched teeth.

Garion shot her a quick glance, recognized the danger signals, and then replied as mildly as he could, 'I suppose you're right, dear. I don't see any reason why we shouldn't have a little outing together. We could ask Arell—and maybe Kail—if they'd like to join us.'

'No, Garion,' she said quite firmly.

'No?'

'Definitely not.'

And so it was that, shortly after breakfast, the Rivan King, hand in hand with his little queen, left the Citadel with a well-stocked basket, crossed the broad meadow behind the city, and strolled into the sunlight-dappled shade beneath the evergreens that mounted steeply toward the glistening, snow-capped peaks that formed the spine of the island.

Once they entered the woods, all traces of discontent dropped away from Ce'Nedra's face. She picked wild-flowers as they wandered among the tall pines and firs and wove them into a garland for herself. The morning sun slanted down through the limbs high overhead, dappling the mossy forest floor with golden light and blue shadows. The resinous smell of the tall evergreens was a heady perfume, and birds swooped and spiraled among the tall, columnlike trunks, caroling to greet the sun.

After a time, they found a glade, a mossy, open clearing embraced by trees, where a brook gurgled and murmured over shining stones to drop into a gleaming forest pool and where a single, soft-eyed deer stood to drink. The deer raised her head from the water swirling about her delicate brown legs, looked at them quite unafraid, and then picked her way back into the forest, her hooves clicking on the stones and her tail flicking.

'Oh, this is just perfect,' Ce'Nedra declared with a soft little smile on her face. She sat on a round boulder and began to unlace her shoes.

Garion put down the basket and stretched, feeling the cares of the past several weeks slowly draining out of him. 'I'm glad you thought of this,' he said, sprawling comfortably on the sun-warmed moss. 'It's really a very good idea.'

'Naturally,' she said. 'All my ideas are good ones.'

'I don't know if I'd go *that* far.' Then a thought occurred to him. 'Ce'Nedra,' he said.

'What?'

'I've been meaning to ask you something. All the Dryads have names that begin with an X, don't they? Xera, Xantha—like that.'

'It's our custom,' she replied, continuing to work on her shoelaces.

'Why doesn't yours, then? Begin with an X, I mean?'

'It does.' She pulled off one of her shoes. 'Tolnedrans just pronounce it a little differently, that's all. So they spell it that way. Dryads don't read or write very much, so they don't worry too much about spelling.'

'X'Nedra?'

'That's fairly close. Make the X a little softer, though.'

'You know, I've been wondering about that for the longest time.'

'Why didn't you ask, then?'

'I don't know. I just never got around to it.'

'There's a reason for everything, Garion,' she told him, 'but you'll never find it out if you don't ask.'

'Now you sound just like Aunt Pol.'

'Yes, dear, I know.' She smiled, pulled off her other shoe and wriggled her toes contentedly.

'Why barefoot?' he asked idly.

'I like the feel of the moss on my feet—and I think that in a little bit I might go swimming.'

'It's too cold. That brook comes right out of a glacier.'

'A little cold water won't hurt me.' She shrugged. Then, almost as if responding to a dare, she stood up and began to take off her clothes.

'Ce'Nedra! What if someone comes along?'

She laughed a silvery laugh. 'What if they do? I'm not

going to soak my clothes just for the sake of propriety. Don't be such a prude, Garion.'

'It's not that. It's—'

'It's what?'

'Never mind.'

She ran on light feet into the pool, squealing delightedly as the icy water splashed up around her. With a long clean dive, she disappeared beneath the surface of the pool, swam to the far side, where a large, mossy log angled down into the crystal-clear water, and surfaced with streaming hair and an impish grin. 'Well?' she said to him.

'Well what?'

'Aren't you coming in?'

'Of course I'm not.'

'Is the mighty Overlord of the West afraid of cold water?'

'The mighty Overlord of the West has better sense than to catch cold for the sake of a little splashing around.'

'Garion, you're getting positively stodgy. Take off your crown and relax.'

'I'm not wearing my crown.'

'Take off something else, then.'

'Ce'Nedra!'

She laughed another silvery peal of laughter and began kicking her bare feet, sending up showers of sparkling water drops that gleamed like jewels in the midmorning sunlight. Then she lay back and her hair spread like a deep copper fan upon the surface of the pool. The garland of flowers she had woven for herself earlier had come apart as a result of her swimming, and the individual blossoms floated on the water, bobbing in the ripples.

Garion sat on a mossy hummock with his back resting comfortably against a tree trunk. The sun was warm, and the smell of trees and grass and wildflowers filled his nostrils. A breeze carrying the salt tang of the sea sighed among the green limbs of the tall fir trees surrounding the little glade, and golden sunlight fell in patches on the floor of the forest.

An errant butterfly, its patterned wings a blaze of iridescent blue and gold, flitted out from among the tall tree trunks into the sunlight. Drawn by color or scent or some other, more mysterious urge, it wavered through the lucid air to the pool and the flowers bobbing there. Curiously it moved from flower to floating flower, touching each of them lightly with its wings. With a breathless expression Ce'Nedra slowly sank her head into the water until only her upturned face was above the surface. The butterfly continued its curious investigation, coming closer and closer to the waiting queen. And then it hovered over her face, its soft wings brushing her lips ecstatically.

'Oh, fine.' Garion laughed. 'Now my wife is consorting with butterflies.'

'I'll do whatever it takes in order to get a kiss,' she replied, giving him an arch look.

'If it's kisses you want, I'll take care of that for you,' he said.

'That's an interesting thought. I think I'd like one right now. My other lover seems to have lost interest.' She pointed at the butterfly, which had settled with quivering wings on a bush near the foot of the pool. 'Come and kiss me, Garion.'

'You're right in the middle of the deepest part of the pool,' he pointed out.

'So?'

'I don't suppose you'd consider coming out.'

'You offered kisses, Garion. You didn't make any conditions.'

Garion sighed, stood up, and began to remove his clothing. 'We're both going to regret this,' he predicted. 'A cold in the summertime lasts for months.'

'You're not going to catch cold, Garion. Come along now.'

He groaned and then waded manfully into the icy water. 'You're a cruel woman, Ce'Nedra,' he accused, wincing at the shocking chill.

'Don't be such a baby. Come over here.'

Gritting his teeth, he plowed through the water toward her, stubbing his toe on a large rock in the process. When he reached her, she slid her cold, wet little arms around his neck and glued her lips to his. Her kiss was lingering and it pulled him slightly off balance. He felt her lips tighten slightly as she grinned impishly, even in the midst of the kiss, and then without any warning, she lifted her legs, and her weight pulled him under.

He came up spluttering and swearing.

'Wasn't that fun?' she giggled.

'Not really,' he grumbled. 'Drowning isn't one of my favorite sports.'

She ignored that. 'Now that you're all wet, you might as well swim with me.'

They swam together for about a quarter of an hour and then emerged from the pool, shivering and with their lips turning blue.

'Make a fire, Garion,' Ce'Nedra said through chattering teeth.

'I didn't bring any tinder,' he said, 'or a flint.'

'Do it the other way, then.'

'What other way?' he asked blankly.

'You know—' She made a sort of mysterious gesture.

'Oh. I forgot about that.'

'Hurry, Garion. I'm freezing.'

He gathered some twigs and fallen branches, cleared a space in the moss, and concentrated his will on the pile of wood. At first, a small tendril of smoke arose, then a tongue of bright orange flame. Within a few minutes, a goodly little fire was crackling just beside the moss-covered hummock upon which the shivering Ce'Nedra was huddled.

'Oh, that's much better,' she said, stretching her hands out to the fire. 'You're a useful person to have around, my Lord.'

'Thank you, my Lady. Would my Lady like to consider putting on some clothes?'

'Not until she's dry, she wouldn't. I *hate* pulling on dry clothes over wet skin.'

'Let's hope nobody comes along, then. We're not really dressed for company, you know.'

'You're *so* conventional, Garion.'

'I suppose so,' he admitted.

'Why don't you come over here beside me?' she invited. 'It's much warmer here.'

He couldn't really think of any reason why he shouldn't, so he joined her on the warm moss.

'See,' she said, putting her arms about his neck. 'Isn't this much nicer?' She kissed him—a serious kind of kiss that made his breath catch in his throat and his heart pound.

When she finally released her grip about his neck, he looked around the glade nervously. A fluttering movement near the foot of the pool caught his eye. He coughed, looking slightly embarrassed.

'What's the matter?' she asked him.

'I think that butterfly is watching,' he said with a slight flush.

'That's all right.' She smiled, sliding her arms about his neck and kissing him again.

The world seemed unusually quiet as spring gently slipped into summer that year. The secession of the Vordues crumbled under the onslaughts of the armored Mimbrate 'brigands,' and the Vodue family finally capitulated, pleading with an almost genuine humility to be readmitted to the Empire. While they were not fond of Varana's tax-collectors, they all ran out into the streets to greet his legions as they returned.

The news from Cthol Murgos was sketchy at best, but it appeared that things in the far south remained at an impasse, with Kal Zakath's Malloreans holding the plains and Urgit's Murgos firmly entrenched in the mountains.

Periodic reports forwarded to Garion by Drasnian Intelligence seemed to indicate that the re-emergent Bear-cult was doing little more than mill around out in the countryside.

Garion enjoyed this respite from crisis and, since there was no really pressing business, he took to sleeping late, sometimes lying in bed in a kind of luxurious doze until two or three hours past sunrise.

On one such morning about midsummer, he was having

an absolutely splendid dream. He and Ce'Nedra were leaping from the loft in the barn at Faldor's farm into the soft hay piled below. He was awakened rather rudely as his wife bolted from the bed and ran into an adjoining chamber where she was violently and noisily sick.

'Ce'Nedra!' he exclaimed, jumping out of bed to follow her. 'What are you doing?'

'I'm throwing up,' she replied, raising her pale face from the basin she was holding on her knees.

'Are you sick?'

'No,' she drawled sarcastically, 'I'm doing it for fun.'

'I'll get one of the physicians,' he said, grabbing up a robe.

'Never mind.'

'But you're sick.'

'Of course I am, but I don't need a physician.'

'That doesn't make any sense, Ce'Nedra. If you're sick, you need a doctor.'

'I'm supposed to be sick,' she told him.

'*What?*'

'Don't you know anything, Garion? I'll probably get sick every morning for the next several months.'

'I don't understand you at all, Ce'Nedra.'

'You're impossibly dense. People in my condition *always* get sick in the morning.'

'Condition? What condition?'

She rolled her eyes upward almost in despair. 'Garion,' she said with exaggerated patience, 'do you remember that little problem we had last fall? The problem that made us send for Lady Polgara?'

'Well—yes.'

'I'm *so* glad. Well, we don't have that problem any more.'

He stared at her, slowly comprehending. 'You mean—?'

'Yes, dear,' she said with a pale smile. 'You're going to be a father. Now, if you'll excuse me, I think I'll throw up again.'

Chapter Thirteen

They did not match. No matter how hard Garion twisted and turned the sense of the two passages, there was no apparent way to make them match. Despite the fact that they both seemed to describe the same period of time, they simply went off in opposite directions. It was a bright, golden autumn morning outside, but the dusty library seemed somehow dim, chill, and uninviting.

Garion did not think of himself as a scholar and he had approached the task that Belgarath had laid upon him with some reluctance. The sheer volume of the documents he was obliged to read was intimidating, for one thing, and this gloomy little room with its smell of ancient parchment and mildewed leather bindings always depressed him. He had done unpleasant things before, and, although he was a bit grim about it, he nonetheless dutifully spent at least two hours a day confined in this prisonlike cell, struggling with ancient books and scrolls written in often-times difficult script. At least, he told himself, it was better than scrubbing pots in a scullery.

He set his teeth together and laid the two scrolls side by side on the table to compare them again. He read slowly and aloud, hoping perhaps to catch with his ears what his eyes might miss. The Darine Codex seemed relatively clear and straightforward. 'Behold,' it said, 'in the day that Aldur's Orb burns hot with crimson fire shall the name of the Child of Dark be revealed. Guard well the son of the Child of Light for he shall have no brother. And it shall come to pass that those which once were one and now are two shall be rejoined, and in that rejoining shall one of them be no more.'

The Orb *had* turned crimson, and the name of the Child of Dark—Zandramas—had been revealed. That matched what had taken place. The information that the son of the Child of Light—his son—would have no brother had concerned Garion a bit. At first he had taken it to mean that he and Ce'Nedra would only have one child, but the more he thought about that, the more he realized that his reasoning there was flawed. All it really said was that they would only have one son. It said nothing about daughters. The more he thought about it, the more the notion of a whole cluster of chattering little girls gathered about his knee appealed to him.

The last passage, however—the one about the two which once were one—didn't really make any sense yet, but he was quite certain that it would, eventually.

He moved his hand over to trace the lines of the Mrin Codex, peering hard at them in the flickering yellow candlelight. He read slowly and carefully once more. 'And the Child of Light shall meet with the Child of Dark and shall overcome him—' That obviously referred to the meeting with Torak. '—and the Darkness shall flee.' The Dark Prophecy *had* fled when Torak had died. 'But behold, the stone which lies at the center of the Light—' The Orb, obviously. '—shall—' One word seemed to be blotted at that point. Garion frowned, trying to make out what word might lie beneath that irregular splotch of ink. Even as he stared at it, a strange kind of weariness came over him, as if the effort to push aside that blot to see what lay beneath were as difficult as moving a mountain. He shrugged and went on, '—and this meeting will come to pass in a place which is no more, and there will the choice be made.'

That last fragment made him want to howl in frustration. How could a meeting—or anything else—happen in a place which is no more? And what was the meaning of the word 'choice'? What choice? Whose choice? Choice between what and what?

He swore and read it again. Once again he felt that peculiar lassitude when his eyes reached the blot on the page. He shrugged it off and went on. No matter what the word under the blot might be, it was still only one word, and one single word could not be *that* important. Irritably he put the scroll aside and considered the discrepancy. The most immediate explanation was that this spot, like so many others, was a place where the Mrin Prophet's well-known insanity had simply got the best of him. Another possibility was that this particular copy was not precisely accurate. The scribe who had copied it off had perhaps inadvertently skipped a line or two at the time when he had blotted the page. Garion recalled an occasion when he had done that himself, turning a perfectly bland proclamation into a horrendous declaration that he was on the verge of naming himself military dictator of all the kingdoms lying on this side of the Eastern Escarpment. When he had caught the blunder, he had not just erased the offending lines, he had shudderingly burned the whole sheet to make sure that no one ever saw it.

He stood up, stretching to relieve his cramped muscles and going to the small, barred window of the library. The autumn sky was a crisp blue. The nights had turned chilly in the past few weeks, and the higher meadows lying above the city were touched with frost when the sun arose. The days, however, were warm and golden. He checked the position of the sun to gauge the time. He had promised to meet with Count Valgon, the Tolnedran ambassador, at midday and he did not want to be late. Aunt Pol had stressed the importance of punctuality, and Garion always did his best to be on time.

He turned back to the table and absently rerolled the two scrolls, his mind still wrestling with the problem of the conflicting pasages. Then he blew out the candles and left the library, carefully closing the door behind him.

Valgon, as always, was tedious. Garion felt that there was an innate pomposity in the Tolnedran character that made it impossible for them to say what they meant without extensive embellishment. The discussion that day had to do with 'prioritizing' the unloading of merchant vessels in the harbor at Riva. Valgon seemed terribly fond of the word 'prioritizing,' finding a way to insert it into the discussion at least once in every other sentence. The essense of Valgon's presentation seemed to be a request —or a demand—that Tolnedran merchantmen should always have first access to the somewhat limited wharves at the foot of the city.

'My dear Valgon,' Garion began, seeking some diplomatic way to refuse, 'I actually believe that this matter needs—' He broke off, looking up as the great carved doors to the throne room swung inward.

One of the towering, gray-cloaked sentries who always stood guard outside when Garion was in the throne room stepped in, cleared his throat, and announced in a voice that probably could have been heard on the other side of the island, 'Her Royal Majesty, Queen Ce'Nedra of Riva, Imperial Princess of the Tonedran Empire, Commander of the Armies of the West, and beloved wife of his Majesty, Belgarion of Riva, Godslayer, Lord of the Western Sea, and Overlord of the West!'

Ce'Nedra, demure and tiny, entered on the sentry's heels, her shoulders unbowed by the weight of all those vast titles. She wore a teal-green velvet gown, gathered beneath the bodice to conceal her expanding waistline, and her eyes were sparkling mischievously.

Valgon turned and bowed smoothly.

Ce'Nedra touched the sentry's arm, strained up on tiptoe, and whispered to him. The sentry nodded, turned back toward the throne at the front of the hall, and cleared his throat again. 'His Highness, Prince Kheldar of Drasnia, nephew of the beloved late King Rhodar, and cousin to King Kheva, Lord of the Marches of the North!'

Garion started up from the throne in astonishment.

Silk entered grandly. His doublet was a rich pearl gray, his fingers glittered with rings, and a heavy gold chain with a large pendant sapphire hung about his neck. 'That's all right, gentlemen,' he said to Garion and Count Valgon with an airy wave of his hand, 'you needn't rise.' He extended his arm grandly to Ce'Nedra, and the two of them came down the broad, carpeted aisle past the three flowing firepits in the floor.

'Silk!' Garion exclaimed.

'The very same,' Silk replied with a mocking little bow. 'Your Majesty is looking well—considering.'

'Considering what?'

Silk winked at him.

'I am quite overwhelmed to meet so famous a merchant prince again,' Valgon murmured politely. 'Your Highness has become a legend in recent years. Your exploits in the East are the absolute despair of the great commercial houses in Tol Honeth.'

'One *has* had a certain modest success,' Silk responded, breathing on a large ruby ring on his left hand and then polishing it on the front of his doublet. 'In your next report, please convey my regards to your new Emperor. His handling of the Vordue situation was masterly.'

Valgon permitted himself a faint smile. 'I'm sure his Imperial Majesty will appreciate your good opinion, Prince Kheldar.' He turned to Garion. 'I know that your Majesty and his old friend will have many things to discuss,' he said. 'We can take up this other matter at a later date, perhaps.' He bowed. 'With your Majesty's permission, I will withdraw.'

'Of course, Valgon,' Garion replied. 'And thank you.'

The Tolnedran bowed again and quietly left the throne room.

Ce'Nedra came down to the foot of the throne and linked her arm affectionately with Silk's. 'I hope you didn't mind being interrupted, Garion,' she said. 'I know that you and Valgon were having an absolutely *fascinating* talk.'

Garion made a face. 'What was the idea behind all that formality?' he asked curiously. 'The business with all those titles, I mean?'

Silk grinned. 'Ce'Nedra's idea. She felt that if we over-whelmed Valgon with enough titles, we could persuade him to go away. Did we interrupt anything important?'

Garion gave him a sour look. 'He was talking about the problem of getting Tonedran merchant vessels unloaded. I think that, if he'd thrown the word "prioritizing" at me about one more time, I'd have jumped up and strangled him.'

'Oh?' Ce'Nedra said, all wide-eyed and girlish. 'Let's call him back, then.'

'I take it that you're unfond of him,' Silk suggested.

'He's a Honethite,' Ce'Nedra replied, making an indelicate little sound. 'I despise the Honeths.'

'Let's go someplace where we can talk,' Garion said, looking around at the formal throne room.

'Whatever your Majesty wishes,' Silk said with a grand bow.

'Oh, stop that!' Garion said, coming down from the dais and leading the way to the side door.

When they reached the quiet, sunlit sanctuary of the royal apartment, Garion sighed with relief as he took off his crown and shrugged out of his formal state robes. 'You have no idea how hot that thing gets,' he said, tossing the robe in a heap on a chair in the corner.

'It also wrinkles, dear,' Ce'Nedra reminded him, picking up the robe, folding it carefully, and hanging it over the chair back.

'Perhaps I could find one for you in Mallorean satin— suitable color and interwoven with silver thread,' Silk suggested. 'It would look very rich—tastefully understated—and not nearly so heavy.'

'That's a thought,' Garion said.

'And I'm sure I could offer it to you at a *very* attractive price.'

Garion gave him a startled look, and Silk laughed.

'You never change, do you, Silk?' Ce'Nedra said.

'Of course not,' the little thief replied, sprawling unasked in a chair.

'What brings you to Riva?' Garion asked him, taking a chair across the table from his friend.

'Affection—at least mostly. I haven't seen you two for

several years now.' He looked around. 'I don't suppose you've got anything to drink handy?'

'We could probably find something.' Garion grinned at him.

'We have a rather pleasant little wine,' Ce'Nedra offered, going to a dark, polished sideboard. 'We've been trying to keep Garion here away from ale.'

One of Silk's eyebrows went up.

'He has an unfortunate tendency to want to sing when he drinks ale,' the Queen explained. 'I wouldn't want to put you through that.'

'All right,' Garion said to her.

'It's not so much his voice,' Ce'Nedra went on relentlessly. 'It's the way he goes looking for the right notes—and doesn't find them.'

'Do you *mind*?' Garion asked her.

She laughed a shimmering laugh and filled two silver goblets with a blood-red Tolnedran wine.

'Aren't you joining us?' Silk asked.

She made a face. 'The heir to the Rivan Throne doesn't care much for wine,' she replied, delicately placing one hand on her swelling abdomen. 'Or perhaps he enjoys it too much. It makes him start kicking, and I'd rather that he didn't break too many of my ribs.'

'Ah,' Silk said delicately.

She brought the goblets to the table and set them down. 'Now, if you two gentlemen will excuse me, it's time for my visit to the baths.'

'Her hobby,' Garion said. 'She spends at least two hours of every afternoon down in the women's baths—even when she isn't dirty.'

She shrugged. 'It relaxes my back. I've been carrying this burden lately.' Once again she touched her abdomen. 'And it seems to get heavier every day.'

'I'm glad that it's the women who have the babies,' Silk said. 'I'm sure I wouldn't really have the strength for it.'

'You're a nasty little man, Kheldar,' she retorted tartly.

'Of course I am,' he smirked.

She gave him a withering look and went in search of Lady Arell, her usual companion in the baths.

'She looks absolutely blooming,' Silk observed, 'and she's not nearly as bad-tempered as I'd expected.'

'You should have been around a few months ago.'

'Bad?'

'You can't imagine.'

'It happens, I suppose—or so I've been told.'

'What have you been up to lately?' Garion asked, leaning back in his chair. 'We haven't heard much about you.'

'I've been in Mallorea,' Silk replied, sipping at his wine. 'The fur trade isn't very challenging any more, and Yarblek's been handling that end of the business. We felt that there was a great deal of money to be made in Mallorean silks, carpets, and uncut gemstones, so I went over to investigate.'

'Isn't it a little dangerous for a western merchant in Mallorea?'

Silk shrugged. 'No worse than Rak Goska—or Tol Honeth, for that matter. I've spent my whole life in dangerous places, Garion.'

'Couldn't you just buy your goods at Yar Marak or Thull Zelik when they come off the Mallorean ships?'

'The prices are better at the source. Everytime an article goes through another pair of hands, the price doubles.'

'That makes sense, I suppose.' Garion looked at his friend, envying the freedom that made it possible for Silk to go anywhere in the world he wanted to go. 'What's Mallorea really like?' he asked. 'We hear stories, but I think that's all they are most of the time.'

'It's in turmoil just now,' Silk replied gravely. 'Kal Zakath's off fighting his war with the Murgos, and the Grolims went all to pieces when they heard about the death of Torak. Mallorean society has always been directed from either Mal Zeth or Mal Yaska—the emperor or the church —but now nobody seems to be in charge. The government bureaucracy tries to hold things together, but Malloreans need strong leadership and right now they don't have it.

All sorts of strange things are beginning to surface—rebellions, new religions, that kind of thing.'

A thought occurred to Garion. 'Have you run across the name Zandramas?' he asked curiously.

Silk looked at him sharply. 'It's odd you should ask that,' he said. 'When I was in Boktor, just before Rhodar died, I was talking with Javelin. Errand happened to be there and he asked Javelin the same question. Javelin told him that it's a Darshivan name and that was about all he knew. When I went back to Mallorea, I asked in a few places, but people got very tight-lipped and white-knuckled every time I mentioned it, so I let it drop. I gathered that it has something to do with one of those new religions mentioned before.'

'Did you happen to hear anything about something called the Sardion—or Cthrag Sardius, maybe?'

Silk frowned, tapping the rim of his goblet thoughtfully against his lower lip. 'It's got a familiar ring to it, but I can't quite put my finger on where I heard it.'

'If you happen to remember, I'd appreciate your telling me anything you can find out about it.'

'Is it important?'

'I think it might be. Grandfather and Beldin have been trying to track it down.'

'I've got some contacts in Mal Zeth and Melcene,' Silk noted. 'When I get back, I'll see what I can find out.'

'You're going back soon, then?'

Silk nodded. 'I'd have stayed there, but a little crisis came up in Yar Nadrak. King Drosta started to get greedy. We've been paying him some very healthy bribes to persuade him to look the other way about some of our activities in his kingdom. He got the notion that we were making a great deal of money and he was toying with the idea of expropriating our holdings in Gar og Nadrak. I had to come back and talk him out of the notion.'

'How did you manage that? I've always had the impression that Drosta does pretty much what he wants in Gar og Nadrak.'

'I threatened him,' Silk said. 'I pointed out that I'm

closely related to the King of Drasnia and hinted that I was on very good terms with Kal Zakath. The prospect of an invasion from either the East or the West didn't appeal to him, so he dropped the idea.'

'*Are* you on good terms with Zakath?'

'I've never met him—but Drosta doesn't know that.'

'You lied? Isn't that dangerous?'

Silk laughed. 'Lots of things are dangerous, Garion. We've both been in tight spots before. Rak Cthol wasn't the safest place in the world, if you'll recall, and Cthol Mishrak made me definitely edgy.'

Garion toyed with his goblet. 'You know something, Silk?' he said. 'I sort of miss all that.'

'All what?'

'I don't know—the danger, the excitement. Things have settled down pretty much for me. About the only excitement I get these days is in trying to maneuver my way around the Tolnedran ambassador. Sometimes I wish—' He left it hanging there.

'You can come to Mallorea with me, if you'd like,' Silk offered. 'I could find interesting work for a man of your talents.'

'I don't think Ce'Nedra would be too pleased if I left just now.'

'That's one of the reasons I never married,' Silk told him. 'I don't have to worry about things like that.'

'Are you going to stop in Boktor on your way back?'

'Briefly, maybe. I visited the people I needed to see on my way here from Yar Nadrak. Porenn's doing very well with Kheva. He's probably going to be a good king when he grows up. And I stopped by to see Javelin, of course. It's more or less expected. He likes to get our impressions of foreign countries—even when we're not acting in any official capacity.'

'Javelin's very good, isn't he?'

'He's the best.'

'I always thought you were.'

'Not by a long way, Garion.' Silk smiled. 'I'm too erratic —brilliant, maybe, but erratic. I get sidetracked too easily.

When Javelin goes after something, he doesn't let anything distract him until he gets it. Right now, he's trying to get to the bottom of this Bear-cult thing.'

'Is he having any luck?'

'Not yet. He's been trying for several years to get somebody into the inner councils of the cult, but he hasn't been able to manage it. I told him that he ought to send in Hunter, but he hasn't been able to manage it. I told him that he ought to send in Hunter, but he told me that Hunter's busy with something else and to mind my own business.'

'Hunter? Who's Hunter?'

'I have no idea,' Silk admitted. 'It's not really a who, you see. It's a name that's applied to the most secret of our spies, and it changes from time to time. Only Javelin knows who Hunter is and he won't tell anybody—not even Porenn. Javelin himself was Hunter for a time—about fifteen years ago. It's not always necessarily a Drasnian, though—or even a man. It can be anybody in the world. It might even be somebody we know—Barak, maybe, or Relg—or maybe somebody in Nyissa.'

'Mandorallen, perhaps?' Garion suggested, smiling.

Silk considered that. 'No, Garion,' he concluded, 'I don't think Mandorallen has the right equipment. It can surprise you though. On several occasions, Hunter has even been a Murgo.'

'A Murgo? How could you possibly trust a Murgo?'

'I didn't say we always have to *trust* Hunter.'

Garion shook his head helplessly. 'I'll never understand spies and spying.'

'It's a game,' Silk told him. 'After you've played for a while, the game itself gets to be more important than which side you're on. Our reasons for doing things sometimes get pretty obscure.'

'I've noticed that,' Garion said. 'And as long as the subject has come up, what's your *real* reason for coming to Riva?'

'It's nothing all that secret, Garion,' Silk replied urbanely, adjusting the cuffs of his gray doublet. 'I realized a few years ago that a traveling merchant tends to lose track of things. If you want to stay on top of a local situation, you need to have an agent on the scene— somebody who can take advantage of opportunities when they arise. I've located some markets for certain Rivan products—glass, good boots, those wool capes, that sort of thing—and I decided that it might not be a bad idea to have a representative here.'

'That's really a very good idea, Silk. Things are a little static down in the city. We could use some new businesses to liven things up.'

Silk beamed at him.

'And I can always use the additional revenue,' Garion added.

'What?'

'There *are* a few taxes, Silk—nothing too burdensome, but I'm sure you understand. A kingdom is very expensive to run.'

'Garion!' Silk's voice was anguished.

'It's one of the first things I learned. People don't mind taxes so much if they're sure that everybody's paying the same. I can't really make exceptions at all—not even for an old friend. I'll introduce you to Kail. He's my chief administrator. He'll set things up for you.'

'I'm terribly disappointed in you, Garion,' Silk said with a crestfallen look.

'As you've said so many times, business is business, after all.'

There was a light tap on the door.

'Yes?' Garion answered.

'The Rivan Warder, your Majesty,' the sentry outside announced.

'Send him in.'

The tall, graying Rivan Warder entered quietly. 'Prince Kheldar,' he greeted Silk with a brief nod, then turned to Garion. 'I wouldn't bother you, your Majesty,' he apologized, 'but a matter of some urgency has come up.'

'Of course, Brand,' Garion replied politely. 'Sit down.'

'Thank you, Belgarion,' Brand said gratefully, sinking into a chair. 'My legs aren't what they used to be.'

'Isn't it a joy to grow older?' Silk said. 'The mind gets better, but everything else starts to fall apart.'

Brand smiled briefly. 'There's been a bit of a squabble in the garrison here in the Citadel, Belgarion,' he said, getting directly to the point. 'I'll discipline the two young men involved myself, but I thought that perhaps if *you* spoke to them, it might head off bloodshed.'

'Bloodshed?'

'They were bickering over something quite unimportant, and one thing led to another. They scuffled a bit and knocked a few of each other's teeth loose. That should have been the end of it, but they started issuing each other formal challenges. I was fairly sure that you would want to keep the swords out of it.'

'Definitely.'

'I can order them to withdraw the challenges, but there's always the possibility that they'll sneak out some night and find a private place to do war on each other. I think that if the king spoke with them, we might be able to head off that sort of foolishness. They're a couple of fairly good young men, and I don't think we want to have them chop each other into dog meat.'

Garion nodded his agreement. 'Send the pair of them to me first thing in the—'

The medallion he always wore gave a peculiar little twitch, and he broke off what he was saying, startled by the flutter against his chest. The amulet suddenly seemed to grow very hot, and there was a strange humming sound in his ears.

'What is it, Garion?' Silk asked him curiously.

Garion started to hold up one hand as he tried to pinpoint the source of the humming sound. Then his amulet gave a violent lurch that was almost like a blow to his chest. The humming shattered, and he heard Ce'Nedra's voice crying to him. *Garion! Help me!*

He sprang to his feet as Brand and Silk stared at him in amazement. 'Ce'Nedra!' he shouted. 'Where are you?'

'Help me, Garion! The baths!'

'Quick!' Garion exclaimed to the others. 'Ce'Nedra needs us—in the baths!' And he ran from the room, grabbing up a plain sword standing sheathed in the corner as he passed.

'What is it?' Silk demanded, running along behind as they burst into the outer corridor.

'I don't know,' Garion shouted. 'She called me for help.' He shook his sword as he ran, trying to free it of its sheath. 'Something's happening down in the baths.'

It was a long way down seemingly endless flights of torchlit stairs to the baths in the cellars of the Citadel. Garion went down those stairs three and four at a time with Silk and Brand hot on his heels. Startled servants and officials jumped out of their way as they rushed down, faces grim and with drawn weapons in their hands.

At the bottom of the last flight of stairs they found the heavy door to the women's baths bolted from the inside. Instantly summoning his will, Garion focused it and commanded, 'Burst!' The iron-bound door blasted inward off its hinges.

The scene inside was one of horror. The Lady Arell lay in a crumpled heap on the tile floor with the hilt of a dagger protruding from between her shoulders. In the center of the steaming pool, a tall, raw-boned woman in a dark cloak was grimly holding something under the water—something that struggled weakly—and floating on the surface above that struggling form was a great fan of coppery red hair.

'Ce'Nedra!' Garion shouted, leaping feet first into the pool with his sword aloft.

The cloaked woman gave him one startled glance and fled, splashing frantically away from the enraged king.

Ce'Nedra's tiny body rose limply to the surface of the pool, and she floated facedown and bobbing slightly in the water. With a cry of anguish, Garion dropped his sword and struggled through the warm, waist-deep water, his desperate arms reaching out toward the limp body floating just beyond his grasp.

Roaring with rage, Brand ran around the tiled walkway surrounding the pool with his sword aloft to pursue the tall woman, who was fleeing through a narrow doorway on the far side of the bath, but Silk was already ahead of him, running swiftly after the woman with a long-bladed dagger held low.

Garion caught up the body of his wife in his arms and struggled toward the edge of the pool. With horror he realized that she was not breathing.

'What can I do?' he cried desperately. 'Aunt Pol, what can I do?' But Aunt Pol was not there. He laid Ce'Nedra on the tiles on the edge of the pool. There was no sign of movement, no flutter of breath, and her face was a ghastly blue-gray color.

'Somebody help me!' Garion cried out, catching the tiny, lifeless form in his arms and holding it very close to him.

Something throbbed sharply against his chest, and he looked into his wife's still face, desperately searching for some sign of life. But Ce'Nedra did not move, and her little body was limp. Again he caught her to him.

Once again he felt that sharp throb—almost like a blow against his heart. He held Ce'Nedra away from him again, searching with tear-filled eyes for the source of that strange, jolting throb. The flickering light of one of the torches stuck in iron rings around the marble walls of the pool seemed to dance on the polished surface of the silver amulet at her throat. Could it have been—? With a trembling hand he put his fingertips to the amulet. He felt a tingling shock in his fingers. Startled, he jerked his hand away. Then he closed his fist about the amulet. He could feel it in his palm, throbbing like a silver heart, beating with a faltering rhythm.

'Ce'Nedra!' he said sharply. 'You've got to wake up. Please don't die, Ce'Nedra!' But there was no sign, no movement from his wife. Still holding the amulet, Garion began to weep. 'Aunt Pol,' he cried brokenly, 'what can I do?'

'Garion?' It was Aunt Pol's startled voice, coming to him across the empty miles.

'Aunt Pol,' he sobbed, 'help me!'

'What is it? What's wrong?'

'It's Ce'Nedra. She—she's been drowned!' and the full horror of it struck him like some great, overwhelming blow, and he began to sob again, great, tearing sobs.

'Stop that!' Aunt Pol's voice cracked like a whip. 'Where?' she demanded. 'When did this happen?'

'Here in the baths. She's not breathing, Aunt Pol. I think she's dead.'

'Stop babbling, Garion!' Her voice was like a slap in the face. 'How long has it been since her breathing stopped?'

'A few minutes—I don't know.'

'You don't have any time to lose. Have you got her out of the water?'

'Yes—but she's not breathing, and her face is like ashes.'

'Listen carefully. You've got to force the water out of her lungs. Put her down on her face and push on her back. Try to do it in the same rhythm as normal breathing, and be careful not to push too hard. You don't want to hurt the baby.'

'But—'

'Do as I say, Garion!'

He turned his silent wife over and began to carefully push down on her ribs. As astonishing amount of water came out of the tiny girl's mouth, but she remained still and unmoving.

Garion stopped and took hold of the amulet again. 'Nothing's happening, Aunt Pol.'

'Don't stop.'

He began pushing on Ce'Nedra's ribs again. He was about ready to despair, but then she coughed, and he almost wept with relief. He continued to push at her back. She coughed again, and then she began to cry weakly. Garion put his hand on the amulet. 'She's crying, Aunt Pol! She's alive!'

'Good. You can stop now. What happened?'

'Some woman tried to kill her here in the baths. Silk and Brand are chasing the woman now.'

There was a long silence. 'I see,' Aunt Pol said finally. 'Now listen, Garion—carefully. Ce'Nedra's lungs will be very weak after this. The main danger right now is congestion and fever. You've got to keep her warm and quiet. Her life—and the baby's—depend on that. As soon as her breathing is stronger, get her into bed. I'll be there as soon as I can.'

Garion moved quickly, gathering up every towel and robe he could find to make a bed for his weakly crying wife. As he covered her with a cloak, Silk returned, his face grim, and Brand, puffing noticeably, was right behind him.

'Is she all right?' the big Warder asked, his face desperately concerned.

'I think so,' Garion said. 'I got her breathing started again. Did the woman get away?'

'Not exactly,' Silk replied. 'She ran upstairs until she reached the battlements. When she got up there, I was right behind her. She saw that there was no way to escape, so she threw herself off.'

Garion felt a surge of satisfaction at that. 'Good,' he said without thinking.

'No. Not really. We needed to question her. Now we'll never find out who sent her here to do this.'

'I hadn't thought of that.'

Brand had gone sadly to the silent body of his niece. 'My poor Arell,' he said, his voice full of tears. He knelt beside her and took hold of the dagger protruding from her back. 'Even in death, she served her queen,' he said almost proudly.

Garion looked at him.

'The dagger's stuck,' Brand explained, tugging at it. 'The woman who killed her couldn't get it out. That's why she was trying to drown Ce'Nedra. If she'd been able to use this knife, we'd have been too late.'

'I'm going to find out who's responsible for this,' Garion

234

declared from between clenched teeth. 'I think I'll have him flayed.'

'Flaying is good,' Silk agreed. 'Or boiling. Boiling has always been my favorite.'

'Garion,' Ce'Nedra said weakly, and all thoughts of vengeance fled from Garion's mind as he turned to her. While he held his wife close to him, he dimly heard Silk speaking quietly to Brand.

'After somebody picks up what's left of our would-be assassin,' the little man was saying in a terse voice, 'I'd like to have all of her clothing brought to me.'

'Her clothing?'

'Right. The woman isn't able to talk anymore, but her clothing might. You'd be surprised at how much you can learn about someone by looking at his undergarments. We want to find out who was behind this, and that dead woman out there is our only clue. I want to find out who she was and where she came from. The quicker I can do that, the quicker we can start heating up the oil.'

'Oil?'

'I'm going to simmer the man who was behind this—slowly and with a great deal of attention to every exquisite detail.'

Chapter Fourteen

Polgara arrived late that same afternoon. No one saw fit to raise the question of how she had crossed the hundreds of intervening leagues in the space of hours instead of weeks. The sentry who had been standing watch atop the battlements and who escorted her to the sickroom, however, had a slightly wild look in his eyes, as if he had just seen something about which he would prefer not to speak.

Garion, at the moment she arrived, was in the midst of a discussion with one of the court physicians about the therapeutic value of bleeding, and the conversation had reached the point where he had just picked up a sword to confront the startled medical man who was approaching the bed with lancet in hand. 'If you try to open my wife's veins with that,' the young king declared firmly, 'I'm going to open yours with this.'

'All right,' Polgara said crisply, 'that will do, Garion.' She removed her cloak and laid it across the back of a chair.

'Aunt Pol,' he gasped with relief.

She had already turned to face the four physicians who had been tending the little queen. 'Thank you for your efforts, gentlemen,' she told them. 'I'll send for you if I need you.' The note of dismissal in her voice was final, and the four quietly filed out.

'Lady Polgara,' Ce'Nedra said weakly from the bed.

Polgara turned to her immediately. 'Yes, dear,' she said, taking Ce'Nedra's tiny hand in hers. 'How do you feel?'

'My chest hurts, and I can't seem to stay awake.'

'We'll have you up and about in no time at all, dear,' Polgara assured her. She looked critically at the bed. 'I think I'm going to need more pillows, Garion,' she said. 'I want to prop her up into a sitting position.'

Garion quickly went through the sitting room to the door leading to the corridor outside.

'Yes, your Majesty?' the sentry said as Garion opened the door.

'Do you want to get me about a dozen or so pillows?'

'Of course, your Majesty.' The sentry started down the corridor.

'On second thought, make that two dozen,' Garion called after him. Then he went back to the bedroom.

'I mean it, Lady Polgara,' Ce'Nedra was saying in a weak little voice. 'If it ever gets to the point where you have to make a choice, save my baby. Don't even think about me.'

'I see,' Polgara replied gravely. 'I hope you've purged yourself of that particular nonsense now.'

Ce'Nedra stared at her.

'Melodrama has always made me just ever so faintly nauseous.'

A slow flush crept up Ce'Nedra's cheeks.

'That's a very good sign,' Aunt Pol encouraged her. 'If you can blush, it means that you're well enough to take note of trivial things.'

'Trivial?'

'Such as being embarrassed about how truly stupid that last statement of yours really was. Your baby's fine, Ce'Nedra. In fact, he's better off right now than you are. He's sleeping at the moment.'

Ce'Nedra's eyes had gone wide, and her hands were placed protectively over her abdomen. 'You can see him?' she asked incredulously.

'See isn't exactly the right word, dear,' Polgara said as she mixed two powders together in a glass. 'I know what he's doing and what he's thinking about.' She added water to the mixture in the glass and watched critically as the contents bubbled and fumed. 'Here,' she instructed,

237

handing the glass to her patient, 'drink this.' Then she turned to Garion. 'Build up the fire, dear. It's autumn, after all, and we don't want her getting chilled.'

Brand and Silk had rather carefully examined the broken body of the would-be assassin and had shifted their attention to her clothing by the time Garion joined them late that evening. 'Have you found out anything yet?' he asked as he entered the room.

'We know that she was an Alorn,' Brand replied in his rumbling voice. 'About thirty-five years old, and she didn't work for a living. At least she didn't do anything strenuous enough to put calluses on her hands.'

'That's not very much to go on,' Garion said.

'It's a start,' Silk told him, carefully examining the hem of a blood-stained dress.

'It sort of points at the Bear-cult then, doesn't it?'

'Not necessarily,' Silk replied, laying aside the dress and picking up a linen shift. 'When you're trying to hide your identity, you pick an assassin from another country. Of course, that kind of thinking might be a little too subtle for the Bear-cult.' He frowned. 'Now, where have I seen this stitch before?' he muttered, still looking at the dead woman's undergarment.

'I'm so very sorry about Arell,' Garion said to Brand. 'We were all very fond of her.' It seemed like such an inadequate thing to say.

'She would have appreciated that, Belgarion,' Brand said quietly. 'She loved Ce'Nedra very much.'

Garion turned back to Silk with a feeling of frustration boiling up in him. 'What are we going to do?' he demanded. 'If we can't find out who was behind this, he'll probably just try again.'

'I certainly *hope* so,' Silk said.

'You *what*?'

'We can save a lot of time if we can catch somebody who's still alive. You can only get so much out of dead people.'

'I wish we'd been a little more thorough when we wiped out the Bear-cult at Thull Mardu,' Brand said.

'I wouldn't get my mind *too* set on the notion that the Bear-cult was responsible for this,' Silk told him. 'There are some other possibilities.'

'Who else would want to hurt Ce'Nedra?' Garion asked.

Silk sprawled in a chair, scratching absently at his cheek and with his forehead furrowed with thought. 'Maybe it wasn't Ce'Nedra,' he mused.

'What?'

'It's altogether possible, you know, that the attempt was directed at the baby she's carrying. There could be people out there in the world who do not want there to be an heir to Iron-grip's throne.'

'Who?'

'The Grolims come to mind rather quickly,' Silk replied. 'Or the Nyissans—or even a few Tolnedrans. I want to keep an open mind on the matter—until I find out a few more things.' He held up the stained undergarment. 'I'm going to start with this. Tomorrow morning, I'm going to take it down to the city and show it to every tailor and seamstress I can find. I might be able to get something out of the weave, and there's a peculiar kind of stitching along the hem. If I can find somebody to identify it for me, it might give us something to work on.'

Brand looked thoughtfully over at the still, blanket-draped form of the woman who had tried to kill Ce'Nedra. 'She would have had to have entered the Citadel by way of one of the gates,' he mused. 'That means that she passed a sentry and that she had to have given him some kind of excuse for coming in. I'll round up every man who's been on sentry duty for the past week and bring them all down here to have a look at her. Once we know exactly when she got in, maybe we can start to backtrack her. I'd like to find the ship she arrived on and have a talk with the captain.'

'What can I do?' Garion asked quickly.

'Probably you should stay close to Ce'Nedra's room,' Silk suggested. 'Any time Polgara leaves for any reason at all, you ought to go in and take her place. There could be other attempts, you know, and I think we'll all feel better if Ce'Nedra's guarded rather closely.'

Under Polgara's watchful eyes, Ce'Nedra spent a quiet night, and her breathing was much stronger the next day. She complained bitterly about the taste of the medicines she was required to drink, and Polgara listened with a great show of interest to the queen's extensive tirade. 'Yes, dear,' she agreed pleasantly. 'Now drink it all down.'

'Does it have to taste so awful?' Ce'Nedra said with a shudder.

'Of course it does. If medicine tasted good, sick people might be tempted to stay sick so that they could enjoy the medicine. The worse it tastes, the quicker you get well.'

Late that afternoon, Silk returned with a disgusted look on his face. 'I hadn't realized how many ways it's possible to attach two pieces of cloth together,' he grumbled.

'No luck, I take it,' Garion said.

'Not really,' Silk replied, throwing himself into a chair. 'I managed to pick up all sorts of educated guesses, though.'

'Oh?'

'One tailor was willing to stake his reputation on the fact that this particular stitch is used exclusively in Nyissa. A seamstress told me very confidently that this was an Ulgo garment. And one half-wit went so far as to say that the owner of the garment was a sailor, since this stitch is *always* used to repair torn sails.'

'What are you talking about, Silk?' Polgara asked curiously as she passed through the sitting room on her way back to Ce'Nedra's bedside.

'I've been trying to get someone to identify the stitching on the hem of this thing,' he said in a disgusted tone, waving the blood-stained shift.

'Here. Let me see it.'

Silk wordlessly handed her the garment.

She glanced at it almost casually. 'Northeastern Drasnia,' she told him, 'from somewhere near the town of Rheon.'

'Are you sure?' Silk came to his feet quickly.

She nodded. 'That kind of stitching was developed

centuries ago—back in the days when all the garments up there were made from reindeer skin.'

'That's disgusting,' Silk said.

'What is?'

'I ran around with this thing all day long—up and down all those stairs and in and out of every tailor shop in Riva —and all I had to do to find out what I wanted to know was show it to you.'

'That's not my fault, Prince Kheldar,' she told him, handing back the shift. 'If you don't know enough to bring these little problems to me by now, then there probably isn't much hope for you.'

'Thanks, Polgara,' he said drily.

'Then the assassin was a Drasnian,' Garion said.

'A *northeastern* Drasnian,' Silk corrected. 'Those people up there are a strange sort—almost worse than the ones who live in the fens.'

'Strange?'

'Standoffish, closemouthed, unfriendly, clannish, secretive. Everybody in northeast Drasnia behaves as if he had all the state secrets in the kingdom tucked up his sleeve.'

'Why would they hate Ce'Nedra so much?' Garion asked with a puzzled frown.

'I wouldn't make too much of the fact that this assassin was a Drasnian, Garion,' Silk told him. 'People who hire other people to do their killing for them don't always go looking for their hirelings close to home—and, although there are a lot of assassins in the world, very few of them are women.' He pursed his lips thoughtfully. 'I *do* think that I'll take a trip up to Rheon and have a look around, however.'

As the chill of winter set in, Polgara finally declared that Ce'Nedra was out of all danger. 'I think I'll stay, though,' she added. 'Durnik and Errand can manage at home for a few months, and I'd probably no sooner get home than I'd have to turn around and come back.'

Garion looked at her blankly.

'You didn't actually think that I was going to let anybody else deliver Ce'Nedra's first baby, did you?'

It snowed heavily just before Erastide, and the steep streets of the city of Riva became virtually impassable. Ce'Nedra's disposition soured noticeably. Her increasing girth made her awkward, and the depth of the snow in the city streets had rather effectively confined her to the Citadel. Polgara took the little queen's outbursts and crying fits calmly, scarcely changing expression, even at the height of the eruptions. 'You *do* want to have this baby, don't you?' she asked pointedly on one such occasion.

'Of course I do,' Ce'Nedra replied indignantly.

'Well then, you have to go through this. It's the only way I know of to fill the nursery.'

'Don't try to be reasonable with me, Lady Polgara,' Ce'Nedra flared. 'I'm not in the mood for reasonableness right now.'

Polgara gave her a faintly amused look, and Ce'Nedra, in spite of herself, began to laugh. 'I'm being silly, aren't I?'

'A bit, yes.'

'It's just that I feel so huge and ugly.'

'That will pass, Ce'Nedra.'

'Sometimes I wish I could just lay eggs—the way birds do.'

'I'd stick to doing it the old way, dear. I don't think you have the disposition for sitting on a nest.'

Erastide came and passed quietly. The celebration on the island was warm, but somewhat restrained. It seemed as if the whole population was holding its breath, waiting for a much larger reason for celebration. Winter ground on with each week adding more snow to the already high-piled drifts. A month or so after Erastide there was a brief thaw, lasting for perhaps two days, and then the frigid chill locked in again, turning the sodden snowbanks into blocks of ice. The weeks plodded by tediously, and everybody waited.

'Would you just look at that?' Ce'Nedra said angrily to Garion one morning shortly after they had arisen.

'At what, dear?' he replied mildly.

'At that!' She pointed disgustedly at the window. 'It's snowing again.' There was a note of accusation in her voice.

'It's not my fault,' he said defensively.

'Did I say that it was?' She turned awkwardly to glare at him. Her tininess made her swollen belly appear all the larger, and she sometimes seemed to thrust it out at him as if it were entirely his doing.

'This is just absolutely insupportable,' she declared. 'Why have you brought me to this frozen—' She stopped in mid-tirade, a strange look crossing her face.

'Are you all right, dear?' Garion asked.

'Don't "dear" me, Garion. I—' She stopped again. 'Oh, my,' she said breathlessly.

'What is it?' He got to his feet.

'Oh, dear,' Ce'Nedra said, putting her hands to the small of her back. 'Oh dear, oh dear, oh dear.'

'Ce'Nedra, that's not very helpful. What's the matter?'

'I think perhaps I'd better go lie down,' she said almost absently. She started across the room, moving at a stately waddle. She stopped. 'Oh, dear,' she said with much more vehemence. Her face was pale, and she put one hand on a chair back to support herself. 'I think that it mght be a good idea if you sent for Lady Polgara, Garion.'

'Is it—? I mean, are you—?'

'Don't babble, Garion,' she said tensely. 'Just open the door and scream for your Aunt Pol.'

'Are you trying to say that—?'

'I'm not trying, Garion. I'm saying it. Get her in here right now.' She waddled to the bedroom door and stopped again with a little gasp. 'Oh, my goodness,' she said.

Garion stumbled to the door and jerked it open. 'Get Lady Polgara!' he said to the startled sentry. 'Immediately! Run!'

'Yes, your Majesty!' the man replied, dropping his spear and sprinting down the hall.

Garion slammed the door and dashed to Ce'Nedra's side. 'Can I do anything?' he asked, wringing his hands.

'Help me to bed,' she told him.

'Bed!' he said. 'Right!' He grabbed her arm and began to tug at her.

'What are you doing?'

'Bed,' he blurted, pointing at the royal four-poster.

'I know what it is, Garion. Help me. Don't yank on me.'

'Oh.' He took her hand, slipped his other arm about her, and lifted her off her feet. He stumbled toward the bed, his eyes wide and his mind completely blank.

'Put me down, you great oaf!'

'Bed,' he urged her, trying with all the eloquence at his command to explain. He carefully set her back down on her feet and rushed on ahead. 'Nice bed,' he said, patting the coverlets encouragingly.

Ce'Nedra closed her eyes and sighed. 'Just step out of my way, Garion,' she said with resignation.

'But—'

'Why don't you build up the fire?' she suggested.

'What?' He stared around blankly.

'The fireplace—that opening in the wall with the burning logs in it. Put some more wood in there. We want it nice and warm for the baby, don't we?' She reached the bed and leaned against it.

Garion dashed to the fireplace and stood staring at it stupidly.

'What's the matter now?'

'Wood,' he replied. 'No wood.'

'Bring some in from the other room.'

What an absolutely brilliant suggestion she had just made! He stared at her gratefully.

'Go into the other room, Garion,' she said, speaking very slowly and distinctly. 'Pick up some wood. Carry it back in here. Put it on the fire. Have you got all that so far?'

'Right!' he said excitedly. He dashed into the other room, picked up a stick of firewood, and dashed back in with it. 'Wood,' he said, holding the stick up proudly.

'Very nice, Garion,' she said, climbing laboriously into

the bed. 'Now put it on the fire and go back out and bring in some more.'

'More,' he agreed, flinging the stick into the fireplace and dashing out the door again.

After he had emptied the woodbin in the sitting room —one stick at a time—he stared around wildly, trying to decide what to do next. He picked up a chair. If he were to swing it against the wall, he reasoned, it ought to break up into manageable pieces.

The door to the apartment opend, and Polgara came in. She stopped to stare at the wild-eyed Garion. 'What on earth are you doing with that chair?' she demanded.

'Wood,' he explained, brandishing the heavy piece of furniture. 'Need wood—for the fire.'

She gave him a long look, smoothing down the front of her white apron. 'I see,' she said. 'It's going to be one of those. Put the chair down, Garion. Where's Ce'Nedra?'

'Bed,' he replied, regretfully setting down the polished chair. Then he looked at her brightly. 'Baby,' he informed her.

She rolled her eyes toward the ceiling. 'Garion,' she said, speaking carefully as if to a child, 'it's much too early for Ce'Nedra to be taking to her bed. She needs to walk around—keep moving.'

He shook his head stubbornly. 'Bed,' he repeated. 'Baby.' He looked around and picked up the chair again.

Polgara sighed, opened the door, and beckoned to the sentry. 'Young man,' she said, 'why don't you take his Majesty here down to that courtyard just outside the kitchen? There's a large pile of logs there. Get him an axe so that he can cut up some firewood.'

Everybody was being absolutely brilliant today. Garion marveled at the suggestion Aunt Pol had just made. He set down the chair again and dashed out with the baffled sentry in tow.

He chopped up what seemed like a cord of wood in the first hour, sending out a positive blizzard of chips as he swung the axe so fast that it seemed almost to blur in the air. Then he paused, pulled off his doublet, and really got down to work. About noon, a respectful cook brought him a slab of freshly roasted beef, a large chunk of bread, and some ale. Garion wolfed down three or four bites, took a couple of gulps of the ale, and then picked up his axe to attack another log. It was altogether possible that he might have finished up with the woodpile outside the kitchen and then gone in search of more trees had not Brand interrupted him shortly before the sun went down.

The big, gray-haired Warder had a broad grin on his face. 'Congratulations, Belgarion,' he said. 'You have a son.'

Garion paused, looking almost regretfully at the remaining logs. Then what Brand had just said finally seeped into his awareness. The axe slid from his fingers. 'A son?' he said. 'What an amazing thing. And so quickly, too.' He looked at the woodpile. 'I only just now got here. I always thought that it took much longer.'

Brand looked at him carefully, then gently took him by the arm. 'Come along now, Belgarion,' he said. 'Let's go up and meet your son.'

Garion bent and carefully picked up an armload of wood. 'For the fire,' he explained. 'Ce'Nedra wants a nice big fire.'

'She'll be very proud of you, Belgarion,' Brand assured him.

When they reached the royal bedchamber, Garion carefully put his armload of wood on the polished table by the window and approached the bed on tiptoe.

Ce'Nedra looked very tired and wan, but there was, nonetheless, a contented little smile on her face. Nestled beside her in a soft blanket was a very small person. The newcomer had a red face and almost no hair. He seemed to be asleep; but as Garion approached, his eyes opened. Gravely, the crown prince looked at his father, then sighed, burped, and went back to sleep.

'Oh, isn't he just beautiful, Garion?' Ce'Nedra said in a wondering little voice.

'Yes,' Garion replied with a great lump coming up into

his throat. 'And so are you.' He knelt beside the bed and put his arm about them both.

'Very nice, children,' Polgara said from the other side of the bed. 'You both did just fine.'

The following day Garion and his newborn son went through a very ancient ceremony. With Polgara at his side in a splendid blue and silver gown, he carried the baby to the Hall of the Rivan King, where the nobles of the island kingdom awaited them. As the three of them entered the Hall, the Orb of Aldur, standing on the pommel of Iron-grip's sword, blazed forth with a great shimmer of blue light. Almost bemused, Garion approached his throne. 'This is my son, Geran,' he announced—in part to the gathered throng, but also, in a peculiar way, to the Orb itself. The choice of his son's name had not been difficult. Though he could not remember his father, Garion had wanted to honor him, and no way seemed more appropriate that to give *his* son his father's name.

He carefully handed the baby to Polgara, reached up, and took down the great sword. Holding it by the blade, he extended it toward the blanket-wrapped infant in Polgara's arms. The shimmering glow of the Orb grew brighter. And then, as if attracted by that light, Geran stretched forth his tiny pink hand and put it on the glowing jewel. A great aura of many-colored light burst from the Orb at the infant touch, surrounding the three of them with a pulsating rainbow that illuminated the entire Hall. A vast chorus filled Garion's ears, rising to an enormous chord that seemed to shake the whole world.

'Hail Geran!' Brand boomed in a great voice, 'heir to the throne of Iron-grip and keeper of the Orb of Aldur!'

'Hail Geran!' the throng echoed in a thunderous shout.

'Hail Geran,' the dry voice in Garion's mind added quietly.

Polgara said nothing. She did not need to speak, since the look in her eyes said everything that needed saying.

Although it was winter and the Sea of the Winds was lashed by storms, the Alorn Kings all journeyed to Riva to celebrate the birth of Geran. Many others, friends and old acquaintances, joined with Anheg, Cho-Hag, and Queen Poreen on the journey to Riva. Barak was there, of course, accompanied by his wife Merel. Hettar and Adara arrived. Lelldorin and Mandorallen came up from Arendia with Ariana and Nerina.

Garion, now somewhat more sensitive to such things, was amazed at how many children his friends had produced. No matter which way he turned, there seemed to be babies, and the sound of little boys and girls running and laughing filled the sober halls of the Citadel. The boy-king Kheva of Drasnia and Barak's son Unrak soon became the closest of friends. Nerina's daughters romped with Adara's sons in endless games involving much giggling. Barak's eldest daughter, Gundred, now a ravishing young lady, cut a broad track through the hearts of whole platoons of young Rivan nobles, all the while under the watchful eye of her huge, red-bearded father, who never actually threatened any of his daughter's suitors, but whose looks said quite plainly that he would tolerate no foolishness. Little Terzie, Gundred's younger sister, hovered on the very brink of womanhood—romping one moment with the younger children and looking the next with devastating eyes at the group of adolescent Rivan boys who always seemed to be around.

King Fulrach and General Brendig sailed over from Sendaria about midway through the celebration. Queen Layla sent her fondest congratulations, but she did not make the trip with her husband. 'She almost got on board the ship,' Fulrach reported, 'but then a gust of wind made waves break over the stones of the quay, and she fainted. We decided not to subject her to the voyage at that point.'

'It's probably best,' Garion agreed.

Durnik and Errand came up from the Vale, naturally, and with them came Belgarath.

The celebration went on for weeks. There were banquets and formal presentations of gifts, both by the visitors and by the ambassadors of various friendly kingdoms. And, of course, there were hours of reminiscences and a fair amount of serious drinking. Ce'Nedra was in her glory, since she and her infant son were the absolute center of attention.

Garion found that the festivities, coupled with his normal duties, left him almost no free time at all. He wished that he could find an hour or two to talk with Barak, Hettar, Mandorallen, and Lelldorin; but no matter how he tried to rearrange his days, the time simply was not there.

Very late one evening, however, Belgarath came looking for him. Garion looked up from a report he had been reading as the old sorcerer entered his study. 'I thought we might want to talk for a bit,' the old man said.

Garion tossed aside the report. 'I haven't meant to neglect you, Grandfather,' he apologized, 'but they're keeping my days pretty well filled up.'

Belgarath shrugged. 'Things are bound to settle down in a while. Did I ever get around to congratulating you?'

'I think so.'

'Good. That's taken care of, then. People always make such a fuss about babies. I don't really care that much for them myself. They're all squally and wet, most of the time, and it's almost impossible to talk to them. You don't mind if I help myself, do you?' He pointed at a crystal decanter of pale wine standing on a table.

'No. Go ahead.'

'You want some?'

'No thanks, Grandfather.'

Belgarath poured himself a goblet of wine and then settled down in a chair across from Garion's. 'How's the king business?' he asked.

'Tedious,' Garion replied ruefully.

'Actually, that's not a bad thing, you know. When it gets exciting, that usually means that something pretty awful is happening.'

'I suppose you're right.'

'Have you been studying?'

Garion sat up quickly. 'I'm glad you brought that up. Things have been so hectic that something sort of important had almost slipped my mind.'

'Oh?'

'How careful were people when they made copies of those prophecies?'

Belgarath shrugged. 'Fairly careful, I suppose. Why do you ask?'

'I think that something got left out of my copy of the Mrin Codex.'

'What makes you think so?'

'There's a passage in there that just doesn't make sense.'

'Maybe not to *you*, but you haven't been studying all that long.'

'That's not what I mean, Grandfather. I'm not talking about an obscure meaning. What I'm getting at is a sentence that starts out and then just stops without going anywhere. I mean, it doesn't have any ending the way it should.'

'You're concerned about grammar?'

Garion scratched at his head. 'It's the only passage I found in there that breaks off that way. It goes, "But behold, the stone which lies at the center of the light shall —" And then there's a blot, and it takes up again with "—and this meeting will come to pass in a place which is no more, and there will the choice be made."'

Belgarath frowned. 'I think I know the passage,' he said.

'The two just don't fit together, Grandfather. The first part is talking about the Orb—at least that's the way I read it—and the second part is talking about a meeting. I don't know what word is under that blot, but I can't for the life of me figure out how the two parts could be hooked together. I think there's something missing. That's why I was asking about how they went about copying these things. Could the scribe who was doing it have skipped a couple of lines?'

'I don't think so, Garion,' Belgarath said. 'The new copy is always compared with the old one by somebody other than the scribe. We *are* fairly careful about things like that.'

'Then what's under that blot?'

Belgarath scratched at his beard thoughtfully. 'I can't

quite recall,' he admitted. 'Anheg's here. Maybe he remembers—or you can ask him to transcribe that part from his copy and send it to you when he gets back to Val Alorn.'

'That's a good idea.'

'I wouldn't worry too much about it, Garion. It's only part of one passage, after all.'

'There are a lot of things in there that are only one passage, Grandfather, and they turned out to be sort of important.'

'If it bothers you so much, chase it down. That's a good way to learn.'

'Aren't you the least bit curious about it?'

'I have other things on my mind. You're the one who found this discrepancy, so I'll give you all the glory of exposing it to the world and working out the solution.'

'You're not being very much help, Grandfather.'

Belgarath grinned at him. 'I'm not really trying to be, Garion. You're grown up enough now to solve your own problems.' He looked over at the decanter. 'I believe I'll have just another little touch of that,' he said.

Chapter Fifteen

'. . . And they shall number twelve, for twelve is a number which is pleasing to the Gods. I know this to be true, for a raven once came to me in a dream and told me so. I have always loved the number twelve, and it is for this reason that the Gods have chosen me to reveal this truth to all the nations. . . .'

Garion scowled at the musty-smelling book. There had been some hope in the earlier pages—some obscure references to Light and Dark and a tantalizing fragment which had stated quite clearly that, 'The holiest of things will always be the color of the sky, save only when it perceives great evil, and then will it burn hot with scarlet flame.' When he had found that passage, he had read on avidly, convinced that he had stumbled across a genuine and hitherto undiscovered prophecy. The rest of the book, unfortunately, proved to be absolute gibberish. The brief biographical note at the beginning of the book indicated that its author had been a Drasnian merchant of some substance during the third millennium and that these secret jottings had been found only after his death. Garion wondered how a man with so disturbed a mind could have even functioned in a normal society.

He closed the book in disgust and added it to the growing pile of ravings that was accumulating on the table in front of him. Next he picked up a slender volume that had been found in a deserted house in Arendia. The first few pages were devoted to the household accounts of a very minor Arendish nobleman. Then, on the fourth page, the mundane broke off quite suddenly. 'The Child of Light shall take up the sword and go in search of that which is hidden,' Garion read. This was immediately followed by a tediously detailed account of the purchase of a dozen or so pigs from a neighbor. Then once again the unknown writer jumped into prophecy. 'The quest of the Child of Light shall be for one whose soul has been reft away, for a stone that is empty at its center and for the babe who will hold the Light in one hand and the Dark in the other.' That definitely seemed to be getting somewhere. Garion pulled one of his guttering candles closer and hunched over the book, reading each page carefully. Those two passages, however, proved to be the only ones in the entire volume that did not speak of the day-to-day business of that forgotten farm somewhere in Arendia.

Garion sighed, leaned back, and looked around at the dimly lighted library. The bound books stood in their dusty rows on the dark shelves, and the linen-covered scrolls lay along the top of each bookcase. The light of his two candles flickered, making the room seem almost to dance.

'There has to be a faster way to do this,' he muttered.

'*Actually there is,*' the dry voice in his mind said to him.

'What?'

'*You said that there had to be a faster way. I said that there is.*'

'Where have you been?'

'*Here and there.*'

Garion knew this other awareness well enough by now to be certain that it would tell him only what it wanted him to know. 'All right,' he said, 'what is this faster way?'

'*You don't have to read every single word the way you have been doing. Open your mind and just leaf through the pages. The things I put in each book will sort of leap out at you.*'

'Are the prophecies always mixed right in with all this other nonsense?'

'*Usually, yes.*'

'Why did you do it that way?'

'*Several reasons. Most of the time I didn't want the man*'

who was doing the actual writing even to know what I was hiding in his book. Then, of course, it's a good way to keep things from falling into unfriendly hands.'

'And friendly ones, too, for that matter.'

'Did you want me to explain, or were you just looking for an excuse to make clever remarks?'

'All right.' Garion sighed, giving up.

'I think I've told you before that the word gives meaning to the event. The word has to be there, but it doesn't have to be right out in the open where just anybody can find it.'

Garion frowned. 'Do you mean that you put all these things in all these books for just a few people to read?'

'The term "a few" isn't really accurate. Try "one" instead.'

'One? Who?'

'You, obviously.'

'Me? Why me?'

'Are we going to go through that again?'

'Are you trying to say that all of this was sort of like a personal letter—just to me?'

'In a manner of speaking, yes.'

'What if I hadn't gotten around to reading it?'

'Why are you reading it now?'

'Because Belgarath told me to.'

'Why do you think Belgarath told you that?'

'Because —' Garion broke off. 'You told him to say it to me?'

'Naturally. He didn't know about it, of course, but I sort of nudged him. All sorts of people have access to the Mrin Codex. That's why I made it so cryptic. These personal instructions to you, however, should be fairly clear—if you pay attention.'

'Why don't you just *tell* me what I'm supposed to do?'

'I'm not permitted to do that.'

'Permitted?'

'We have our rules, my opposite and I. We're very carefully balanced and we have to stay that way. We agreed only to act through our instruments, and if I

intervene in person—with such things as telling you directly what you must do—then my opposite will also be free to step over the line. That's why we both work through what are called prophecies.'

'Isn't that a little complicated?'

'The alternative would be absolute chaos. My opposite and I are limitless. If we confront each other directly, whole suns will be destroyed.'

Garion shuddered and swallowed hard. 'I didn't realize that,' he admitted. Then an idea occurred to him. 'Would you be permitted to tell me about that line in the Mrin Codex—the one that's got the blotted word in the middle of it?'

'That depends on how much you want to know about it.'

'What's the word under the blot?'

'There are several words there. If you look at it in the right kind of light, you should be able to see them. As for these other books, try reading them the way I told you to. I think you'll find that it saves a lot of time—and you really don't have all that much time to spare.'

'What's that supposed to mean?'

But the voice was gone.

The door to the library opened, and Ce'Nedra came in, wearing her nightdress and a warm robe. 'Garion,' she said, 'aren't you *ever* coming to bed?'

'What?' He looked up. 'Oh—yes. Right away.'

'Who was in here with you?'

'Nobody. Why?'

'I heard you talking to someone.'

'I was just reading, that's all.'

'Come to bed, Garion,' she said firmly. 'You can't read the whole library in one evening.'

'Yes, dear,' he agreed.

Not long after that, when spring had begun to touch the lower meadows on the slopes behind the Citadel, the promised letter from King Anheg arrived. Garion immediately took the copy of that baffling passage in the Mrin

Codex to the library to compare it with *his* copy. When he put the two side by side, he began to swear. Anheg's copy was blotted in exactly the same place. 'I told him!' Garion fumed. 'I told him specifically that I needed to see that particular spot! I even showed him!' Swearing angrily, he began to pace up and down, waving both arms in the air.

Rather surprisingly, Ce'Nedra took her husband's near-obsession with the Mrin Codex in stride. Of course, the little queen's attention was almost totally riveted on her new son, and Garion was fairly certain that anything he said or did was only on the very edge of her awareness. Young Prince Geran was grossly overmothered. Ce'Nedra held him in her arms almost every minute that he was awake and frequently even when he was asleep. He was a good-natured baby and seldom cried or fussed. He took his mother's constant attention quite calmly and accepted all the cuddling and cooing and impulsive kisses with equanimity. Garion, however, felt that Ce'Nedra really overdid things just a bit. Since she insisted on holding Geran constantly, it definitely cut into the time when *he* might be able to hold his son. Once he almost asked her when his turn was going to come, but decided at the last minute not to. The thing that he really felt was unfair was Ce'Nedra's sense of timing. Whenever she *did* put Geran in his cradle for a few moments and Garion finally got the chance to pick him up, the little queen's hands seemed almost automatically to go to the buttons on the front of her dress, and she would placidly announce that it was time for Geran to nurse. Garion certainly did not begrudge his son his lunch, but the baby really didn't look all that hungry most of the time.

After a time, however, when he finally became adjusted to Geran's undeniable presence in their lives, the call of the dim, musty library began to reassert itself. The procedure that had been suggested to him by the dry voice worked surprisingly well. After a little practice, he found that he could skim rapidly over page after page of mundane material and that his eye would stop automatically at the prophetic passages buried in the midst of ordinary text. He was surprised to find so many of these passages hidden away in the most unlikely places. In most cases it was obvious that the writers had not even been aware of what they had inserted. A sentence would frequently break off, leap into prophecy, and then take up again exactly where it had stopped. Garion was positive that upon rereading the text, the unconscious prophet who had inserted the material would not even see what he had just written.

The Mrin Codex, however, and to a lesser degree the Darine, remained the core of the whole thing. Passages from other works clarified or expanded, but the two major prophecies put it all down in uncontaminated form. Garion began to cross index as he went along, identifying each new passage with a number and then linking those numbers to the series of letter codes he had assigned to the paragraphs of the Mrin scroll. Each paragraph of the Mrin, he discovered, usually had three or four corroborating or explanatory lines gleaned from other works—all except that crucial blotted passage.

'And how did the search go today, dear?' Ce'Nedra asked brightly one evening when he returned, grouchy and out of sorts, to the royal apartment. She was nursing Geran at the time, and her face was aglow with tenderness as she held her baby to her breast.

'I'm just about to give it all up,' he declared, flinging himself into a chair. 'I think it might be better just to lock up that library and throw away the key.'

She looked at him fondly and smiled. 'Now you know that wouldn't do any good, Garion. You know that after a day or so you wouldn't be able to stand it, and no door is so stout that you can't break it down.'

'Maybe I should just burn all those books and scrolls,' he said morosely. 'I can't concentrate on anything else any more. I *know* there's something hidden under that blot, but I can't find a single clue anywhere to what it might be.'

'If you burn that library, Belgarath will probably turn

you into a radish,' she warned with a smile. 'He's very fond of books, you know.'

'It might be nice to be a radish for a while,' he replied.

'It's really very simple, Garion,' she said with that infuriating placidity. 'Since all the copies are blotted, why don't you go look at the original?'

He stared at her.

'It has to be *somewhere*, doesn't it?'

'Well—I suppose so, yes.'

'Find out where it is, then, and go look—or send for it.'

'I never thought of that.'

'Obviously. It's much more fun to rant and rave and be unpleasant about it.'

'You know, that's really a very good idea, Ce'Nedra.'

'Naturally. You men always want to complicate things so much. Next time you have a problem, dear, just bring it to me. I'll tell you how to solve it.'

He let that pass.

The first thing the following morning, Garion went down into the city and called on the Rivan Deacon in the Temple of Belar. The Rivan Deacon was a sober-faced, gentle man. Unlike the priests of Belar in the major temples on the continent, who were frequently more involved in politics than in the care of their flocks, the leader of the Rivan Church concerned himself almost exclusively with the well-being—physical as well as spiritual—of the common people. Garion had always rather liked him.

'I've never actually seen it myself, your Majesty,' the deacon replied in response to Garion's question, 'but I've always been told that it's kept in that shrine on the banks of the Mrin River—between the edge of the fens and Boktor.'

'Shrine?'

'The ancient Drasnians erected it on the site where the Mrin Prophet was kept chained,' the deacon explained. 'After the poor man died, King Bull-neck directed that a memorial of some sort be put up there. They built the shrine directly over his grave. The original scroll is kept there in a large crystal case. A group of priests is there to protect it. Most people wouldn't be allowed to touch it; but considering the fact that you're the Rivan King, I'm sure that they'll make an exception.'

'Then it's always been there?'

'Except during the time of the Angarak invasion during the fourth millennium. It was taken by ship to Val Alorn for safekeeping just before Boktor was burned. Torak wanted to get his hands on it, so it was felt wiser to get it out of the country.'

'That makes sense,' Garion said. 'Thank you for the information, your Reverence.'

'Glad to be of help, your Majesty.'

It was going to be hard to get away. This week was completely out of the question, since there was that meeting with the port authorities the day after tomorrow. And next week would be even worse. There were always so many official meetings and state functions. Garion sighed as he climbed back up the long stairs to the Citadel with his inevitable guard at his side. It somehow seemed that he was almost a prisoner here on this island. There were always so many demands on his time. He could remember a time, not really that long ago when he started each day on horseback and seldom slept in the same bed two nights in a row. Upon consideration, however, he was forced to admit that even then he had not been free to do as he wished. Though he had not known it, this burden of responsibility had descended upon him on that windy autumn night so many years ago when he, Aunt Pol, Belgarath, and Durnik had crept through the gate at Faldor's farm and out into the wide world that lay before them.

'Well,' he muttered under his breath, 'this is important too. Brand can manage here. They'll just have to get along without me for a while.'

'What was that, your Majesty?' the guard asked politely.

'Just thinking out loud,' Garion replied, a little embarrassed.

Ce'Nedra seemed moody and out of sorts that evening.

She held Geran almost abstractedly, paying scant attention to him as he played with the amulet at her throat with a look of serious concentration on his face.

'What's the matter, dear?' Garion asked her.

'Just a headache, that's all,' she replied shortly. 'And a strange sort of ringing in my ears.'

'You're tired.'

'Maybe that's it.' She arose. 'I think I'll put Geran in his cradle and go to bed,' she declared. 'Maybe a good night's sleep will make me feel better.'

'I can put him to bed,' Garion offered.

'No,' she said with a strange look. 'I want to be sure that he's safely in his cradle.'

'Safe?' Garion laughed. 'Ce'Nedra, this is Riva. It's the safest place in the world.'

'Go tell that to Arell,' she told him and went into the small room adjoining their bedchamber where Geran's cradle stood.

Garion sat up and read until rather late that evening. Ce'Nedra's restless moodiness had somehow communicated itself to him, and he did not feel ready for bed. Finally, he put aside his book and went to the window to look out across the moon-touched waters of the Sea of the Winds lying far below. The long, slow waves seemed almost like molten silver in the pale light, and their stately pace was oddly hypnotic. Finally he blew out the candles and went quietly into the bedroom.

Ce'Nedra was tossing restlessly in her sleep and muttering half-formed phrases—meaningless snatches of fragmentary conversation. Garion undressed and slipped into bed, trying not to disturb her.

'No,' she said in a peremptory tone of voice. 'I won't let you do that.' Then she moaned and tossed her head on the pillow.

Garion lay in the soft darkness, listening to his wife talking in her sleep.

'Garion!' she gasped, coming suddenly awake. 'Your feet are cold!'

'Oh,' he said. 'Sorry.'

She drifted almost immediately back into sleep, and the muttering resumed.

It was the sound of a different voice that awoke him several hours later. The voice was oddly familiar, and Garion lay, still almost asleep, trying to remember exactly where he had heard it before. It was a woman's voice, low and musical and speaking in a peculiarly soothing tone.

Then he suddenly realized that Ce'Nedra was not in the bed beside him and he came fully awake instantly.

'But I have to hide him so that they can't find him,' he heard Ce'Nedra say in a strangely numb voice. He tossed back the covers and slid out of bed.

A faint light gleamed through the open door to the nursery, and the voices seemed to be coming from there. Garion moved quickly to that door, his bare feet making no sound on the carpet.

'Uncover your baby, Ce'Nedra,' the other woman was saying in a calm, persuasive voice. 'You'll hurt him.'

Garion looked through the doorway. Ce'Nedra was standing by the cradle in her white nightdress, her eyes vacant and staring, with another figure beside her. On the chair at the foot of the cradle was a great heap of blankets and pillows. Dreamily, the Rivan Queen was methodically piling the bedclothes on top of her baby.

'Ce'Nedra,' the woman said to her. 'Stop. Listen to me.'

'I have to hide him,' Ce'Nedra replied stubbornly. 'They want to kill him.'

'Ce'Nedra. You'll smother him. Now take all the blankets and pillows out again.'

'But —'

'Do as I said, Ce'Nedra,' the woman said firmly. 'Now.'

Ce'Nedra made a little whimpering sound and began to remove the bedding from the cradle.

'That's better. Now listen to me. You must ignore him when he tells you things like this. He is not your friend.'

Ce'Nedra's face grew puzzled. 'He isn't?'

'He's your enemy. *He* is the one who wants to hurt Geran.'

'My baby?'

'Your baby's all right, Ce'Nedra, but you have to fight this voice that comes to you in the night.'

'Who—?' Garion started, but then the woman turned to look at him, and he broke off, his mouth agape with astonishment. The woman had tawny-colored hair and warm, golden eyes. Her dress was plain and brown, almost earth-colored. Garion knew her. He had met her once before on the moors of eastern Drasnia when he and Belgarath and Silk had been on their way to that dreadful meeting in the haunted ruins of Cthol Mishrak.

Aunt Pol's mother closely resembled her daughter. Her face had that same calm, flawless beauty, and her head that same proud, erect carriage. There was about this timeless face, however, a strange, almost eternal kind of regret that caught at Garion's throat. 'Poledra!' he gasped. 'What—?'

Aunt Pol's mother put one finger to her lips. 'Don't wake her, Belgarion,' she cautioned. 'Let's get her back to bed.'

'Geran—?'

'He's all right. I arrived in time. Just lead her gently back to bed. She'll sleep now without any more of these adventures.'

Garion went to his wife's side and put his arm about her shoulders. 'Come along now, Ce'Nedra,' he said gently to her.

She nodded, her eyes still vacant, and obediently went with him back into the royal bedroom.

'Could you pull back that bolster for me?' he quietly asked Poledra.

She laughed. 'As a matter of fact, I can't,' she said. 'You forget that I'm not really here, Belgarion.'

'Oh,' he said. 'I'm sorry. It just seemed —' He pushed the bolster out of the way, carefully laid Ce'Nedra in bed, and pulled the coverlets up around her chin. She sighed and snuggled down to sleep.

'Let's go into the other room,' Poledra suggested.

He nodded and quietly followed her into the adjoining

room which was still dimly lighted by the glowing embers of the dying fire. 'What was that all about?' he asked, softly closing the door.

'There's someone who hates and fears your son, Belgarion,' she told him gravely.

'He's only a baby,' Garion protested.

'His enemy fears him for what he may become—not for what he is now. It's happened that way before, you'll recall.'

'You mean when Asharak killed my parents?'

She nodded. 'He was actually trying to get at you.'

'But how can I protect Geran from his own mother? I mean—if this man can come to Ce'Nedra in her sleep like that and make her do things, how can I possibly—?'

'It won't happen again, Belgarion. I took care of that.'

'But how could you? I mean, you're—well —'

'Dead? That's not altogether accurate, but no matter. Geran is safe for the moment, and Ce'Nedra won't do this again. There's something else we need to discuss.'

'All right.'

'You're getting very close to something important. I can't tell you everything, but you *do* need to look at the Mrin Codex—the real one, not one of the copies. You must see what's hidden there.'

'I can't leave Ce'Nedra—not now.'

'She's going to be all right, and this is something that only you can do. Go to that shrine on the River Mrin and look at the Codex. It's desperately important.'

Garion squared his shoulders. 'All right,' he said. 'I'll leave in the morning.'

'One other thing.'

'What?'

'You must take the Orb with you.'

'The Orb?'

'You won't be able to see what you have to see without it.'

'I don't quite understand.'

'You will when you get there.'

'All right, Poledra,' he said. Then he made a rueful face.

'I don't know why I'm objecting. I've been doing things I didn't understand all my life now.'

'Everything will become clear in time,' she assured him. Then she looked at him rather critically. 'Garion,' she said in a tone so like Aunt Pol's that he answered automatically.

'Yes?'

'You really shouldn't run around at night without a robe, you know. You'll catch cold.'

The ship he hired at Kotu was small, but well designed for river travel. It was a shallow-draft, broad-beamed little ship that sometimes bobbed like a chip of wood. The oarsmen were sturdy fellows and they made good time rowing against the sluggish current of the Mrin River as it meandered its slow way through the fens.

By nightfall they were ten leagues upriver from Kotu, and the captain prudently moored his ship to a dead snag with one of the tar-smeared hawsers. 'It's not a good idea to try to find the channel in the dark,' he told Garion. 'One wrong turn and we could spend the next month wandering around in the fens.'

'You know what you're doing, Captain,' Garion told him. 'I'm not going to interfere.'

'Would you like a tankard of ale, your Majesty?' the captain offered.

'That might not be a bad idea,' Garion agreed.

Later, he leaned against the railing with his tankard in hand, watching the darting lights of the fireflies and listening to the endless chorus of the frogs. It was a warm spring night, and the damp, rich odor of the fens filled his nostrils.

He heard a faint splash, a fish maybe, or perhaps a diving otter.

'Belgarion?' It was a strange, piping kind of voice, but it was quite distinct. It was also coming from the other side of the railing.

Garion peered out into the velvet darkness.

'Belgarion?' The voice came again. It was somewhere below him.

'Yes?' Garion answered cautiously.

'I need to tell you something.' There was another small splash, and the ship rocked slightly. The hawser that moored her to the snag dipped, and a scampering shadow ran quickly up it and slid over the railing in a curiously fluid way. The shadow stood up, and Garion could clearly hear the water dripping from it. The figure was short, scarcely more than four feet tall, and it moved toward Garion with a peculiarly shuffling gait.

'You are older,' it said.

'That happens,' Garion replied, peering at the form as he tried to make out its face. Then the moon slid out from behind a cloud, and Garion found himself staring directly into the furry, wide-eyed face of a fenling. 'Tupik?' he asked incredulously. 'Is that you?'

'You remember.' The small, furry creature seemed pleased.

'Of course I remember.'

The ship rocked again, and another furry shadow ran up the hawser. Tupik turned with irritation. 'Poppi!' he chittered angrily. 'Go home!'

'No,' she answered quite calmly.

'You must do as I say!' he told her, stamping his feet on the deck.

'Why?'

Tupik stared at her in obvious frustration. 'Are they all like that?' he demanded of Garion.

'All what?'

'Females.' Tupik said the word with a certain disgust.

'Most of them, yes.'

Tupik sighed.

'How is Vordai?' Garion asked them.

Poppi made a peculiarly disconsolate whimpering sound. 'Our mother is gone,' she said sadly.

'I'm sorry.'

'She was very tired,' Tupik said.

'We covered her with flowers,' Poppi said. 'And then we closed up her house.'

'She would have liked that.'

'She said that one day you would come back,' Tupik told him. 'She was very wise.'

'Yes.'

'She said that we should wait until you came and then we were to give you a message.'

'Oh?'

'There is an evil that moves against you.'

'I was beginning to suspect that.'

'Mother said to tell you that the evil has many faces and that the faces do not always agree, but that which is behind it all has no face and that it comes from much farther than you think.'

'I don't quite follow.'

'It is from beyond the stars.'

Garion stared at him.

'That is what we were told to say,' Poppi assured him. 'Tupik said it exactly as mother told it to him.'

'Tell Belgarath about mother,' Tupik said then. 'And tell him that she sent him her thanks.'

'I will.'

'Good-bye, Belgarion,' the fenling said. Poppi made a small, affectionate sound in her throat, pattered over, and nuzzled briefly at Garion's hand.

And then the two of them slipped over the side and vanished in the dark waters of the fens.

Chapter Sixteen

It was a dreary-looking place. The village huddled on the river bank at the edge of a flat, featureless plain covered with coarse, dark-green grass. The underlying soil was alluvial clay, slick, gray, and unwholesome looking, and just beyond the wide bend in the Mrin River lay the endless green and brown expanse of the fens. The village itself consisted of perhaps two dozen dun-colored houses, huddled all together about the square stone structure of the shrine. Rickety docks, constructed of bone-white driftwood, stuck out into the river like skeletal fingers, and fishing nets hung on poles, drying and smelling in the humid, mosquito-infested air.

Garion's ship arrived about noon, and he went immediately up from the creaking dock along the muddy, rutted street to the shrine itself, walking carefully to avoid slipping, and feeling the curious stares of the dull-eyed villagers directed at him and at the great sword of the Rivan King strapped to his back.

The priests of Belar who guarded the shrine were obsequious, almost fawning, when he arrived at the tarnished bronze gates and requested entry. They led him through a flagstone-covered courtyard, pointing proudly at the rotting kennel and the stout, tar-smeared post with its fragment of heavy, rusting chain where the mad prophet of Mrin had spent his last days.

Within the shrine itself stood the customary altar with its great carved-stone bearhead. Garion noted that the interior of the shrine stood in need of a good cleaning and that the priest-guardians themselves were rumpled and unwashed. One of the first manifestations of religious enthusiasm, he had noted, was a powerful aversion to soap and water. Holy places—and those who attended them—always seemed to smell bad.

There was some small problem when they reached the vaulted sanctorum where the yellowed parchment scroll of the original Mrin Codex lay in its crystal case with two man-high candles flanking it. One of the priests, a wild-eyed fanatic whose hair and beard resembled a wind-ravaged strawstack, objected shrilly—almost hysterically—when Garion politely requested that the case be opened. The ranking priest, however, was enough of a politician to recognize the pre-eminent claim of the Rivan King—particularly since he bore Aldur's Orb—to examine any holy object he pleased. Garion realized once again that, in a peculiar way, he himself was a holy object in the minds of many Alorns.

The fanatic at last retreated, muttering the word 'blasphemy' over and over again. The crystal case was opened with a rusty iron key, and a small table and chair were brought into the circle of candlelight so that Garion might examine the Codex.

'I think I can manage now, your Reverences,' he told them rather pointedly. He did not like having people read over his shoulder and he felt no particular need of company. He sat at the table, put his hand on the scroll, and looked directly at the little clot of priests. 'I'll call if I need anything,' he added.

Their expressions were disapproving, but the overpowering presence of the Rivan King made them too timid to protest his peremptory dismissal; they quietly filed out, leaving him alone with the scroll.

Garion was excited. The solution to the problem that had plagued him for all these months lay at last in his hands. With nervous fingers, he untied the silken cord and began to unroll the crackling parchment. The script was archaic, but gorgeously done. The individual letters had not so much been written as they had been meticulously drawn. He perceived almost at once that an entire lifetime had been devoted to the production of this single manuscript. His hands actually trembling with his eagerness, Garion carefully unrolled the scroll, his eyes running over the now-familiar words and phrases, searching for the line that would once and for all clear up the mystery.

And there it was! Garion stared at it incredulously, not believing what he saw. The blot was exactly the same as it was on all the copies. He almost screamed with frustration.

With a sick feeling of defeat, he read once again that fatal line: 'And the Child of Light shall meet with the Child of Dark and shall overcome him, and the Darkness shall flee. But behold, the Stone which lies at the center of the Light shall —' And there was that accursed blot again.

A peculiar thing happened as he read it again. An odd sort of indifference seemed to come over him. Why was he making such a fuss about a single blotted word? What difference could one word make? He almost rose from his chair with the intention of putting the scroll back in its case and leaving this foul-smelling place for home. Then he stopped quite suddenly, remembering all the hours he had spent trying to puzzle out the meaning of that blot on the page. Perhaps it wouldn't hurt to read it one more time. He had, after all, come a very long way.

He started over again, but his distaste became so acute that he could hardly stand it. Why was he wasting his time with this nonsense? He had traveled all this way to wear out his eyes on this moldering scrap of insane gibberish—this stinking, half-rotten sheet of poorly tanned sheepskin. He shoved the Codex away in disgust. This was sheer idiocy. He pushed back the chair and stood up, shifting Iron-grip's great sword on his back. His ship would still be there, moored to that rickety dock. He could be halfway to Kotu by nightfall and back at Riva within the week. He would lock the library once and for all and tend to his business. A king, after all, did not have time for all this idle, brainsickly speculation. Decisively, he turned his back on the scroll and started toward the door.

As soon as he was no longer looking at the scroll, however, he stopped. What was he doing? The puzzle was still there. He had made no effort to solve it. He *had* to find out. But as he turned back and looked at the scroll again, that same wave of insupportable disgust almost overwhelmed him. It was so strong that it made him feel faint. Once again he turned his back, and once again the feeling vanished. There was something about the scroll itself that was trying to drive him away.

He began to pace up and down, carefully keeping his eyes away from the scroll. What had the dry voice in his mind told him? 'There are several words there. If you look at them in the right kind of light, you should be able to see them.' *What* kind of light? The candles in this vaulted room obviously weren't what the voice had meant. Sunlight? That hardly seemed likely. Poledra had said that he *must* read the hidden words, but how could he, when the Codex literally drove him away each time he looked at it?

Then he stopped. What else had she said? Something about not being able to see without . . .

The wave of disgust which struck him was so strong that he felt his stomach constrict. He spun quickly so that his back was toward that hateful document; as he did so, the hilt of Iron-grip's sword jabbed him painfully in the side of the head. Angrily he reached over his shoulder to grasp the handle and push it back, but instead, his hand touched the Orb. The feeling of revulsion evaporated instantly, and his mind became clear, and his thoughts lucid. The light! Of course! He had to read the Codex by the light of the Orb! That is what both Poledra and the dry voice had been trying to tell him. Awkwardly, he reached up and back, seizing the Orb. 'Come off,' he muttered to it. With a faint click, the Orb came free in his hand. The sudden weight of the huge sword strapped across his back very nearly drove him to his knees. In astonishment, he realized that the seeming weightlessness of the great weapon had been the work of the Orb itself. Struggling under that gross weight, he fumbled with the buckle at his chest, unfastened it, and felt the enormous bulk slide free. Iron-grip's sword fell to the floor with a loud clatter.

Holding the Orb in front of him, Garion turned and looked directly at the scroll. He could almost hear an angry snarl hovering in the air, but his mind remained clear. He stepped to the table and pulled the scroll open with one hand, holding the glowing Orb above it with the other.

At last he saw the meaning of the blot that had frustrated him for so long. It was not some random splotch of spilled ink. The message was there—all of it, but the words had all been written down on top of one another! The entire prophecy lay in that one single spot! By the blue, unwavering light of Aldur's Orb, his eyes seemed actually to plunge down and down beneath the surface of the parchment, and the words, hidden for eons, rose like bubbles out of the substance of the scroll.

'But Behold,' the crucial passage read, 'the Stone which lies at the center of the Light shall burn red, and my voice shall speak unto the Child of Light and reveal the name of the Child of Dark. And the Child of Light will take up the Guardian's sword and go forth to seek out that which is hidden. Long will be his quest, and it shall be threefold. And ye shall know that the quest hath begun when the Keeper's Line is renewed. Guard well the seed of the Keeper, for there shall be no other. Guard it well, for should that seed fall into the hands of the Child of Dark and be taken to the place where the evil dwells, then blind choice alone can decide the outcome. Should the Keeper's seed be reft away, then must the Beloved and Eternal lead the way. And he shall find the path to the place where the evil dwells in the Mysteries. And in each Mystery shall lie but a part of the path, and he must find them all—all— or the path will lead awry, and the Dark shall triumph. Hasten therefore to the meeting where the three-fold quest will end. And this meeting will come to pass in a place which is no more, and there will the choice be made.'

Garion read it again, and then a third time, feeling an ominous chill as the words echoed and thundered through his consciousness. Finally he rose and went to the door of the candlelit, vaulted chamber. 'I'll need something to write with,' he told the priest standing just outside. 'And send someone down to the river. Have him tell the captain of my ship to get things ready. Just as soon as I finish here, I have to leave for Kotu.'

The priest was staring wide-eyed at the incandescently glowing Orb in Garion's hand. 'Don't just stand there, man, move!' Garion told him. 'The whole world's hanging on this!'

The priest blinked and then scurried away.

The following day, Garion was in Kotu, and about a day and a half later, he reached Aldurford in northern Algaria. As luck had it, a herd of half-wild Algarian cattle was being driven across that wide, shallow place in the mighty river on their way to Muros, and Garion went immediately in search of the herd master.

'I'm going to need two horses,' he said, skipping the customary courtesies. 'The best you have. I have to be in the Vale of Aldur before the week is out.'

The herd master, a fierce-looking Algar warrior in black leather, looked at him speculatively. 'Good horses are expensive, your Majesty,' he ventured, his eyes coming alight.

'That's beside the point. Please have them ready in a quarter of an hour—and throw some food in a saddlebag for me.'

'Doesn't your Majesty even want to discuss the price?' the herd master's voice betrayed his profound disappointment.

'Not particularly,' Garion told him. 'Just add it all up, and I'll pay it.'

The herd master sighed. 'Take them as a gift, your Majesty,' he said. Then he looked mournfully at the Rivan King. 'You *do* realize, of course, that you've absolutely ruined my whole afternoon.'

Garion gave him a tight, knowing grin. 'If I had the time, good herd master, I'd haggle with you for the whole day—right down to the last penny—but I have urgent business in the south.'

The herd master shook his head sadly.

'Don't take it so hard, my friend,' Garion told him. 'If you like, I'll curse your name to everyone I meet and tell them all how badly you cheated me.'

The herd master's eyes brightened. 'That would be extremely kind of your Majesty,' he said. He caught Garion's amused look. 'One *does* have a certain reputation to maintain, after all. The horses will be ready whenever you are. I'll select them for you myself.'

Garion made good time as he galloped south. He kept his horses fresh and strong by changing mounts every two or three leagues. The long journey in quest of the Orb had taught him many ways to conserve the strength of a good horse, and he utilized them all. When a steep hill stood in his path, he slowed to a walk and made up the lost time on the long downhill slope on the other side. When he could, he went around rough terrain. He stopped for the night late and was on the move again at first light in the morning.

Steadily he moved south through the knee-high sea of waving prairie grass lying lush and green under the warm spring sun. He avoided the man-made mountain of the Algarian Stronghold, knowing that King Cho-Hag and Queen Silar, and certainly Hettar and Adara, would insist that he stop over for a day or so. Regretfully, he also passed a league or so to the west of Poledra's cottage. He hoped that there would be time later to visit Aunt Pol, Durnik, and Errand. Right now he had to get to Belgarath with the passage of the Codex he had so carefully copied and which now rode in the inside pocket of his doublet.

When at last he arrived at Belgarath's squat, round tower, his legs were so tired that they trembled under him as he swung down from his lathered horse. He went immediately to the large, flat-faced rock that was the door to the tower. 'Grandfather!' he shouted at the windows above, 'Grandfather, it's me!'

There was no answer. The squat tower loomed silently

up out of the tall grass, etched sharply against the sky. Garion had not even considered the possibility that the old man might not be here. 'Grandfather!' he called again. There was still no answer. A red-winged blackbird swooped in, landed atop the tower, and peered curiously down at Garion. Then it began to preen its feathers.

Almost sick with disappointment, Garion stared at the silent rock that always swung aside for Belgarath. Although he knew that it was a serious breach of etiquette, he pulled in his concentration, looked at the rock, and said, 'Open.'

The stone gave a startled little lurch and swung obediently aside. Garion went in and quickly mounted the stairs, remembering at the last instant to step up over the one where the loose stone still lay unrepaired. 'Grandfather!' he called up the stairway.

'Garion?' the old man's voice coming from above sounded startled. 'Is that you?'

'I called,' Garion said, coming up into the cluttered, round room at the top of the stairs. 'Didn't you hear me?'

'I was concentrating on something,' the old man replied. 'What's the matter? What are you doing here?'

'I finally found that passage,' Garion told him.

'What passage?'

'The one in the Mrin Codex—the one that was missing.'

Belgarath's expression grew suddenly tense, even wary. 'What are you talking about, boy? There's no missing passage in the Mrin Codex.'

'We talked about it at Riva. Don't you remember? It's the place where there's that blot on the page. I pointed it out to you.'

Belgarath's look grew disgusted. 'You came here and interrupted me over *that*?' His tone was scathing.

Garion stared at him. This was not the Belgarath he knew. The old man had never treated him so coldly before. 'Grandfather,' he said, 'what's wrong with you? This is very important. Somebody has somehow obscured a part of the Codex. When you read it, there's a part you don't see.'

'But *you* can see it?' Belgarath said in a voice filled almost with contempt. '*You*? A boy who couldn't even read until he was almost grown? The rest of us have been studying that Codex for thousands of years, and now you come along and tell us that we've been missing something?'

'Listen to me, Grandfather. I'm trying to explain. When you come to that place, something happens to your mind. You don't pay any attention to it because, for some reason, you don't want to.'

'Nonsense!' Belgarath snorted. 'I don't need some rank beginner trying to tell *me* how to study.'

'Won't you at least look at what I found?' Garion begged, taking the parchment out of his inside pocket and holding it out.

'No!' Belgarath shouted, slapping the parchment away. 'Take that nonsense away from me. Get out of my tower, Garion!'

'Grandfather!'

'Get out of here!' The old man's face was pale with anger, and his eyes flashed.

Garion was so hurt by his grandfather's words that tears actually welled up in his eyes. How could Belgarath talk to him this way?

The old man became even more agitated. He began to pace up and down, muttering angrily to himself. 'I have work to do—important work—and you come bursting in here with this wild tale about something being missing. How dare you? How dare you interrupt me with this idiocy? Don't you know who I am?' He gestured at the parchment Garion had picked up and was holding again. 'Get that disgusting thing out of my sight!'

And then Garion suddenly understood. Whatever or whoever it was that was trying to conceal the words hidden in that strange blot of ink was growing desperate, driving Belgarath into this uncharacteristic rage to keep him from reading the passage. There was only one way to break that strange compulsion not to see. Garion laid the parchment on a table, then coldly and deliberately unbuckled the heavy belt running across his chest, removed Iron-grip's sword from his back, and stood it against the wall. He put his hand to the Orb on the pommel of the sword and said, 'Come off.' The Orb came free in his hand, glowing at his touch.

'What are you doing?' Belgarath demanded of him.

'I'm going to have to *make* you see what I'm talking about, Grandfather,' Garion said unhappily. 'I don't want to hurt you, but you have to look.' He walked slowly and deliberately toward Belgarath, the Orb extended before him.

'Garion,' Belgarath said, backing away apprehensively, 'be careful with that.'

'Go to the table, Grandfather,' Garion told him grimly. 'Go to the table and read what I found.'

'Are you threatening me?' Belgarath demanded incredulously.

'Just do it, Grandfather.'

'We don't behave this way toward each other, Garion,' the old man said, still backing away from the glowing Orb.

'The table,' Garion repeated. 'Go over there and read.'

Sweat was standing out on Belgarath's forehead. Reluctantly, almost as if it were causing him some obscure kind of pain, he went to the table and bent over the parchment sheet. Then he shook his head. 'I can't see it,' he declared, though a burning candle stood right beside the sheet. 'It's too dark in here.'

'Here,' Garion said, reaching forth with the glowing Orb, 'I'll light it for you.' The Orb flared, and its blue light fell across the sheet and filled the room. 'Read it, Grandfather,' Garion said implacably.

Belgarath stared at him with an almost pleading expression. 'Garion —'

'Read it.'

Belgarath dropped his eyes to the page lying before him, and suddenly he gasped. 'Where—? How did you get this?'

'It was under that blot. Can you see it now?'

'Of course I can see it.' Excitedly Belgarath picked

up the sheet and read it again. His hands were actually trembling. 'Are you sure this is exactly what it said?'

'I copied it word for word, Grandfather—right off the original scroll.'

'How were you able to see it?'

'The same way you are—by the light of the Orb. Somehow that makes it clear.'

'Astonishing,' the old man said. 'I wonder —' He went quickly to a cabinet standing by the wall, rummaged around for a moment, and then came back to the table with a scroll in his hands. He quickly unrolled it. 'Hold the Orb closer, boy,' he said.

Garion held out the Orb and watched with his grandfather as the buried words slowly rose to the surface just as they had in the shrine.

'Absolutely amazing,' Belgarath marveled. 'It's blurred, and some of the words aren't clear, but it's there. It's all there. How is it possible that none of us noticed this before —and how did *you* discover it?'

'I had help, Grandfather. The voice told me that I had to read it in a certain kind of light.' He hesitated, knowing how much pain what he had to say would cause the old man. 'And then, Poledra came to visit us.'

'Poledra?' Belgarath spoke his wife's name with a little catch in his voice.

'Someone was making Ce'Nedra do something in her sleep—something very dangerous—and Poledra came and stopped her. Then she told me that I had to go to the shrine in Drasnia and read the Codex and she specifically told me to take the Orb along. When I got there and started reading, I almost left. It all seemed so stupid somehow. Then I remembered what they had told me and I put it together. As soon as I started reading by the light of the Orb, that feeling that I was wasting my time disappeared. Grandfather, what causes that? I thought it was only me, but it affected you, too.'

Belgarath thought a moment, frowning. 'It was an interdiction,' he explained finally. 'Someone at some time put his will to that one spot and made it so repulsive that no one could even see it.'

'But it's right there—even on your copy. How is it that the scribe who copied it could see it well enough to write it down, but we couldn't?'

'Many of the scribes in the old days were illiterate,' Belgarath explained. 'You don't have to be able to read in order to copy something. All those scribes were doing was drawing exact duplicates of the letters on the page.'

'But this—what was it you called it?'

'Interdiction. It's a fancy word for what happens. I think Beldin invented it. He's terribly impressed by his own cleverness sometimes.'

'The interdiction made the scribes pile all the words on top of each other—even though they didn't know what the words meant?'

Belgarath grunted, his eyes lost in thought. 'Whoever did this is very strong—and very subtle. I didn't even suspect that someone was tampering with my mind.'

'When did it happen?'

'Probably at the same time the Mrin Prophet was speaking the words originally.'

'Would the interdiction keep working after the person who caused it was dead?'

'No.'

'Then —'

'Right. He's still around somewhere.'

'Could it be this Zandramas we keep hearing about?'

'That's possible, I suppose.' Belgarath picked up the sheet Garion had copied. 'I can see it by ordinary light now,' he said. 'Apparently once you break the interdiction for somebody, it stays broken.' He carefully read the sheet again. 'This is really important, Garion.'

'I was fairly sure it was,' Garion replied. 'I don't understand it all, though. The first part is fairly simple—the part about the Orb turning red and the name of the Child of Dark being revealed. It sort of looks as if I'm going to have to make another one of those trips.'

'A long one, if this is right.'

278

'What's this next part mean?'

'Well, as nearly as I can make it out, this quest of yours —whatever it is—has already started. It began when Geran was born.' The old man frowned. 'I don't like this part that says that blind choice might make the decision, though. That's the sort of thing that makes me very nervous.'

'Who is the Beloved and Eternal?'

'Probably me.'

Garion looked at him.

Belgarath shrugged. 'It's a little ostentatious,' he admitted, 'but some people do call me "the Eternal Man"— and when my Master changed my name, he added the syllable "Bel" to my old one. In the old language "Bel" meant "beloved."' He smiled a bit sadly. 'My Master had a way with words sometimes.'

'What are these mysteries it talks about?'

'It's an archaic term. In the old days they used the word "mystery" instead of "prophecy." As cryptic as some of them are, it sort of makes sense, I guess.'

'Ho! Garion! Belgarath!' The voice came to them from outside the tower.

'Who's that?' Belgarath asked. 'Did you tell anybody you were coming here?'

'No,' Garion frowned, 'not really.' He went to the window and looked down. A tall, hawk-faced Algar with a flowing black scalp lock sat astride a lathered and exhausted-looking horse. 'Hettar!' Garion called down to him, 'What's the matter?'

'Let me in, Garion,' Hettar replied. 'I have to talk with you.'

Belgarath joined Garion at the window. 'The door's around on the other side,' he called down. 'I'll open it for you. Be careful of the stone on that fifth step,' he cautioned, as the tall man started around the tower. 'It's loose.'

'When are you going to fix that, Grandfather?' Garion asked. He felt the faint, familiar surge as the old man opened the door.

'Oh, I'll get to it one of these days.'

Hettar's hawklike face was bleak as he came up into the round room at the top of the tower.

'What's all the urgency, Hettar?' Garion asked. 'I've never seen you ride a horse into the ground like that.'

Hettar took a deep breath. 'You've got to go back to Riva immediately, Garion,' he said.

'Is something wrong there?' Garion asked, a sudden chill coming over him.

Hettar sighed. 'I hate to be the one to have to tell you this, Garion, but Ce'Nedra sent word for me to get you as fast as I possibly could. You've got to go back to Riva at once.'

Garion steeled himself, a dozen dreadful possibilities arising in his imagination. 'Why?' he asked quietly.

'I'm sorry, Garion—more sorry than I can possibly say —but Brand has been murdered.'

Part Three

ALORIA

CHEREK

Jarviksholm

Val Alorn

Gulf
of
Cherek

The Bore

Kotu

The Fens

Aldurford

ISLE
OF THE
WINDS

Riva

Arctic Circle

DRASNIA

Rheon

Mrin R.

Boktor

North Caravan Route

Lake
Atun

North Road

ALGARIA

Aldur River

The Stronghold

The Escarpment

The Vale of Aldur

ALORIA

Being

ISLE OF THE WINDS,

CHEREK, DRASNIA,

and

ALGARIA

SHELLY
SHAPIRO

Chapter Seventeen

Lieutenant Bledik was one of those sober-minded young Sendarian officers who took everything very seriously. He arrived at the Lion Inn in the port city of Camaar promptly on time and was escorted upstairs by the aproned innkeeper. The rooms in which Garion and the others were staying were airy and well-furnished and looked out over the harbor. Garion stood at the window holding aside one of the green drapes and looking out as if it might be possible to penetrate all those leagues of open water and see what was happening at Riva.

'You sent for me, your Majesty?' Bledik asked with a respectful bow.

'Ah, Lieutenant, come in,' Garion said, turning from the window. 'I have an urgent message for King Fulrach. How fast do you think you can get to Sendar?'

The lieutenant considered it. One look at his sober face told Garion that the young man always considered everything. Bledik pursed his lips, absently adjusting the collar of his scarlet uniform. 'If I ride straight through and change horses at every hostel along the way, I can be at the palace by late tomorrow afternoon.'

'Good,' Garion said. He handed the young officer the folded and sealed letter to the Sendarian king. 'When you see King Fulrach, tell him that I've sent Lord Hettar of Algaria to all of the Alorn Kings to tell them that I'm calling a meeting of the Alorn Council at Riva and that I'd like to have him there as well.'

'Yes, your Majesty.'

'And tell him that the Rivan Warder has been murdered.'

Bledik's eyes widened, and his face went pale. 'No!' he gasped. 'Who was responsible?'

'I don't know any of the details yet, but, as soon as we can hire a ship, we're going across to the island.'

'Garion, dear,' Polgara said from her chair by the window, 'you explained everything in the letter. The lieutenant has a long way to go, and you're delaying him.'

'You're probably right, Aunt Pol,' he admitted. He turned back to Bledik. 'Will you need any money or anything?' he asked.

'No, your Majesty.'

'You'd better get started then.'

'At once, your Majesty.' The lieutenant saluted and went out.

Garion began to pace up and down on the costly Mallorean carpet while Polgara, dressed in a plain blue traveling gown, continued to mend one of Errand's tunics, her needle flashing in the sunlight streaming through the window. 'How can you be so calm?' he demanded of her.

'I'm not, dear,' she replied. 'That's why I'm sewing.'

'What's taking them so long?' he fretted.

'Hiring a ship takes time, Garion. It's not exactly like buying a loaf of bread.'

'Who could possibly have wanted to hurt Brand?' he burst out. He had asked that same question over and over in the week or more since they had left the Vale. The big, sad-faced Warder had been so totally devoted to Garion and the Rivan Throne that he had possessed virtually no separate identity. So far as Garion knew, Brand had not had an enemy in the world.

'That's one of the first things we'll want to find out when we get to Riva,' she said. 'Now please try to calm yourself. Pacing about doesn't accomplish anything and it's very distracting.'

It was almost evening when Belgarath, Durnik, and Errand returned, bringing with them a tall, gray-haired

Rivan whose clothing carried those distinctive smells of salt-water and tar that identified him as a sailor.

'This is Captain Jandra,' Belgarath introduced him. 'He's agreed to ferry us across to the Isle.'

'Thank you, Captain,' Garion said simply.

'My pleasure, your Majesty,' Jandra replied with a stiff bow.

'Have you just come in from Riva?' Polgara asked him.

'Yesterday afternoon, my Lady.'

'Have you any idea at all about what happened there?'

'We didn't get too many details down at the harbor, my Lady. Sometimes the people up at the Citadel are sort of secretive—no offense, your Majesty. There are all kinds of rumors going about the city, though—most of them pretty farfetched. About all I can say for certain is that the Warder was attacked and killed by a group of Chereks.'

'*Chereks!*' Garion exclaimed.

'Everyone agrees on that point, your Majesty. Some people say that all the assassins were killed. Others say that there were some survivors. I couldn't really say for sure, but I know that they *did* bury six of them.'

'Good,' Belgarath grunted.

'Not if there were only six to begin with, father,' Polgara told him. 'We need answers, not bodies.'

'Uh—pardon me, your Majesty,' Jandra said a little uncomfortably. 'It might not be my place to say this, but some of the rumors in the city say that the Chereks were officials of some kind from Val Alorn and that they were sent by King Anheg.'

'Anheg? That's absurd.'

'That's what some people are saying, your Majesty. I don't put much stock in it myself, but it might just be the kind of talk you wouldn't want going much further. The Warder was well-liked in Riva, and a lot of people have taken to polishing their swords—if you take my meaning.'

'I think I'd better get home as soon as possible,' Garion said. 'How long will it take us to get to Riva?'

The captain thought it over. 'My ship isn't as fast as a Cherek warship,' he apologized. 'Let's say three days—if the weather holds. We can leave on the morning tide, if you can be ready.'

'We'll do that, then,' Garion said.

It was late summer on the Sea of the Winds, and the weather held clear and sunny. Jandra's ship plowed steadily through the sparkling, sun-touched waves, heeling to one side under a quartering wind. Garion spent most of the voyage pacing moodily up and down the deck. When, on the third day out from Camaar, the jagged shape of the Isle of the Winds appeared low on the horizon ahead, a kind of desperate impatience came over him. There were so many questions that had to be answered and so many things that had to be done that even the hour or so that it would take to reach the harbor seemed an intolerable delay.

It was midafternoon when Jandra's ship rounded the headland at the harbor mouth and made for the stone quays at the foot of the city. 'I'm going on ahead,' Garion told the others. 'Follow me as soon as you can.' And even as the sailors were making fast the hawsers, he leaped across to the salt-crusted stones of the quay and started up toward the Citadel, taking the steps two at a time.

Ce'Nedra was waiting for him at the massive main doors of the Citadel, garbed in a black mourning dress. Her face was pale, and her eyes full of tears. 'Oh, Garion,' she cried as he reached her. She threw her arms about his neck and began to sob against his chest.

'How long ago did it happen, Ce'Nedra?' he asked, holding her in his arms. 'Hettar didn't have too many details.'

'It was about three weeks ago,' she sobbed. 'Poor Brand. That poor, dear man.'

'Do you know where I can find Kail?'

'He's been working at Brand's desk,' she replied. 'I don't think he's slept for more than a few hours any night since it happened.'

'Aunt Pol and the others should be along shortly. I'm going to talk with Kail. Would you bring them as soon as they get here?'

'Of course, dear,' she replied, wiping her eyes with the back of her hand.

'We'll talk later,' he said. 'Right now I've got to find out what happened.'

'Garion,' she said gravely, 'they were Chereks.'

'That's what I'd heard,' he said, 'and that's why I've got to get to the bottom of this as quickly as possible.'

The corridors of the Citadel were muted and oddly silent. As Garion strode toward that group of rooms in the west wing from which Brand had always conducted the day-to-day business of the kingdom, the servants and functionaries he encountered bowed soberly and stood aside for him.

Kail was dressed in deepest black, and his face was gray with fatigue and deep sorrow. The orderly stacks of documents on the top of Brand's heavy desk, however, gave evidence that despite his grief he had been working not only at his own duties but at his father's as well. He looked up as Garion entered the room and started to rise.

'Don't,' Garion said. 'We have too much to do for formalities.' He looked at his weary friend. 'I'm sorry, Kail,' he said sadly. 'I'm more sorry than I can possibly tell you.'

'Thank you, your Majesty.'

Garion sank into the chair across the desk from him, his own weariness coming over him in a wave. 'I haven't been able to get any details,' he said. 'Could you tell me exactly what happened?'

Kail nodded and leaned back in his chair. 'It was about a month ago,' he began, 'not long after you left for Drasnia. A trade deputation from King Anheg arrived. All their credentials seemed to be in order, but they were a bit vague about exactly what the purpose of their visit was. We extended them the customary courtesies, and most of the time they stayed in the rooms we assigned them. Then, late one night, my father had been discussing some matters with Queen Ce'Nedra and was on his way back to his own quarters when he encountered them in the corridor leading to the royal apartments. He asked if he could help them, and they attacked him without any warning whatsoever.' Kail stopped, and Garion could see his jaws tightly clenched. He drew in a deep breath and passed one weary hand across his eyes. 'Your Majesty, my father wasn't even armed. He did his best to defend himself, and he was able to call for help before they cut him down. My brothers and I ran to his aid—along with several of the Citadel guards—and we did our best to capture the assassins, but they absolutely refused to surrender.' He frowned. 'It was almost as if they were deliberately throwing their lives away. We had no choice but to kill them.'

'All of them?' Garion asked with a sinking feeling in the pit of his stomach.

'All but one,' Kail replied. 'My brother, Brin, hit him across the back of the head with the butt of an axe. He's been unconscious ever since.'

'Aunt Pol's with me,' Garion said. 'She'll wake him— if anybody can.' His face went bleak. 'And when he *does* wake up, he and I are going to have a little talk.'

'I want some answers, too,' Kail agreed. He paused, his face troubled. 'Belgarion, they carried a letter from King Anheg. That's why we let them into the Citadel.'

'I'm sure there's a logical explanation.'

'I have the letter. It's over his seal and his signature.'

'I've called a meeting of the Alorn Council,' Garion told him. 'As soon as Anheg gets here, we'll be able to clear this up.'

'If he comes,' Kail added sombrely.

The door opened quietly, and Ce'Nedra led the others into the room.

'All right,' Belgarath said crisply, 'let's see if we can sort this out. Did any of them survive?'

'One, Ancient One,' Kail replied, 'but he's unconscious.'

'Where is he?' Polgara asked.

'We put him in a room in the north tower, my Lady. The physicians have been tending his injuries, but they haven't been able to revive him yet.'

'I'll go at once,' she said.

Errand crossed the room to where Kail sat and word-lessly laid a sympathetic hand on the young Rivan's shoulder. Kail's jaws clenched again, and tears suddenly welled up in his eyes.

'They had a letter from Anheg, Grandfather,' Garion told the old man. 'That's how they got inside the Citadel.'

'Do you have the letter anywhere?' Belgarath asked Kail.

'Yes, Ancient One. It's right here.' Kail began to leaf through a stack of documents.

'That seems to be the best place to start,' the old man said. 'The entire Alorn alliance is hanging on this, so we'd better get it straightened out fast.'

It was late evening by the time Polgara completed her examination of the lone surviving assassin. When she came into the royal apartment where the discussions had been continuing, her face was bleak. 'I'm sorry, but there's absolutely nothing I can do with him,' she reported. 'The entire back of his skull has been crushed. He's only barely alive; if I try to wake him, he'll die immediately.'

'I need some answers, Aunt Pol,' Garion said. 'How long do you think it's going to be until he wakes up?'

She shook her head. 'I doubt that he ever will—and even if he does, it's unlikely that he's going to be able to say anything coherent. About all that's holding his brains together right now is his scalp.'

He looked at her helplessly. 'Couldn't you—?'

'No, Garion. There's nothing left of his mind to work with.'

Two days later, King Cho-Hag, Chief of the Clan-Chiefs of the Algar horsemen, arrived, accompanied by Queen Silar and Adara, Garion's tall, dark-haired cousin. 'A very sad occasion,' Cho-Hag said to Garion in his quiet voice as they clasped hands on the quay.

'It seems lately that about the only time we all get together is to attend funerals,' Garion agreed. 'Where's Hettar?'

'I think he's at Val Alorn,' Cho-Hag replied. 'He'll probably come here with Anheg.'

'That's something we're going to have to talk about,' Garion said.

Cho-Hag lifted one eyebrow.

'The people who killed Brand were Chereks,' Garion explained quietly. 'They had a letter from Anheg.'

'Anheg could not have had anything to do with it,' Cho-Hag declared. 'He loved Brand like a brother. There had to be somebody else behind it.'

'I'm sure you're right, but there's a great deal of suspicion here in Riva right now. There are some people who are even talking war.'

Cho-Hag's face went grim.

'That's why we have to get to the truth in a hurry,' Garion told him. 'We've got to head that kind of thinking off before it gets completely out of hand.'

The next day King Fulrach of Sendaria arrived in the harbor; with him on their stout, broad-beamed ship was the one-armed General Brendig, the ancient but still-vigorous Earl of Seline and, surprisingly, Queen Layla herself, the lady whose fear of sea travel had become almost legendary. That same afternoon, Queen Porenn, still in deepest mourning for her husband, disembarked from the black-painted Drasnian vessel that had carried her from Boktor, along with her son, the boy-king Kheva and the bone-thin Margrave Khendon, the man known as Javelin.

'Oh, my dear Garion,' Porenn said, embracing him at the foot of the gangway. 'I cannot tell you how sorry I am.'

'We've all lost one of our dearest friends,' he replied. He turned to Kheva. 'Your Majesty,' he said with a formal bow.

'Your Majesty,' Kheva replied, also bowing.

'We heard that there's some mystery surrounding the assassination,' Porenn said. 'Khendon here is very good at clearing up mysteries.'

'Margrave,' Garion greeted the Drasnian Chief of Intelligence.

'Your Majesty,' Javelin responded. He turned and

extended one hand to a young woman with honey-blond hair and soft brown eyes who was coming down the gangway. 'You do remember my niece, don't you?'

'Margravine Liselle,' Garion greeted her.

'Your Majesty,' she replied with a formal curtsy. Although she was probably not even aware of it, the hint of a dimple in each of her cheeks gave her expression a slightly impish cast. 'My uncle has pressed me into service as his secretary. He pretends failing eyesight, but I think perhaps it's just an excuse to avoid giving me a genuine assignment. Older relatives tend to be overprotective sometimes, don't you think?'

Garion smiled briefly. 'Has anyone heard from Silk?' he asked.

'He's at Rheon,' Javelin replied, 'trying to gather information about the activities of the Bear-cult. We've sent messengers, but sometimes he can be hard to find. I expect he'll be along soon, though.'

'Has Anheg arrived yet?' Queen Porenn asked.

Garion shook his head. 'Cho-hag and Fulrach are here, but there's no word from Anheg yet.'

'We've heard that some people suspect him,' the little blond queen said. 'It simply cannot be true, Garion.'

'I'm sure he'll be able to explain everything as soon as he arrives.'

'Did any of the assassins survive?' Javelin asked.

'One,' Garion told him, 'but I'm afraid that he won't be much help to us. One of Brand's sons bashed in his head. It doesn't appear that he's ever going to wake up.'

'Pity,' Javelin murmured briefly, 'but a man doesn't always have to be able to talk in order to provide information.'

'I hope you're right,' Garion said fervently.

The discussions at supper and later that evening were subdued. Though no one stated it openly, they were all reluctant to speak of the bleak possibility which faced them. To raise that question without Anheg's being present might have solidified the doubts and suspicions and given the entire meeting a tone none of them were willing to assume.

'When is Brand's funeral to be held?' Porenn asked quietly.

'As soon as Anheg arrives, I guess,' Garion replied.

'Have you made any decisions concerning his office?' Fulrach asked.

'I don't quite follow you.'

'The position of Warder originated a long time ago in order to fill the vacuum that existed after the Nyissans murdered King Gorek and his family. Now that you occupy the throne, do you really *need* a Warder?'

'To be honest with you, I hadn't really thought about it. Brand's always been here. He seemed as permanent as the stones of the Citadel itself.'

'Who's been doing his work since he was killed, your Majesty?' the silvery-haired old Earl of Seline asked.

'His second son, Kail.'

'You have many other responsibilities, Belgarion,' the Earl pointed out. 'You really do need someone here to manage the day-to-day details—at least until the present crisis has passed. I don't think, however, that any final decision about the post of Warder needs to be made just now. I'm sure that if you asked him, Kail would continue to perform his father's duties without a formal appointment.'

'He's right, Garion,' Ce'Nedra said. 'Kail's absolutely devoted to you. He'll do anything you ask him to do.'

'If this young man is doing an adequate job, it's probably best to let him continue,' Seline suggested. Then he smiled briefly. 'There's an old Sendarian adage that says, "If it isn't broken, don't try to fix it."'

The following morning an ungainly-looking ship with elaborate structures fore and aft wallowed into the harbor under an obviously top-heavy spread of sail. Garion, who stood atop the battlements of the Citadel talking quietly with Javelin, frowned as he looked down at it. 'What kind of ship is that?' he asked. 'I don't recognize the construction.'

'It's Arendish, your Majesty. They feel the need to make everything look like a castle.'

'I didn't know that the Arends even *had* any ships.'

'They don't have very many,' Javelin replied. 'Their vessels have a tendency to capsize whenever they encounter a stiff breeze.'

'I guess we'd better go down and see who it is.'

'Right,' Javelin agreed.

The passengers aboard the clumsy Arendish vessel proved to be old friends. Mandorallen, the mighty Baron of Vo Mandor, stood at the rail, gleaming in full armor. At his side stood Lelldorin of Wildantor, and with them were their wives, Nerina and Ariana, both ornately gowned in dark, rich brocades.

'We came instantly upon our receipt of the news of thy tragedy, Garion,' Mandorallen shouted across the intervening water as the Arendish crew laboriously maneuvered their awkward ship toward the quay upon which Garion and Javelin waited. 'Duty and affection, both for thee and thy foully murdered Warder, impell us to aid thee in thy rightful search for vengeance. Korodullin himself would have joined us but for an illness which hath laid him low.'

'I suppose I should have expected this,' Garion murmured.

'Are they likely to complicate matters?' Javelin asked quietly.

Garion shuddered. 'You have no idea.'

It was not until two days later that the *Seabird*, with Barak at the tiller, rounded the headland and sailed into the harbor. The rails were lined with burly Cherek warriors in chain-mail shirts. Their faces were alert, and their eyes were wary as Barak steered his ship up to the quay.

When Garion reached the foot of the long flight of stone steps leading down from the Citadel, a sizeable crowd had gathered. The mood of that crowd was ugly, and most of the men who stood there with grim faces had weapons at their sides.

'It looks as if we've got a situation on our hands here,'

Garion said quietly to Kail, who had accompanied him. 'I think we'd better try to put the best face on this meeting.'

Kail looked at the angry faces of the townspeople pressing toward the wharves. 'Perhaps you're right, Belgarion,' he agreed.

'We're going to have to put on a show of cordiality when we greet Anheg.'

'You ask a great deal, Belgarion.'

'I hate to put it this way, Kail, but I'm not *asking*. Those Chereks along the rail are Anheg's personal bodyguard. If anything starts here, there's going to be a lot of bloodshed—and probably the beginning of a war that none of us wants. Now smile, and let's go welcome the King of Cherek.'

To give it the best possible appearance, Garion led Kail up the gangway to the deck of Barak's ship so that his meeting with King Anheg could take place in full view of the angry crowd. Barak, clad in a formal green doublet and looking even larger than he had the last time Garion had seen him, strode down the deck to meet them. 'This is a very bleak time for us all,' he declared as he shook hands first with Garion and then with Kail. 'Anheg and Hettar are below with the ladies.'

'Ladies?' Garion asked.

'Islena and Merel.'

'You've heard the rumors?' Garion asked him.

Barak nodded. 'That's one of the reasons we brought our wives.'

'Good idea,' Garion said approvingly. 'A man who's coming someplace to pick a fight doesn't usually bring his wife along, and we all want to give this the best possible appearance.'

'I'll go down and get Anheg,' Barak said, casting a quick glance at the ugly crowd gathered at the foot of his gangway.

King Anheg's brutish, black-bearded face was haggard and drawn when he emerged from belowdecks in his usual blue robe.

'Anheg, my friend,' Garion said in a voice intended to

carry to the crowd. He hurried forward and caught the Cherek king in a rough embrace. 'I think we should smile,' he whispered. 'We want to let those people know that we're still the best of friends.'

'Are we, Garion?' Anheg asked in a subdued voice.

'Nothing has changed at all, Anheg,' Garion said firmly.

'Let's get on with this, then.' Anheg raised his voice. 'The royal house of Cherek extends its condolences to the Rivan Throne in this hour of grief,' he declared formally.

'Hypocrite!' a voice from the crowd bellowed.

Anheg's face went bleak, but Garion moved quickly to the rail, his eyes angry. 'Any man who insults my friend insults me,' he said in a dreadfully quiet voice. 'Does anyone here want to say anything to *me*?'

The crowd drew back nervously.

Garion turned back to Anheg. 'You look tired,' he said.

'I've been tearing the palace apart—and most of Val Alorn as well—ever since I heard about what happened, but I haven't been able to find a single clue.' The black-bearded Cherek king stopped and looked straight into Garion's face. His eyes had a pleading look in them. 'I swear to you, Garion, upon my life, that I had nothing whatsoever to do with the death of Brand.'

'I know that, Anheg,' Garion said simply. He glanced at the still-angry crowd. 'Maybe we'd better get Hettar and the ladies and go on up to the Citadel. The others are all there, and we want to get started.' He turned to Kail. 'As soon as we get there, I want you to send down some men to disperse these people. Have them seal off the foot of this quay. I don't want any trouble here.'

'Is it that bad?' Anheg asked very quietly.

'Just a precaution,' Garion said. 'I want to keep things under control until we get to the bottom of this.'

Chapter Eighteen

The funeral of Brand, the Rivan Warder, took place the following day in the Hall of the Rivan King. Garion, dressed all in black, sat on the basalt throne with Ce'Nedra at his side as the Rivan Deacon delivered the eulogy to the crowded Hall.

The presence of King Anheg of Cherek at that sorrowful ceremony caused an angry undertone among the members of the Rivan nobility, and it was only their profound respect for Brand and Garion's flinty gaze that prevented the whispers at the back of the Hall from becoming open accusations. Anheg, seated between Porenn and Cho-Hag, remained stony-faced throughout the services and he left the Hall immediately upon their conclusion.

'I've never seen him like this,' Barak said quietly to Garion after the ceremony. 'No one has ever accused him of murder before, and he doesn't know how to deal with it.'

'No one's accusing him now,' Garion replied quickly.

'Turn around and look at the faces of your subjects, Garion,' Barak said sadly. 'There's an accusation in every single eye.'

Garion sighed. 'I don't have to look. I know exactly what they're thinking.'

'When do you want to start the meetings?'

'Let's wait a bit,' Garion decided. 'I don't particularly want Anheg going through the corridors of the Citadel while all these mourners are drifting about with daggers in their belts.'

'Sound thinking,' Barak agreed.

They gathered about midafternoon in the blue-draped council chamber in the south tower. As soon as Kail had closed the door, Anheg rose and faced them. 'I want to state right at the outset that I had absolutely nothing to do with what happened here,' he declared. 'Brand was always one of my closest friends, and I'd have cut off my arm before I'd have hurt him. You have my word for that —both as a king and as an Alorn.'

'No one's accusing you of anything, Anheg,' Cho-Hag said quietly.

'Ha! I'm not nearly as stupid as I look, Cho-Hag—and even if I were, I still have ears. The people here in Riva have done everything short of spitting in my face.'

The silvery-haired Earl of Seline leaned back in his chair. 'I think perhaps that all of these suspicions—totally unfounded, of course—stem from that letter the assassins presented when they came here. Might it not be the quickest way to proceed to begin by examining that document?'

'Not a bad idea,' Garion said. He turned to Kail. 'Could we see the letter?'

'Ah—Ancient Belgarath has it, Sire,' Kail said.

'Oh—that's right,' Belgarath said. 'I'd almost forgotten.' He reached inside his gray tunic, drew out a folded parchment, and handed it to the old Sendarian nobleman.

'It looks more or less in order,' the Earl mused after he had read it.

'Let me see that,' Anheg demanded. He held the document distastefully, scowlng as he read. 'That's my signature, all right,' he admitted, 'and my seal, but I certainly didn't write this.'

Garion had a thought. 'Do you always read everything they bring you to sign?' he asked. 'I know that there are times when they bring me whole stacks of things to sign, and I just write my name at the bottom of each one. What I'm getting at is—could someone have slipped this into a pile of other documents so that you signed it without knowing what it said?'

Anheg shook his head. 'That happened to me once,' he

said. 'Now I read everything before I sign it. Not only that, I dictate every document I put my name to. That way I know it says exactly what I want it to say.' He thrust the letter toward Garion. 'Look at this,' he said, pointing at the second paragraph. '"Foreasmuch as trade is the lifeblood of both our kingdoms —" and so on. Blast it, Garion! I've never used the word "foreasmuch" in my entire life.'

'How do we reconcile this, then?' the Earl of Seline asked. 'We have authenticated the signature and seal. King Anheg declares that he not only reads everything he signs but that he also dictates every letter and proclamation personally. And yet we find textual inconsistencies in the document.'

'Seline,' Anheg said acidly, 'did you ever dabble in law? You sound a greal deal like a lawyer.'

The Earl laughed. 'Merely trying to be concise, your Majesty,' he said.

'I *hate* lawyers.'

The damning letter was central to the discussions for the remainder of the day, but nothing was resolved. Garion went wearily to bed that night as confused and filled with doubts as he had been when they started.

He slept badly and woke late. As he lay in the canopied royal bed, still trying to sort out his thoughts, he could hear voices coming from the adjoining room. Almost idly he began to identify those voices. Ce'Nedra was there, of course, and Aunt Pol. Queen Layla's giddy laugh made her easily identifiable. Nerina and Ariana, because of their Mimbrate dialect, were as easy. There were others as well, but the individuality of their voices was lost in the general chatter.

Garion slowly sat up, feeling almost as if he had not slept at all. He pushed the down-filled comforter aside and swung his feet to the floor. He did not really want to face this day. He sighed and stood up. Briefly he looked at the solid black doublet and hose he had worn the day before, then shook his head. To continue to dress in mourning might in some obscure way be taken as a silent accusation. That must be avoided at all costs. The situation involving King Anheg was so delicate at the moment that the slightest hint could push it into crisis. He crossed to the heavy wardrobe where he kept his clothes, selected one of his customary blue doublets, and began to dress.

The conversation in the adjoining room broke off suddenly at the sound of a knock on the door.

'Am I welcome here?' he heard Queen Islena ask in a subdued voice.

'Of course you are,' Aunt Pol replied.

'I had thought that —' Islena faltered, then began again. 'Considering everything, I had thought that perhaps it might be better if I stayed away.'

'Nonsense,' Queen Layla declared. 'Do come in, Islena.'

There was a general murmur of agreement.

'I swear to you all that my husband is innocent of this atrocity,' Islena said in a clear voice.

'No one is saying that he was not, Islena,' Aunt Pol replied quietly.

'Not openly perhaps, but there are ugly suspicions everywhere.'

'I'm certain that Garion and the others will get to the bottom of it,' Ce'Nedra said firmly. 'Then everything will be cleared up.'

'My poor Anheg did not sleep at all last night,' Islena told them sadly. 'I know that he looks brutish, but inside he's really very sensitive. This has hurt him deeply. Once he even cried.'

'Our lords will requite the tears thy husband hath shed upon the body of the foul villain who lurks behind this monstrous act,' the Baroness Nerina declared. 'And the foolish men who doubt his true fidelity shall be covered with shame for their lack of trust, once the truth is out.'

'I can only hope that you're right,' Islena said.

'This is a mournful topic, ladies,' Garion's cousin Adara told the rest of them, 'and it has nothing to do with the real reason we're all here.'

'And what reason is that, gentle Adara?' Ariana asked.

'The baby, Ariana,' Adara replied. 'We've come to see

your baby again, Ce'Nedra. I'm sure he's not still sleeping, so why don't you bring him in here so that we can all fuss over him?'

Ce'Nedra laughed. 'I thought you'd never ask.'

The council meeting began again about midmorning. The kings and their advisors gathered once more in the blue-draped council chamber. The golden sunlight of a late summer morning streamed in through the windows and a gentle sea breeze stirred the draperies. There was no particular formality in these sessions, and the monarchs and the others lounged comfortably in the velvet-upholstered chairs scattered about the room.

'I really don't think we'll accomplish too much by chewing on that letter for another day,' Belgarath began. 'Let's agree that it's obviously a forgery of some kind and move on.' He looked at Kail. 'Did your father have any enemies here on the island?' he asked. 'Someone wealthy enough and powerful enough to hire Cherek assassins?'

Kail frowned. 'No one can go through life without stepping on a few toes, Ancient One,' he replied, 'but I don't think anybody was holding that kind of grudge.'

'In truth, my friend,' Mandorallen told him, 'some men, when they feel that they have been offended, will nurture their rancor in silence and with dissembling guise conceal their enmity until opportunity doth present itself to revenge themselves. The history of Arendia is replete with stories of such acts.'

'It's a possibility,' King Fulrach agreed. 'And it might be better if we start close to home before we begin to go further afield.'

'A list might be useful,' Javelin suggested. 'If we write down the name of every man on the Isle of the Winds whom Brand might possibly have offended, we can start eliminating them. Once we have the list narrowed down, we can start investigating. If the man behind this is a Rivan, he'd either have had to visit Cherek or had some contact with Chereks sometime in the recent past.'

It took the remainder of the morning to compile the list. Kail sent for certain documents, and they all considered each of the decisions Brand had made during the past five years. Since the Warder had functioned as the kingdom's chief magistrate, there had been many decisions and usually a winner and a loser in each case.

After lunch, they began the winnowing process, discarding the names of those men without sufficient wealth or power to be able to obtain the services of paid assassins.

'It's narrowing down a bit,' Javelin said as he struck off another name. He held up the list. 'We've got this down to almost manageable proportions.'

There was a respectful knock on the door. One of the guards posted there spoke briefly with someone outside, then came over to Barak and murmured something to him. The big red-bearded man nodded, rose, and followed him from the room.

'How about this one?' Javelin asked Kail, pointing at another name.

Kail scratched at one cheek. 'I don't think so,' he replied.

'It was a dispute over land,' Javelin pointed out, 'and some people get very intense where land is concerned.'

'It was only a pasture,' Kail recalled, 'and not a very big one. The man has more land than he can keep track of anyway.'

'Why did he go to the law, then?'

'It was the other man who brought the matter to my father.'

Barak came back into the room. 'Anheg,' he said to his cousin, 'Greldik's here. He's got something fairly important to tell you.'

Anheg started to rise, then looked around. 'Have him come in here,' he said shortly. 'I don't want anybody thinking that I've got any secrets.'

'We've all got secrets, Anheg,' Queen Porenn murmured.

'My situation is somewhat peculiar, Porenn.' He pushed his dented crown back into place from where it had slipped down over one ear.

The bearded and fur-clad Greldik pushed past the

guards and came into the chamber at that point. 'You've got trouble at home, Anheg,' he growled bluntly.

'What kind of trouble?'

'I just came back from Jarviksholm,' Greldik replied. 'They're very unfriendly there.'

'There's nothing new about that.'

'They tried to sink me,' Greldik said. 'They've lined the tops of the cliffs on both sides of the inlet leading up to the city with catapults. The boulders were coming down like hailstones for a while.'

Anheg scowled. 'Why would they do that?'

'Probably because they didn't want me to see what they're doing.'

'What could they be doing that they'd want to keep *that* secret?'

'They're building a fleet.'

Anheg shrugged. 'Lots of people build ships in Cherek.'

'A hundred at a time?'

'*How many?*'

'I was busy dodging boulders, so I couldn't get an exact count, but the entire upper end of the inlet is lined with yards. The keels have all been laid, and they're starting on the ribs. Oh, they're working on the city walls, too.'

'The walls? They're already higher than the walls of Val Alorn.'

'They're even higher now.'

Anheg scowled. 'What are they up to?'

'Anheg, when you build a fleet and start strengthening your fortifications, it usually means that you're getting ready for a war. And when you try to sink the ship of a man known to be friendly to the crown, that usually means that the war is going to be with your king.'

'He does have a point, Anheg,' Barak said.

'Who's in control at Jarviksholm right now?' Garion asked curiously.

'The Bear-cult,' Anheg said in disgust. 'They've been filtering into the town from all over Cherek for the past ten years.'

'This is very serious, Anheg,' Barak said.

'It's also totally out of character,' Javelin pointed out. 'The cult has never been interested in confrontational politics before.'

'*What* kind of politics?' Anheg asked.

'Another way of saying open war with the crown,' the Drasnian Chief of Intelligence explained.

'Say what you mean, man.'

'An occupational peculiarity,' Javelin shrugged. 'Always before, the cult has tried to work from within—trying to gather enough support to be able to coerce the kings of the Alorn nations to follow *their* policies. I don't think they've ever even considered open rebellion before.'

'There's a first time for everything, I guess,' Hettar suggested.

Javelin was frowning. 'It's not at all like them,' he mused, 'and it's a direct reversal of a policy they've followed for the past three thousand years.'

'People change sometimes,' General Brendig said.

'Not the Bear-cult,' Barak told him. 'There isn't room enough in a cultist's mind for more than one idea.'

'I think you'd better get off your behind and get back to Val Alorn, Anheg,' Greldik suggested. 'If they get those ships in the water, they'll control the whole west coast of Cherek.'

Anheg shook his head. 'I have to stay here,' he declared. 'I've got another matter that's more important right now.'

Greldik shrugged. 'It's your kingdom,' he said, 'at least for the time being.'

'Thanks, Greldik,' Anheg said drily. 'You have no idea how that notion comforts me. How long will it take you to get to Val Alorn?'

'Three—maybe four days. It depends on how I catch the tides at the Bore.'

'Go there,' Anheg told him. 'Tell the fleet admirals that I want them to move out of Val Alorn and take up stations off the Halberg straits. I think that when this council is over, I'll want to take a little journey up to Jarviksholm. It shouldn't take much to burn out those shipyards.'

Greldik's answering grin was positively vicious.

After the council adjourned for the evening, Kail caught up with Garion in the torchlit corridor. 'I think there's something you should consider, Belgarion,' he said quietly.

'Oh?'

'This moving of the Cherek fleet concerns me.'

'It's Anheg's fleet,' Garion replied, 'and his kingdom.'

'There is only this Greldik's unsupported word about the shipyards at Jarviksholm,' Kail pointed out. 'And the Halberg straits are only three days from Riva.'

'Aren't we being overly suspicious, Kail?'

'Your Majesty, I agree completely that King Anheg deserves every benefit of doubt concerning the assassination of my father, but this coincidence that puts the Cherek fleet within striking distance of Riva is an altogether different matter. I think we should quietly look to our defenses—just to be on the safe side.'

'I'll think about it,' Garion said shortly and moved on down the corridor.

About noon on the following day, Silk arrived. The little man was richly dressed in a gray velvet doublet; as had become his custom of late, his fingers glittered with costly jewels. After only the briefest of greetings to his friends, he went into private discussions with Javelin.

When Belgarath entered the council chamber that afternoon, he had a self-satisfied smirk on his face and the letter from King Anheg in his hand.

'What is it, father?' Polgara asked curiously. 'You look like the ship's cat on a fishing boat.'

'I'm always pleased when I solve a riddle, Pol.' He turned to the rest of them. 'As it turns out, Anheg *did* write this letter.'

King Anheg jumped to his feet, his face livid.

Belgarath held up one hand. '*But*,' he continued, 'what Anheg wrote is *not* what the letter seems to say.' He laid the sheet of parchment on the table. 'Have a look,' he invited them.

When Garion looked at the letter, he could clearly see red-colored letters lying behind the ones which spelled out the message that seemed to place responsibility for Brand's death at Anheg's door.

'What is this, Belgarath?' King Fulrach asked.

'Actually, it's a letter to the Earl of Maelorg,' the old man replied. 'It has to do with Anheg's decision to raise the taxes on the herring fishery.'

'I wrote *that* letter four years ago,' Anheg declared, a baffled look crossing his face.

'Exactly,' Belgarath said. 'And if memory serves me, didn't the Earl of Maelorg die last spring?'

'Yes,' Anheg said. 'I attended the funeral.'

'It appears that, after his death, someone got into his papers and filched this letter. Then they went to a great deal of trouble to bleach out the original message—all but the signature, of course—and to write one that introduced this so-called trade deputation.'

'Why couldn't we see it before?' Barak asked.

'I had to tamper with it a bit,' the old man admitted.

'Sorcery?'

'No. Actually I used a solution of certain salts. Sorcery might have raised the old message, but it probably would have erased the new one, and we might need that later on for evidence.'

Barak's expression was slightly disappointed.

'Sorcery is not the *only* way to do things, Barak.'

'How did you find out?' Garion asked the old man, 'That there was another message, I mean?'

'The bleach the fellow used leaves a very faint odor on the page.' The sorcerer made a wry face. 'It wasn't until this morning that I finally realized what I was smelling.' He turned to Anheg. 'I'm sorry it took me so long to exonerate you,' he said.

'That's quite all right, Belgarath,' Anheg said expansively. 'It gave me the chance to find out who my *real* friends are.'

Kail rose to his feet, his face a study in conflicting emotions. He went to Anheg's chair and dropped to one knee. 'Forgive me, your Majesty,' he said simply. 'I must confess that I suspected you.'

'Of course I forgive you.' Anheg laughed suddenly. 'Belar's teeth,' he said. 'After I read that letter, I even suspected myself. Get up, young man. Always stand on your feet—even when you've made a mistake.'

'Kail,' Garion said, 'would you see to it that word of this discovery gets the widest possible circulation? Tell the people down in the city to stop sharpening their swords.'

'I'll see to it at once, your Majesty.'

'That still leaves us with an unsolved riddle,' the Earl of Seline noted. 'We know that King Anheg wasn't behind this, but who was?'

'We already have a good start on that,' Lelldorin declared. 'We've got that list of men who might have had reason to hate Brand.'

'I think we're following the wrong track there,' Queen Porenn disagreed. 'The murder of the Rivan Warder was one thing, but trying to make it look as if Anheg had been responsible is something else entirely.'

'I don't quite follow you, Porenn,' Anheg admitted.

'If you had a very close friend—you *do* have a few friends, don't you, Anheg, dear?—and if this friend of yours was also a high-ranking official in your government, and the king of another country had him murdered, what would you do?'

'My warships would sail on the next tide,' he replied.

'Exactly. The murder of Brand may not have been the result of a personal grudge. It might have been an attempt to start a war between Riva and Cherek.'

Anheg blinked. 'Porenn, you are an extraordinary woman.'

'Why, thank you, Anheg.'

The door opened, and Silk and Javelin entered. 'Our most excellent Prince Kheldar here has a very interesting report for us,' Javelin announced.

Silk stepped forward and bowed grandiosely. 'Your Majesties,' he said, 'and dear friends. I can't say for certain just how relevant this is to your current discussions, but it's a matter that should be brought to your attention, I think.'

'Have you ever noticed how a little prosperity makes certain people very pompous?' Barak asked Hettar.

'I noticed that,' Hettar agreed mildly.

'I thought you might have.'

Silk flashed his two friends a quick grin. 'Anyway,' he continued in a more conversational tone, 'I've spent the past several months in the town of Rheon on the eastern frontier of dear old Drasnia. Interesting town, Rheon. Very picturesque—particularly now that they've doubled the height of the walls.'

'Kheldar,' Queen Porenn said, tapping her fingers impatiently on the arm of her chair, 'you *do* plan to get to the point eventually, don't you?'

'Why, of course, Auntie dear,' he replied mockingly. 'Rheon has always been a fortified town, largely because of its proximity to the Nadrak border. It is also filled with a citizenry so archconservative that most of them disapprove of the use of fire. It's a natural breeding-ground for the Bear-cult. After the attempt on Ce'Nedra's life last summer, I sort of drifted into town to do a bit of snooping.'

'That's an honest way to put it,' Barak said.

'I'm going through an honest phase,' Silk shrugged. 'Enjoy it while you can, because it's starting to bore me. Now, it seems that the Bear-cult has a new leader—a man named Ulfgar. After Grodeg got that Murgo axe stuck in his back at Thull Mardu, the cult was pretty well demoralized. Then this Ulfgar comes out of nowhere and begins to pull them all together. This man can quite literally talk the birds out of the trees. Always before the leadership of the cult was in the hands of the priesthood, and always before it was centered in Cherek.'

'Tell me something new,' Anheg growled sourly.

'Ulfgar does not appear to be a priest of Belar,' Silk continued, 'and his center of power is at Rheon in eastern Drasnia.'

'Kheldar, *please* come to the point,' Porenn said.

'I'm getting there, your Majesty,' he assured. 'In the last few months, very quietly, our friend Ulfgar has been calling in his cohorts. Cultists have been drifting up from

Algaria and filtering into Rheon from all over Drasnia. The town is literally bulging with armed men. I'd guess that Ulfgar currently has a force at Rheon at least equal to the entire Drasnian army.' He looked at young King Kheva. 'Sorry, cousin,' he said, 'but it rather looks as if you now have only the second biggest army in Drasnia.'

'I can correct that if I have to, cousin,' Kheva replied firmly.

'You're doing a wonderful job with this boy, Auntie,' Silk congratulated Porenn.

'Kheldar,' she said acidly, 'am I going to have to put you on the rack to pull this story out of you?'

'Why, Auntie dearest, what a shocking thing to suggest. This mysterious Ulfgar has resurrected a number of very ancient rituals and ceremonies—among them a permanent means of identifying kindred spirits—so to speak. At his orders, every cultist in Aloria has had a distinctive mark branded on the sole of his right foot. The chances are rather good that anyone you see limping is a new convert to the Bear-cult.'

Barak winced. 'That would *really* hurt,' he said.

'They wear it rather proudly,' Silk told him, 'Once it heals, anyway.'

'What does this mark look like?' King Cho-Hag asked.

'It's a symbolic representation of a bear paw,' Silk explained. 'It's shaped sort of like the letter U with a couple of marks at its open end to represent claws.'

'After Kheldar told me this,' Javelin took up the story, 'we paid a short visit to that surviving assassin. His right foot has been branded with that particular mark.'

'So now we know,' Hettar said.

'We do indeed,' Belgarath replied.

'Prithee,' Mandorallen said, frowning in perplexity. 'I have always been advised that the aim of this obscure religious denomination hath been the reunification of Aloria, that titanic empire of the north which existed under the reign of King Cherek Bear-shoulders, the mightiest ruler of antiquity.'

'It may very well still be,' Belgarath told him, 'but if

this Ulfgar had succeeded in putting Riva and Cherek at each other's throats, he might have been able to topple Drasnia and possibly Algaria as well. With Anheg and Garion concentrating on destroying each other, it probably wouldn't have been all that difficult for him to have taken their two kingdoms as well.'

'Particularly with that fleet his people are building at Jarviksholm,' Anheg added.

'His strategy seems at once very simple and yet very complex,' General Brendig mused, 'and I think it came very close to working.'

'Too close,' Polgara said. 'What are we going to do about this, father?'

'I think we'll have to take steps,' Belgarath replied. 'This fellow Ulfgar still wants to reunite Aloria—but with himself as the successor to Bear-shoulders. The cult has tried subversion for three millennia. Now apparently they're going to try open war.'

Garion's face grew bleak. 'Well,' he said, 'if it's a war they want, they've come to the right place.'

'I might drink to that,' Anheg agreed. He thought for a moment. 'If you're open to any suggestions, I think it might be a good idea if we destroy Jarviksholm before we move on Rheon. We don't want those Cherek cultists coming up behind us on the moors of eastern Drasnia and we *definitely* don't want a cult fleet in the Sea of the Winds. If even half of what Greldik says is true, we're going to have to burn out those shipyards before they get their warships into the water. You could mount a very successful attack on Rheon, Garion, and then come home to find a hostile force occupying Riva itself.'

Garion considered that. 'All right then,' he agreed. 'We'll go to Jarviksholm first. Then we'll go to Rheon and have a little chat with this Ulfgar. I really want to look at a man who thinks he's big enough to fill Bear-shoulders' shoes.'

Chapter Nineteen

'I'm sorry, Kail,' Garion told his friend as they sat together in Garion's study with the morning sun streaming golden through the window, 'but I have to have you and your brothers here at Riva. I'm taking most of our forces with me, and someone has to stay here to defend the city in case some of the cultists' ships slip around behind us.'

Kail's face was angry. 'That's not the real reason is it?' he accused.

'Not entirely, no,' Garion admitted. 'I know how much you all loved your father and I know how much you want revenge on the people responsible for his murder.'

'Isn't that only natural?'

'Of course it is, but people caught up in those feelings don't think clearly. They get rash and do things that put them in danger. Your family has shed enough blood already—first your brother Olban, Arell, and now your father—so I'm not taking any chances with the rest of you.'

Kail stood up, his face red with suppressed anger. 'Does your Majesty have any further instructions for me?' he asked stiffly.

Garion sighed. 'No, Kail,' he said, 'not at the moment. You know what to do here.'

'Yes, your Majesty.' Kail bowed curtly, turned and left the room.

Belgarath came into Garion's study through the other door.

'He didn't like it,' Garion said.

'I didn't think he would.' The old man shrugged,

scratching at one bearded cheek. 'But he's too important here in the Citadel for us to be risking his life. He'll be angry for a while, but he'll get over it.'

'Is Aunt Pol staying behind, too?'

Belgarath made a face. 'No. She insists on going. At least the other ladies have sense enough to realize that a battlefield is no place for a woman. I think we ought to leave Errand here, too. He has no sense of personal danger, and that's not a good trait when the fighting starts. You'd better finish here. The morning tide's turning, and we're almost ready to start.'

As the *Seabird* moved out of the harbor that sunny morning with a flotilla of stout Rivan ships following her, Garion and the others gathered in the spacious, low-beamed aft cabin, poring over maps and discussing stategy.

'The inlet that runs up to Jarviksholm is very narrow,' Anheg advised them, 'and it's got more twists and turns to it than a Tolnedran trade agreement. It's going to slow us to a crawl.'

'And then those catapults on top of the cliffs will sink half the fleet,' Barak added gloomily.

'Is there any way we can come at the city from behind?' Hettar asked.

'There's a road coming up from Halberg,' Barak replied; 'but it goes through several passes fifteen leagues or so to the south of the city. Those passes are ideal for ambushes.'

General Brendig had been studying the map. 'What's this terrain like?' he asked, pointing at a spot on the south side of the mouth of the inlet.

'Rough,' Barak said, 'and steep.'

'That's a description of most of Cherek,' Silk observed.

'Is it passable?' Brendig persisted.

'Oh, you could climb it,' Barak said, 'but you'd be in plain view of the catapultists up on the cliffs. There'd be a whole army waiting for you by the time you got to the top.'

'Not if you did it at night,' Brendig said.

'At night?' the big man scoffed. 'Brendig, do you really want to take up nighttime mountain climbing at your age?'

Brendig shrugged. 'If it's the only way to get there.'

Mandorallen had also been studying the map. 'Prithee, my Lord,' he said to Barak, 'is this slope to the north also gentle enough to afford access to the cliff top?'

Barak shook his head. 'It's a sheer face.'

'Then we must needs seek other means to neutralize the catapults on that side.' The knight thought a moment, then he smiled. 'We have the means at our immediate disposal,' he declared.

'I'd be interested to know what they are,' King Fulrach said to him.

'It is the simplest possible solution, your Majesty.' Mandorallen beamed. 'To convey siege engines up the south slope would be tiresome—particularly during the hours of darkness. It would, moreover, be totally unnecessary, since the means of destroying the engines on the north side are already in place.'

'I don't quite follow what you're suggesting,' Garion admitted.

'I do,' Hettar said. 'All we have to do is climb the south slope at night, capture the catapults on top and then start lobbing boulders at the engines across the inlet.'

'And once you distract *those* people, I can sweep up the inlet with fireboats and burn out the shipyards,' Anheg added.

'But doesn't that still leave the city intact?' King Fulrach asked dubiously.

Garion stood up and began to pace up and down, thinking hard. 'Once we start throwing rocks back and forth across the inlet and the fireboats start moving up toward the yards, it's going to attract quite a bit of attention from the city, wouldn't you say?'

'I could almost guarantee that,' Brendig replied.

'Then wouldn't that be a perfect time to mount an attack on the landward side of the town? Everybody's going to be lining the front wall. The back side will be only lightly defended. If we strike fast enough, we could be inside before most of the defenders knew we were coming.'

'Very good, Belgarion,' King Cho-Hag murmured.

'It's all going to have to be carefully timed, though,' Barak said thoughtfully. 'We'll have to work out a way to pass signals back and forth.'

'That's not really a problem, Barak,' Aunt Pol told the big man. 'We can take care of that.'

'You know,' Anheg said, 'I think it might work. If we get lucky, we could take Jarviksholm in a single day.'

'I never cared much for long sieges anyway,' Silk noted, carefully polishing one of his rings.

Two days later they found the Cherek fleet standing at anchor off the Halberg straits, a narrow passage leading through a cluster of small, rocky islets jutting up out of the coastal waters of the west coast of the Cherek peninsula. The islets were topped with scrubby trees and they stood out, green against the snowfields covering the higher mountains lying inland. Garion stood at the rail of the *Seabird*, drinking in the beauty of that wild coast. A light step behind him and a familiar fragrance announced his Aunt Pol's approach.

'It's lovely, isn't it, Garion?' she said.

'Breathtaking,' he agreed.

'It always seems this way,' she mused. 'Somehow it's when you're on your way to something very ugly that you come across these glimpses of beauty.' She looked at him gravely. 'You *will* be careful at Jarviksholm, won't you?'

'I'm always careful, Aunt Pol.'

'Really? I seem to remember a number of incidents not too many years ago.'

'I was a child then.'

'Some things never change, I'm afraid.' She suddenly put her arms about his neck and sighed. 'Oh, my Garion,' she said, 'I've missed you in the past few years, do you know that?'

'I've missed you, too, Aunt Pol. Sometimes I wish —' He left it hanging.

'That we could have just stayed at Faldor's farm?'

'It really wasn't such a bad place, was it?'

'No. It was a very good place—for a child. But you're grown now. Would you really have been content there? Life was quite placid at Faldor's.'

'If we hadn't left, I'd never have known what it was like to live any other way.'

'But if we hadn't left, you never would have met Ce'Nedra, would you?'

'I suppose I hadn't thought about that.'

'Let's go below, shall we,' she suggested. 'That breeze is really rather brisk.'

They encountered King Anheg and Barak in a narrow companionway just outside the main cabin belowdecks. 'Barak,' Anheg was saying acidly, 'you're getting to be worse than an old woman.'

'I don't care what you say, Anheg,' the red-bearded Barak growled. 'You're not going to take the *Seabird* up that inlet until all those catapults have been cleared. I didn't spend that much money on her to have somebody drop boulders on her decks from those cliffs. My boat, my rules.'

The lean-faced Javelin approached from down the companionway. 'Is there some problem, my Lords?' he asked.

'I was just laying down a few rules for Anheg here,' Barak replied. 'He's going to be in charge of my ship while I'm gone.'

'Were you going somewhere, my Lord of Trellheim?'

'I'll be going with Garion when he mounts his attack on the city.'

'As you think best, my Lord. How long do you think it's going to take to reach the mouth of the inlet?'

Barak tugged at his luxuriant red beard. 'Those Rivan ships carrying Garion's troops aren't quite as fast as our warships,' he mused. 'I make it about a day and a half. Wouldn't you agree, Anheg?'

'About that, yes.'

'That should put us there tomorrow evening, then?' Javelin asked.

'Right,' Barak said, 'and that's when the fun starts.'

Aunt Pol sighed. 'Alorns!'

After a few shouted conferences from ship to ship, the combined fleet heeled over sharply in the quickening breeze and beat northward along the rugged west coast of the Cherek peninsula toward Jarviksholm.

The following morning, Garion went up on deck with Barak and Hettar to watch the sun come up above the forested and snow-capped peaks of Cherek. The shadows back in the wooded valleys were a kind of misty blue, and the sun sparkled on the waves.

A mail-shirted Cherek sailor, who had been ostensibly coiling a rope, turned from his task, then suddenly plunged a dagger directly at Garion's unprotected back as the king stood at the rail.

The attack might well have proved fatal had Durnik not shouted a quick warning. Garion half-turned in time to see the dagger go skittering across the deck. At the same time, he heard a startled exclamation and a splash. He wheeled about to see a desperately clutching hand sink beneath the waves about thirty yards to port. He looked questioningly at Polgara, but she shook her head.

'I forgot about the mail shirt,' Durnik said apologetically. 'It's sort of hard to swim with one of those on, isn't it?'

'More than sort of,' Barak assured him.

'You'll want to question him, I suppose,' Durnik said. 'I can fish him out, if you like.'

'What do you think, Hettar?' Barak asked.

Hettar considered the notion for several moments, looking out at the bubbles coming up from somewhere far beneath the surface. 'These are Cherek waters, aren't they?'

Barak nodded.

'Then I think we should consult King Anheg and get his opinion.'

'Anheg's sleeping late this morning,' Barak told him, also looking out at the bubbles.

'I'd hate to wake him,' Hettar said. 'He's had a lot on

315

his mind lately, and I'm sure he needs his rest.' The tall Algar turned to Durnik with an absolutely straight face. 'I'll tell you what, Durnik. The very moment King Anheg wakes up, we'll bring the matter immediately to his attention.'

'Have you ever translocated anything before, Durnik?' Polgara asked her husband.

'No, not really. I knew how it was done, of course, but I've never had the occasion to try it myself. I threw him just a little farther than I'd intended, I'm afraid.'

'You'll get better with practice, dear,' she assured him. Then she turned to Garion. 'Are you all right?' she asked.

'I'm fine, Aunt Pol. He didn't even get close to me—thanks to Durnik.'

'He's always been very useful to have around,' she replied, giving Durnik a warm smile.

'Where did the fellow come from, Barak?' Hettar asked.

'Val Alorn, of all places. He always seemed like a good man, too. He did his work and kept his mouth shut. I'd never have suspected that he might have had religious convictions.'

'Maybe it's time for us to examine everybody's feet,' Hettar suggested.

Barak looked at him quizzically.

'If Silk's right, then all the Bear-cultists have that brand on the soles of their right feet. It's probably easier in the long run to examine feet rather than have Garion offer his back to every dagger aboard your ship.'

'You might be right,' Barak agreed.

They sailed into the wide mouth of the inlet that wound its way up to Jarviksholm just as the sun was setting. 'Shouldn't we have waited until after dark to come this close?' Garion asked as he and the other kings stood on the foredeck of the *Seabird*.

Anheg shrugged. 'They knew we were coming. They've been watching us ever since we left the Halberg straits. Besides, now that they know that we're here, those catapultists up there will concentrate on watching the ships.

That ought to make it easier for you and Brendig to slip up behind them when the time comes.'

'That makes sense, I guess.'

Barak came forward with the one-armed General Brendig. 'As close as we can figure it, we ought to start about midnight,' he said. 'Garion and the rest of us will climb up first and circle around until we're behind the city. Brendig and his men can follow us up and start taking over the catapults. As soon as it gets light enough to see, he's going to start throwing boulders across the inlet.'

'Will that give Garion time enough to get into position?' King Fulrach asked.

'It should be plenty of time, your Majesty,' Brendig assured him. 'Lord Barak says that once we get to the top, the terrain is fairly flat.'

'There are trees, too,' Barak told them. 'That should give us plenty of concealment.'

'How much open space are we going to have to charge across when we attack the city?' Garion asked.

'Oh, maybe five hundred yards,' Barak replied.

'That's quite a ways.'

'It's about as far as *I* want to run.'

Evening settled slowly over the calm waters of the inlet, purpling the sheer cliffs rising on either side. Garion used the last bit of light carefully to examine every inch of the steep slope which he and his men would be climbing in just a few hours. A flicker of movement just overhead caught his eye, and he looked up in time to see a ghostly white shape sliding silently through the calm, purple air. A single soft white feather slowly sifted down to settle on the deck not far away. Gravely, Hettar went over and picked it up.

A moment or two later, Aunt Pol, wrapped in her blue cloak, came down the deck and joined them. 'You're going to have to be very careful when you approach the shipyards,' she told Anheg, who stood nearby with Brendig. 'They've moved catapults down to the beaches to try to hold you off.'

'I expected that,' he replied with an indifferent shrug.

'You'd better pay attention to her, Anheg,' Barak said in a threatening tone, 'because if you get my ship sunk, I'll pull out your beard one whisker at a time.'

'What a novel way to address one's king,' Silk murmured to Javelin.

'How heavily is the rear of the city defended?' Garion asked Polgara.

'The walls are high,' she answered, 'and the gate looks impressive. There aren't very many men there, though.'

'Good.'

Hettar silently handed her the feather.

'Why, thank you,' she said to him. 'I would have missed that.'

The slope of the hill leading to the rolling plateau high above was even steeper than Garion's examination from the deck of the *Seabird* had led him to believe. Clumps of broken rock, almost invisible in the midnight darkness, rolled treacherously underfoot, and the stiff limbs of the scrubby bushes that choked the hillside seemed almost to push deliberately at his face and chest as he struggled upward. His mail shirt was heavy, and he was soon dripping with sweat.

'Rough going,' Hettar observed laconically.

A pale sliver of a moon had risen when they finally crested that brutal slope. As they reached the top, they found that the plateau above was covered with a dense forest of fir and spruce trees.

'This might take us a little longer than I'd thought,' Barak muttered, eyeing the thick undergrowth.

Garion paused to get his breath. 'Let's stop for a moment,' he told his friends. He stared glumly at the forest barring their way. 'If all of us start crashing through that, we're going to alert the catapultists along the top of the cliff,' he said. 'I think we'd better send out some scouts to see if we can find a path or a track of some kind.'

'Give me a while,' Silk told him.

'You'd better take some men with you.'

'They'd just slow me down. I'll be back before long.' The little man vanished into the trees.

'He never changes, does he?' Hettar murmured.

Barak laughed shortly. 'Did you really think he would?'

'How long thinkest thou it will be until dawn, my Lord?' Mandorallen asked the big Cherek.

'Two—maybe three hours,' Barak replied. 'That hill took a long time.'

Lelldorin, his bow slung acros his back, joined them at the edge of the dark wood. 'General Brendig's started up,' he told them.

'I wonder how he's going to manage that climb with only one arm,' Barak said.

'I don't think you need to worry too much about Brendig,' Hettar replied. 'He usually does what he sets out to do.'

'He's a good man,' Barak agreed.

They waited in the warm summer darkness as the moon slowly climbed the eastern sky. From far below Garion could hear the calls of Anheg's men and the rasp of windlasses as the sailors strove to make enough noise to cover any inadvertent sounds Brendig's men might make as they struggled up the brushy slope. Finally Silk returned, appearing soundlessly out of the bushes. 'There's a road about a quarter of a mile south of here,' he reported quietly. 'It seems to go toward Jarviksholm.'

'Excellent,' Mandorallen said gaily. 'Let us proceed, my Lords. The city doth await our coming.'

'I hope not,' Garion said. 'The whole idea is to surprise them.'

The narrow road Silk had found proved to be a wood-cutter's track, and it meandered in a more or less easterly direction, leading them inland. Behind him Garion could hear the jingle of mail shirts and the steady, shuffling tread of his soldiers as they moved through the tag end of night in the deep shadows of the surrounding forest. There was a sense of inexorable purpose involved in this leading a mass of faceless men through the darkness. A tense excitement had been building in him since they had left the ships. His impatience to begin the attack was so strong now that it was all he could do to keep himself from breaking into a run.

They reached a large cleared area. At the far side of that open field, the white ribbon of a well-traveled highway cut due north across the moonlit pastureland. 'That's the Halberg road,' Barak told them. 'We're almost there.'

'I'd better see how Brendig's doing,' Garion said. He carefully reached out, skirting the thoughts of the troops massed at his back and seeking the familiar touch of Durnik's mind. *'Durnik,'* he said silently, *'can you hear me?'*

'Garion?' the smith's thought came back.

'Right,' Garion replied. *'Have you captured the catapults yet?'*

'We've still got a dozen or so to take. Brendig's moving slowly to keep down unnecessary noise.'

'Will you have them all by the time it starts getting light?'

'I'm sure we will.'

'Good. Let me know when you capture the last one.'

'I will.'

'How are they doing?' Lelldorin asked. The young bowman's voice was tight with excitement.

'They'll be ready when it's time,' Garion replied.

'What thinkest thou, my Lord?' Mandorallen asked Barak. 'Might it not be the proper moment to select some few stout trees to serve as rams to reduce the city gates?'

'I'll deal with the gate,' Garion told them firmly.

Barak stared at him. 'You mean that you're going to—?' He made a gesture with one thick-fingered hand.

Garion nodded.

'That hardly seems proper, Garion,' Barak objected disapprovingly.

'Proper?'

'There are certain ways that things are done. City gates are supposed to be knocked in with battering rams.'

'While the people inside pour boiling pitch down on the men trying to break in?'

'That's part of the risk,' Barak explained. 'Without a little risk, a battle isn't very much fun.'

Hettar laughed quietly.

'I hate to fly in the face of tradition,' Garion said, 'but I'm not going to let a lot of people get killed unnecessarily just for the sake of an old custom.'

A hazy ground fog, glowing in the moonlight, lay low on the broad, open expanse between the edge of the forest and the towering walls of Jarviksholm. Off to the east, the first pale glimmer of the approaching dawn stained the velvet sky. There were ruddy torches along the top of the heavy battlements of the city; by their light Garion could see a number of armed men.

'How close do you need to get to break in the gate?' Silk whispered to Garion.

'The closer, the better,' Garion replied.

'All right. We'll have to move up a bit, then. The fog and the tall grass should help.'

'I'll go along with you,' Barak said. 'Is it likely to make much noise?'

'Probably,' Garion said.

The big man turned to Hettar and Mandorallen. 'Use that as your signal. When Garion knocks the gate down, you start the charge.'

Hettar nodded.

Garion drew in a deep breath. 'All right,' he said, 'let's go.' Crouched low, the three of them started across the open field toward the city. When they were no more than a hundred yards from the gate, they sank down in the tall grass.

'*Garion*,' Durnik's thought came from out of the growing light, '*we've captured all the catapults.*'

'*Can you see the ones on the north cliffs yet?*'

'*It's probably going to be just a few more minutes.*'

'*Tell Brendig to start just as soon as he can make them out.*'

They waited as the eastern sky grew steadily lighter. Then a series of solid thuds came from beyond the city, followed after an interval by the sound of heavy rocks crashing through timbers and by startled shouts and cries of pain.

'We've started,' Durnik reported.

'Garion,' Polgara's thought came to him, 'are you in position?'

'Yes, Aunt Pol.'

'We're going to start up the inlet now.'

'Let me know when you're in sight of the city.'

'Be careful, Garion.'

'I will.'

'What's happening?' Barak whispered, eyeing the men atop the city walls.

'They've started dropping rocks on the north cliff,' Garion replied softly, 'and Anheg's got the fleet moving.'

Barak ground his teeth together. 'I told him to wait until all the catapults were out of action.'

'Don't worry so much about that ship of yours,' Silk murmured. 'It's very hard to aim a catapult when you're dodging boulders.'

'Somebody might get lucky.'

They waited tensely as the light slowly grew stronger. Garion could smell the salt tang of the sea and the heavy odor of evergreens as he surveyed the stout gate.

'We can see the city now, Garion,' Aunt Pol reported.

Shouts of alarm came from inside the city, and Garion saw the armed men atop the walls running along the parapet, making for the seaward side of Jarviksholm. 'Are we ready?' he whispered to his two friends.

'Let's do it,' Silk said tensely.

Garion rose to his feet and concentrated. He felt something that was almost like an inrushing of air as he drew in and concentrated his will. He seemed to be tingling all over as the enormous force built up in him. Grimly he drew Iron-grip's sword, which he had left sheathed until now in order to conceal that telltale blue fire. The Orb leaped joyously into flame. 'Here we go,' he said from between clenched teeth. He pointed the sword at the gate, standing solid and impenetrable-looking a hundred yards in front of him. 'Burst!' he commanded, and all his clenched-in will surged into the sword and out through its flaming tip.

The one thing that he had overlooked, of course, was the Orb's desire to be helpful. The force which struck the gates of Jarviksholm was, to put it very mildly, excessive. The logs disappeared entirely, and chunks and splinters of that tar-smeared gate were later found as much as five miles distant. The solid stone wall in which the gate had been mounted also blew apart, and many of the huge, rough-hewn blocks sailed like pebbles to splash into the harbor and the inlet far from the city. Most of the back wall of Jarviksholm crumbled and fell in on itself. The noise was awful.

'Belar!' Barak swore in amazement as he watched the nearly absolute destruction.

There was a stunned silence for a moment, and then a great shout came from the edge of the woods as Hettar and Mandorallen led the charge of the massed Rivans and Chereks into the stunned city.

It was not what warriors call a good fight. The Bear-cult was not composed entirely of able-bodied men. It had also attracted into its ranks old men, women, and children. Because of the raging fanaticism of the cult, the warriors entering the city frequently found it necessary to kill those who might otherwise have been spared. By late afternoon, there were only a few small pockets of resistance remaining in the northwest quarter of Jarviksholm, and much of the rest of the city was on fire.

Garion, half-sickened by the smoke and the slaughter, stumbled back through the burning city, over that shattered wall, and out into the open fields beyond. He wandered, tired and sick, for a time until he came across Silk, seated comfortably on a large rock, casually watching the destruction of the city. 'Is it just about finished?' the little man asked.

'Nearly,' Garion replied. 'They only have a few buildings left in their control.'

'How was it?'

'Unpleasant. A lot of old people and women and children got killed.'

'That happens sometimes.'

'Did Anheg say what he was going to do with the survivors? I think there's been enough killing already.'

'It's hard to say,' Silk replied. 'Our Cherek cousins tend sometimes to be a bit savage, though. Some things are likely to happen in the next day or so that you probably won't want to watch—like that.' He pointed toward the edge of the wood where a crowd of Chereks were working on something. A long pole was raised and set into the ground. A crosspiece was attached to the top of the pole, and a man was tied by his outspread arms to that crosspiece.

'No!' Garion exclaimed.

'I wouldn't interfere, Garion,' Silk advised. 'It is Anheg's kingdom, after all, and he can deal with traitors and criminals in any way he sees fit.'

'That's barbaric!'

'Moderately so, yes. As I said, though, Chereks have a certain casual brutality in their nature.'

'But shouldn't we at least question the prisoners first?'

'Javelin's attending to that.'

Garion stared at the crowd of soldiers working in the last ruddy light of the setting sun. 'I'm sorry,' he said, choking in revulsion, 'but that's going entirely too far. I'm going to put a stop to it right now.'

'I'd stay out of it, Garion.'

'Oh, no—not when he starts crucifying women!'

'He's *what*?' Silk turned to stare at the soldiers. Suddenly the blood drained from the little man's face, and he sprang to his feet. With Garion close on his heels, he ran across the intervening turf. 'Have you lost your mind entirely?' he demanded hotly of the bony Chief of Drasnian Intelligence, who sat calmly at a rough table in the center of the group of soldiers.

'What seems to be your problem, Kheldar?'

'Do you know who that is that you just crucified?'

'Naturally. I questioned her myself.' His fingers moved

almost idly, but Silk stood directly in front of the table, cutting off Garion's view of the thin man's hands.

'Get her down from there!' Silk said, though his voice seemed for some reason to have lost the edge of its outrage.

'Why don't you attend to your own business, Kheldar?' Javelin suggested. 'Leave me to mine.' He turned to a burly Cherek standing nearby. 'Prince Kheldar and the Rivan King will be leaving now,' he said coldly. 'Would you escort them, please. I think that they should be somewhere at least a quarter of a mile from here.'

'I'll kill him,' Silk fumed as he and Garion were herded away. 'I'll kill him with my own two bare hands.'

As soon as the soldiers had led them to a spot some distance from Javelin and had turned to go back to their grisly work, however, the little man regained his composure with astonishing speed.

'What was that all about?' Garion asked.

'The girl he just crucified is his own niece, Liselle,' Silk replied quite calmly.

'You can't be serious!'

'I've known her since she was a child. He promised to explain later. His explanation had better be very good, though, or I'm going to carve out his tripes.' He removed a long dagger from under his pearl-gray doublet and tested the edge with his thumb.

It was after dark when Javelin came looking for them. 'Oh, put that away, Kheldar,' he said disgustedly, looking at Silk's dagger.

'I may need it in a minute,' Silk replied. 'Start talking, Javelin, and you'd better make it very convincing, or I'll have your guts in a pile right between your feet.'

'You seem upset.'

'You noticed. How clever of you.'

'I did what I did for a very specific reason.'

'Wonderful. I thought you were just amusing yourself.'

'I can do without the sarcasm, Silk. You should know by now that I never do anything without a reason. You can put your mind at rest about Liselle. She's probably already been released.'

'Released?'

'Escaped, actually. There were dozens of cultists hiding in those woods. Your eyes must be going bad on you if you didn't see them. Anyway, by now, every prisoner we crucified has been released and is on the way to safety back in the mountains.'

'Exactly what is this all about, Javelin?'

'It's really very simple. We've been trying for years to get someone into the upper echelons of the Bear-cult. They have just rescued a genuine heroine—a martyr to the cause. Liselle's clever enough to use that to work her way into their higher councils.'

'How did she get here in the first place?'

Javelin shrugged. 'She put on a mail shirt, and I slipped her on board Trellheim's ship. After the fighting was nearly over, I just slipped her in with the other prisoners.'

'Won't the others who were just rescued say that she was never in the city?'

'No, your Majesty, I don't think so,' Javelin replied. 'She's going to say that she lived in the northeast quarter of Jarviksholm. The others we crucified all came from the southwest quarter. Jarviksholm is a fairly good-sized town. Nobody could really say for sure that she wasn't there all along.'

'I still can't believe that you would actually do that to her,' Silk said.

'It took a fair amount of convincing and a great deal of fast talking on her part to persuade me,' Javelin admitted.

Silk stared at him.

'Oh, yes,' Javelin said. 'Hadn't you guessed? The whole thing was her idea in the first place.'

Suddenly Garion heard a hollow rushing sound, and a moment later Ce'Nedra's voice came to him quite clearly.

'*Garion!*' she cried out in anguish. '*Garion, come home immediately! Someone has stolen our baby!*'

Chapter Twenty

Polgara looked at Garion critically as they stood together in a high, open meadow above the still-burning city of Jarviksholm while the pale light of dawn washed the stars out of the sky. 'Your wing feathers are too short,' she told him.

Garion made the feathers longer.

'Much better,' she said. Then her look became intense, and she also shimmered into the shape of a speckled falcon. 'I've never liked these hard feathers,' she murmured, clicking her hooked beak. Then she looked at Garion, her golden eyes fierce. 'Try to remember everything I told you, dear. We won't go too high on your first flight.' She spread her wings, took a few short steps with her taloned feet, and lifted herself effortlessly into the air.

Garion tried to imitate what she had just done and drove himself beak-first into the turf.

She swooped back in. 'You have to use your tail, too, Garion,' she said. 'The wings give the power, but the tail gives direction. Try it again.'

The second attempt was a bit smoother. He actually flew for about fifty yards before he crashed into a tree.

'That was very nice, dear. Just try to watch where you're going.'

Garion shook his head, trying to clear the ringing from his ears and the speckles of light from in front of his eyes.

'Straighten your feathers, dear, and let's try it again.'

'It's going to take months for me to learn this, Aunt

Pol. Wouldn't it just be faster to sail to Riva on the *Seabird*?'

'No, dear,' she said firmly. 'You just need a bit of practice, that's all!'

His third attempt was somewhat more successful. He was beginning to get the knack of co-ordinating his wings and tail, but he still felt clumsy and he seemed to do a great deal of clawing ineffectually at the air.

'Garion, don't fight with it. Let it lift you.'

They circled the meadow several times in the shadowless luminosity of dawn. Garion could see the smoke rising black from the city and the burned-out shipyards in the harbor as he followed Polgara in a steady upward spiral. As his confidence increased, he began to feel a fierce exhilaration. The rush of cool morning air through his feathers was intoxicating, and he found that he could lift himself higher and higher almost effortlessly. By the time the sun was fully up, the air was no longer an enemy, and he had begun to master the hundreds of minute muscular adjustments necessary to get the greatest possible efficiency out of his feathers.

Belgarath swooped in to join them with Durnik not far behind. 'How's he doing?' the fierce-looking falcon asked Polgara.'

'He's almost ready, father.'

'Good. Let him practice for another fifteen minutes or so, and then we'll get started. There's a column of warm air rising off that lake over there. That always makes it easier.' He tilted on one wing and veered away in a long, smooth arc.

'This is really very fine, Pol,' Durnik said. 'I should have learned how to do this years ago.'

When they moved into the column of air rising from the surface of the warm waters of the lake, Garion learned the secret of effortless flight. With his wings spread and unmoving, he let the air lift him up and up. Objects on the ground far below shrank as he rose higher and higher. Javiksholm now looked like a toy village, and its harbor was thick with miniature ships. The hills and forests were

328

bright green in the morning sunshine. The sea was azure, the snowfields on the higher peaks were so intensely white that they almost hurt his eyes.

'How high would you say we are?' he heard Durnik ask Belgarath.

'Several thousand feet.'

'It's sort of like swimming, isn't it? It doesn't really matter how deep the water is, because you're only using the top of it anyway.'

'I never really thought of it that way.' Belgarath looked over at Aunt Pol. 'This should be high enough,' he said in the shrill, falcon's whistle. 'Let's go to Riva.'

The four of them beat steadily southwest, leaving the Cherek coast behind and flying out over the Sea of the Winds. For a time, a following breeze aided them, but at midday the breeze dropped, and they had to work for every mile. Garion's shoulders ached, and the unaccustomed effort of flying made the muscles in his chest burn. Grimly, he flew on. Far below him he could see the miles-long waves on the Sea of the Winds, looking from this height almost like ripples roughening the surface in the afternoon sunlight.

The sun was low over the western horizon when the rocky coast of the Isle of the Winds came into view. They flew southward along the east coast and spiraled down at last toward the uplifted towers and battlements of the Citadel, standing grim and gray over the city of Riva.

A sentry, leaning idly on his spear atop the highest parapet, looked startled as the four speckled falcons swooped in to land around him, and his eyes bulged with astonishment as they shimmered into human form. 'Y-your Majesty,' he stammered to Garion, awkwardly trying to bow and hold onto his spear at the same time.

'What happened here?' Garion demanded.

'Someone has abducted your son, Sire,' the sentry reported. 'We've sealed off the island, but we haven't caught him yet.'

'Let's go down,' Garion said to the others. 'I want to talk to Ce'Nedra.'

But that, of course, was nearly impossible. As soon as Garion entered the blue-carpeted royal apartment, she flew into his arms and collapsed in a storm of hysterical weeping. He could feel her tiny body trembling violently against him, and her fingers dug into his arms as she clung to him. 'Ce'Nedra,' he pleaded with her, 'you've got to stop. You have to tell us what happened.'

'He's gone, Garion,' she wailed. 'S-somebody came into the n-nursery and t-took him!' She began to cry again.

Ariana, Lelldorin's blond Mimbrate wife, stood not far away, and the dark-haired Adara stood at the window, looking on with a grieved expression.

'Why don't you see what you can do, Pol,' Belgarath said quietly. 'Try to get her calmed down. I'll need to talk to her—but probably later. Right now, I think the rest of us should go talk to Kail.'

Polgara had gravely removed her cloak, folded it carefully, and laid it across the back of a chair. 'All right, father,' she replied. She came over and gently took the sobbing little queen out of Garion's arms. 'It's all right, Ce'Nedra,' she said soothingly. 'We're here now. We'll take care of everything.'

Ce'Nedra clung to her. 'Oh, Lady Polgara,' she cried.

'Have you given her anything?' Aunt Pol asked Ariana.

'Nay, my Lady Polgara,' the blond girl replied. 'I feared that in her distraught condition those potions which most usually have a calming effect might do her injury.'

'Let me have a look at your medicine kit.'

'At once, Lady Polgara.'

'Come along,' Belgarath said to Garion and Durnik, a steely glint coming into his eyes. 'Let's go find Kail and see if we can get to the bottom of this.'

They found Kail sitting wearily at a table in his father's office. Spread before him was a large map of the island, and he was pouring over it intently.

'It happened sometime yesterday morning, Belgarion,' he said gravely after they had exchanged the briefest of greetings. 'It was before daybreak. Queen Ce'Nedra looked in on the prince a few hours past midnight, and everything was fine. A couple of hours later, he was gone.'

'What have you done so far?' Belgarath asked him.

'I ordered the island sealed,' Kail replied, 'and then we searched the Citadel from one end to the other. Whoever took the prince was nowhere in the fortress, but no ship has arrived or departed since I gave that order, and the harbor master reports that nobody sailed after midnight yesterday. So far as I know the abductor has not left the Isle of the Winds.'

'Good,' Garion said, a sudden hope welling up in him.

'At the moment, I have troops searching house by house in the city, and ships are patrolling every inch of the coastline. The island is completely sealed off.'

'Have you searched the forests and mountains?' the old man asked.

'We want to finish the search of the city first,' Kail said. 'Then we'll seal the city and move the troops out into the surrounding countryside.'

Belgarath nodded, staring at the map. 'We want to move carefully,' he said. 'Let's not back this child stealer into a corner—at least not until we have my great-grandson safely back where he belongs.'

Kail nodded his agreement. 'The safety of the prince is our primary concern,' he said.

Polgara quietly entered the room. 'I gave her something that will make her sleep,' she said, 'and Ariana's watching her. I don't think it would do any good to try to question her just yet, and sleep is what she needs right now.'

'You're probably right, Aunt Pol,' Garion said, 'but I'm not going to sleep—not until I find what happened to my son.'

Early the following morning, they gathered again in Kail's orderly study to pore once again over the map. Garion was about to ask Kail about the search of the city, but he stopped as he felt a sudden tug of the great sword strapped across his back. Absently, still staring at the yellowed parchment map on Kail's desk, he adjusted the strap. It tugged at him again, more insistently this time.

'Garion,' Durnik said curiously, 'does the Orb sometimes glow like that when you aren't actually holding the sword?'

Garion looked over his shoulder at the flaring Orb. 'What's it doing that for?' he asked, baffled.

The next tug nearly jerked him off his feet.'Grandfather,' he said, a bit alarmed.

Belgarath's expression grew careful. 'Garion,' he said in a level voice, 'I want you to take the sword out of its scabbard. I think the Orb is trying to tell you something.'

Garion reached back over his shoulder and drew Irongrip's great sword from its sheath with a steely slither. Without even stopping to think how irrational it might sound, he spoke directly to the glowing stone on the pommel. 'I'm awfully busy right now. Can't this wait?'

The answer was a steady pull toward the door.

'What is it *doing*?' Garion demanded irritably.

'Let's just follow it,' Belgarath told him.

Helplessly, Garion followed the powerful urging through the door and out into the torchlit corridor, with the others trailing curiously along behind him. He could sense the peculiarly crystalline awareness of the Orb and feel its overwhelming anger. Not since the dreadful night in Cthol Mishrak when he had faced the maimed God of Angarak had he felt so much outrage emanating from that living stone. The sword continued to pull him down the corridor, moving faster and faster until he was half running to keep up.

'What's it trying to do, father?' Polgara asked in a puzzled tone. 'It's never done anything like this before.'

'I'm not sure,' the old man replied. 'We'll just have to follow it and find out. I think it might be important, though.'

Kail stopped briefly in front of a sentry posted in the corridor. 'Would you go get my brothers?' he asked the man. 'Have them come to the royal apartment.'

'Yes sir,' the sentry replied, with a quick salute.

Garion stopped at the dark, polished door to the apartment, opened it, and went inside with the sword still pulling at him.

Queen Layla was just in the act of drawing a blanket over the exhausted Adara, who lay asleep on the couch, and she looked up with astonishment. 'What on earth—?' she began.

'Hush, Layla,' Polgara told her. 'Something's happening that we don't quite understand.'

Garion steeled himself and went on into the bedroom. Ce'Nedra lay in the bed, tossing and whimpering in her sleep. At her bedside sat Queen Islena and Barak's wife Merel. Ariana dozed in a deep chair near the window. He was only able to give the ladies attending his wife the briefest of glances, however, before the sword pulled him on into the nursery, where the sight of the empty cradle wrenched at his heart. The great sword dipped over the cradle, and the Orb glowed. Then the stone flickered with a pulsating light for a moment.

'I think I'm starting to understand,' Belgarath said. 'I won't absolutely swear to this, but I think it wants to follow Geran's trail.'

'Can it do that?' Durnik asked.

'It can do almost anything, and it's totally committed to the Rivan line. Let it go, Garion. Let's see where it leads you.'

In the corridor outside, Kail's two brothers, Verdan and Brin, met them. Verdan, the eldest of the three, was as burly as an ox, and Brin, the youngest, only slightly less so. Both men wore mail shirts and helmets and had heavy broadswords belted to their sides.

'We think that the Orb may be trying to lead us to the prince,' Kail explained tersely to them. 'We might need you two when we find him.'

Brin flashed a broad, almost boyish grin. 'We'll have the abductor's head on a pole before nightfall, then,' he said.

'Let's not be too hasty about removing heads,' Belgarath told him. 'I want the answers to some questions first.'

'One of you stay with Ce'Nedra at all times,' Aunt Pol told Queen Layla, who had curiously trailed along behind them. 'She'll probably wake up sometime this afternoon.

Let Ariana sleep for now. Ce'Nedra might need her when she awakens.'

'Of course, Polgara,' the plump queen of Sendaria replied.

'And you,' Aunt Pol said firmly to Errand, who was just coming down the hall. 'I want you to stay in the royal apartment and do exactly what Layla tells you to do.'

'But —' he started to protest.

'No buts, Errand. What we have to do might be dangerous, and that's something you haven't quite learned to understand yet.'

He sighed. 'All right, Polgara,' he said disconsolately.

With the Orb on the pommel of the massive sword pulling him along, Garion followed the unseen track of his son's abductor out through one of the side gates with the rest of them close on his heels.

'It seems to want to go toward the mountains,' Garion said. 'I thought the trail would lead down into the city.'

'Don't think, Garion,' Polgara told him. 'Just go where the Orb leads you.'

The trail led across the meadow rising steeply behind the Citadel and then into the forest of dark fir and spruce where Garion and Ce'Nedra had often strolled on their summer outings.

'Are you sure it knows what it's doing?' Garion asked as he pushed his way through a tangled patch of undergrowth. 'There's no path here at all. I don't think anyone would have come this way.'

'It's following some kind of trail, Garion,' Belgarath assured him. 'Just keep up with it.'

They struggled through the thick underbrush for an hour or so. Once a covey of grouse exploded from under Garion's feet with a heart-stopping thunder of wings.

'I'll have to remember this place,' Brin said to Kail. 'The hunting here might be very good.'

'We're hunting other game at the moment. Keep your mind on you work.'

When they reached the upper edge of the forest, Garion stared up at the steep, rock-strewn meadow rising above the timberline. 'Is there a pass of any kind through these mountains?' he asked.

'Off to the left of that big peak,' Brin replied, pointing. 'I use it when I go out to hunt wild stags, and the shepherds take their flocks through it to the pastures in the interior valleys.'

'Also the shepherdesses,' Verdan added drily. 'Sometimes the game my brother chases doesn't have horns.'

Brin threw a quick, nervous glance at Polgara, and a slow blush mounted his cheeks.

'I've always been rather fond of shepherdesses,' Belgarath noted blandly. 'For the most part, they're gentle, understanding girls—and frequently lonely, aren't they, Brin?'

'That will do, father,' Aunt Pol said primly.

It took the better part of the day to go over the pass and through the green meadows lying in the hidden valleys among the mountains beyond. The sun hovered just above the gleaming, almost molten-looking sea on the western side of the Isle when they crested a boulder-covered ridge and started down the long, rocky slope toward the cliffs and the frothy surf pounding endlessly aganst the western coast.

'Could a ship have landed on this side?' Garion asked Kail as they went downhill.

Kail was puffing noticeably from the strenuous trek across the island and he mopped his streaming face with his sleeve. 'There are a few places where it's possible, Belgarion—if you know what you're doing. It's difficult and dangerous, but it *is* possible.'

Garion's heart sank. 'Then he could very well have gotten away,' he said.

'I had ships out there, Belgarion,' Kail said to him, pointing at the sea. 'I sent them out as soon as we found out that the prince had been taken. About the only way someone could have gotten all the way across the island to this side in time to sail away before those ships got around here would be if he could fly.'

'We've got him, then,' the irrepressible Brin exclaimed,

loosening his sword in its scabbard and searching the boulder-strewn slope and the brink of the cliffs with a hunter's trained eye.

'Hold it a second,' Durnik said sharply. He lifted his head and sniffed at the onshore breeze. 'There's somebody up ahead.'

'What?' Garion said, a sudden excitement building up in him.

'I just caught a distinct whiff of somebody who doesn't bathe regularly.'

Belgarath's face took on an intense expression. 'Pol,' he said, 'why don't you take a quick look down there?'

She nodded tersely, and her forehead furrowed with concentration. Garion felt and heard the whispered surge as she probed the empty-looking terrain ahead. 'Chereks,' she said after a moment, 'about a dozen of them. They're hiding behind those boulders at the edge of the cliffs. They're watching us and planning an ambush.'

'Chereks?' Brin exclaimed. 'Why would Chereks want to attack us?'

'They're Bear-cultists,' she told him, 'and nobody knows why those madmen do anything.'

'What do we do?' Brin asked in a half whisper.

'An ambusher always has the advantage,' Verdan replied, 'unless the person about to be ambushed knows that he's there. Then it's the other way around.' He looked down the slope grimly, his big hand on his sword hilt.

'Then we just go down there and spring their trap?' Brin asked eagerly.

Kail looked at Belgarath. 'What do you think, Ancient One? We have the advantage now. They're going to expect us to be startled when they jump out at us, but we'll be ready for them. We could have half of them down before they realize their mistake.'

Belgarath squinted at the setting sun. 'Normally, I'd say no,' he said. 'These little incidental fights aren't usually very productive, but we're losing the light.' He turned to Aunt Pol. 'Is Geran anywhere in the vicinity?'

'No,' she replied. 'There's no sign of him.'

336

Belgarath scratched at his beard. 'If we leave the Chereks there, they're going to follow us, and I don't think I want them creeping along behind—particularly once it gets dark.' His lined old face tightened into a wolfish grin. 'All right, let's indulge ourselves.'

'Save a few of them though, father,' Polgara said. 'I have some questions I'd like answered. And try not to get yourselves hurt, gentlemen. I'm a little tired for surgery today.'

'No surgery today, Lady Polgara,' Brin promised blithely. 'A few funerals, perhaps, but no surgery.'

She raised her eyes toward the sky. 'Alorns,' she sighed.

The ambush did not turn out at all as the hidden Bear-cultists had anticipated. The fur-clad Cherek who leaped howling at Garion was met in midair by the flaming sword of the Rivan King and was sheared nearly in two at the waist by the great blade. He fell to the suddenly blood-drenched grass, writhing and squealing. Kail coolly split a charging cultist's head while his brothers fell on the startled attackers and savagely but methodically began to hack them to pieces.

One cultist leaped atop a large rock, drawing a bow with his arrow pointed directly at Garion, but Belgarath made a short gesture with his left hand, and the bowman was suddenly hurled backward in a long, graceful arc that carried him out over the edge of the nearby cliff. His arrow went harmlessly into the air as he fell shrieking toward the foamy breakers five hundred feet below.

'Remember, I need a few of them alive!' Polgara sharply reminded them, as the carnage threatened to get completely out of hand.

Kail grunted, then neatly parried the thrust of a desperate Cherek. His big left fist swung in a broad arc and smashed solidly into the side of the Cherek's head, sending him spinning to the turf.

Durnik was using his favorite weapon, a stout cudgel perhaps three feet long. Expertly, he slapped a cultist's sword out of his hand and cracked him sharply alongside the head. The man's eyes glazed, and he tumbled limply to the ground. Belgarath surveyed the fight, selected a likely candidate and then levitated him about fifty feet into the air. The suspended man was at first apparently unaware of his new location and kept slashing ineffectually at the surrounding emptiness.

The fight was soon over. The last crimson rays of the setting sun mingled with the scarlet blood staining the grass near the edge of the cliff, and the ground was littered with broken swords and scraps of bloody bearskin. 'For some reason, that makes me feel better,' Garion declared, wiping his sword on the fallen body of one of the cultists. The Orb, he noted, was also blazing with a kind of fiery satisfaction.

Polgara was coolly inspecting a couple of unconscious survivors. 'These two will sleep for a while,' she noted, rolling back an eyelid to examine the glazed eye underneath. 'Bring that one down, father,' she said, pointing at the man Belgarath had suspended in midair, 'In one piece, if you can manage it. I'd like to question him.'

'Of course, Pol.' The old man's eyes were sparkling, and his grin very nearly split his face.

'Father,' she said, 'when *are* you ever going to grow up?'

'Why, Polgara,' he said mockingly, 'what a thing to say.'

The floating cultist had finally realized his situation and had dropped his sword. He stood tremblng on the insubstantial air, with his eyes bulging in terror and his limbs twitching violently. When Belgarath gently lowered him to the ground, he immediately collapsed in a quivering heap. The old man firmly grasped him by the front of his fur tunic and hauled him roughly into a half-standing position. 'Do you know who I am?' he demanded, thrusting his face into that of the cringing captive.

'You—I —'

'Do you?' Belgarath's voice cracked like a whip.

'Yes,' the man choked.

'Then you know that if you try to run away, I'll just

hang you back up in the air again and leave you there. You know that I can do that, don't you?'

'Yes?'

'That won't be necessary, father,' Polgara said coolly. 'This man is going to be very co-operative.'

'I will say nothing, witch-woman,' the captive declared, though his eyes were still a bit wild.

'Ah, no, my friend,' she told him with a chilly little smile. 'You will say everything. You'll talk for weeks if I need you to.' She gave him a hard stare and made a small gesture in front of his face with her left hand. 'Look closely, friend,' she said. 'Enjoy every single detail.'

The bearded Bear-cultist stared at the empty air directly in front of his face, and the blood drained from his cheeks. His eyes started from his head in horror, and he shrieked, staggering back. Grimly, she made a sort of hooking gesture with her still-extended hand, and his retreat stopped instantly. 'You can't run away from it,' she said, 'and unless you talk—right now—it will stand in front of your face until the day you die.'

'Take it away!' he begged in an insane shriek. 'Please, I'll do anything—anything!'

'I wonder where she learned to do that,' Belgarath murmured to Garion. 'I could never do it to anybody— and I've tried.'

'He'll tell you whatever he knows now, Garion,' Polgara said then. 'He's aware of what will happen if he doesn't.'

'What have you done with my son?' Garion demanded of the terrified man.

The prisoner swallowed hard, and then he straightened defiantly. 'He's far beyond your reach now, King of Riva.'

The rage welled up in Garion again, and, without thinking, he reached over his shoulder for his sword.

'Garion!' Polgara said sharply.

The cultist flinched back, his face going pale. 'Your son is alive,' he said hastily. Then a smug look crossed his face. 'But the next time you meet him, he will kill you.'

'What are you talking about?'

'Ulfgar has consulted the oracles. You are not the Rivan

339

King we have awaited for all these centuries. It's the *next* King of Riva who will unite Aloria and lead us against the kingdoms of the south. It is your son, Belgarion, and he will lead us because he will be raised to share our beliefs.'

'Where is my son?' Garion shouted at him.

'Where you will never find him,' the prisoner taunted. 'We will raise and nurture him in the true faith, as befits an Alorn monarch. And when he is grown, he will come and kill you and take his crown and his sword and his Orb from your usurping hand.' The man's eyes were bulging, his limbs shook with religious ecstasy, and there was foam on his lips. 'You will die by your own son's hand, Belgarion of Riva,' he shrieked, 'and King Geran will lead all Alorns against the unbelievers of the south, as Belar commanded.'

'We're not getting too far with this line of questioning,' Belgarath said. 'Let me try for a while.' He turned to the wild-eyed captive. 'How much do you know about this Ulfgar?' he asked.

'Ulfgar is the Bear-lord, and he has even more power than you, old man.'

'Interesting notion,' Belgarath murmured. 'Have you ever met this master sorcerer—or even seen him, for that matter?'

'Well —' the captive hedged.

'I didn't think so. How did you know he wanted you to come here and abduct Belgarion's son, then?'

The captive bit his lip.

'Answer me!'

'He sent a messenger,' the man replied sullenly.

A sudden thought occurred to Garion. 'Was this Ulfgar of yours behind the attempt to kill my wife?' he demanded.

'Wife!' The cultist sneered. 'No Alorn takes a Tolnedran mongrel to wife. You—Iron-grip's heir—should know that better than any man. Naturally we tried to kill the Tolnedran wench. It was the only way to rid Aloria of the infection you brought here.'

'You're starting to irritate me, friend,' Garion said bleakly. 'Don't do that.'

'Let's get back to this messenger,' Belgarath said. 'You say that the baby is where we can't reach him, but you're still here, aren't you? Could it just possibly be that it was the messenger who was the actual abductor and that you and your friends are merely underlings?'

The cultist's eyes grew wild, and he looked this way and that like a trapped animal. His limbs began to tremble violently.

'I think we're approaching a question that you don't want to answer, friend,' Belgarath suggested.

It came almost like a blow. There was a wrenching kind of feeling to it, almost as if someone were reaching inside a skull to twist and crush the brain within. The captive shrieked, gave Belgarath one wild look, then spun, took three quick steps, and hurled himself off the edge of the cliff behind him.

'Question me now!' he shrieked as he plummeted down into the twilight that was rising out of the dark, angry waters surging about the rocks at the foot of the cliff. Then, even as he fell, Garion heard peal upon peal of insane laughter fading horribly as the fanatic dropped away from them.

Aunt Pol started quickly toward the edge, but Belgarath reached out and took her arm. 'Let him go, Pol,' he said. 'It wouldn't be a kindness to save him now. Someone put something in his mind that crushed out his sanity as soon as he was asked that certain question.'

'Who could possibly do that?' she asked.

'I don't know, but I'm certainly going to find out.'

The shrieking laughter, still fading, continued to echo up to where they stood. And then it ended abruptly far below.

Chapter Twenty-one

A sudden summer storm had come howling in off the Great Western Sea two days after the fight on the cliffs and it raked the island with shrieking winds and sheets of rain that rattled against the windows of the council chamber high in the south tower. The bone-thin Javelin, who had arrived with the others aboard the *Seabird* that morning, slouched in his chair, looking out at the raging storm and thoughtfully tapping his fingers together. 'Where did the trail finally lead?' he asked.

'Right down to the water's edge in a secluded cove,' Garion replied.

'Then I think we'll have to assume that his abductor made a clean escape with the prince. The timing might have been a little tight, but the men aboard the ships that were patrolling the coast would have been concentrating on the shore line, and a ship that had gotten well out to sea before they arrived could have escaped their notice.'

Barak was piling an armload of logs in the cavernous fireplace. 'Why were those others left behind, then?' he asked. 'That doesn't make any sense at all.'

'We're talking about Bear-cultists, Barak,' Silk told him. 'They're not *supposed* to make sense.'

'There's a certain logic to it, though,' the Earl of Seline pointed out. 'If what that cultist said before he died is true, this Ulfgar has declared war on Belgarion. Isn't it entirely possible that those men were left behind specifically to waylay him? One way or another, he was certain to follow that trail.'

'There's still something that doesn't quite ring true,' Javelin frowned. 'Let me think about it for a bit.'

'We can sort out their motives later,' Garion said. 'The important thing right now is to find out where they've taken my son.'

'Rheon, most likely,' Anheg said. 'We've destroyed Jarviksholm. Rheon's the only strong point they've got left.'

'That's not entirely certain, Anheg,' Queen Porenn disagreed. 'This scheme to abduct Prince Geran was obviously planned quite some time ago, and you destroyed Javiksholm only last week. It's unlikely that the abductors even knew about it. I don't think we can rule out the possibility that the prince was taken to Cherek.'

Anheg rose and began pacing up and down, a dark scowl on his face. 'She's got a point,' he admitted finally. 'These child stealers were Chereks, after all. It's quite possible that they tried to take him to Jarviksholm, but when they found the city destroyed, they had to go someplace else. We could very well find them holed up in a fishing village somewhere on the west coast.'

'What do we do now, then?' Garion asked helplessly.

'We split up,' King Cho-Hag said quietly. 'Anheg turns out all his forces, and they search every village and farm in Cherek. The rest of us go to Rheon and deal with those people there.'

'There's only one difficulty with that,' Anheg said. 'A baby is a baby. How do my men recognize Garion's son if they do run across him?'

'That's no real problem, Anheg,' Polgara told him from her chair by the fire where she sat sipping a cup of tea. 'Show them your palm, Garion.'

Garion held up his right hand to show the King of Cherek the silvery mark there.

'I'd almost forgotten that,' Anheg grunted. 'Does Prince Geran have the same mark?'

'All heirs to the Rivan Throne have that mark on their palms,' she replied. 'It's been that way since the birth of Iron-grip's first son.'

'All right,' Anheg said. 'My men will know what to

look for, but will the rest of you have enough men to take Rheon? With the Algar and Drasnian cultists there, Ulfgar's got quite an army.'

General Brendig rose and went over to a large map tacked up on one of the walls. 'If I leave immediately for Sendar, I can put together a sizeable army in a few days. A forced march could put us in Darine within a week.'

'I'll have ships waiting there to ferry you and your men to Boktor, then,' Anheg promised.

'And I'll go south and raise the clans,' Hettar said. 'We'll ride straight north to Rheon.'

Garion was also peering at the map. 'If Anheg's ships take me and my troops to Boktor, we can join with the Drasnian pikemen there and march toward Rheon from the west,' he said. 'Then the ships can go back to Darine and pick up Brendig.'

'That would save some time,' Brendig agreed.

'With the Rivans and Drasnians, you're going to have enough troops to encircle Rheon,' Silk said. 'You might not have enough men to take the city, but you *will* have enough to keep anybody from going in or out. Then all you have to do is sit and wait for Brendig and Hettar. Once they join you, you'll have an overwhelming force.'

'It's a sound plan, Garion,' Barak said approvingly.

Mandorallen stood up. 'And when we arrive at this fortified city on the moors of eastern Drasnia, I will undertake with siege engines and diverse other means to weaken the walls so that we may more easily gain access when we make our final assault,' he noted. 'Rheon will fall, and we will bring this miscreant Ulfgar to swift and terrible justice.'

'Not *too* swift, I hope,' Hettar murmured. 'I was thinking along the lines of something more lingering.'

'We'll have time to think about that after we catch him,' Barak said.

The door opened, and Ce'Nedra, pale and wan-looking and accompanied by Queen Layla and the other ladies, entered. 'Why are you all still here?' she demanded. 'Why aren't you taking the world apart to find my baby?'

'That's hardly fair, Ce'Nedra,' Garion chided her gently.

'I'm not trying to be fair. I want my baby.'

'So do I, but we're not going to accomplish much by dashing around in circles, are we?'

'I'll raise an army myself, if I have to,' she declared hotly. 'I did it before and I can certainly do it again.'

'And just where would you take them, dear?' Polgara asked her.

'Wherever it is that they've got my baby.'

'And where is that? If you know something that we don't, shouldn't you share it with us?'

Ce'Nedra stared at her helplessly, her eyes filling with tears.

Belgarath had not contributed anything to the discussions, but rather had sat brooding out at the storm from a deep-cushioned chair by the window. 'I've got the feeling that I'm missing something,' he muttered as Adara and Nerina led the distraught Ce'Nedra to a chair near the council table.

'What did you say, Belgarath?' Anheg asked, removing his dented crown and tossing it on the table.

'I said that I think I'm missing something,' the old man replied. 'Anheg, just how extensive is your library?'

The Cherek King shrugged, scratching at his head. 'I don't know that I could match the university library at Tol Honeth,' he admitted, 'but I've gathered *most* of the significant books in the world.'

'How does your collection stack up in the area of the mysteries?'

'Of what?'

'Prophecies—not so much the Mrin Codex or the Darine—but the others; the Gospels of the Seers at Kell, the Grolim Prophecies of Rak Cthol, the Oracles of Ashaba.'

'I've got that one,' Anheg told him, 'the Ashaba thing. I picked it up about a dozen years ago.'

'I think I'd better go to Val Alor and have a look at it.'

'This is hardly the time for side trips, Grandfather,' Garion objected.

'Garion, we know that something's happening that goes beyond an insurrection by a group of religious fanatics. That passage you found in the Mrin Codex was very specific. It instructed me to look into the mysteries, and I think that if I don't do exactly that, we're all likely to regret it.' He turned to Anheg. 'Where's your copy of the Ashabine Oracles?'

'In the library—up on the top shelf. I couldn't make any sense out of it, so I stuck it up there. I always meant to get back to it one day.' Then a thought occurred to him. 'Oh, by the way, there's a copy of the Mallorean Gospels in the monastery at Mar Terrin.'

Belgarath blinked.

'That's one of the other books you wanted to see, wasn't it? The one by the Seers of Kell?'

'How could you possibly know what's in the library at Mar Terrin?'

'I heard about it a few years back. I have people who keep their eyes open for rare books. Anyway, I made the monks an offer for it—quite generous, I thought—but the negotiations fell through.'

'You're a positive sink of information, Anheg. Can you think of anything else?'

'I can't help you with the Grolim Prophecies of Rak Cthol, I'm afraid. The only copy I know of was in Ctuchik's library, and that was probably buried when you blew Rak Cthol off its mountaintop. You could go dig for it, I suppose.'

'Thanks, Anheg,' Belgarath said drily. 'You have no idea how much I appreciate your help.'

'I can't believe that I'm hearing this,' Ce'Nedra said accusingly to Belgarath. 'Someone has stolen my baby— your great-grandson—and instead of trying to find him, you're planning to go off chasing obscure manuscripts.'

'I'm not abandoning the child, Ce'Nedra. I'm just looking for him in a different place, that's all.' He looked at her with a great sympathy in his eyes. 'You're still very young,' he said, 'and all you can see is the one reality that your baby has been taken from you. There are two kinds of reality, however. Garion is going to follow your child in *this* reality. I'm going to follow him in the other. We're all after the same thing and this way we cover all the possibilities.'

She stared at him for a moment, and then she suddenly covered her face with her hands and began to cry. Garion rose, went to her, and put his arms around her. 'Ce'Nedra,' he said soothingly, 'Ce'Nedra, it's going to be all right.'

'Nothing will be all right,' she sobbed brokenly. 'I'm so afraid for my baby, Garion. Nothing will ever be all right again.'

Mandorallen rose to his feet, tears standing in his eyes. 'As I am thy true knight and champion, dearest Ce'Nedra, I vow upon my life that the villain Ulfgar will never see another summer.'

'That sort of gets to the point,' Hettar murmured. 'Why don't we all go to Rheon and nail Ulfgar to a post someplace—with very long nails?'

Anheg looked at Cho-hag. 'Your son has a remarkably firm grasp of the realities of this situation,' he observed.

'He's the delight of my twilight years,' Cho-Hag said proudly.

The argument with Ce'Nedra began immediately upon their return to the royal apartment. Garion tried reason first, then commands. Finally, he resorted to threats.

'I don't care what you say, Garion, I *am* going to Rheon.'

'You are *not*!'

'I am *so*!'

'I'll have you locked in the bedroom.'

'And as soon as you leave, I'll order someone to unlock the door—or I'll chop it down—and I'll be on the next boat out of the harbor.'

'Ce'Nedra, it's too dangerous.'

'So was Thull Mardu—and Cthol Mishrak—and I didn't flinch from either one. I'm going to Rheon, Garion —either with you or by myself. I'm going to get my baby back—even if I have to tear down the city walls with my bare hands.'

'Ce'Nedra, please.'

'No!' she exclaimed, stamping her foot. 'I'm going, Garion, and nothing you can say or do is going to stop me!'

Garion threw his arms in the air. 'Women!' he said in a despairing tone.

The fleet left at dawn the following morning, sailing out of the harbor into rough seas and the dirty scud and wrack of the tail-end of the storm.

Garion stood on the aft deck of the *Seabird* beside Barak, whose thick hands firmly grasped the tiller. 'I didn't think I was ever going to have to do this again,' he said morosely.

'Oh, sailing in rough weather isn't all that bad.' Barak shrugged as the wind tossed his red beard.

'That's not what I meant. I thought that after Torak died, I could live out my life in peace.'

'You got lucky,' Barak told him.

'Are you trying to be funny?'

'All anybody ever got out of peace was a fat behind and cobwebs in his head,' the big man said sagely. 'Give me a nice friendly little war any time.'

When they were some leagues at sea, a detachment of ships separated from the fleet to sail due east toward Sendar, bearing with them King Fulrach, General Brendig, the Earl of Seline, and the heavily sedated Queen Layla.

'I hope Brendig gets to Darine on time,' Anheg said, standing at the rail. 'I'm really going to need those ships during the search.'

'Where do you plan to start?' Queen Porenn asked him.

'The cult's largely concentrated on the west coast,' he replied. 'If Prince Geran's abductors went to Cherek, they'd most likely head for a cult stronghold. I'll start along the coast and work my way inland.'

'That seems like sound strategy.' she agreed, 'Deploy your men and sweep the area.'

'Porenn,' he said with a pained look, 'I love you like a sister, but please don't use military terms when you talk to me. It sets my teeth on edge to hear that sort of language in a woman's mouth.'

The passage through the Cherek Bore delayed them for two days. Although Greldik and a few other hardy souls were willing—even eager—to attempt the Great Maelstrom in the heavy seas that were the aftermath of the storm, cooler and more prudent heads prevailed. 'I'm sure the sea will quiet down in a bit,' Barak shouted across to his friend, 'and Rheon isn't going anyplace. Let's not lose any ships if we don't have to.'

'Barak,' Greldik shouted back, 'you're turning into an old woman.'

'Anheg said the same thing just before Jarviksholm,' Barak noted.

'He's a wise king.'

'It isn't his ship.'

After they passed the Bore and entered the calmer waters of the Gulf of Cherek, King Anheg took a sizeable portion of the fleet and sailed northward toward Val Alorn. Before making the transfer to one of Anheg's ships, Belgarath stood on deck, talking quietly with Garion and Polgara. 'As soon as I finish at Val Alorn, I'll go on down to Mar Terrin,' he told them. 'If I don't get back before you arrive at Rheon, be careful. The cult's pretty fanatic, and this war they've started is directed at you personally, Garion.'

'I'll watch out for him, father,' Polgara assured him.

'I can more or less take care of myself, Aunt Pol,' Garion told her.

'I'm sure you can, dear,' she replied, 'but old habits die hard.'

'How old am I going to have to be before you realize that I'm grown up?'

'Why don't you check back with me in a thousand years or so?' she said. 'Maybe we can talk about it then.'

He smiled, then sighed. 'Aunt Pol,' he said, 'I love you.'

'Yes, dear,' she replied, patting his cheek, 'I know, and I love you, too.'

At Kotu, the ship carrying Hettar and his wife and parents turned south toward Aldurford. 'I'll meet you at Rheon in about three weeks,' the hawk-faced Algar called across to the *Seabird*. 'Save a little bit of the fighting for me.'

'Only if you hurry,' Lelldorin shouted back blithely.

'I'm not sure which is worse,' Polgara murmured to Ce'Nedra, 'Arends or Alorns.'

'Could they possibly be related?' Ce'Nedra asked.

Aunt Pol laughed, then wrinkled her nose as she looked at the wharves of Kotu. 'Come, dear,' she said, 'Let's go below. Harbors always have the most distressing odors about them.'

The fleet passed Kotu and filed into the mouth of the Mrin River. The current was sluggish, and the fens lay green and soggy on either side. Garion stood near the bow of the *Seabird*, idly watching the gray-green reeds and scrubby bushes slide by as the oarsmen pulled steadily upstream.

'Ah, there you are, Garion,' Queen Porenn said, coming up behind him. 'I thought we might talk for a few minutes.'

'Of course.' He had a rather special feeling for this small, blonde woman, whose courage and devotion bespoke at once an enormous affection and an iron-clad resolve.

'When we reach Boktor, I want to leave Kheva at the palace. I don't think he's going to like it very much, but he's just a little young for battles. If he gets stubborn about it, could you order him to stay behind?'

'Me?'

'You're the Overlord of the West, Garion,' she reminded him. 'I'm only his mother.'

'Overlord of the West is an over-rated title, I'm afraid.' He tugged absently at one ear. 'I wonder if I could possibly persuade Ce'Nedra to stay in Boktor as well,' he mused.

'I doubt it,' she said. 'Kheva might accept you as his superior, but Ce'Nedra looks upon you as her husband. There's a difference, you know.'

He made a wry face. 'You're probably right,' he admitted. 'It's worth a try, though. How far up the Mrin can we go by boat?'

'The north fork runs into a series of shallows about twenty leagues above Boktor,' she replied. 'I supppose we could portage around them, but it wouldn't accomplish very much. Ten leagues farther upstream you come to another stretch of shallows, and then there are the rapids. We could spend a great deal of time pulling the boats out of the water and then putting them back in again.'

'Then it would be faster just to start marching when we get to the first shallows?'

She nodded. 'It's likely to take several days for my generals to assemble their troops and get their supplies together,' she added. 'I'll instruct them to follow us as quickly as they can. Once they join us, we can go on to Rheon and lay siege until Brendig and Hettar arrive.'

'You know, you're really very good at this, Porenn.'

She smiled sadly. 'Rhodar was a very good teacher.'

'You loved him very much, didn't you?'

She sighed. 'More than you can possibly imagine, Garion.'

They reached Boktor the following afternoon, and Garion accompanied Queen Porenn and her slightly sullen son to the palace, with Silk tagging along behind. As soon as they arrived, Porenn sent a messenger to the headquarters of the Drasnian military forces.

'Shall we take some tea while we're waiting, gentlemen?' the little blonde queen offered as the three of them sat comfortably in a large, airy chamber with red velvet drapes at the windows.

'Only if you can't find anything stronger,' Silk replied with an impudent grin.

'Isn't it a trifle early in the day for that, Prince Kheldar?' she asked him reprovingly.

'I'm an Alorn, Auntie dear. It's never too early in the day.'

'Kheldar, please don't call me that. It makes me feel positively antique.'

'But you *are*, Porenn—my aunt, I mean, not antique, of course.'

'Are you ever serious about anything?'

'Not if I can help it.'

She sighed and then laughed a warm tinkle of a laugh.

Perhaps a quarter of an hour later, a stocky man with a red face and a somewhat gaudy orange uniform was shown into the room. 'Your Majesty sent for me?' he asked, bowing respectfully.

'Ah, General Haldar,' she replied. 'Are you acquainted with his Majesty, King Belgarion?'

'We met briefly, ma'am—at your late husband's funeral.' He bowed floridly to Garion. 'Your Majesty.'

'General.'

'And of course you've met Prince Kheldar.'

'Of course' the general replied. 'Your Highness.'

'General.' Silk looked at him closely. 'Isn't that a new decoration, Haldar?' he asked.

The red-faced general touched the cluster of medals on his chest somewhat deprecatingly. 'That's what generals do in peacetime, Prince Kheldar. We give each other medals.'

'I'm afraid that the peacetime is at an end, General Haldar,' Porenn said rather crisply. 'You've heard what happened at Jarviksholm in Cherek, I presume.'

'Yes, your Majesty,' he replied. 'It was a well-executed campaign.'

'We are now going to proceed against Rheon. The Bear-cult has abducted King Belgarion's son.'

'*Abducted?*' Haldar's expression was incredulous.

'I'm afraid so. I think the time has come to eliminate the cult entirely. That's why we're moving on Rheon. We have a fleet in the harbor loaded with Belgarion's Rivans. Tomorrow,we'll sail up to the shallows and disembark. We'll march overland toward Rheon. I want you to muster the army and follow us as quickly a you possibly can.'

Haldar was frowning as if something he had heard had distracted him. 'Are you sure that the Rivan Prince was abducted, you Majesty?' he asked. 'He was not killed?'

'No,' Garion answered firmly. 'It was clearly an abduction.'

Haldar began to pace up and down agitatedly. 'That doesn't make any sense,' he muttered, almost to himself.

'Do you understand your instructions, General?' Porenn asked him.

'What? Oh, yes, your Majesty. I'm to gather the army and catch up with King Belgarion's Rivans before they reach Rheon.'

'Precisely. We'll besiege the town until the rest of our forces arrive. We'll be joined at Rheon by Algars and elements of the Sendarian army.'

'I'll start at once, your Majesty,' he assured her. His expression was still slightly abstracted, and his frown was worried.

'Is there anything wrong, General?' she asked him.

'What? Oh, no, your Majesty. I'll go to headquarters and issue the necessary orders immediately.'

'Thank you, General Haldar. That will be all.'

'He certainly heard something he didn't like,' Silk observed after the general had left.

'We've all heard things lately that we haven't liked,' Garion said.

'It wasn't quite the same, though,' Silk muttered. 'Excuse me for a bit. I think I'm going to go ask a few questions.' He rose from his chair and quietly left the room.

Early the next morning, the fleet weighed anchor and began to move slowly upstream from Boktor. Though the day had dawned clear and sunny, by noon a heavy cloud cover had swept in off the Gulf of Cherek to turn the Drasnian countryside gray and depressing.

'I hope it doesn't rain,' Barak growled from his place at the tiller. 'I hate slogging through mud on my way to a fight.'

The shallows of the Mrin proved to be a very wide stretch of river where the water rippled over gravel bars.

'Have you ever considered dredging this?' Garion asked the Queen of Drasnia.

'No,' she replied. 'As a matter of policy I don't want the Mrin navigable beyond this point. I'd rather not have Tolnedran merchantmen bypassing Boktor.' She smiled sweetly at Ce'Nedra. 'I'm not trying to be offensive, dear,' she said, 'but your countrymen always seem to want to avoid customs. As things now stand, I control the North Caravan Route and I need that customs revenue.'

'I understand, Porenn,' Ce'Nedra assured her. 'I'd do it that way myself.'

They beached the fleet on the northern bank of the river, and Garion's forces began to disembark. 'You'll lead the ships back downriver and across to Darine, then?' Barak said to the bearded Greldik.

'Right,' Greldik said. 'I'll have Brendig and his Sendars back here within a week.'

'Good. Tell him to follow us to Rheon as quickly as he can. I've never been happy with the idea of long sieges.'

'Are you going to send *Seabird* back with me?'

Barak scratched at his beard thoughtfully. 'No,' he said finally. 'I think I'll leave her here.'

'Believe me, I'm not going to get her sunk, Barak.'

'I know, but I just feel better about the idea of having her here in case I need her. Will you come to Rheon with Brendig? There's bound to be some good fighting.'

Greldik's face grew mournful. 'No,' he replied. 'Anheg ordered me to come back to Val Alorn when I finish freighting the Sendars here.'

'Oh. That's too bad.'

Greldik grunted sourly. 'Have fun at Rheon,' he said, 'and try not to get yourself killed.'

'I'll make a special point of it.'

By the time the troops and supplies had all been unloaded, it was late afternoon. The clouds continued to roll in, though there was as yet no rain. 'I think we may as well set up a camp here,' Garion said to the others as they all stood on the gently sloping riverbank. 'We wouldn't get too far before dark anyway, and if we get a good night's sleep, we can start early in the morning.'

'That makes sense,' Silk agreed.

'Did you find out anything about Haldar?' Queen Porenn asked the rat-faced little man. 'I know there was something about him that was bothering you.'

'Nothing really very specific.' Silk shrugged. 'He's been doing a lot of traveling lately, though.'

'He's a general, Kheldar, and my Chief of Staff. Generals *do* have to make inspection tours from time to time, you know.'

'But usually not alone,' Silk replied. 'When he makes these trips, he doesn't even take his aide along.'

'I think you're just being overly suspicious.'

'It's my nature to be suspicious, Auntie dear.'

She stamped her foot. '*Will* you stop calling me that?'

He looked at her mildly. 'Does it really bother you, Porenn?' he asked.

'I've told you that it bothers me.'

'Maybe I ought to try to remember that, then.'

'You're absolutely impossible, do you know that?'

'Of course I do, Auntie dear.'

For the next two days the Rivan army marched steadily eastward across the desolate, gray-green moors, a wasteland of barren, sparsely vegetated hills interspersed with rank patches of thorn and bramble springing up around dark pools of stagnant water. The sky remained gray and threatening, but there was as yet no rain.

Garion rode at the head of the column with a bleakly determined look on his face, speaking infrequently except to issue commands. His scouts reported at intervals, announcing that there was no sign of cult forces ahead and with equal certainty that there was as yet no evidence that the Drasnian pike men under General Haldar were coming up from the rear.

When they stopped for a hasty midday meal on that second day, Polgara approached him gravely. Her blue cloak seemed to whisper through the tall grass as she came, and her familiar fragrance came to him on the vagrant breeze. 'Let's walk a bit, Garion,' she said quietly. 'There's something we need to discuss.'

'All right.' His reply was short, even curt.

She did something then that she had rarely done in the past several years. With a kind of solemn affection, she linked her arm in his, and together they walked away from the army and the rest of their friends, moving up a grassy knoll.

'You've grown very grim in the past few weeks, dear,' she said as they stopped at the crest of the knoll.

'I think I've got reason enough, Aunt Pol.'

'I know that you've been hurt very deeply by all of this, Garion, and that you're filled with a great rage; but don't let it turn you into a savage.'

'Aunt Pol, I didn't start this,' he reminded her. 'They tried to kill my wife. Then they murdered one of my closest friends and tried to start a war between me and Anheg. And now they've stolen my son. Don't you think that a little punishment might be in order?'

'Perhaps,' she replied, looking directly into his face, 'but you must not allow your sense of outrage to run away with you and make you decide to start wading in blood. You have tremendous power, Garion, and you could very easily use it to do unspeakable things to your enemies. If you do that, the power will turn you into something as vile as Torak was. You'll begin to take pleasure in the horrors you inflict. In time, that pleasure will come to own you.'

He stared at her, startled by the intensity in her voice and by the way the single white lock at her brow seemed to blaze up suddenly.

'It's a very real danger, Garion. In a peculiar way, you're in more peril right now than you were when you faced Torak.'

'I'm not going to let them get away with what they've done,' he said stubbornly. 'I'm not just going to let them go.'

'I'm not suggesting that, dear. We'll be at Rheon soon, and there'll be fighting. You're an Alorn, and I'm sure that you'll be very enthusiastic about the fighting. I want you to promise me that you won't let that enthusiasm and your sense of outrage push you over the line into wanton slaughter.'

'Not if they surrender,' he replied stiffly.

'And what then? What will you do with your prisoners?'

He frowned. He hadn't really considered that.

'For the most part, the Bear-cult is composed of the ignorant and the misguided. They're so obsessed with a single idea that they can't even comprehend the enormity of what they've done. Will you butcher them for stupidity? Stupidty is unfortunate, but it hardly deserves *that* kind of punishment.'

'What about Ulfgar?' he demanded.

She smiled a bleak little smile. 'Now *that*,' she said, 'is another matter.'

A large, blue-banded hawk spiraled down out of the murky sky. 'Are we having a little family get-together?' Beldin asked harshly, even as he shimmered into his own form.

'Where have you been, uncle?' Aunt Pol asked him quite calmly. 'I left word with the twins for you to catch up with us.'

'I just got back from Mallorea,' he grunted, scratching at his stomach. 'Where's Belgarath?'

'At Val Alorn,' she replied, 'and then he's going on to Mar Terrin. He's trying to follow the trail that's supposed to be hidden in the mysteries. You've heard about what's happened?'

'Most of it, I think. The twins showed me the passage that was hidden in the Mrin Codex, and I heard about the Rivan Warder and Belgarion's son. You're moving against Rheon, right?'

'Naturally,' she answered. 'That's the source of the infection.'

The hunchback looked speculatively at Garion. 'I'm sure you're an expert tactician, Belgarion,' he said, 'but your reasoning escapes me this time.'

Garion looked at him blankly.

'You're moving to attack a superior force in a fortified city, right?'

'I suppose you could put it that way.'

'Then why is more than half your army camped at the shallows of the Mrin, two days behind you? Don't you think you might need them?'

'What are you talking about, uncle?' Aunt Pol asked sharply.

'I thought I was speaking quite plainly. The Drasnian army's camped at the shallows. They don't show signs of planning to move at any time in the near future. They're even fortifying their positions.'

'That's impossible.'

He shrugged. 'Fly back and have a look for yourself.'

'We'd better go tell the others, Garion,' Aunt Pol said gravely. 'Something has gone terribly wrong somewhere.'

Chapter Twenty-two

'What is that man thinking of?' Queen Porenn burst out in a sudden uncharacteristic fury. 'I specifically ordered him to catch up with us.'

Silk's face was bleak. 'I think we should have checked the inestimable General Haldar's feet for that telltale brand,' he said.

'You're not serious!' Porenn exclaimed.

'He's deliberately disobeying your orders, Porenn, and he's doing it in such a way as to endanger you and all the rest of us.'

'Believe me, I'll get to the bottom of this as soon as I get back to Boktor.'

'Unfortunately, we're not going in that direction just now.'

'Then I'll go back to the shallows alone,' she declared. 'If necessary, I'll relieve him of his command.'

'No,' he said firmly, 'you won't.'

She stared at him incredulously. 'Kheldar, do you realize to whom you're speaking?'

'Perfectly, Porenn, but it's too dangerous.'

'It's my duty.'

'No,' he corrected. 'Actually, your duty is to stay alive long enough to raise Kheva to be King of Drasnia.'

She bit her lip. 'That's unfair, Kheldar.'

'Life is hard, Porenn.'

'He's right, your Majesty,' Javelin said. 'General Haldar has already committed treason by disobeying you. I don't think he'd hesitate to add your murder to that crime.'

'We're going to need some men,' Barak rumbled, 'a few,

anyway. Otherwise we're going to have to stop and wait for Brendig.'

Silk shook his head. 'Haldar's camped at the shallows. If what we suspect is true, he can keep Brendig from ever disembarking his troops.'

'Well,' Ce'Nedra demanded angrily, 'what do we do now?'

'I don't think we've got much choice,' Barak said. 'We'll have to turn around and go back to the shallows and arrest Haldar for treason. Then we turn around and come back with the pikemen.'

'That could take almost a week,' she protested.

'What other alternatives do we have? We have to have those pikemen.'

'I think you're overlooking something, Barak,' Silk said. 'Have you noticed a slight chill in the air the last two days?'

'A little—in the mornings.'

'We're in northeastern Drasnia. Winter comes very early up here.'

'Winter? But it's only early autumn.'

'We're a long way north, my friend. We could get the first snowfall at any time now.'

Barak started to swear.

Silk motioned Javelin aside, and the two of them spoke together briefly.

'It's all falling apart, isn't it, Garion?' Ce'Nedra said, her lower lip trembling.

'We'll fix it, Ce'Nedra,' he said, taking her in his arms. 'But how?'

'I haven't quite worked that out yet.'

'We're vulnerable, Garion,' Barak said seriously. 'We're marching directly into cult territory with a vastly inferior force. We're wide open to ambush.'

'You'll need somebody to scout on ahead,' Beldin said, looking up from the piece of cold meat he had been tearing with his teeth. He stuffed the rest of the chunk in his mouth and wiped his fingers on the front of his filthy tunic. 'I can be fairly unobtrusive if I want to be.'

'I'll take care of that, uncle,' Polgara told him. 'Hettar's coming north with the Algar clans. Could you go to him and tell him what's happened? We need him as quickly as he can get here.'

He gave her an appraising look, still chewing on the chunk of meat. 'Not a bad idea, Pol,' he admitted. 'I thought that married life might have made your wits soft, but it looks as if it's only your behind that's getting flabby.'

'Do you mind, uncle?' she asked acidly.

'I'd better get started,' he said. He crouched, spread his arms, and shimmered into the form of a hawk.

'I'll be away for a few days,' Silk said, coming back to join them. 'We might be able to salvage this yet.' Then he turned on his heel and went directly to his horse.

'Where's he going?' Garion asked Javelin.

'We need men,' Javelin replied. 'He's going after some.'

'Porenn,' Polgara said, trying to look back down over her shoulder, 'does it seem to you that I've been putting on a few extra pounds in the past months?'

Porenn smiled gently. 'Of course not, Polgara,' she said. 'He was only teasing you.'

Polgara, however, still had a slightly worried look on her face as she removed her blue cloak. 'I'll go on ahead,' she told Garion. 'Keep your troops moving, but don't run. I don't want you to blunder into something before I have a chance to warn you.' Then she blurred, and the great snowy owl drifted away on soft, noiseless wings.

Garion moved his forces carefully after that, deploying them into the best possible defensive posture as they marched. He doubled his scouts and rode personally to the top of every hill along the way to search the terrain ahead. The pace of their march slowed to no more than five leagues a day; though the delay fretted him, he felt that he had no real choice in the matter.

Polgara returned each morning to report that no apparent dangers lay ahead and then she flew away again on noiseless wings.

'How does she manage that?' Ce'Nedra asked. 'I don't think she's sleeping at all.'

'Pol can go for weeks without sleep,' Durnik told her. 'She'll be all right—if it doesn't go on for *too* long.'

'Belgarion,' Errand said in his light voice, pulling his chestnut stallion in beside Garion's mount, 'you did know that we're being watched, didn't you?'

'What?'

'There are men watching us.'

'Where?'

'Several places. They're awfully well hidden. And there are other men galloping back and forth between that town we're going to and the army back at the river.'

'I don't like that very much,' Barak said. 'It sounds as if they're trying to co-ordinate something.'

Garion looked back over his shoulder at Queen Porenn, who rode beside Ce'Nedra. 'Would the Drasnian army attack us if Haldar ordered them to?' he asked.

'No,' she said quite firmly. 'The troops are absolutely loyal to me. They'd refuse that kind of order.'

'What if they thought they were rescuing you?' Errand asked.

'Rescuing?'

'That's what Ulfgar is suggesting,' the young man replied. 'The general's supposed to tell his troops that our army here is holding you prisoner.'

'I think they *would* attack under those circumstances, your Majesty,' Javelin said, 'and if the cult and the army catch us between them, we could be in very deep trouble.'

'What *else* can go wrong?' Garion fumed.

'At least it isn't snowing,' Lelldorin said. 'Not yet, anyway.'

The army seemed almost to crawl across the barren landscape as the clouds continued to roll ponderously overhead. The world seemed locked in a chill, colorless gray, and each morning the scum of ice lying on the stagnant pools was thicker.

'We're never going to get there at this rate, Garion,' Ce'Nedra said impatiently one gloomy midday as she rode beside him.

'If we get ambushed, we might not get there at all,

Ce'Nedra,' he replied. 'I don't like this any more than you do, but I don't think we've really got much choice.'

'I want my baby.'

'So do I.'

'Well, do something then.'

'I'm open to suggestions.'

'Can't you—?' She made a vague sort of gesture with one hand.

He shook his head. 'You know that there are limits to that sort of thing, Ce'Nedra.'

'What good is it then?' she demanded bitterly, pulling her gray Rivan cloak more tightly about her against the chill.

The great white owl awaited them just over the next rise. She sat on a broken limb of a dead-white snag, observing them with her unblinking golden eyes.

'Lady Polgara,' Ce'Nedra greeted her with a formal inclination of her head.

Gravely the white owl returned her a stiff little bow. Garion suddenly laughed.

The owl blurred, and the air around it wavered briefly. Then Polgara was there, seated sedately on the limb with her ankles crossed. 'What's so amusing, Garion?' she asked him.

'I've never seen a bird bow before,' he replied. 'It just struck me as funny, that's all.'

'Try not to let it overwhelm you, dear,' she said primly. 'Come over here and help me down.'

'Yes, Aunt Pol.'

After he had helped her to the ground, she looked at him soberly. 'There's a large cult force lying in wait two leagues ahead of you,' she told him.

'How large?'

'Half again as large as yours.'

'We'd better go tell the others,' he said grimly, turning his horse.

'Is there any way we could slip around them?' Durnik asked after Polgara had told them all of the cultists lying in ambush ahead.

'I don't think so, Durnik,' she replied. 'They know we're here, and I'm sure we're being watched.'

'We must needs attack them, then,' Mandorallen asserted. 'Our cause is just, and we must inevitably prevail.'

'That's an interesting superstition, Mandorallen,' Barak told him, 'but I'd prefer to have the numbers on my side.' The big man turned to Polgara. 'How are they deployed? What I mean is —'

'I know what the word means, Barak.' She scraped a patch of ground bare with her foot and picked up a stick. 'This trail we're following runs through a ravine that cuts through that low range of hills just ahead. At about the deepest part of the ravine, there are several gullies running up the sides. There are four separate groups of cultists, each one hiding in a different gully.' She sketched out the terrain ahead with her stick. 'They obviously plan to let us march right into the middle of them and then attack us from all sides at once.'

Durnik was frowning as he studied her sketch. 'We could easily defeat any one of those groups,' he suggested, rubbing thoughtfully at one cheek. 'All we really need is some way to keep the other three groups out of the fight.'

'That sort of sums it up,' Barak said, 'but I don't think they'll stay away just because they weren't invited.'

'No,' the smith agreed, 'so we'll probably have to put up some kind of barrier to prevent their joining in.'

'You've thought of something, haven't you, Durnik?' Queen Porenn observed.

'What manner of barrier could possibly keep the villains from rushing to the aid of their comrades?' Mandorallen asked.

Durnik shrugged. 'Fire would probably work.'

Javelin shook his head and pointed at the low gorse bushes in the field beside them. 'Everything in this area is still green,' he said. 'I don't think it's going to burn very well.'

Durnik smiled. 'It doesn't have to be a *real* fire.'

'Could you do that, Polgara?' Barak asked, his eyes coming alight.

She considered it a moment. 'Not in three places at once,' she replied.

'But there *are* three of us, Pol,' the smith reminded her. 'You could block one group with an illusion of fire; I could take the second; and Garion the third. We could pen all three groups in their separate gullies, and then, after we've finished with the first group, we could move on to the next.' He frowned slightly. 'The only problem with it is that I'm not sure exactly how to go about creating the illusion.'

'It's not too difficult, dear,' Aunt Pol assured him. 'It shouldn't take long for you and Garion to get the knack of it.'

'What do you think?' Queen Porenn asked Javelin.

'It's dangerous,' he told her, 'very dangerous.'

'Do we have any choice?'

'Not that I can think offhand.'

'That's it, then,' Garion said. 'If the rest of you will tell the troops what we're going to do, Durnik and I can start learning how to build imaginary bonfires.'

It was perhaps an hour later when the Rivan troops moved out tensely, each man walking through the gray-green gorse with his hand close to his weapon. The low range of hills lay dark ahead of them, and the weedy track they followed led directly into the boulder-strewn ravine where the unseen Bear-cultists waited in ambush. Garion steeled himself as they entered that ravine, drawing in his will and carefully remembering everything Aunt Pol had taught him.

The plan worked surprisingly well. As the first group of cultists dashed from the concealment of their gully with their weapons aloft and shouts of triumph on their lips, Garion, Durnik, and Polgara instantly blocked the mouths of the other three gullies. The charging cult members faltered, their triumph changing to chagrin as they gaped at the sudden flames that prevented their comrades from joining the fray. Garion's Rivans moved immediately to take advantage of that momentary hesitation. Step by step the first group of cultists were pushed back into the narrow confines of the gully that had concealed them.

Garion could pay only scant attention to the progress of the fight. He sat astride his horse with Lelldorin at his side, concentrating entirely upon projecting the images of flame and the sense of heat and the crackle of fire across the mouth of the gully opposite the one where the fight was in progress. Dimly through the leaping flames, he could see the members of the cult trying to shield their faces from an intense heat that was not really there. And then the one thing that had not occurred to any of them happened. The trapped cult-members in Garion's gully began to throw bucketsful of water hastily dipped from a stagnant pond on the imaginary flames. There was, of course, no hiss of steam nor any other visible effect of that attempt to quench the illusion. After several moments a cult member, cringing and wincing, stepped through the fire. 'It isn't real!' he shouted back over his shoulder. 'The fire isn't real!'

'*This* is, though,' Lelldorin muttered grimly, sinking an arrow into the man's chest. The cultist threw up his arms and toppled over backward into the fire—which had no effect on his limp body. That, of course, gave the whole thing away. First a few and then a score or more cult-members ran directly through Garion's illusion. Lelldorin's hands blurred as he shot arrow after arrow into the milling ranks at the mouth of the gully. 'There're too many of them, Garion,' he shouted. 'I can't hold them. We'll have to fall back.'

'Aunt Pol!' Garion yelled. 'They're breaking through!'

'Push them back,' she called to him. 'Use your will.'

He concentrated even more and pushed a solid barrier of his will at the men emerging from the gully. At first it seemed that it might even work, but the effort he was exerting was enormous, and he soon began to tire. The edges of his hastily erected barrier began to fray and tatter and the men he was trying so desperately to hold back began to find those weak spots.

Dimly, even as he bent all of his concentration on maintaining the barrier, he heard a sullen rumble, almost like distant thunder.

'Garion!' Lelldorin cried. 'Horsemen—hundreds of them!'

In dismay, Garion looked quickly up the ravine and saw a sudden horde of riders coming down the steep cut from the east. 'Aunt Pol!' he shouted, even as he reached back over his shoulder to draw Iron-grip's great sword.

The wave of riders, however, veered sharply just as they reached him and crashed directly into the front ranks of the cultists who were on the verge of breaking through his barrier. This new force was composed of lean, leather-tough men in black, and their eyes had a peculiar angularity to them.

'Nadraks! By the Gods, they're Nadraks!' Garion heard Barak shout from somewhere across the ravine.

'What are *they* doing here?' Garion muttered, half to himself.

'Garion!' Lelldorin exclaimed. 'That man in the middle of the riders—isn't that Prince Kheldar?'

The new troops charging into the furious mêlée quickly turned the tide of battle. They charged directly into the faces of the startled cultists who were emerging from the mouths of the gullies, inflicting dreadful casualties.

Once he had committed his horsemen, Silk dropped back to join Garion and Lelldorin in the center of the ravine. 'Good day, gentlemen,' he greeted them with aplomb. 'I hope I didn't keep you waiting.'

'Where did you get all the Nadraks?' Garion demanded, trembling with sudden relief.

'In Gar og Nadrak, of course.'

'Why would they want to help us?'

'Because I paid them.' Silk shrugged. 'You owe me a great deal of money, Garion.'

'How did you find so many so fast?' Lelldorin asked.

'Yarblek and I have a fur-trading station just across the border. The trappers who brought in their furs last spring were just lying around, drinking and gambling, so I hired them.'

'You got here just in time,' Garion said.

'I noticed that. Those fires of yours were a nice touch.'

'Up until the point where they started throwing

water on them. That's when things started to get tense.'

A few hundred of the trapped cultists managed to escape the general destruction by scrambling up the steep sides of the gullies and fleeing out onto the barren moors; but for most of their fellows, there was no escape.

Barak rode out of the gully where the Rivan troops were mopping up the few survivors of the initial charge. 'Do you want to give them the chance to surrender?' he asked Garion.

Garion remembered the conversation he and Polgara had had several days previously. 'I suppose we should,' he said after a moment's thought.

'You don't *have* to, you know,' Barak told him. 'Under the circumstances, no one would blame you if you wiped them out to the very last man.'

'No,' Garion said, 'I don't think I really want to do that. Tell the ones that are left that we'll spare their lives if they throw down their weapons.'

Barak shrugged. 'It's up to you.'

'Silk, you lying little thief!' a tall Nadrak in a felt coat and an outrageous fur hat exclaimed. He was roughly searching the body of a slain cultist. 'You said that they all had money on them and that they were loaded down with gold chains and bracelets. All this one has on him is fleas.'

'Perhaps I exaggerated just a trifle, Yarblek,' Silk said urbanely to his partner.

'I ought to gut you, do you know that?'

'Why, Yarblek,' Silk replied with feigned astonishment, 'is that any way to talk to your brother?'

'Brother!' the Nadrak snorted, rising and planting a solid kick in the side of the body that had so sorely disappointed him.

'That's what we agreed when we went into partnership —that we were going to treat each other like brothers.'

'Don't twist words on me, you little weasel. Besides, I stuck a knife in my brother twenty years ago—for lying to me.'

As the last of the trapped and outnumbered cultists threw down their arms in surrender, Polgara, Ce'Nedra, and Errand came cautiously up the ravine, accompanied by the filthy, hunchbacked Beldin.

'Your Algar reinforcements are still several days away,' the ugly little sorcerer told Garion. 'I tried to hurry them along, but they're very tenderhearted with their horses. Where did you get all the Nadraks?'

'Silk hired them.'

Beldin nodded approvingly. 'Mercenaries always make the best soldiers,' he said.

The coarse-faced Yarblek had been looking at Polgara, his eyes alight with recognition. 'You're still as handsome as ever, girl,' he said to her. 'Have you changed your mind about letting me buy you?'

'No, Yarblek,' she replied. 'Not yet, anyway. You arrived at an excellent time.'

'Only because some lying little thief told me there was loot to be had.' He glared at Silk and then nudged the body he was standing over with his foot. 'Frankly, I'd make more money plucking dead chickens.'

Beldin looked at Garion. 'If you intend to see your son again before he has a full beard, you'd better get moving,' he said.

'I've got to make some arrangements about the prisoners,' Garion replied.

'What's to arrange?' Yarblek shrugged. 'Line them up and chop off their heads.'

'Absolutely not!'

'What's the point of fighting if you can't butcher the prisoners when it's over?'

'Someday when we have some time, I'll explain it to you,' Silk told him.

'Alorns!' Yarblek sighed, casting his eyes toward the murky sky.

'Yarblek, you mangy son of a dog!' It was a raven-haired woman in leather breeches and a tight-fitting leather vest. There was at once a vast anger and an overwhelming physical presence about her. 'I thought you said we could make a profit by picking over the dead. These vermin don't have a thing on them.'

'We were misled, Vella,' he replied somberly, giving Silk a flinty look.

'I told you not to trust that rat-faced little sneak. You're not only ugly, Yarblek, you're stupid as well.'

Garion had been looking curiously at the angry woman. 'Isn't that the girl who danced in the tavern that time in Gar og Nadrak?' he asked Silk, remembering the girl's overwhelming sensuality that had stirred the blood of every man in that wayside drinking establishment.

The little man nodded. 'She married that trapper— Tekk—but he came out second best in an argument with a bear a few years back, and his brother sold her to Yarblek.'

'Worst mistake I ever made,' Yarblek said mournfully. 'She's almost as fast with her knives as she is with her tongue.' He pulled back one sleeve and showed them an angry red scar. 'And all I was trying to do was to be friendly.'

She laughed. 'Ha! You know the rules, Yarblek. If you want to keep your guts on the inside, you keep your hands to yourself.'

Beldin's eyes had a peculiar expression in them as he looked at her. 'Spirited wench, isn't she?' he murmured to Yarblek. 'I admire a woman with a quick wit and a ready tongue.'

A wild hope suddenly flared in Yarblek's eyes. 'Do you like her?' he asked eagerly. 'I'll sell her to you, if you want.'

'Have you lost your mind entirely, Yarblek?' Vella demanded indignantly.

'Please, Vella, I'm talking business.'

'This shabby old troll couldn't buy a tankard of cheap ale, much less me.' She turned to Beldin. 'Have you even got two coins to rub together, you jackass?' she demanded.

'Now you've gone and spoiled the whole negotiation,' Yarblek accused her plaintively.

Beldin, however gave the dark-haired woman a wicked, lopsided grin. 'You interest me, girl,' he told her, 'and nobody's done that for longer than I can remember. Try to work on your threats and curses a bit, though. The rhythm isn't quite right.' He turned to Polgara. 'I think I'll go back and see what those Drasnian pikemen are up to. Somehow I don't believe that we want them creeping up behind us.' Then he spread his arms, crouched, and became a hawk.

Vella stared incredulously after him as he soared away. 'How did he do that?' she gasped.

'He's very talented,' Silk replied.

'He is indeed.' She turned on Yarblek with fire in her eyes. 'Why did you let me talk to him like that?' she demanded. 'You know how important first impressions are. Now he'll never make a decent offer for me.'

'You can tell for yourself that he doesn't have any money.'

'There are other things than money, Yarblek.'

Yarblek shook his head and walked away muttering to himself.

Ce'Nedra's eyes were as hard as green agates. 'Garion,' she said in a deceptively quiet voice, 'one day very soon we'll want to talk about these taverns you mentioned— and dancing girls—and a few other matters as well.'

'It was a long time ago, dear,' he said quickly.

'Not nearly long enough.'

'Does anybody have anything to eat?' Vella demanded, looking around. 'I'm as hungry as a bitch wolf with ten puppies.'

'I can probably find something for you,' Polgara replied.

Vella looked at her, and her eyes slowly widened. 'Are you who I think you are?' she asked in an awed voice.

'That depends on who you think I am, dear.'

'I understand that you dance,' Ce'Nedra said in a chilly voice.

Vella shrugged. 'All women dance. I'm just the best, that's all.'

'You seem very sure of yourself, Mistress Vella.'

'I just recognize facts.' Vella looked curiously at Ce'Nedra. 'My, you're a tiny one, aren't you?' she asked. 'Are you really full-grown?'

'I am the Queen of Riva,' Ce'Nedra replied, drawing herself up to her full height.

'Good for you, girl,' Vella said warmly, clapping her on the shoulder. 'I always enjoy seeing a woman get ahead.'

It was midmorning of a gray, cloudy day when Garion crested a hill and looked across a shallow valley at the imposing bulk of Rheon. The town stood atop a steep hill, and its walls reared up sharply out of the rank gorse covering the slopes.

'Well,' Barak said quietly as he joined Garion, 'there it is.'

'I didn't realize the walls were quite so high,' Garion admitted.

'They've been working on them,' Barak said, pointing. 'You can see that new stonework on the parapet.'

Flying defiantly above the city, the scarlet banner of the Bear-cult, a blood-red flag with the black outline of a shambling bear in the center, snapped in the chill breeze. For some reason that flag raised an almost irrational rage in Garion. 'I want that thing down,' he said from between clenched teeth.

'That's why we came,' Barak told him.

Mandorallen, burnished in his armor, joined them.

'This isn't going to be easy, is it?' Garion said to them.

'It won't be so bad,' Barak replied, 'Once Hettar gets here.'

Mandorallen had been assessing the town's fortifications with a professional eye. 'I foresee no insurmountable difficulties,' he declared confidently. 'Immediately upon the return of the several hundred men I dispatched to procure timbers from that forest lying some leagues to the north, I shall begin the construction of siege engines.'

'Can you actually throw a rock big enough to knock a hole in walls that thick?' Garion asked dubiously.

''Tis not the single stroke that reduces them, Garion,' the knight replied. ''Tis the repetition of blow after blow. I will ring the town with engines and rain stones upon their walls. I doubt not that there will be a breach or two 'ere my Lord Hettar arrives.'

372

'Won't the people inside repair them as fast as you break them?' Garion asked.

'Not if you've got other catapults throwing burning pitch at them,' Barak told him. 'It's very hard to concentrate on anything when you're on fire.'

Garion winced. 'I hate using fire on people,' he said, briefly remembering Asharak the Murgo.

'It's the only way, Garion,' Barak said soberly. 'Otherwise you're going to lose a lot of good men.'

Garion sighed. 'All right,' he said. 'Let's get started then.'

Reinforced by Yarblek's trappers, the Rivans drew up in a wide circle around the fortified town. Though their combined numbers were not yet sufficient to mount a successful assault on those high, grim walls, they were nonetheless enough to seal the town effectively. The construction of Mandorallen's siege engines took but a few days; once they were completed and moved into position, the steady twang of tightly twisted ropes uncoiling with terrific force and the sharp crack of heavy rocks shattering against the walls of Rheon was almost continual.

Garion watched from a vantage point atop a nearby hill as rock after rock lofted high into the air to smash down on those seemingly impregnable walls.

'It's a sad thing to watch,' Queen Porenn noted as she joined him. A stiff breeze tugged at her black gown and stirred her flaxen hair as she moodily watched Mandorallen's engines pound relentlessly at the walls. 'Rheon has stood here for almost three thousand years. It's been like a rock guarding the frontier. It seems very strange to attack one of my own cities—particularly when you consider the fact that half of our forces are Nadraks, the very people Rheon was built to hold off in the first place.'

'Wars are always a little absurd, Porenn,' Garion agreed.

'More than just a little. Oh, Polgara asked me to tell you that Beldin has come back. He has something to tell you.'

'All right. Shall we go back down, then?' He offered the Queen of Drasnia his arm.

Beldin was lounging on the grass near the tents, gnawing the shreds of meat off a soup bone and exchanging casual insults with Vella. 'You've got a bit of a problem, Belgarion,' he told Garion. 'Those Drasnian pike men have broken camp and they're marching this way.'

Garion frowned. 'How far away is Hettar?' he asked.

'Far enough to turn it into a race,' the little hunchback replied. 'I expect that the whole outcome is going to depend on which army gets here first.'

'The Drasnians wouldn't really attack us, would they?' Ce'Nedra asked.

'It's hard to say,' Porenn replied. 'If Haldar has convinced them that Garion is holding me prisoner, they might. Javelin took a horse and rode back to see if he could find out exactly what's going on.'

Garion began to pace up and down, gnawing worriedly on one fingernail.

'Don't bite your nails, dear,' Polgara told him.

'Yes, ma'am,' he replied automatically, still lost in thought. 'Is Hettar coming as fast as he can?' he asked Beldin.

'He's pushing his horses about as hard as they can be pushed.'

'If there was only some way to slow down the pikemen.'

'I've got a couple of ideas,' Beldin said. He looked at Polgara. 'What do you say to a bit of flying, Pol?' he asked her. 'I might need some help with this.'

'I don't want you to hurt those men,' Queen Porenn said firmly. 'They're my people—even if they are being misled.'

'If what I've got in mind works, nobody's going to get hurt,' Beldin assured her. He rose to his feet and dusted off the back of his filthy tunic. 'I've enjoyed chatting with you, girl,' he said to Vella.

She unleashed a string of expletives at him that turned Ce'Nedra's face pale.

'You're getting better at that,' he approved. 'I think you're starting to get the hang of it. Coming, Pol?'

Vella's expression was indecipherable as she watched the blue-banded hawk and the snowy owl spiral upward.

Chapter Twenty-three

Later that day, Garion rode out to continue his observations of the ongoing siege of the town of Rheon and he found Barak, Mandorallen, and Durnik in the midst of a discussion. 'It has to do with the way walls are built, Mandorallen,' Durnik was trying to explain. 'A city wall is put together to withstand exactly what you're trying to do to that one.'

Mandorallen shrugged. 'It becomes a test then, Goodman, a test to discover which is the stronger—their walls or mine engines.'

'That's the kind of test that could take months,' Durnik pointed out. '*But* if instead of throwing rocks at the *outside* of the wall, you lobbed them all the way over to hit the *inside* of the wall on the far side, you'd stand a pretty fair chance of toppling them outward.'

Mandorallen frowned, mulling it over in his mind.

'He could be right, Mandorallen,' Barak said. 'City walls are usually buttressed from the inside. They're built to keep people out, not in. If you bang your rocks against the inside of the walls, you won't have the strength of the buttresses to contend with. Not only that—if the walls fall outward, they'll provide us with natural ramps into the city. That way we won't need scaling ladders.'

Yarblek sauntered over to join the discussion, his fur cap at a jaunty angle. After Durnik had explained his idea, the rangy-looking Nadrak's eyes narrowed thoughtfully. 'He's got a point, Arend,' he said to Mandorallen. 'And after you've pounded the walls from the inside for a while, we can throw a few grappling hooks over the tops of them. If the walls have already been weakened, we should be able to pull them down.'

'I must admit the feasibility of these most unorthodox approaches to the art of the siege,' Mandorallen said. 'Though they both do fly in the face of long-established tradition, they show promise of shortening the tedious procedure of reducing the walls.' He looked curiously at Yarblek. 'I had not previously considered this notion of using grappling hooks so,' he admitted.

Yarblek laughed coarsely. 'That's probably because you're not a Nadrak. We're an impatient people, so we don't build very good walls. I've pulled down some pretty stout-looking houses in my time—for one reason or another.'

'I think, though, that we don't want to yank down the walls too soon,' Barak cautioned. 'The people inside outnumber us just now, and we don't want to give them any reason to come swarming out of that place—and if you pull a man's walls down, it usually makes him very grouchy.'

The siege of Rheon continued for two more days before Javelin returned astride an exhausted horse. 'Haldar's put his own people in most of the positions of authority in the army,' he reported, once they had all gathered in the large, dun-colored tent that served as the headquarters of the besieging army. 'They're all going around making speeches about Belgarion taking Queen Porenn prisoner. They've about halfway persuaded the troops that they're coming to her rescue.'

'Was there any sign of Brendig and the Sendars yet?' Garion asked him.

'I didn't see them personally, but Haldar has his troops moving at a forced march, and he's got a lot of scouts out behind him. I think he believes that Brendig's right on his heels. On the way back, I ran into Lady Polgara and the sorcerer Beldin. They seem to be planning something, but I didn't have time to get any details.' He slumped in his chair with a look of exhaustion on his face.

'You're tired, Khendon,' Queen Porenn said. 'Why

don't you get a few hours' sleep, and we'll gather here again this evening.'

'I'm all right, your Majesty,' he said quickly.

'Go to bed, Javelin,' she said firmly. 'Your contributions to our discussions won't be very coherent if you keep falling asleep in your chair.'

'You might as well do as she says, Javelin,' Silk advised. 'She's going to mother you whether you like it or not.'

'That will do, Silk,' Poreen said.

'But you *will*, Auntie. You're known far and wide as the little mother of Drasnia.'

'I said, that will do.'

'Yes, mother.'

'I think you're walking on very thin ice, Silk,' Yarblek said.

'I always walk on thin ice. It gives my life a certain zest.'

The gloomy day was slowly settling into an even gloomier evening as Garion and his friends gathered once more in the large tent near the center of the encampment. Yarblek had brought a number of rolled-up rugs with him and several iron braziers, and these contributions to their headquarters added certain garish, even barbaric, touches to the interior of the tent.

'Where's Silk?' Garion asked, looking around as they all seated themselves around the glowing braziers.

'I think he's out snooping,' Barak replied.

Garion made a face. 'I wish that just once he'd be where he's supposed to be.'

Javelin looked much more alert after his few hours' sleep. His expression, however, was grave. 'We're starting to run out of time,' he told them. 'We've got three armies converging on this place. Lord Hettar is coming up from the south, and General Brendig is coming in from the west. Unfortunately, the Drasnian pikemen are very likely to get here first.'

'Unless Pol and Beldin can slow them down,' Durnik added.

'I have every confidence in Lady Polgara and Master Beldin,' Javelin said, 'but I think we should decide what we're going to do in the event that they aren't successful. It's always best to prepare for the worst.'

'Wisely spoken, my Lord,' Mandorallen murmured.

'Now,' the Chief of Drasnian Intelligence continued, 'we don't truly want to fight the pikemen. First of all, they aren't really our enemies; secondly, a battle with them is going to weaken our forces to the point that a sortie in force from the city could conceivably defeat us.'

'What are you leading up to, Javelin?' Porenn asked him.

'I think that we're going to have to get into the city.'

'We haven't got enough men,' Barak said flatly.

'And 'twill take several more days to reduce the walls,' Mandorallen added.

Javelin held up one hand. 'If we concentrate the siege engines on one section of wall, we should be able to bring it down within one day,' he declared.

'But that just announces which quarter we'll attack from,' Lelldorin protested. 'The forces in the city will be concentrated there to repel us.'

'Not if the rest of their city's on fire,' Javelin replied.

'Absolutely out of the question,' Garion said flatly. 'My son could be in that town, and I'm not going to risk his life by setting the whole place on fire.'

'I still say that we haven't got enough men to take the city,' Barak maintained.

'We don't have to take the *whole* city, my Lord of Trellheim,' Javelin said. 'All we need to do is get our men inside. If we take one quarter of the town and fortify it, we can hold off the cult from the inside and Haldar from the outside. Then we simply sit tight and wait for Lord Hettar and General Brendig.'

'It's got some possibilities,' Yarblek said. 'The way things stand right now, we're caught in a nutcracker. If those pikemen get here first, about all your friends are going to be able to do when they arrive is to pick up the pieces.'

'No fire,' Garion declared adamantly.

'I do fear me that however we proceed, we may not

gain entry into the city 'ere the walls are breached,' Mandorallen observed.

'The walls aren't really any problem,' Durnik said quietly. 'No wall is any better than its foundation.'

'It is quite impossible, Goodman,' Mandorallen told him. 'A wall's foundation hath the entire weight resting upon it. No engine in the world can move such a mass.'

'I wasn't talking about an engine,' Durnik said.

'What have you got in mind, Durnik?' Garion asked him.

'It's not really going to be that hard, Garion,' Durnik said. 'I did a bit of looking around. The walls aren't resting on rock. They're resting on packed dirt. All we have to do is soften that dirt a bit. There's plenty of underground water in this region. If we put our heads together, you and I ought to be able to bring it up under one section of wall without anybody inside the city knowing what we've done. Once the ground is soft enough, a few dozen of Yarblek's grappling hooks ought to be enough to topple it.'

'Can it be done, Garion?' Lelldorin asked doubtfully.

Garion thought it through. 'It's possible,' he conceded. 'It's very possible.'

'And if we did it at night, we could be in position to rush into the city just as soon as the wall falls,' Barak said. 'We could get inside without losing a single man.'

'It's a novel solution,' Silk observed from the doorway of the tent. 'A little unethical, perhaps, but novel all the same.'

'Where have you been, you little sneak?' Yarblek demanded.

'In Rheon, actually,' Silk replied.

'You were inside the city?' Barak asked in surprise.

Silk shrugged. 'Of course. I thought it might be appropriate to get a friend of ours out of there before we took the place apart.' He stepped aside with a mocking little bow to admit the honey-blonde Margravine Liselle.

'Now *that* is a splendid-looking young woman,' Yarblek breathed in admiration.

Liselle smiled at him, the dimples dancing in her cheeks.

'How did you get inside?' Garion asked the rat-faced little man.

'You really wouldn't want to know, Garion,' Silk told him. 'There's always a way in or out of a city, if you're really serious about it.'

'You two don't smell too good,' Yarblek noted.

'It has to do with the route we took,' Liselle replied, wrinkling her nose.

'You're looking well,' Javelin said conversationally to his niece, 'all things considered.'

'Thank you, uncle,' she replied. Then she turned to Garion. 'Are the rumors going about the city true, your Majesty?' she asked. 'Has your son been abducted?'

Garion nodded grimly. 'It happened just after we took Jarviksholm. That's why we're here.'

'But Prince Geran doesn't seem to be in Rheon,' she told him.

'Are you sure?' Ce'Nedra demanded.

'I think so, your Majesty. The cultists inside the city are baffled. They seem to have no idea who took your son.'

'Ulfgar may be keeping it a secret,' Javelin said. 'Only a small group may know.'

'Perhaps, but it doesn't look that way. I wasn't able to get close enough to him to make sure, but he has the look of a man whose plans have gone all awry. I don't think he expected this attack on Rheon. His fortifications are not nearly as complete as they might appear from the outside. The north wall in particular is rather flimsy. His reinforcement of the walls seems a desperation move. He was not expecting a siege. If he'd been behind the abduction, he would have been prepared for the attack— unless he thought you could never trace it to him.'

'This is most excellent news, my Lady,' Mandorallen praised her. 'Since we know of the weakness of the north fortifications, we can concentrate our efforts there. If Goodman Durnik's plan proves workable, a weakening of the foundations of the north wall should bring it down most speedily.'

'What can you tell us about Ulfgar?' Barak asked the girl.

'I only saw him briefly at a distance. He spends most of his time inside his house, and only his closest cohorts are allowed near him. He made a speech, though, just before he sent his forces to attack you. He speaks very passionately and he had the crowd absolutely under his control. I *can* tell you one thing about him, though. He's not an Alorn.'

'He's not?' Barak looked dumbfounded.

'His face doesn't give away his nationality, but his speech is not that of an Alorn.'

'Why would the cult accept an outsider as their leader?' Garion demanded.

'They aren't aware of the fact that he is an outsider. He mispronounces a few words—just a couple, actually, and only a trained ear would catch them. If I'd been able to get closer to him, I might have been able to steer him toward those words that would have betrayed his origins. I'm sorry that I can't be of more help.'

'How strong is his grip on the cult?' Javelin asked.

'It's absolute,' she replied. 'They'll do anything he tells them to do. They look upon him as something very akin to a God.'

'We're going to have to take him alive,' Garion said grimly. 'I have to have some answers.'

'That may be extremely difficult, your Majesty,' she said gravely. 'It's widely believed in Rheon that he's a sorcerer. I didn't actually see any evidence of it myself, but I talked with a number of people who have, or at least who claimed they have done so.'

'You have performed a great service for us, Margravine,' Queen Porenn said gratefully. 'It shall not be forgotten.'

'Thank you, your Majesty,' Liselle replied simply, with a formal little curtsy. Then she turned back to Garion. 'What information I was able to glean says quite strongly that the cult forces within the walls are not nearly so formidable as we were led to believe. Their numbers are impressive, but they include a great many young boys and old men. They appear to be counting rather desperately on a force that's marching toward the city under the command of a hidden cult-member.'

'Haldar,' Barak said.

She nodded.

'And that brings us right back to the absolute necessity of getting inside those walls,' Javelin told them. He looked at Durnik. 'How long do you estimate that it's going to take for the ground under the north wall to soften enough to topple the structure?'

Durnik sat back, staring thoughtfully at the ceiling of the tent. 'We want to take them by surprise,' he said, 'so I don't think we want the water to come gushing out—not at first, anyway. A gradual seepage would be far less noticeable. It's going to take a while to saturate the ground.'

'And we're going to have to be very careful,' Garion added. 'If this Ulfgar really is a sorcerer, he'll hear us if we make too much noise.'

'There'll be plenty of noise when the wall comes down,' Barak said. 'Why don't you just blow it apart the way you did the back wall of Jarviksholm?'

Garion shook his head. 'There are a couple of moments after you unleash your will when you're absolutely vulnerable to attack by anybody who has the same kind of talent. I'd sort of like to be alive and sane when I find my son.'

'How long will it take to soak the ground under the wall?' Javelin asked.

Durnik scratched at his cheek. 'Tonight,' he replied, 'and all day tomorrow. By midnight tomorrow, the wall ought to be sufficiently undermined. Then, just before we attack, Garion and I can speed up the flow of water and wash out most of the dirt. It's going to be very wet and soft already, and a good stream of water ought to cut it right out from under the wall. If we lob stones at it from the far side and get a few dozen grappling hooks into it, we should be able to pull it down in short order.'

'You might want to pick up the pace with your engines,'

Yarblek said to Mandorallen. 'Give them time to get used to the idea of rocks coming out of the sky. That way they won't pay any attention when you start pounding on their walls tomorrow night.'

'Midnight tomorrow, then?' Barak said.

'Right,' Garion said firmly.

Javelin looked at his niece. 'Do you have the layout of the north quarter of the city fairly well in mind?' he asked.

She nodded.

'Make a sketch for us. We'll need to know where to set up our defenses once we get inside.'

'Right after I bathe, uncle.'

'We need that sketch, Liselle.'

'Not nearly as badly as I need a bath.'

'You too, Kheldar,' Queen Porenn said firmly.

Silk gave Liselle a speculative look.

'Never mind, Kheldar,' she said. 'I can wash my own back, thank you.'

'Let's go find some water, Durnik,' Garion said, getting to his feet. 'Underground, I mean.'

'Right,' the smith replied.

There was no moon, of course. The clouds that had hovered over the area for the past week and more obscured the sky. The night air was chill as Garion and Durnik moved carefully across the shallow valley toward the besieged city.

'Cold night,' Durnik murmured as they walked through the rank gorse.

'Umm,' Garion agreed. 'How deep do you think the water might be lying?'

'Not too deep,' Durnik replied. 'I asked Liselle how deep the wells are in Rheon. She said that they were all fairly shallow. I think we'll hit water at about twenty-five feet.'

'What gave you this idea, anyway?'

Durnik chuckled softly in the darkness. 'When I was much younger, I worked for a farmer who gave himself great airs. He thought it might impress his neighbors if he had a well right inside his house. We worked at it all one winter and finally tapped into an artesian flow. Three days later, his house collapsed. He was very upset about it.'

'I can imagine.'

Durnik looked up at the looming walls. 'I don't know that we need to get any closer,' he said. 'It might be hard to concentrate if they see us and start shooting arrows at us. Let's work around to the north side.'

'Right.'

They moved even more carefully now, trying to avoid making any sound in the rustling gorse.

'This should do it,' Durnik whispered. 'Let's see what's down there.'

Garion let his thoughts sink quietly down through the hard-packed earth under the north wall of the city. The first few feet were difficult, since he kept encountering moles and earthworms. An angry chittering told him that he had briefly disturbed a badger. Then he hit a layer of rock and probed his thought along its flat surface, looking for fissures.

'Just to your left,' Durnik murmured. 'Isn't that a crack?'

Garion found it and wormed his way downward. The fissure seemed to grow damper and damper the deeper he went. 'It's wet down there,' he whispered, 'but the crack's so narrow that the water's barely seeping up.'

'Let's widen the crack—but not too much. Just enough to let a trickle come up.'

Garion bent his will and felt Durnik's will join with his. Together they shouldered the crack in the rock a bit wider. The water lying beneath the rock layer gushed upward. Together they pulled back and felt the water begin to erode the hard-packed dirt under the wall, seeping and spreading in the darkness beneath the surface.

'Let's move on,' Durnik whispered. 'We ought to open up six or eight places under the wall in order to soak the ground thoroughly. Then tomorrow night we can push the cracks wide open.'

'Won't that wash out this whole hillside?' Garion asked, also whispering.

'Probably.'

'That's going to make it a little hard for our troops when they rush this place.'

'There's not much question about the fact that they're going to get their feet wet,' Durnik said, 'but that's better than trying to scale a wall with somebody pouring boiling oil on your head, wouldn't you say?'

'Much, much better,' Garion agreed.

They moved on through the chill night. Then something brushed Garion's cheek. At first he ignored it, but it came again—soft and cold and damp. His heart sank. 'Durnik,' he whispered, 'it's starting to snow.'

'I thought that's what it was. I think this is all going to turn very unpleasant on us.'

The snow continued to fall through the remainder of the night and on into the next morning. Though there were occasional flurries that swirled around the bleak fortress, the snowfall for the most part was intermittent. It was a wet, sodden kind of snow that turned to slush almost as soon as it touched the ground.

Shortly before noon, Garion and Lelldorin donned heavy wool cloaks and stout boots and went out of the snow-clogged encampment toward the north wall of Rheon. When they were perhaps two hundred paces from the base of the hill upon which the city rested, they sauntered along with a great show of casualness, trying to look like nothing more dangerous than a pair of soldiers on patrol. As Garion looked at the fortress city, he saw the red and black bear-flag once more, and once again that banner raised an irrational rage in him. 'Are you sure that you'll be able to recognize your arrows in the dark?' he asked his friend. 'There are a lot of arrows sticking in the ground out there, you know.'

Lelldorin drew his bow and shot an arrow in a long arc toward the city. The feathered shaft rose high in the air and then dropped to sink into the snow-covered turf about fifty paces from the beginning of the slope. 'I made the arrows myself, Garion,' he said, taking another shaft from the quiver at his back. 'Believe me, I can recognize one of them as soon as my fingers touch it.' He leaned back and bent his bow again. 'Is the ground getting soft under the wall?'

Garion sent out his thought toward the slope of the hill and felt the chill, musty dampness of the soil lying under the snow. 'Slowly,' he replied, 'it's still pretty firm, though.'

'It's almost noon, Garion,' Lelldorin said seriously, reaching for another arrow. 'I know how thoroughly Goodman Durnik thinks things through, but is this really working?'

'It takes a while,' Garion told him. 'You have to soak the lower layers of earth first. Then the water starts to rise and saturate the dirt directly under the wall itself. It takes time; but if the water started gushing out of rabbit holes, the people on top of the wall would know that something's wrong.'

'Think of how the rabbits would feel.' Lelldorin grinned and shot another arrow.

They moved on as Lelldorin continued to mark the jumping-off line of the coming night's assault with deceptive casualness.

'All right,' Garion said. 'I know that *you* can recognize your own arrows, but how about the rest of us? One arrow feels just like another to me.'

'It's simple,' the young bowman replied. 'I just creep up, find my arrows and string them all together with twine. When you hit that string, you stop and wait for the wall to topple. Then you charge. We've been making night assaults on Mimbrate houses in Asturia for centuries this way.'

Throughout the remainder of that snowy day, Garion and Durnik periodically checked the level of moisture in the soil of the north slope of the steep knoll upon which the city of Rheon stood. 'It's getting very close to the saturation point, Garion,' Durnik reported as dusk began to fall. 'There are a few places on the lower slope where the water's starting to seep through the snow.'

'It's a good thing it's getting dark,' Garion said, shifting the weight of his mail shirt nervously. Armor of any kind always made him uncomfortable, and the prospect of the upcoming assault on the city filled him with a peculiar emotion, part anxiety, and part anticipation.

Durnik, his oldest friend, looked at him with an understanding that pierced any possible concealment. He grinned a bit wryly. 'What are a pair of sensible Sendarian farm boys doing fighting a war in the snow in eastern Drasnia?' he asked.

'Winning—I hope.'

'We'll win, Garion,' Durnik assured him, laying an affectionate hand on the younger man's shoulder. 'Sendars always win—eventually.'

About an hour before midnight, Mandorallen began to move his siege engines, leaving only enough of them on the eastern and western sides to continue the intermittent barrage that was to mask their real purpose. As the hour wore on, Garion, Lelldorin, Durnik, and Silk crept forward at a half crouch toward the invisible line of arrows sticking up out of the snow.

'Here's one,' Durnik whispered as his outstretched hands encountered the shaft of an arrow.

'Here,' Lelldorin murmured, 'let me feel it.' He joined the smith, the both of them on their knees in the slush. 'Yes, it's one of mine, Garion,' he said very quietly. 'They should be about ten paces apart.'

Silk moved quickly to where the two of them crouched over the arrow. 'Show me how you recognize them,' he breathed.

'It's in the fletching,' Lelldorin replied. 'I always use twisted gut to attach the feathers.'

Silk felt the feathered end of the arrow. 'All right,' he said. 'I can pick them out now.'

'Are you sure?' Lelldorin asked.

'If my fingertips can find the spots on a pair of dice, they can certainly tell the difference between gut and linen twine,' Silk replied.

'All right. We'll start here.' Lelldorin attached one end of a ball of twine to the arrow. 'I'll go this way, and you go that.'

'Right.' Silk tied the end of his ball of string to the same shaft. He turned to Garion and Durnik. 'Don't overdo it with the water, you two,' he said. 'I don't particularly want to get buried in a mud slide out here.' Then he moved off, crouched low and groping for the next arrow. Lelldorin touched Garion's shoulder briefly, then disappeared in the opposite direction.

'The ground's completely soaked now,' Durnik murmured. 'If we open those fissures about a foot wider, it's going to flush most of the support out from under the wall.'

'Good.'

Again they sent their probing thoughts out through the sodden earth of the hillside, located the layer of rock, and then swept back and forth along its irregular upper side until they located the first fissure. Garion felt a peculiar sensation as he began to worm his thought down that narrow crack where the water came welling up from far below, almost as if he were extending some incredibly long though invisible arm with slender, supple fingers at its end to reach down into the fissure. 'Have you got it?' he whispered to Durnik.

'I think so.'

'Let's pull it apart then,' Garion said, bracing his will.

Slowly, with an effort that made the beads of sweat stand out on their foreheads, the two of them forced the fissure open. A sharp, muffled crack reverberated up from beneath the sodden slope of the hillside as the rock broke under the force of their combined wills.

'Who's there?' a voice demanded from atop the city wall.

'Is it open wide enough?' Garion whispered, ignoring that alarmed challenge.

'The water's coming up much faster,' Durnik replied after a moment's probing. 'There's a lot of pressure under that layer of rock. Let's move on to the next place.'

A heavy twang came from somewhere behind them, and a peculiar slithering whistle passed overhead as the line from one of Yarblek's catapult-launched grappling hooks arched up and over the north wall. The hook made a steely clink as it slapped against the inside of the wall, and then there was a grating sound as the points dug in.

Crouched low, Garion and Durnik moved carefully on to their left, trying to minimize the soggy squelching sound their feet made in the slush and probing beneath the earth for the next fissure. When Lelldorin came back to rejoin them, they had already opened two more of those hidden cracks lying beneath the saturated slope; behind and above them, there was a gurgling sound as the soupy mud oozed out of the hillside to cascade in a brown flood down the snowy slope. 'I got all the way to the end of the line of arrows,' Lelldorin reported. 'The string's in place on this side.'

'Good,' Garion said, panting slightly from his exertions. 'Go back and tell Barak to start moving the troops into place.'

'Right.' Lelldorin turned and went off into the swirl of a sudden snow flurry.

'We'll have to be careful with this one,' Durnik murmured, searching along under the soil. 'There are a lot of fractures in the rock here. If we pull it too far apart, we'll break up the whole layer and turn loose a river.'

Garion grunted his agreement as he sent the probing fingers of his will out toward the fissure.

When they reached the last of their subterranean wellsprings, Silk came out of the dark behind them, his nimble feet making no sound as he moved through the slush.

'What kept you?' Durnik whispered to the little man. 'You only had about a hundred yards to go.'

'I was checking the slope,' Silk replied. 'The whole thing is starting to ooze through the snow like cold gravy. Then I went up and pushed my foot against one of the foundation stones of the wall. It wobbled like a loose tooth.'

'Well,' Durnik said in a tone of self-satisfaction, 'it worked after all.'

There was a pause in the snowy darkness. 'You mean you weren't actually sure?' Silk asked in a strangled voice.

'The theory was sound,' the smith answered in an offhand sort of way. 'But you can never be actually positive about a theory until you try it.'

'Durnik, I'm getting too old for this.'

Another grappling hook sailed overhead.

'We've got one more to open,' Garion murmured. 'Barak's moving the troops into place. Do you want to go back and tell Yarblek to send up the signal to Mandorallen?'

'With pleasure,' Silk replied. 'I want to get out of there before we're all hip-deep in mud anyway.' He turned and went off into the dark.

Perhaps ten minutes later, when the last fissure had been opened and the entire north slope of the hill had turned into a slithering mass of oozing mud and freely running water, an orange ball of blazing pitch arched high in the air over the city. In response to that prearranged signal, Mandorallen's engines emplaced to the south began a continuous barrage, lofting their heavy stones high over the roof tops of Rheon to slam against the inside of the north wall. At the same time, the lines on Yarblek's grappling hooks tautened as the Nadrak mercenaries began to move their teams of horses away from the wall. There was an ominous creaking and grinding along the top of the hill as the weakened wall began to sway.

'How much longer do you think it's going to stand?' Barak asked as he came out of the darkness with Lelldorin at his side to join them.

'Not very,' Durnik replied. 'The ground's starting to give way under it.'

The groaning creak above them grew louder, punctuated by the continual sharp crashes along the inside as Mandorallen's catapults stepped up the pace of their deadly rain. Then, with a sound like an avalanche, a section of the wall collapsed with a peculiarly sinuous motion as the upper portion toppled outward and the lower sank into the sodden earth. There was a great, splashing rumble as the heavy stones cascaded into the slush and mud of the hillside.

'A man should never try to put up stonework resting only on dirt,' Durnik observed critically.

'Under the circumstances, I'm glad they did,' Barak told him.

'Well, yes,' Durnik admitted, 'but there *are* right ways to do things.'

The big Cherek chuckled. 'Durnik, you're an absolute treasure, do you know that?'

Another section of the wall toppled outward to splash onto the slope. Shouts of alarm and the clanging of bells began to echo through the streets of the fortified town.

'You want me to move the men out?' Barak asked Garion, his voice tense with excitement.

'Let's wait until the whole wall comes down,' Garion replied. 'I don't want them charging up the hill with all those building stones falling on top of them.'

'There it goes.' Lelldorin laughed gleefully, pointing toward the last, toppling section of the wall.

'Start the men,' Garion said tersely, reaching over his shoulder for the great sword strapped to his back.

Barak drew in a deep breath. 'Charge!' he roared in a vast voice.

With a concerted shout, the Rivans and their Nadrak allies plunged up through the slush and mud and began clambering over the fallen ruins of the north wall and on into the city.

'Let's go!' Barak shouted. 'We'll miss all the fighting if we don't hurry!'

Chapter Twenty-four

The fight was short and in many cases very ugly. Each element of Garion's army had been thoroughly briefed by Javelin and his niece, and they had all been given specific assignments. Unerringly, they moved through the snowy, firelit streets to occupy designated houses. Other elements, angling in from the edges of the breach in the north wall, circled the defensive perimeter Javelin had drawn on Liselle's map to pull down the houses and fill the streets with obstructing rubble.

The first counterattack came just before dawn. Howling Bear-cultists clad in shaggy furs swarmed out of the narrow streets beyond the perimeter to swarm up over the rubble of the collapsed houses, only to run directly into a withering rain of arrows from the rooftops and upper windows. After dreadful losses, they fell back.

As dawn broke pale and gray along the snowy eastern horizon, the last few pockets of resistance inside the perimeter crumbled, and the north quarter of Rheon was secure. Garion stood somberly at a broken upper window of a house overlooking the cleared area that marked the outer limits of that part of the town that was under his control. The bodies of the cultists who had mounted the counterattack lay sprawled in twisted, grotesque heaps, already lightly dusted with snow.

'Not a bad little fight,' Barak declared, coming into the room with his blood-stained sword still in his hand. He dropped his dented shield in a corner and came over to the window.

'I didn't care much for it,' Garion replied, pointing at

the wind-rows of the dead lying below. 'Killing people is a very poor way of changing their minds.'

'They started this war, Garion. You didn't.'

'No,' Garion corrected. 'Ulfgar started it. He's the one I actually want.'

'Then we'll have to go get him for you,' Barak said, carefully wiping his sword with a bit of tattered cloth.

During the course of the day, there were several more furious counterattacks from inside the city, but the results were much the same as had been the case with the first. Garion's positions were too secure and too well covered by archers to fall to these sporadic sorties.

'They don't actually fight well in groups, do they?' Durnik said from the vantage point of the upper storey of that half-ruined house.

'They don't have that kind of discipline,' Silk replied. The little man was sprawled on a broken couch in one corner of the room, carefully peeling an apple with a small, sharp knife. 'Individually, they're as brave as lions, but the concept of unified action hasn't quite seeped into their heads yet.'

'That was an awfully good shot,' Barak congratulated Lelldorin, who had just loosed an arrow through the shattered window.

Lelldorin shrugged. 'Child's play. Now, that fellow creeping along the roof-line of the house several streets back—that's a bit more challenging.' He nocked another arrow, drew, and released all in one smooth motion.

'You got him,' Barak said.

'Naturally.'

As evening approached, Polgara and Beldin returned to the camp outside the city. 'Well,' the gnarled sorcerer said with a certain satisfaction, 'you won't have to worry about the pikemen for a while.' He held out his twisted hands to one of Yarblek's glowing braziers.

'You didn't hurt them, did you?' Porenn asked quickly.

'No,' he grinned. 'We just bogged them down. They were going through a marshy valley, and we diverted a river into it. The whole place is a quagmire now. They're perched on hummocks and in the branches of trees waiting for the water to subside.'

'Won't that stall Brendig as well?' Garion asked.

'Brendig's marching around that valley,' Polgara assured him, sitting near one of the braziers with a cup of tea. 'He should be here in a few days.' She looked at Vella. 'This tea is really excellent,' she said.

'Thank you, Lady Polgara,' the dark-haired dancer replied. Her eyes were fixed on Ce'Nedra's copper curls, radiant in the golden candlelight. She sighed enviously. 'If I had hair like that, Yarblek could sell me for double the price.'

'I'd settle for half,' Yarblek muttered. 'Just to avoid all those incidental knifings.'

'Don't be such a baby, Yarblek,' she told him. 'I didn't really hurt you all that much.'

'You weren't the one who was doing the bleeding.'

'Have you been practicing your curses, Vella?' Beldin asked.

She demonstrated—at some length.

'You're getting better,' he congratulated her.

For the next two days, Garion's forces worked to heap obstructions along the rubble-choked perimeter of the north quarter of Rheon to prevent a counterattack in force from crossing that intervening space. Garion and his friends observed the process from a large window high up in the house which they had converted into a headquarters.

'Whoever's in charge over there doesn't seem to have a very good grasp of basic strategy,' Yarblek noted. 'He's not making any effort to block off *his* side of that open space to keep us out of the rest of his city.'

Barak frowned. 'You know, Yarblek, you're right. That should have been his first move after we secured this part of town.'

'Maybe he's too arrogant to believe that we can take more of his houses,' Lelldorin suggested.

'Either that or he's laying traps for us back out of sight,' Durnik added.

'That's possible, too,' Barak agreed. 'More than possible. Maybe we ought to do a little planning before we start any more attacks.'

'Before we can plan anything, we have to know exactly what kind of traps Ulfgar has waiting for us,' Javelin said.

Silk sighed and made a wry face. 'All right. After dark I'll go have a look.'

'I wasn't really suggesting that, Kheldar.'

'Of course you weren't.'

'It's a very good idea, though. I'm glad you thought of it.'

It was some time after midnight when Silk returned to the large, firelit room in Garion's headquarters. 'It's a very unpleasant night out there,' the little man said, shivering and rubbing his hands together. He went over to stand in front of the fire.

'Well, are they planning any surprises for us?' Barak asked him, lifting a copper tankard.

'Oh, yes,' Silk replied. 'They're building walls across the streets several houses back from our perimeter and they're putting them just around corners so you won't see them until you're right on top of them.'

'With archers and tubs of boiling pitch in all the houses nearby?' Barak asked glumly.

'Probably.' Silk shrugged. 'Do you have any more of that ale? I'm chilled to the bone.'

'We'll have to work on this a bit,' Javelin mused.

'Good luck,' Barak said sourly, going to the ale keg. 'I *hate* fighting in towns. Give me a nice open field any time.'

'But the towns are where all the loot is,' Yarblek said to him.

'Is that all you ever think about?'

'We're in this life to make a profit, my friend,' the raw-boned Nadrak replied with a shrug.

'You sound just like Silk.'

'I know. That's why we went into partnership.'

It continued to snow lightly throughout the following day. The citizens of Rheon made a few more probing attacks on Garion's defensive perimeter, but for the most part they contented themselves with merely shooting arrows at anything that moved.

About midmorning the next day, Errand picked his way over the rubble of the fallen north wall and went directly to the house from which Garion was directing operations. When he entered, his young face was tight with exhilaration, and he was panting noticeably. 'That's exciting,' he said.

'What is?' Garion asked him.

'Dodging arrows.'

'Does Aunt Pol know you're here?'

'I don't think so. I wanted to see the city, so I just came.'

'You're going to get us both in trouble, do you know that?'

Errand shrugged. 'A scolding doesn't hurt all that much. Oh, I thought you ought to know that Hettar's here—or he will be in an hour or so. He's just a few miles to the south.'

'Finally!' Garion said with an explosive release of his breath. 'How did you find out?'

'Horse and I went out for a ride. He gets restless when he's penned up. Anyway, we were up on that big hill to the south, and I saw the Algars coming.'

'Well, let's go meet them.'

'Why don't we?'

When Garion and his young friend reached the top of the hill south of Rheon, they saw wave upon wave of Algar clansmen flowing over the snowy moors at a brisk canter. A single horseman detached himself from the front rank of that sea of horses and men and pounded up the hill, his long black scalplock flowing behind him. 'Good morning, Garion,' Hettar said casually as he reined in. 'You've been well, I trust?'

'Moderately.' Garion grinned at him.

'You've got snow up here.'

Garion looked around in feigned astonishment. 'Why, I do believe you're right. I hadn't even noticed that.'

Another rider came up the hill, a man in a shabby,

hooded cloak. 'Where's your Aunt, Garion?' the man called when he was halfway up the hill.

'Grandfather?' Garion exclaimed with surprise. 'I thought you were going to Mar Terrin.'

Belgarath made an indelicate sound. 'I did,' he replied as he reined in his horse, 'and it was an absolutely wasted trip. I'll tell you about it later. What's been going on here?'

Briefly Garion filled them in on the events of the past several weeks.

'You've been busy,' Hettar noted.

'The time goes faster when you keep occupied.'

'Is Pol inside the city, then?' Belgarath asked him.

'No. She and Ce'Nedra and the other ladies are staying in the camp we built when we first got here. The cultists have been counterattacking against our positions inside, so I didn't think it was entirely safe for them to be there.'

'That makes sense. Why don't you round up everybody and bring them to the camp. I think we need to talk about a few things.'

'All right, Grandfather.'

It was shortly after noon when they gathered in the main tent in the Rivan encampment outside the city.

'Were you able to find anything useful, father?' Polgara asked Belgarath as the old man entered the tent.

Belgarath sprawled in a chair. 'Some tantalizing hints was about all,' he replied. 'I get the feeling that Anheg's copy of the Ashabine Oracles has been rather carefully pruned somewhere along the way—or more likely at the very beginning. The modifications seem to be a part of the original text.'

'Prophets don't usually tamper with their own prophecies,' Polgara noted.

'*This* one would have—particularly if parts of the prophecy said things he didn't want to believe.'

'Who was it?'

'Torak. I recognized his tone and his peculiar turn of phrase almost immediately.'

'Torak?' Garion exclaimed, feeling a sudden chill.

Belgarath nodded. 'There's an old Mallorean legend

that says that after he destroyed Cthol Mishrak, Torak had a castle built at Ashaba in the Karandese Mountains. Once he moved in, an ecstasy came over him, and he composed the Ashabine Oracles. Anyway, the legend goes on to say that after the ecstasy had passed, Torak fell into a great rage. Apparently there were things in the prophecy that he didn't like. That could very well account for the tampering I detected. We've always been told that the word gives meaning to the event. Torak may have believed that by altering the word, he could change the event.'

'Can you do that?'

'No. But Torak was so arrogant that he may have believed he could.'

'But that puts us at a dead end, doesn't it?' Garion asked with a sinking feeling. 'I mean—the Mrin Codex said that you had to look at all the mysteries, and if the Ashabine Oracles aren't correct—' He lifted his hands helplessly.

'There's a true copy somewhere,' Belgarath replied confidently. 'There has to be—otherwise the Codex would have given me different instructions.'

'You're operating on pure faith, Belgarath,' Ce'Nedra accused him.

'I know,' he admitted. 'I do that when I don't have anything else to fall back on.'

'What did you find at Mar Terrin?' Polgara asked.

Belgarath made a vulgar sound. 'The monks there may be very good at comforting the spirits of all those slaughtered Marags, but they're very bad at protecting manuscripts. The roof leaks in their library, and the copy of the Mallorean Gospels, naturally, was on a shelf right under the leak. It was so soggy that I could barely get the leaves apart, and the ink had run and smeared all over the pages. It was almost totally illegible. I spoke with the monks at some length about that.' He scratched at one bearded cheek. 'It looks as if I'm going to have to go a bit further afield to get what we need.'

'You found nothing at all, then?' Beldin asked.

Belgarath grunted. 'There was one passage in the

Oracles that said that the Dark God will come again.'

Garion felt a sudden chill grip his stomach. 'Torak?' he said. 'Is that possible?'

'I suppose you *could* take it to mean that, but if that's what it really means, then why would Torak have gone to the trouble of destroying so many of the other passages? If the entire purpose of the Oracles was to predict his own return, I expect that he'd have been overjoyed to keep them intact.'

'You're assuming that old burnt-face was rational,' Beldin growled. 'I never noticed that quality in him very often.'

'Oh, no,' Belgarath disagreed. 'Everything Torak did was perfectly rational—as long as you accepted his basic notion that he was the sole reason for creation. No, I think the passage means something else.'

'Could you read any part of the Mallorean Gospels at all, father?' Aunt Pol asked him.

'Just one little fragment. It said something about a choice between the Light and the Dark.'

Beldin snorted. 'Now *that* would be something very unusual,' he said. 'The Seers at Kell haven't made a choice about anything since the world was made. They've been sitting on the fence for millennia.'

Late the following afternoon, the Sendarian army came into view on the snowy hilltops to the west. Garion felt a peculiar twinge of pride as the solid, steady men he had always thought of as his countrymen marched purposefully through the snow toward the now-doomed city of Rheon.

'I might have gotten here sooner,' General Brendig apologized as he rode up, 'but we had to march around that quagmire where the Drasnian pikemen are bogged down.'

'Are they all right?' Queen Porenn asked him quickly.

'Perfectly, your Majesty,' the one-armed man replied. 'They just can't go anywhere, that's all.'

'How much rest will your troops need before they'll be

ready to join the assault, Brendig?' Belgarath asked him.

Brendig shrugged. 'A day ought to do it, Ancient One.'

'That will give us time enough to make our plans,' the old man said. 'Let's get your men bivouaced and then Garion can brief you on the way things stand here.'

In the strategy meeting in the garishly carpeted main tent that evening, they smoothed out the rough edges of their relatively simple plan of attack. Mandorallen's siege engines would continue to pound the city throughout the next day and on into the following night. On the next morning, a feigned assault would be mounted against the south gate to draw as many cultists as possible away from the hastily erected fortification inside the city. Another force would march out of the secure enclave in the north quarter of Rheon to begin the house-by-house occupation of the buildings facing the perimeter. Yet another force, acting on an inspired notion of General Brendig's, would use scaling ladders as bridges to go across the housetops and drop in behind the newly erected walls inside the city.

'The most important thing is to take Ulfgar alive,' Garion cautioned. 'We have to get some answers from him. I need to know just what part he played in the abduction of my son and where Geran is, if he knows.'

'And I want to know just how many of the officers in my army he's subverted,' Queen Porenn added.

'It looks as if he's going to be doing a lot of talking,' Yarblek said with an evil grin. 'In Gar og Nadrak we have a number of very entertaining ways of loosening people's tongues.'

'Pol will handle that,' Belgarath told him firmly. 'She can get the answers we need without resorting to that sort of thing.'

'Are you getting soft, Belgarath?' Barak asked.

'Not likely,' the old man replied, 'but if Yarblek here gets carried away, it might go a little too far, and you can't get answers out of a dead man.'

'But afterward?' Yarblek asked eagerly.

'I don't really care what you do with him afterward.'

The next day, Garion was in a small, curtained-off area

in the main tent going over his maps and his carefully organized lists, trying to determine if there was anything he had overlooked. He had begun of late to feel as if the entire army were resting directly on his shoulders.

'Garion,' Ce'Nedra said, entering his cubicle, 'some friends have arrived.'

He looked up.

'Brand's three sons,' she told him, 'and that glass blower Joran.'

Garion frowned. 'What are they doing here?' he asked. 'I told them all to stay at Riva.'

'They say that they've got something important to tell.'

He sighed. 'You'd better have them come in, then.'

Brand's three gray-cloaked sons and the serious-faced Joran entered and bowed. Their clothes were mud-splattered, and their faces weary.

'We are not deliberately disobeying your orders, Belgarion,' Kail assured him quickly, 'but we discovered something very important that you have to know.'

'Oh? What's that?'

'After you left Riva with the army, your Majesty,' Kail's older brother Verdan explained, 'we decided to go over the west coast of the island inch by inch. We thought there might be some clues that we overlooked in our first search.'

'Besides,' Brin added, 'we didn't have anything else to do.'

'Anyway,' Verdan continued, 'we finally found the ship those Chereks had used to come to the island.'

'Their ship?' Garion asked, suddenly sitting up. 'I thought that whoever it was who abducted my son used it to get off the island.'

Verdan shook his head. 'The ship had been deliberately sunk, your Majesty. They filled it with rocks and then chopped holes in the bottom. We sailed right over it five times until a calm day when there wasn't any surf. It was lying on the bottom in about thirty feet of water.'

'How did the abductor get off the island, then?'

'We had that same thought, Belgarion,' Joran said. 'It occurred to us that, in spite of everything, the abductor might still be on the Isle of the Winds. We started searching. That's when we found the shepherd.'

'Shepherd?'

'He'd been alone with his flock up in the meadows on the western side of the Isle,' Kail explained. 'He was completely unaware of what had happened in the city. Anyway, we asked him if he had seen anything unusual at about the time Prince Geran was taken from the Citadel, and he said that he had seen a ship sail into a cove on the west coast at about that time and that somebody carrying something wrapped in a blanket got on board. Then the ship put out to sea, leaving the others behind. Belgarion, it was the same cove where the trail the Orb was following ended.'

'Which way did the ship go?'

'South.'

'There's one other thing, Belgarion,' Joran added. 'The shepherd was positive that the ship was Nyissan.'

'Nyissan?'

'He was absolutely certain. He even described the snake banner she was flying.'

Garion got quickly to his feet. 'Wait here,' he told them. Then he went to the flap in the partition. 'Grandfather, Aunt Pol, could you step in here for a moment?'

'What is it, dear?' Polgara asked as she and the old sorcerer came into Garion's makeshift office, with Silk trailing curiously behind.

'Tell them,' Garion said to Kail.

Quickly, Brand's second son repeated what they had just told Garion.

'Salmissra?' Polgara suggested to her father.

'Not necessarily, Pol. Nyissa is full of intrigue, and the Queen isn't behind it all—particularly after what you did to her.' He frowned. 'Why would a Cherek abandon one of his own boats to ride aboard a Nyissan scow? That doesn't make sense.'

'That's another question we'll have to ask Ulfgar, once we get our hands on him,' Silk said.

At dawn the next morning, a large body of troops

comprised of elements from all the forces gathered for the siege began to march across the valley to the south of the city toward the steep hill and Rheon. They carried scaling ladders and battering rams in plain sight to make the defenders believe that this was a major assault.

In the quarter of the city occupied by Garion's troops, however, Silk led a sizeable detachment of men through the dawn murk across the roof tops to clear away the cult archers and the smeared men with their boiling pitch pots occupying those houses on either side of the hastily built walls erected to bar entrance into the rest of the city.

Garion, flanked by Barak and Mandorallen, waited in a snowy street near the perimeter of the occupied quarter. 'This is the part I hate,' he said tensely. 'The waiting.'

'I must confess to thee that I myself find this lull just before a battle unpleasant,' Mandorallen replied.

'I thought Arends loved a battle.' Barak grinned at his friend.

'It is our favorite pastime,' the great knight admitted, checking one of the buckles under his armor. 'This interim just 'ere we join with the enemy, however, is irksome. Sober, even melancholy, thoughts distract the mind from the main purpose at hand.'

'Mandorallen,' Barak laughed, 'I've missed you.'

The shadowy form of Yarblek came up the street to join them. He had put aside his felt overcoat and now wore a heavy steel breast-plate and carried a wicked-looking axe. 'Everything's ready,' he told them quietly. 'We can start just as soon as the little thief gives us the signal.'

'Are you sure your men can pull down those walls?' Barak asked him.

Yarblek nodded. 'Those people didn't have time enough to set the stones in mortar,' he said. 'Our grappling hooks can jerk down the walls in a few minutes.'

'You seem very fond of that particular tool,' Barak observed.

Yarblek shrugged. 'I've always found that the best way to get through a wall is to yank it down.'

'In Arendia, our preference is for the battering rams,' Mandorallen said.

'Those are good, too,' Yarblek agreed, 'but the trouble with a ram is that you're right under the wall when it falls. I've never particularly enjoyed having building stones bouncing off the top of my head.'

They waited.

'Has anybody seen Lelldorin?' Garion asked.

'He went with Silk,' Barak replied. 'He seemed to think that he could find more targets from up on a roof.'

'He was ever an enthusiast.' Mandorallen smiled. 'I must confess, however, that I have never seen his equal with the longbow.'

'There it is,' Barak said, pointing at a flaming arrow arching high above the rooftops. 'That's the signal.'

Garion drew in a deep breath and squared his shoulders. 'All right. Sound your horn, Mandorallen, and let's get started.'

The brazen note of Mandorallen's horn shattered the stillness. From every street and alleyway, Garion's army poured out to begin the final assault on Rheon. Rivans, Algars, Nadraks, and the solid men of Sendaria crunched through the snow toward the perimeter with their weapons in their hands. Three score of Yarblek's leather-clad mercenaries ran on ahead, their grappling hooks swinging from their hands.

With Barak at his side, Garion clambered over the treacherous, sliding rubble of the houses that had been pulled down to form the perimeter and over the half-frozen bodies of arrow-stitched cultists who had fallen earlier. A few—though not many—cultists had escaped the hasty floor-by-floor search of Silk's men in the houses facing the perimeter and they desperately showered the advancing troops with arrows. At Brendig's sharp command, detachments of Sendars veered and broke into each house to neutralize those remaining defenders efficiently.

The scene beyond the perimeter was one of enormous confusion. Advancing behind a wall of shields, Garion's army swept the streets clear of the now-desperate cultists.

The air was thick with arrows and curses, and several houses were already shooting flames out through their roofs.

True to Yarblek's prediction, the loosely stacked walls blocking the streets some way into the city fell easily to the dozens of grappling hooks that sailed up over their tops to bite into the other sides.

The grim advance continued, and the air rang with the steely clang of sword against sword. Somehow in all the confusion, Garion became separated from Barak and found himself fighting shoulder to shoulder beside Durnik in a narrow alleyway. The smith carried no sword or axe, but fought instead with a large, heavy club. 'I just don't like chopping into people,' he apologized, felling a burly opponent with one solid blow. 'If you hit somebody with a club, there's a fair chance that he won't die, and there isn't all that blood.'

They pushed deeper into the city, driving the demoralized inhabitants before them. The sounds of heavy fighting at the southern end of town gave notice that Silk and his men had reached the south wall and opened the gates to admit the massed troops whose feigned attack had fatally divided the cult forces.

And then Garion and Durnik burst out of the narrow alleyway into the broad, snowy central square of Rheon. Fighting raged all over the square; but on the east side, a thick knot of cultists was tightly packed about a high-wheeled cart. Atop the cart stood a black-bearded man in a rust-colored brocade doublet.

A lean Nadrak with a slender spear in his hand arched back, took aim, and hurled his weapon directly at the man on the cart. The black-bearded man raised one hand in a peculiar gesture, and the Nadrak spear suddenly sheered off to the right to clatter harmlessly on the snow-slick cobblestones. Garion clearly heard and felt the rushing surge that could only mean one thing. 'Durnik!' he shouted. 'That man on the cart. That's Ulfgar!'

Durnik's eyes narrowed. 'Let's take him, Garion,' he said.

Garion's anger at this stranger who was the cause of all this warfare and carnage and destruction suddenly swelled intolerably, and his rage communicated itself to the Orb on the pommel of his sword. The Orb flared, and Iron-grip's burning sword suddenly flamed out in searing blue fire.

'There! It's the Rivan King!' the black-bearded man on the cart screamed. 'Kill him!'

Momentarily Garion's eyes locked on the eyes of the man on the cart. There was hate there and, at the same time, an awe and a desperate fear. But, blindly obedient to their leader's command, a dozen cultists ran through the slush toward Garion with their swords aloft. Suddenly they began to tumble into twitching heaps in the sodden snow in the square as arrow after arrow laced into their ranks.

'Ho, Garion!' Lelldorin shouted gleefully from a nearby housetop, his hands blurring as he loosed his arrows at the charging cultists.

'Ho, Lelldorin!' Garion called his reply, even as he ran in amongst the fur-clad men, flailing about him with his burning sword. The attention of the group around the cart was riveted entirely on the horrifying spectacle of the enraged King of Riva and his fabled sword. They did not, therefore, see Durnik the smith moving in a catlike crouch along the wall of a nearby house.

The man on the cart raised one hand aloft, seized a ball of pure fire, and hurled it desperately at Garion. Garion flicked the fireball aside with his flaming blade and continued his grim advance, swinging dreadful strokes at the desperate men garbed in bearskins in front of him without ever taking his eyes off of the pasty-faced man in the black beard. His expression growing panicky, Ulfgar raised his hand again, but suddenly seemed almost to lunge forward off the cart into the brown slush as Durnik's cudgel cracked sharply across the back of his head.

There was a great cry of chagrin as the cult-leader fell. Several of his men tried desperately to lift his inert body, but Durnik's club, whistling and thudding solidly, felled them in their tracks. Others tried to form a wall with their bodies in an effort to keep Garion from reaching the body lying face-down in the snow, but Lelldorin's steady rain of arrows melted the center of that fur-clad wall. Garion, feeling strangely remote and unaffected by the slaughter, marched into the very midst of the disorganized survivors, swinging his huge sword in great, sweeping arcs. He barely felt the sickening shear as his sword cut through bone and flesh. After he had cut down a half dozen or so, the rest broke and ran.

'Is he still alive?' Garion panted at the smith.

Durnik rolled the inert Ulfgar over and professionally peeled back one of his eyelids to have a look. 'He's still with us,' he said. 'I hit him rather carefully.'

'Good,' Garion said. 'Let's tie him up—and blindfold him.'

'Why blindfold?'

'We both saw him use sorcery, so we've answered that particular question, but I think it might be a little hard to do that sort of thing if you can't see what you're aiming at.'

Durnik thought about it for a moment as he tied the unconscious man's hands. 'You know, I believe you're right. It would be difficult, wouldn't it?'

Chapter Twenty-five

With the fall of Ulfgar, the cult's will to resist broke. Though a few of the more rabid continued to fight, most threw down their weapons in surrender. Grimly, Garion's army rounded them up and herded them through the snowy, blood-stained streets into the town's central square.

Silk and Javelin briefly questioned a sullen captive with a bloody bandage wrapped around his head, then joined Garion and Durnik, who stood watch over their still-unconscious prisoner. 'Is that him?' Silk asked curiously, absently polishing one of his rings on the front of his gray doublet.

Garion nodded.

'He doesn't look all that impressive, does he?'

'The large stone house over there is his,' Javelin said, pointing at a square building with red tiles on its roof.

'Not any more,' Garion replied. 'It's mine now.'

Javelin smiled briefly. 'We'll want to search it rather thoroughly,' he said. 'People sometimes forget to destroy important things.'

'We might as well take Ulfgar in there, too,' Garion said. 'We need to question him, and that house is as good as any.'

'I'll go get the others,' Durnik offered, pulling off his pot-shaped helmet. 'Do you think it's safe enough to bring Pol and the other ladies into the city yet?'

'It should be,' Javelin replied. 'What little resistance there is left is in the southeast quarter of the city.'

Durnik nodded and went on across the square, his mail shirt jingling.

Garion, Silk and Javelin picked up the limp form of the black-bearded man and carried him toward the stately house with the banner of a bear flying from a staff in front of it. As they started up the stairs, Garion glanced at a Rivan soldier standing guard over some demoralized prisoners huddled miserably in the slush. 'Would you do me a favor?' he asked the gray-cloaked man.

'Of course, your Majesty,' the soldier said, saluting.

'Chop that thing down.' Garion indicated the flagstaff with a thrust of his jaw.

'At once, your Majesty.' the soldier grinned. 'I should have thought of it myself.'

They carried Ulfgar into the house and through a polished door. The room beyond that door was luxuriously furnished, but the chairs were mostly overturned, and there were sheets of parchment everywhere. A crumpled heap of them had been stuffed into a large stone fireplace built into the back wall, but the fireplace was cold.

'Good,' Javelin muttered. 'He was interrupted before he could burn anything.'

Silk looked around at the room. Rich, dark-colored tapestries hung on the walls, and the green carpeting was thick and soft. The chairs were all upholstered in scarlet velvet, and unlighted candles stood in silver sconces along the wall. 'He managed to live fairly well, didn't he?' the little man murmured as they unceremoniously dumped the prisoner in the rust-colored doublet in one corner.

'Let's gather up these documents,' Javelin said. 'I want to go over them.'

Garion unstrapped his sword, dropped his helmet on the floor and shrugged himself out of his heavy mail shirt. Then he sank wearily onto a soft couch. 'I'm absolutely exhausted,' he said. 'I feel as if I haven't slept for a week.'

Silk shrugged. 'One of the privileges of command.'

The door opened, and Belgarath came into the room.

'Durnik said I could find you here,' he said, pushing back the hood of his shabby old cloak. He crossed the room and nudged the limp form in the corner. 'He isn't dead, is he?'

'No,' Garion replied. 'Durnik put him to sleep with a club that's all.'

'Why the blindfold?' the old man asked, indicating the strip of blue cloth tied across the captive's face.

'He was using sorcery before we captured him. I thought it might not be a bad idea to cover his eyes.'

'That depends on how good he is. Durnik sent soldiers out to round up the others and then he went over to the encampment to get Pol and the other ladies.'

'Can you wake him up?' Silk asked.

'Let's have Pol do it. Her touch is a little lighter than mine, and I don't want to break anything accidently.'

It was perhaps three-quarters of an hour later when they all finally gathered in the green-carpeted room. Belgarath looked around, then straddled a straight-backed chair in front of the captive. 'All right, Pol,' he said bleakly. 'Wake him up.'

Polgara unfastened her blue cloak, knelt beside the prisoner and put one hand on each side of his head. Garion heard a whispered rushing sound and felt a gentle surge. Ulfgar groaned.

'Give him a few minutes,' she said, rising to her feet. 'Then you can start questioning him.'

'He's probably going to be stubborn about it,' Brin predicted with a broad grin.

'I'll be terribly disappointed in him if he isn't,' Silk said as he rifled through a drawer in a large, polished cabinet.

'Have you barbarians blinded me?' Ulfgar said in a weak voice as he struggled into a sitting position.

'No,' Polgara told him. 'Your eyes are covered to keep you out of mischief.'

'Are my captors women, then?' There was contempt in the black-bearded man's voice.

'This one of them is,' Ce'Nedra said, pushing her dark green cloak slightly to one side. It was the note in her voice that warned Garion and saved the prisoner's life. With blazing eyes, she snatched one of the daggers from Vella's belt and flew at the blindfolded man with the gleaming blade held aloft. At the last instant, Garion caught her upraised arm and wrested the knife from her grasp.

'Give me that!' she cried.

'No, Ce'Nedra.'

'He stole my baby!' she screamed. 'I'll kill him!'

'No, you won't. We can't get any answers out of him if you cut his throat.' With one arm still about her, he handed the dagger back to Vella.

'We have a few questions for you, Ulfgar,' Belgarath said to the captive.

'You're going to have to wait a long time for the answers.'

'I'm *so* glad he said that,' Hettar murmured. 'Who wants to start cutting on him?'

'Do whatever you wish,' Ulfgar sneered. 'My body is of no concern to me.'

'We'll do everything we can to change your mind about that,' Vella said in a chillingly sweet voice as she tested the edge of her dagger with her thumb.

'Just what was it you wanted to know, Belgarath?' Errand asked, turning from his curious examination of a bronze statue standing in the corner. 'I can give you the answers, if you want.'

Belgarath looked at the blond boy sharply. 'Do you know what's in his mind?' he asked, startled.

'More or less, yes.'

'Where's my son?' Garion asked quickly.

'That's one thing he doesn't know,' Errand replied. 'He had nothing to do with the abduction.'

'Who did it then?'

'He's not sure, but he thinks it was Zandramas.'

'Zandramas?'

'That name keeps cropping up, doesn't it?' Silk said.

'Does he know who Zandramas is?'

'Not really. It's just a name he's heard from his Master.'

'Who is his Master?'

'He's afraid even to think the name,' Errand said. 'It's a man with a splotchy face, though.'

The prisoner was struggling desperately, trying to free himself from the ropes which bound him. 'Lies!' he screamed. 'All lies!'

'This man was sent here by his Master to make sure that you and Ce'Nedra didn't have any children,' Errand continued, ignoring the screaming captive, 'or to see to it that, if you did, the children didn't live. He couldn't have been behind the abduction, Belgarion. If *he* had been the one who crept into the nursery at Riva, he would have killed your son, not taken him away.'

'Where does he come from?' Liselle asked curiously as she removed her scarlet cloak. 'I can't quite place his accent.'

'That's probably because he's not really a man,' Errand told her. 'At least not entirely. He remembers being an animal of some sort.'

They all stared at the boy and then at Ulfgar.

At that point the door opened again, and the hunchbacked Beldin came into the room. He was about to say something, but stopped, staring at the bound and blindfolded prisoner. He stumped across the floor, bent, and ripped the blue cloth away from the man's eyes to stare into his face. 'Well, dog,' he said. 'What brings you out of your kennel?'

'You!' Ulfgar gasped, his face growing suddenly pale.

'Urvon will have your heart for breakfast when he finds out how badly you've botched things,' Beldin said pleasantly.

'Do you know this man?' Garion asked sharply.

'He and I have known each other for a long, long time, haven't we, Harakan?'

The prisoner spat at him.

'I see you still need a bit of housebreaking.' Beldin grinned.

'Who is he?' Garion demanded.

'His name is Harakan. He's a Mallorean Grolim—one

of Urvon's dogs. The last time I saw him, he was whining and fawning all over Urvon's feet.'

Then, quite suddenly, the captive vanished.

Beldin unleased a string of foul curses. Then he, too, flickered out of sight.

'What happened?' Ce'Nedra gasped. 'Where did they go?'

'Maybe Beldin isn't as smart as I thought,' Belgarath said. 'He should have left that blindfold alone. Our prisoner translocated himself outside the building.'

'Can you do that?' Garion asked incredulously. 'Without being able to see what you're doing, I mean?'

'It's very, very dangerous, but Harakan seems to have been desperate. Beldin's following him.'

'He'll catch him, won't he?'

'It's hard to say.'

'I still have questions that have to be answered.'

'I can answer them for you, Belgarion,' Errand told him quite calmly.

'You mean that you still know what's in his mind—even though he's not here any more?'

Errand nodded.

'Why don't you start at the beginning, Errand?' Polgara suggested.

'All right. This Harakan, I guess his real name is, came here because his Master, the one Beldin called Urvon, sent him here to make sure that Belgarion and Ce'Nedra never had any children. Harakan came here and gained control of the Bear-cult. At first he stirred up all kinds of talk against Ce'Nedra, hoping that he could force Belgarion to set her aside and marry someone else. Then, when he heard that she was going to have a baby, he sent someone to try to kill her. That didn't work, of course, and he started to get desperate. He was terribly afraid of what Urvon would do to him if he failed. He tried to gain control of Ce'Nedra when she was asleep once, to make her smother the baby, but someone—he doesn't know who—stepped in and stopped him.'

'It was Poledra,' Garion murmured. 'I was there that night.'

'Is that when he came up with the idea of murdering Brand and laying the blame at King Anheg's door?' General Brendig asked.

Errand frowned slightly. 'Killing Brand was an accident,' he replied. 'As closely as Harakan could work it out, Brand just happened along and caught the cultists in that hallway when they were about to do what he really sent them to Riva to do.'

'And what was that?' Ce'Nedra asked him.

'They were on their way to the royal apartments to kill you and your baby.'

Her face paled.

'And then they were supposed to kill themselves. *That* was what was supposed to start the war between Belgarion and King Anheg. Anyway, something went wrong. Brand got killed instead of you and your baby, and we found out that the cult was responsible instead of Anheg. He didn't dare go back to Urvon and admit that he had failed. Then Zandramas took your baby and got away from the Isle of the Winds with him. Harakan couldn't follow because Belgarion was already marching on Rheon by the time he found out about it. He was trapped here, and Zandramas was getting away with your baby.'

'That Nyissan ship!' Kail exclaimed. 'Zandramas stole your son, Belgarion, and then sailed off to the south and left us all floundering around here in Drasnia.'

'What about the story we got from that Cherek cultist right after the abduction?' Brin asked.

'A Bear-cultist isn't usually very bright,' Kail replied. 'I don't think this Zandramas would have had too much difficulty in persuading those Chereks that the abduction was on Harakan's orders, and all that gibberish about the prince being raised in the cult so that one day he could claim the Rivan throne is just the kind of brainsick nonsense men like that would believe.'

'That's why they were left behind, then,' Garion said. 'We were *supposed* to capture at least one of them and get

414

the carefully prepared story that sent us off here to Rheon, while Zandramas sailed away to the south with my son.'

'It looks as if we've all been very carefully manipulated,' Javelin said, sorting through some parchment sheets he had stacked on a polished table. 'Harakan as well as the rest of us.'

'We can be clever, too,' Belgarath said. 'I don't think Zandramas realizes that the Orb will follow Geran's trail. If we move fast enough, we can sneak up from behind and take this clever manipulator by surprise.'

It won't work across water, the dry voice in Garion's mind said laconically.

'What?'

The Orb can't follow your son's trail over water. The ground stays in one place. Water keeps moving around— wind, tides, that sort of thing.'

'Are you sure?'

But the voice was gone.

'There's a problem, Grandfather,' Garion said. 'The Orb can't find a trail on water.'

'How do you know that?'

Garion tapped his forehead. '*He* just told me.'

'That complicates things a bit.'

'Not too much,' Silk disagreed. 'There are very few places where a Nyissan ship can land without being searched from keel to topmast. Most monarchs don't care much for the idea of having drugs and poisons slipped into their kingdoms. Zandramas would definitely not want to sail into some port and get caught with the heir to the Rivan Throne aboard ship.'

'There are many hidden coves along the coast of Arendia,' Lelldorin suggested.

Silk shook his head. 'I don't think so,' he said. 'I think the ship would have just stayed out to sea. I'm sure Zandramas wanted to get as far away from the Alorn kingdoms as possible—and as quickly as possible. If this ruse that sent us here to Rheon hadn't worked, Garin would have had every man and every ship in the West out looking for his son.'

'How about southern Cthol Murgos?' General Brendig suggested.

Javelin frowned. 'No,' he said. 'There's a war going on down there and the whole west coast is being patrolled by Murgo ships. The only safe place for a Nyissan ship to land is in Nyissa itself.'

'And that brings us back to Salmissra, doesn't it?' Polgara said.

'I think that if there had been any kind of official involvement in this, my people would have found out about it, Lady Polgara,' Javelin said. 'I've got Salmissra's palace thoroughly covered. The actual orders would have had to come from Sadi, Salmissra's Chief Eunuch, and we watch him all the time. I don't think this came out of the palace.'

The door opened and Beldin, his face as dark as a thundercloud, entered. 'By the Gods!' he swore. 'I lost him!'

'Lost him?' Belgarath asked. 'How?'

'When he got to the street, he turned himself into a hawk. I was right on his tail, but he went into the clouds and changed form on me again. When he came out, he was mixed up in the middle of a flock of geese flying south. Naturally, when the geese saw me, they flew off squawking in all directions. I couldn't tell which one of them he was.'

'You must be getting old.'

'Why don't you shut up, Belgarath?'

'He's not important anymore, anyway.' Belgarath shrugged. 'We got what we need out of him.'

'I think I'd prefer it if he were safely dead. If nothing else, the loss of one of his favorite dogs would irritate Urvon, and I'll go out of my way to do that any day in the week.'

'Why do you keep calling him a dog?' Hettar asked curiously.

'Because he's one of the Chandim—and that's what they are—the Hounds of Torak.'

'Would you like to explain that?' Queen Porenn asked him.

Beldin took a deep breath to get his irritation under control. 'It's not too complicated,' he said. 'When they built Cthol Mishrak in Mallorea, Torak set certain Grolims the task of guarding the city. In order to do that, they became hounds.'

Garion shuddered, the memory of the huge dog-shapes they had encountered in the City of Night coming back to him with painful clarity.

'Anyway,' Beldin continued, 'after the Battle of Vo Mimbre when Torak was put to sleep for all those centuries, Urvon went into the forbidden area around the ruins and managed to persuade a part of the pack of hounds that he was acting on behalf of old burnt-face. He took them back to Mal Yaska with him and gradually changed them back into Grolims, even though he had to kill about half of them in the process. Anyhow, they call themselves the Chandim—a sort of secret order within the Grolim church. Thy're absolutely loyal to Urvon. They're pretty fair sorcerers and they dabble a bit in magic as well. Underneath it all, though, they're still dogs—very obedient and much more dangerous in packs than they are as individuals.'

'What a fascinating little sidelight,' Silk observed, looking up from a parchment scroll he had found in one of the cabinets.

'You have a very clever mouth, Kheldar,' Beldin said testily. 'How would you like to have me brick it up for you?'

'No, that's quite all right, Beldin.'

'Well, what now, Belgarath?' Queen Porenn asked.

'Now? Now we go after Zandramas, of course. This hoax with the cult has put us a long way behind, but we'll catch up.'

'You can count on that,' Garion said. 'I dealt with the Child of Dark once before and I can do it again if I have to.' He turned back to Errand. 'Do you have any idea of why Urvon wants my son killed?'

'It's something he found in a book of some kind. The book says that if your son ever falls into the hands of

Zandramas, then Zandramas will be able to use him to do something. Whatever it is, Urvon would be willing to destroy the world to prevent it.'

'What is it that Zandramas would be able to do?' Belgarath asked, his eyes intent.

'Harakan doesn't know. All he knows is that he's failed in the task Urvon set him.'

Belgarath smiled slowly, a cold, wintery kind of smile. 'I don't think we need to waste any time chasing Harakan,' he said.

'Not chase him?' Ce'Nedra exclaimed. 'After all he's done to us?'

'Urvon will take care of him for us and Urvon will do things to him that we couldn't even begin to think of.'

'Who is this Urvon?' General Brendig asked.

'Torak's third disciple,' Belgarath replied. 'There used to be three of them—Ctuchik, Zedar, and Urvon. But he's the only one left.'

'We still don't know anything about Zandramas,' Silk said.

'We know a few things. We know that Zandramas is now the Child of Dark, for example.'

'That doesn't fit together, Belgarath,' Barak rumbled. 'Why would Urvon want to interfere with the Child of Dark? They're on the same side, aren't they?'

'Apparently not. It begins to look as if there's a little dissension in the ranks on the other side.'

'That's always helpful.'

'I'd like to know a bit more before I start gloating, though.'

It was midafternoon before the last fanatic resistance collapsed in the southeastern quarter of Rheon and the demoralized prisoners were herded through the streets of the burning town to join the others in the town square.

Garion and General Brendig stood on the second floor balcony of the house where they had taken Harakan, talking quietly with the small, black-gowned Queen of Drasnia. 'What will you do with them now, your Majesty?'

General Brendig asked her, looking down at the frightened prisoners in the square.

'I'm going to tell them the truth and let them go, Brendig.'

'Let them go?'

'Of course.'

'I afraid I don't quite follow you.'

'They're going to be just a little upset when I tell them that they've been duped into betraying Aloria by a Mallorean Grolim.'

'I don't think they'll believe you.'

'Enough of them will,' she replied placidly, adjusting the collar of her black dress. 'I'll manage to convince at least some of them of the truth, and they'll spread the word. Once it becomes general knowledge that the cult fell under the domination of this Grolim Harakan, it's going to be more difficult for them to gain new converts, don't you think?'

Brendig considered that. 'I suppose you're right,' he admitted. 'But will you punish the ones who won't listen?'

'That would be tyranny, General, and one should always try to avoid the appearance of tyranny—particularly when it's unncessary. Once word of this gets around, I think that anyone who starts babbling about the divine mission of Aloria to subjugate the southern kingdoms is going to be greeted with a barrage of stones.'

'All right, then, what are you going to do about General Haldar?' he asked seriously. 'You're not just going to let *him* go, too, are you?'

'Haldar's quite another matter,' she replied. 'He's a traitor, and that sort of thing ought to be discouraged.'

'When he finds out what happened here, he'll probably try to run.'

'Appearances can be deceiving, General Brendig,' she told him with a chill smile 'I may look like a helpless woman, but I have a very long arm. Haldar can't run far enough or fast enough to escape me. And when my people catch him, he'll be brought back to Boktor in chains to stand trial. I think the outcome of that trial will be fairly predictable.'

'Would you excuse me?' Garion asked politely. 'I need to go talk with my grandfather.'

'Of course, Garion,' Queen Porenn said with a warm little smile.

He went back downstairs and found Silk and Javelin still ransacking the chests and cabinets in the green-carpeted room. 'Are you finding anything useful?' he asked.

'Well, quite a bit, actually,' Javelin replied. 'I expect that by the time we're finished, we'll have the name of every cult member in Aloria.'

'It just proves something I've always said,' Silk noted as he continued to read. 'A man should never put anything down in writing.'

'Have either of you any idea where I can find Belgarath?'

'You might try the kitchens at the back of the house,' Silk replied. 'He said something about being hungry. I think Beldin went with him.'

The kitchen in Harakan's house had escaped the general ransacking by Yarblek's men, who appeared to be more interested in loot than food, and the two old sorcerers sat comfortably at a table near a low, arched window picking at the remains of a roasted chicken. 'Ah, Garion, my boy,' Belgarath said expansively. 'Come in and join us.'

'Do you suppose there's anything to drink around here?' Beldin asked, wiping his fingers on the front of his tunic.

'There should be,' Belgarath replied. 'It's a kitchen, after all. Why don't you look in that pantry?'

Beldin rose and crossed the kitchen floor toward the pantry.

Garion bent slightly to look out the low window at the houses burning one street over. 'It's starting to snow again,' he observed.

Belgarath grunted. 'I think we'll want to get out of here as quickly as we can,' he said. 'I don't really want to spend the winter here.'

'Ah, ha!' Beldin said from the pantry. He emerged with a triumphant grin carrying a small wooden cask.

'You'd better taste it first,' Belgarath told him. 'It might be vinegar.'

Beldin set the cask on the floor and bashed in its top with his fist. Then he licked his fingers and smacked his lips. 'No,' he said, 'it's definitely not vinegar.' He rummaged through a nearby cupboard and produced three earthenware cups.

'Well, brother,' Belgarath said, 'what are your plans?'

Beldin dipped into the cask with one of the cups. 'I think I'll see if I can track down Harakan. I'd like to finish him off before I go back to Mallorea. He's not the kind you want lurking in alleys behind you as you go by.'

'You're going to Mallorea, then?' Belgarath tore a wing off the chicken lying on the table.

'That's probably the only place where we can get any solid information about this Zandramas.' Beldin belched.

'Javelin says that he thinks it's a Darshivan name,' Garion told him.

Beldin grunted. 'That could help a little. This time I'll start there. I couldn't get anything at all at Mal Zeth, and those half-wits in Karanda fell over in a dead faint every time I mentioned the name.'

'Did you try Mal Yaska?' Belgarath asked him.

'Hardly. Urvon's got my description posted on every wall in that place. For some reason, he's afraid that someday I might show up and yank out several yards of his guts.'

'I wonder why.'

'I told him so, that's why.'

'You'll be in Darshiva, then?'

'For the time being—at least, I will after I've got Harakan safely under the ground. If I find out anything about Zandramas, I'll get word to you.'

'Keep your eyes open for clear copies of the Mallorean Gospels and the Ashabine Oracles, too,' Belgarath told him. 'According to the Codex, I'm supposed to find clues in them.'

'And what are you going to do?'

'I think we'll go on down to Nyissa and see if the Orb can pick up the trail of my great-grandson.'

'The fact that some Rivan shepherd saw a Nyissan ship is a pretty slender lead, Belgarath.'

'I know, but at the moment it's the only one we've got.'

Garion absently pulled a few fragments off the picked-over chicken and put them in his mouth. He suddenly realized that he was ravenously hungry.

'Are you going to take Polgara with you?' Beldin asked.

'I don't think so. Garion and I are likely to be out of touch, and we'll need somebody here in the north to keep an eye on things. The Alorns are feeling muscular at the moment and they're going to need a firm hand to keep them out of mischief.'

'That's a normal condition for Alorns. You realize that Polgara's not going to be happy when you tell her she has to stay behind, don't you?'

'I know,' Belgarath replied with a gloomy look. 'Maybe I'll just leave her a note. That worked pretty well last time.'

'Just try to make sure she's not in the vicinity of anything breakable when she gets the note.' Beldin laughed. 'Like large cities and mountain ranges. I heard what happened when she got the last note you left.'

The door opened, and Barak stuck his head into the kitchen. 'Oh,' he said. 'There you are. There are a couple of people out here who want to see you. Mandorallen found them on the outskirts of town—a very strange pair.'

'How do you mean strange?' Garion asked.

'The man's as big as a house. He's got arms like tree trunks, but he can't talk. The girl's pretty enough, but she'd blind.'

Belgarath and Beldin exchanged a quick look. 'How do you know she's blind?' Belgarath asked.

'She's got a cloth tied across her eyes.' Barak shrugged. 'I just assumed that was what it meant.'

'I guess we'd better go talk to her,' Beldin said, rising from his seat. 'A seeress wouldn't be in this part of the world unless it was pretty important.'

'A seeress?' Garion asked.

'One of those people from Kell,' Belgarath explained.

'They're always blindfolded, and their guides are always mutes. Let's go see what she has to say.'

When they entered the large main room, they found the others curiously eyeing the two strangers. The blindfolded seeress was a slight girl in a white robe. She had dark blond hair, and a serene smile touched her lips. She stood quietly in the center of the room, patiently waiting. Beside her stood one of the largest men Garion had ever seen. He wore a kind of sleeveless kirtle of coarse, undyed cloth belted at the waist, and he carried no weapon except for a stout, polished staff. He towered above even Hettar, and his bare arms were awesomely muscled. In a curious way, he seemed almost to hover over his slender mistress, his eyes watchful and protective.

'Has she said who she is?' Belgarath quietly asked Polgara as they joined the others.

'No,' she replied. 'All that she says is that she has to speak with you and Garion.'

'Her name is Cyradis,' Errand said from nearby.

'Do you know her?' Garion asked him.

'We met once—in the Vale. She wanted to find out something about me, so she came there, and we talked.'

'What did she want to find out?'

'She didn't say.'

'Didn't you ask her?'

'I think that if she'd wanted me to know, she'd have told me.'

'I would speak with thee, Ancient Belgarath,' the seeress said then in a light, clear voice, 'and with thee, also, Belgarion.'

They drew closer.

'I am permitted a short time here to tell thee certain truths. First, know that your tasks are not yet completed. Necessity doth command yet one more meeting between the Child of Light and the Child of Dark; and mark me well—this meeting shall be the last, for it is during this meeting that the final choice between the Light and the Dark shall be made.'

'And where will this meeting take place, Cyradis?' Belgarath asked her, his face intent.

'In the presence of the Sardion—in the place which is no more.'

'And where is that?'

'The path to that dread place lies in the mysteries, Ancient One. Thou must seek it there.' She turned her face toward Garion, half-reaching out to him with one slender hand. 'Thy heart is sore, Belgarion,' she said with a great sympathy in her voice, 'for Zandramas, the Child of Dark, hath reft away thy son and even now doth flee with him toward the Sardion. It lies upon thee to bar the path of Zandramas to that stone—for the stars and the voices of the earth proclaim that the power of the Dark doth reside in the Sardion, even as the power of the Light doth reside in the Orb of Aldur. Should Zandramas reach the Dark Stone with the babe, the Dark shall triumph, and its triumph shall be eternal.'

'Is my baby all right?' Ce'Nedra demanded, her face pale and a dreadful fear in her eyes.

'Thy child is safe and well, Ce'Nedra,' Cyradis told her. 'Zandramas will protect him from all harm—not out of love, but out of Necessity.' The seeress' face grew still. 'Thou must steel thy heart, however,' she continued, 'for should there be no other way to prevent Zandramas from reaching the Sardion with thine infant son, it falls to thee —or to thy husband—to slay the child.'

'Slay?' Ce'Nedra exclaimed. 'Never!'

'Then the Dark shall prevail,' Cyradis said simply. She turned back to Garion. 'My time grows short,' she said to him. 'Heed what I say. Thy choice of companions to aid thee in this task of thine must be guided by Necessity and not thine own preference. Shouldst thou choose awry, then shalt thou fail thy task, and Zandramas will defeat thee. Thy son shall be lost to thee forever, and the world as thou knowest it shall be no more.'

Garion's face was bleak. 'Go ahead,' he told her shortly. 'Say the rest of what you have to say.' Her suggestion that either he or Ce'Nedra could ever under any circumstances kill their own child had filled him with a sudden anger.

'Thou wilt leave this place in the company of Ancient

Belgarath and his most revered daughter. Thou must also take with thee the Bearer of the Orb and thy wife.'

'Absurd!' he burst out. 'I'm not going to expose Ce'Nedra—or Errand—to that kind of danger.'

'Then thou wilt surely fail.'

He looked at her helplessly.

'Thou must have with thee as well the Guide and the Man with Two Lives—and one other whom I will reveal to thee. Thou wilt be joined at some later times by others —the Huntress, the Man Who Is No Man, the Empty One, and by the Woman Who Watches.'

'That's fairly typical seer gibberish,' Beldin muttered sourly.

'The words are not mine, gentle Beldin,' she told him. 'These are the names as they are written in the stars—and in the prophecies. The incidental and worldly names which were given them at the time of their births are of no moment in the timeless realm of the two Necessities which contend with each other at the center of all that is or ever will be. Each of these companions hath a certain task, and all tasks must be completed 'ere the meeting which is to come, else the Prophecy which hath guided thy steps since time began will fail.'

'And what is my task, Cyradis?' Polgara asked her coolly.

'It is as it hath ever been, Holy Polgara. Thou must guide, and nurture, and protect, for thou art the mother —even as Ancient Belgarath is the father.' The faintest of smiles touched the blindfolded girl's lips. 'Others will aid thee in thy quest from time to time, Belgarion,' she continued, 'but those I have named must be with thee at that final meeting.'

'What about us?' Barak demanded, 'Hettar and Mando-rallen and Lelldorin and me?'

'The tasks of each of you are complete, most Dreadful Bear, and the responsibility for them hath descended to your sons. Shouldst thou or the Bowman or the Horse Lord or the Knight Protector seek to join with Belgarion in this quest, thy presence will cause him to fail.'

'Ridiculous!' the big man spluttered. 'I'm certainly not staying behind.'

'That choice is not thine to make.' She turned back to Garion, laying her hand on the massive arm of her mute protector. 'This is Toth,' she said, slumping as if a great weariness were about to overcome her. 'He hath guided my faltering steps since the day that other sight came upon me and I bound up mine eyes that I might better see. Though it doth rend my soul, he and I must now part for a little while. I have instructed him to aid thee in thy search. In the stars he is called the Silent Man, and it is his destiny to be one of thy companions.' She began to tremble as if in exhaustion. 'One last word for thee, Belgarion,' she said in a quavering voice. 'Thy quest will be fraught with great peril, and one of thy companions shall lose his life in the course of it. Prepare thine heart therefore, for when this occurs, thou must not falter, but must press on to the completion of the task which hath been laid upon thee.'

'Who?' he said quickly. 'Which one of them is going to die?'

'That hath not been revealed to me,' she said. And then with an obvious effort, she straightened. 'Remember me,' she said, 'for we shall meet anon.' With that she vanished.

'Where did she go?' General Brendig exclaimed.

'She was never really here,' Errand replied.

'It was a projection, Brendig,' Belgarath said. 'But the man—Toth—is solid. Now how did they work that? Do you know, Errand?'

Errand shrugged. 'I can't tell, Belgarath. But it took the combined power of all the Seers at Kell.'

'What absolute nonsense!' Barak burst out angrily, pounding one huge fist on the table. 'Nothing in this world could make me stay behind!' Mandorallen, Hettar, and Lelldorin vehemently nodded their agreement.

Garion looked at Polgara. 'Could she possibly have been lying?' he asked.

'Cryadis? No. A seeress isn't capable of lying. She may have concealed a few things, but she could not have lied. What she told us was what she saw in the stars.'

'How can she see the stars with that blindfold over her eyes?' Lelldorin objected.

Polgara spread her hands. 'I don't know. The seers perceive things in ways we don't entirely understand.'

'Maybe she read them wrong,' Hettar suggested.

'The Seers at Kell are usually right,' Beldin growled, 'so I wouldn't necessarily want to bet my life on that.'

'That brings us right to the point,' Garion said. 'I'm going to have to go alone.'

'*Alone?*' Ce'Nedra gasped.

'You heard what she said. Somebody who goes with me is going to get killed.'

'That hath ever been a possibility, Garion,' Mandorallen said soberly.

'But never a certainty.'

'I won't let you go by yourself,' Barak declared.

Garion felt a peculiar wrench, almost as if he had been rudely pushed aside. He was powerless as a voice which was not his came from his lips. 'Will you people stop all this babbling?' it demanded. 'You've been given your instructions. Now follow them.'

They all stared at Garion in amazement. He spread his hands helplessly, trying to let them know that he had no control over the words coming from his mouth.

Belgarath blinked. 'This must be important, if it can make *you* take a hand directly,' he said to the awareness that had suddenly usurped Garion's voice.

'You don't have time to sit around debating the issue, Belgarath. You have a very long way to go and only so much time.'

'Then what Cyradis said was true?' Polgara asked.

'As far as it went. She's still not taking sides, though.'

'Then why did she come at all?' Beldin asked.

'She has her own task, and this was part of that. She must also give instructions to Zandramas.'

'I don't suppose you could give us a hint or two about this place we're supposed to find?' Belgarath asked hopefully.

'Belgarath, don't do that. You know better. You have to stop at Prolgu on your way south.'

'Prolgu?'

'Something that has to occur is going to happen there. Time is running out on you, Belgarath, so stop wasting it.'

'You keep talking about time. Could you be a bit more specific?'

'He's gone, Grandfather,' Garion said, regaining control of his voice.

'He always does that,' Belgarath complained. 'Just when the conversation gets interesting, he leaves.'

'You know why he does it, Belgarath,' Beldin said.

Belgarath sighed. 'Yes, I suppose I do.' He turned to the others. 'That's it, then,' he said. 'I guess we do exactly what Cyradis told us to do.'

'You're surely not going to take Ce'Nedra with you,' Porenn objected.

'Of course I'm going, Porenn,' Ce'Nedra declared with a little toss of her head. 'I'd have gone anyway—no matter what that blind girl said.'

'But she said that one of Garion's companions would die.'

'I'm not his companion, Porenn. I'm his wife.'

There were actual tears in Barak's eyes. 'Isn't there anything I can say to persuade you to change your mind?' he pleaded.

Garion felt the tears also welling up in his own eyes. Barak had always been one of the solid rocks in his life, and the thought of beginning this search without the big red-bearded man at his side left a great emptiness inside him. 'I'm afraid we don't have any choice, Barak,' he said very sadly. 'If it were up to me —' He left it hanging, unable to go on.

'This hath rent mine heart, dearest Ce'Nedra,' Mandorallen said, kneeling before the queen. 'I am thy true knight, thy champion and protector, and yet I am forbidden to accompany thee on thy perilous quest.'

Great, glistening tears suddenly streamed down

Ce'Nedra's cheeks. She put her arms about the great knight's neck. 'Dear, dear Mandorallen,' she said brokenly, kissing his cheek.

'I've got some people working on a few things in Mallorea,' Silk said to Yarblek. 'I'll give you a letter to them so that they can keep you advised. Don't make any hasty decisions, but don't pass up any opportunities, either.'

'I know how to run the business, Silk,' Yarblek retorted. 'At least as well as you do.'

'Of course you do, but you get excited. All I'm saying is that you should try to keep your head.' The little man looked down rather sadly at his velvet doublet and all the jewels he was wearing. He sighed. 'Oh, well, I've lived without all this before, I suppose.' He turned to Durnik. 'I guess we should start packing,' he said.

Garion looked at him in perplexity.

'Weren't you listening, Garion?' the little man asked him. 'Cyradis told you whom you were supposed to take along. Durnik's the Man with Two Lives, Errand is the Bearer of the Orb, and in case you've forgotten, I'm the Guide.'

Garion's eyes widened.

'Naturally I'm going with you,' Silk said with an impudent grin. 'You'd probably get lost if I weren't along to show you the way.'

Here ends Book I of *The Malloreon*

Book II, *King of the Murgos*,

begins the quest for Garion's son across strange new lands
to the place that is no more and a conflict of opposing
destinies that will decide the fate of all mankind.

A SELECTED LIST OF FANTASY TITLES
AVAILABLE FROM CORGI AND BLACK SWAN

THE PRICES SHOWN BELOW WERE CORRECT AT THE TIME OF GOING
TO PRESS. HOWEVER TRANSWORLD PUBLISHERS RESERVE THE RIGHT
TO SHOW NEW RETAIL PRICES ON COVERS WHICH MAY DIFFER FROM
THOSE PREVIOUSLY ADVERTISED IN THE TEXT OR ELSEWHERE.

☐	14803 2	MALLOREON 2: KING OF THE MURGOS	*David Eddings*	£6.99
☐	14804 0	MALLOREON 3: DEMON LORD OF KARANDA	*David Eddings*	£6.99
☐	14805 9	MALLOREON 4: SORCERESS OF DARSHIVA	*David Eddings*	£6.99
☐	14806 7	MALLOREON 5: SEERESS OF KELL	*David Eddings*	£6.99
☐	14807 5	BELGARIAD 1: PAWN OF PROPHECY	*David Eddings*	£6.99
☐	14808 3	BELGARIAD 2: QUEEN OF SORCERY	*David Eddings*	£6.99
☐	14809 1	BELGARIAD 3: MAGICIAN'S GAMBIT	*David Eddings*	£6.99
☐	14810 5	BELGARIAD 4: CASTLE OF WIZARDRY	*David Eddings*	£6.99
☐	14811 3	BELGARIAD 5: ENCHANTER'S END GAME	*David Eddings*	£6.99
☐	14252 2	THE LEGEND OF DEATHWALKER	*David Gemmell*	£6.99
☐	14253 0	DARK MOON	*David Gemmell*	£6.99
☐	14254 9	WINTER WARRIORS	*David Gemmell*	£6.99
☐	14255 7	ECHOES OF THE GREAT SONG	*David Gemmell*	£6.99
☐	14256 5	SWORD IN THE STORM	*David Gemmell*	£6.99
☐	14257 3	MIDNIGHT FALCON	*David Gemmell*	£6.99
☐	14674 9	HERO IN THE SHADOWS	*David Gemmell*	£6.99
☐	14675 7	RAVENHEART	*David Gemmell*	£6.99
☐	14676 5	STORMRIDER	*David Gemmell*	£6.99
☐	14180 1	TO RIDE PEGASUS	*Anne McCaffrey*	£5.99
☐	08661 4	DECISION AT DOONA	*Anne McCaffrey*	£4.99
☐	08453 0	DRAGONFLIGHT	*Anne McCaffrey*	£5.99
☐	13763 4	THE ROWAN	*Anne McCaffrey*	£5.99
☐	12848 1	THE LIGHT FANTASTIC	*Terry Pratchett*	£5.99
☐	14028 7	MEN AT ARMS	*Terry Pratchett*	£6.99
☐	14029 5	SOUL MUSIC	*Terry Pratchett*	£6.99
☐	13703 0	GOOD OMENS	*Terry Pratchett & Neil Gaiman*	£6.99
☐	13841 X	THE ANTIPOPE	*Robert Rankin*	£6.99
☐	13922 X	THE BOOK OF ULTIMATE TRUTHS	*Robert Rankin*	£6.99
☐	13681 6	ARMAGEDDON THE MUSICAL	*Robert Rankin*	£5.99
☐	14590 4	SNUFF FICTION	*Robert Rankin*	£5.99
☐	99777 3	THE SPARROW	*Mary Doria Russell*	£7.99
☐	99811 7	CHILDREN OF GOD	*Mary Doria Russell*	£6.99

All Transworld titles are available by post from:

Bookpost, P.O. Box 29, Douglas, Isle of Man IM99 1BQ

Credit cards accepted. Please telephone 01624 836000,
fax 01624 837033, Internet http://www.bookpost.co.uk or
e-mail: bookshop@enterprise.net for details.

**Free postage and packing in the UK. Overseas customers allow
£2 per book (paperbacks) and £3 per book (hardbacks).**